DEAD SHIFT

DEAD SHIFT

A RHO AGENDA NOVEL

RICHARD PHILLIPS

47NORTH

Text copyright © 2015 Richard Phillips

Published by 47North, Seattle

www.apub.com

Amazon, the Amazon logo, and 47North are trademarks of Amazon.com, Inc., or its affiliates.

ISBN-13: 9781477828397
ISBN-10: 1477828397

Cover design by Jason Blackburn

Library of Congress Control Number: 2014958521

Printed in the United States of America

This novel is dedicated to my loving wife, Carol, and to Sienna Farall and Jeremy Loethen, the most wonderful daughter and son-in-law a man could have.

Author's Note

Many of the ideas in this novel on the containment of
artificial intelligence are based upon Nick Bostrom's
Superintelligence: Paths, Dangers, Strategies.

"I think, therefore I am."
—René Descartes

: CHAPTER 1

Jamal Glover removed his gaze from the displays that formed a sixty-degree arc around his zero-gravity chair, stepped out of the full-immersion workstation, and placed his white-striped black fedora atop his head, applying a jaunty tilt. All around him, his fellow cyber-warriors climbed out of their scorpion-shaped cockpits, blinking their eyes as the simulated session came to a close. Of all these elite hackers, Jamal was the best. Not bad for a twenty-year-old black kid from the Bronx. Actually his birthday wasn't until tomorrow, but he was rounding up.

Everything about Jamal announced his presence. He had long since adopted a 1920s-style swagger, from his black-and-white spats, up to his chalk-striped black suit, to his fedora. It was a retro look that said, "You wish you were me. Admit it."

He'd fallen in love with that distant era during the years he'd lived with his Gram, after his folks had died in a car accident. She was a fine, spirited woman and although she'd been gone for three years, the fondness endured.

Jamal looked up at the glass-enclosed balcony that overlooked the multitiered room where he and his compatriots had just finished the evaluation session, surprised to see Admiral Jonathan Riles looking down on them. The War Room was the NSA director's brainchild, and even though the group of NSA hackers whom Riles had nicknamed the Dirty Dozen hadn't been conducting a live cyber-attack, they had been wringing out the brand-new cyber-attack workstations. So, on second thought, it made sense that the director would be interested in this day's results.

As Jamal stepped back and looked out across the three tiers of workstations, he had to admit that the Scorpions added a major new cool factor to the room. Before today the War Room had looked very much like a NASA control room. Now it looked like something out of the latest science-fiction movie. And based upon the kick-ass performance of his Scorpion, he had no doubt that these systems exceeded specifications.

Glancing up at the twenty-foot-high screen that filled the front wall, Jamal felt a grin crease his lips. Although this had just been a simulation, the results still counted and Jamal's name remained firmly entrenched in the number one spot atop the big board. He had to give Admiral Riles credit. Although most people thought of hackers as geeky loners, Riles had recognized that the best of them shared a passion for recognition that only competitive computer gaming could provide.

Riles had directed his team of computer scientists to create a system that scored every cyber-attack session, live or simulated, and maintained a current ranking for every cyber-warrior. The NSA's current top twelve formed the Dirty Dozen and got to come to work every day in the War Room. The other poor bastards found themselves stuck in cubicles, desperately trying to work their way into the top twelve. It was the vision that had recruited a nineteen-year-old Jamal, straight out of MIT, despite big-money offers from the likes of Google. To be the best of the best and to have the big board rub it in all of his competitors' faces was what made him look forward to coming to work every single day.

"Jamal, tomorrow I'm going to wipe that grin right off your face."

Jamal turned to look at Caroline "Goth Girl" Brown's features, her pale skin emphasized by her shaved and tattooed scalp. The effect was so dramatic that her face appeared to be backlit, making her dark-brown eyes loom unnaturally large. The way that Caroline avoided any makeup formed a statement that matched her piercings. It was also what made her such a tempting target for his razor-sharp wit.

"There's nothing wrong with being number two. Accept it and be happy."

Caroline started to say something, but only issued a hiss from her lips as she shouldered past him and stormed out of the chamber. To Jamal's left, he heard Gary Charles's distinctive chuckle.

"If eyes could kill, you'd be a smoking pile of ash right now. Don't be surprised if you feel her sticking pins in a little Jamal doll tonight."

Turning to meet the heavyset man's laughing blue eyes, Jamal shrugged with feigned innocence.

"Apparently it was something I said."

"Or maybe she just doesn't like you."

Jamal shook his head. "Life is hard at the top, looking down on all you little people who wish you could be me for a day."

Again Gary laughed. "You're so full of shit. I'm going to laugh my ass off when someone knocks you off that pedestal."

"Ain't happening."

"We'll see," Gary said, raising his left eyebrow. "Hey, you want to swing by the pizza place before you head home?"

"I would, but Jill will have dinner waiting."

"Lucky man. Where'd you find a girlfriend who is that hot and cooks too?"

"Craigslist."

Seeing Gary shake his head, Jamal continued. "Oh, I almost forgot. Jill's throwing me a surprise birthday party tomorrow night."

"How is it a surprise if you already know about it?"

"Because she thinks it is. I can't help it if I stumble across other people's secrets. It's what I do."

"I don't know how the hell she puts up with you."

"Me either. So, you coming?"

Gary grinned. "Ask me next year when you're old enough to buy some beer."

"Jill's buying wine."

"Gag."

Jamal turned toward the exit, calling back over his shoulder as he walked out the door. "You know you'll be there."

As Jamal made his way to the elevator and then out through the security lobby, he replayed today's test in his head. If the exercise had been designed to test the cyber-warriors, he would now be sitting in an after-action review. But since its purpose had been to wring out the new equipment, the data had been automatically collected and would be reviewed by Dr. David Kurtz and his computer science team. That was fine with Jamal. It meant he would get to have dinner with Jill instead of having her watch him eat her reheated lasagna.

Jamal stepped out of the massive black-glass NSA headquarters building and began the long walk to his parking spot, thankful that the mid-May sun had sunk behind some clouds. It wouldn't be right in his eyes as he drove from Fort Meade to the house he'd rented in Columbia, Maryland. With any luck at all he'd be home right around sunset.

Unfortunately, an accident kept him sitting in bumper-to-bumper traffic for an extra half hour and he didn't pull into his driveway until forty minutes past eight. When the garage door began rumbling upward on its tracks, something pulled Jamal out of his own thoughts. Normally he had to concentrate to notice his physical surroundings. It was one of the oddities of his personality that made Jill laugh at him. But tonight, with purple twilight painting the western sky, Jamal found himself hesitating to pull forward into the garage.

What was it that bothered him? Jill's car sat in its usual space on the right-hand side of the garage. The living room shutters were closed, but she had probably shut them to block the glare of the late afternoon sun and just hadn't gotten around to opening them again. A new thought occurred to Jamal. Perhaps Jill had a bit of a romantic surprise waiting for him on the eve of his twentieth birthday, something that involved candles, wine, and her long golden hair cascading down over a red lace negligee. If so, it wouldn't do to keep her waiting while he sat outside in the driveway.

Jamal pulled into the garage, stepped out of his restored black Packard coupe, and pressed the button that closed the garage door. The clatter it made on the rails reminded him that he had intended to call the garage door repairman to tune up the system. Oh well. Tomorrow was Saturday and since he wasn't scheduled to work this weekend, he'd make the call in the morning.

When Jamal opened the door that led from the garage into the short hall that connected the kitchen to the living room, the pitch darkness of the interior startled him, sending a shiver across his scalp that threatened to straighten his short, curly hair. He froze in the doorway as the garage light cast his shadow against the far wall.

"Jill?"

No answer. Except for the dying vibrations of his voice and the sudden thunder of his pounding heart, there was no sound at all. But the smell of freshly baked lasagna filled his nostrils, along with another much less pleasant smell.

Jamal reached for the light switch on the wall to his left. The switch toggled beneath his finger and the LED hall light came on, obliterating his shadow as it revealed the living room to his left and the kitchen entry on his right. The sound of the door closing behind him alerted Jamal to the fact that he had released it. From where he stood, he could see that the living room was unoccupied, but only a thin sliver of the kitchen was visible.

Jamal took a deep breath and stepped around the corner into the kitchen. The vision that awaited dropped him to his knees. Jill lay slumped against the oven, her head propped up at an angle that made her appear to be trying to call out to him, either through her bloody mouth or through the great gaping wound in her throat. For a moment her open blue eyes transfixed him, before his gaze widened to take in the horrible scene in its entirety.

So much blood had sprayed across the stovetop that her attacker must have slipped up behind her and cut her throat as she set the lasagna atop the stove to cool. The sight of the large blue oven mitts that still covered Jill's hands confirmed Jamal's deduction.

With tears streaming down his face, Jamal moved to her side and tugged off those mitts to take her two hands in his. They were the only parts of his lover that weren't completely soaked in her blood. Kneeling in a bloody pool, Jamal reached out and pulled her to him, hugging her limp form to his chest as sobs wracked his body.

The noise behind him was the faint sound of soft-soled sneakers on tile, but it brought his head around. The man who stood at the kitchen entrance was dressed in black, although no mask covered the fine East Asian features of his handsome face. Weaponless he waited, his open hands hanging loosely at his sides.

Jamal released his hold on Jill, letting his fury pull his six-foot body erect, but the ease with which the killer slipped his punch and dropped him on his face surprised Jamal. As he lay facedown, locked in some sort of immobilizing hold, Jamal felt a sharp sting as a needle slid into the side of his neck, releasing a swirling fog that robbed him of his rage. As Jamal's surroundings faded to nothing, an overwhelming sense of loss accompanied him into the dark.

CHAPTER 2

Qiang Chu watched as two of his men loaded Jamal Glover's unconscious body onto the Boeing 757F owned and operated by International Shipping Service, or ISS. Although Steve Grange himself wasn't on this flight, the medical pioneer was making final preparations to receive this precious cargo at his Sonoma Valley compound, fifty miles north of San Francisco.

But that didn't mean that Grange could afford to waste the seven hours of total flight time it would take to get from Baltimore to Kansas City and then to Oakland. It was why a closely held corporation, under the covert control of the Chinese government, had chartered the cargo jet and loaded several custom shipping containers outfitted with specialized MRI and computing systems designed by Grange. It was why Grange had assigned his mind digitization specialist, Dr. Vicky Morris, and a four-person support team to conduct the medical procedures Jamal Glover would undergo in flight.

Qiang was very pleased with how smoothly the kidnapping had gone. In his experience, such operations rarely came off exactly as planned, but tonight's mission had been executed with flawless precision. The bloody body of the young NSA hacker's murdered girlfriend would be discovered sometime tomorrow, but the evidence Qiang and his team had planted would launch investigators down a false path.

He'd made certain that Jamal's fingerprints were the only prints on the murder weapon. Those same prints were also all over the woman's bloody body. Fabricated text messages and e-mails on her cell phone would provide ample evidence of her ongoing fling with a secret lover. When all of that was combined with what appeared to be Jamal's hasty preparations for travel and his missing automobile, police would come to the obvious conclusion that Jamal Glover had killed his girlfriend in a jealous rage and then fled, using his NSA skills to disappear.

~ ~ ~

Steve Grange had pioneered the research that had led to revolutionary technological breakthroughs in the area of brain-to-machine interfaces. One of those breakthroughs, MRI mind scraping, had become very effective at noninvasive digitization of a subject's memories. For the California phase of Grange's plan to succeed, the billionaire science prodigy needed today's memories pulled from Jamal's brain in high resolution. And since every minute counted, the MRI mind scraping couldn't wait until Jamal arrived at Grange's California laboratory. The MRI machine on this plane had been engineered with special noise cancellation technology to eliminate interference from external vibrations such as those produced by the aircraft.

Long before the plane reached ten thousand feet, the medical team had finished strapping Jamal's body to the MRI platform. Qiang swiveled his leather chair to watch as the doctors inserted an IV needle into the young man's arm and started a drip that fed a hallucinogenic drug cocktail into his veins, one designed to continuously alter his quasi-conscious state in ways that would enhance the memory digitization.

Examining the displays that showed Jamal's vital signs, Dr. Morris nodded with satisfaction and switched on the torus-shaped MRI scanner that surrounded Jamal's head. Although Qiang was familiar with the rhythmic buzzing-gong sound produced by MRI scanners, this one seemed louder and higher pitched than he recalled. Then again, that might be because this was happening inside a cargo jet that was approaching its cruising altitude of thirty-five thousand feet.

Grange had designed and built this particular MRI machine for one specific purpose, but despite all the high-tech manipulation of magnetic pulses and precisely directed frequencies of radio energy that bombarded the NSA man's head, it was one loud, annoying-ass procedure.

Qiang leaned back in one of the big cargo aircraft's less than comfortable seats and closed his eyes. While he prepared to take himself into the deep meditation that would ensconce him in the isolation of his mind palace, his thoughts turned to the fate that awaited Jamal in California. Despite the bloody death of the NSA hacker's girlfriend, there was no doubt in Qiang's mind.

Of these two young people, she'd been the lucky one.

CHAPTER 3

Two hours before sunrise, Steve Grange stood outside his mansion, looking out over the moonlit vineyards that surrounded his home and the adjacent castle-shaped winery that rose to alter the skyline a half mile east of the Sonoma Highway. Beyond that, above the ridgeline that formed Sonoma Valley's western wall, the waning gibbous moon shone bright enough to cast distinct shadows from the castle battlements.

Tall, slender, and elegant, even in his jeans, black T-shirt, and Nikes, Grange ran a hand through his sandy hair and sucked in a deep breath of the cool night air. Despite all he'd accomplished during his forty-eight years of life, Grange had never felt a sense of anticipation as intense as the one that wrapped him in this pre-dawn moonlight. What others didn't dare dream, he would usher into reality over the coming days.

The truck that had just turned off the highway onto the private lane that led to Grange Castle Winery appeared to be a standard delivery vehicle, but nothing could be further from the truth.

Even though it was exactly what Grange expected and it was precisely on schedule, the sight of it brought a tightness to his chest he hadn't felt since that Christmas morning when he'd unwrapped his first personal computer.

"Sir, your car is ready."

Grange turned to see Carlos, his diminutive, dark-eyed chauffeur, standing at the top of the steps that led from the backyard up to the pool deck.

"Fine."

Grange watched the man turn and walk back through the sliding glass doors that led through the drawing room to the twelve-foot-tall front doors. Grange's encrypted cell phone warbled and he lifted it to his ear.

"Yes?"

Qiang Chu's Mandarin-accented voice delivered the expected confirmation. "Package delivery complete."

"Status?"

"It's being prepped right now."

"On my way."

Grange ended the call and took two calming breaths before walking back through the house to the driveway. Carlos held open the red Tesla's door and Grange climbed into the driver's seat. He accelerated out of the semicircular driveway and down the narrow paved road that ran from his house to the castle-shaped winery. Although Carlos was his driver, nobody drove the Tesla but Grange himself. He loved the vehicle's silent power and drive. After all, those were two of his defining traits.

As he approached the castle's rear service gate, the Tesla's headlights illuminated the nonpublic portion of the winery and the paved courtyard beyond. On the far side of the courtyard, a forty-foot roll-aside steel door stood open, and Grange drove inside, parking the Tesla alongside the delivery truck that had been backed up to a loading dock.

Grange climbed out of the car as the huge door rumbled closed on its track behind him. The budget he had thrown at the project had brought the illegal phase of construction to completion six months ago. The non-secret, legal construction of the Grange Castle Winery was finally approaching completion. Wine production had begun and enough of the interior was finished to allow for the hosting of parties.

Considering that this winery was being built with the sole purpose of masking the secret work below the wine caves, he was in no hurry to bring construction to a close. It enabled Grange to disguise the staff of the hidden underground facility as members of the construction crew.

When he looked around, he was surprised to see that Qiang Chu had silently moved up beside him. He knew that by now he should be used to the stealth with which the lean assassin moved, but it just didn't seem natural.

Grange nodded, noting the complete lack of emotion on the dark-haired man's angular features.

"Is our subject being prepped?"

"Dr. Landon's team has taken him below," Qiang said.

"Any problems during transit?"

"Everything is going precisely as planned."

Maybe it was paranoia, but Grange found himself not liking that answer. When things proceeded too smoothly, it was usually because some government agency wanted its targets overconfident. A mirthless smile spread across Qiang's lips, indicating he had guessed what Grange was thinking—one more of the spooky things about this man that put Grange on edge whenever he was near.

"We weren't followed. My people at the airport made sure of that. And there's been no police chatter from the far end. That means they haven't found the girl's body yet."

The smile disappeared from Qiang's face as he continued. "Focus on your work, Mr. Grange."

Grange felt the muscles in his jaw clench, but he refused to be baited by a man of inferior intellect. Besides, Grange was more important to Qiang's Chinese masters than the assassin.

Turning his back on the smaller man, Grange shifted his thoughts to what waited for him below the wine caves. When he reached the freight elevator, he stepped inside and turned to face the panel of elevator buttons. There were three of them, marked SL1 through SL3, and a separate red button marked "Emergency." But Grange wasn't headed for one of the three wine cave sublevels.

With his right hand, he simultaneously pressed the SL1 and SL3 buttons and then pressed the SL2 button twice. Beneath his hand, the panel slid aside to reveal a scanner that Grange placed his palm against. After a brief pause, the elevator started down, descending a hundred feet before decelerating to a smooth stop. When the doors opened, he felt a rush of over-pressurized air whoosh inside, pushing the air that had accompanied him down from the surface out through vents in the back of the car.

In front of him, a short, white-tiled hallway passed between two dark-clad Chinese guards, ending at what appeared to be another closed elevator door. Grange ignored the two men, walked directly to the panel to the right of the ten-foot square doorway, and placed his right palm, fingers spread, on the glass plate. There was no line of visible laser light that swept across the panel; the doors just parted and slid silently into their wall slots to allow him entry.

The white tile floor of the room was reflected in the stainless steel walls. Two doors on the wall to his right were labeled with the standard stick figures that indicated the entry to the men's and women's locker rooms. On the wall to Grange's left, an open doorway led into a fully appointed break room, outfitted with a stocked pantry, refrigerators, sinks, and a pair of single-cup coffee makers.

Directly to his front, an automated security booth led to a closed steel doorway designed for personnel entry. To its left, a much larger steel door provided freight and equipment access to the area beyond.

Grange turned right and entered the men's locker room, where shiny metal benches separated three rows of steel lockers. Beyond these he could see a half dozen empty shower stalls and another door that led to the toilets and sinks. Grabbing a clean set of scrubs and slippers from the racks arrayed along the blue-tiled wall to his left, Grange moved to the locker adorned with his nameplate. He pressed his right thumb to the fingerprint reader and felt it unlatch.

Without hesitation, he stripped out of his clothes and shoes, placed them inside the locker, and donned the light-blue scrubs and slippers before heading for the security booth that formed the only entry or exit from the inner facility. Grange knew it wouldn't have passed fire code. The thought brought a slight smile to his lips. That was the least of the laws being violated on this level.

When he closed the locker, Grange felt and heard the lock slide back into place. Then he turned and walked back out the way he had entered the locker room, accompanied by the distinctive squeak of the rubber slippers on the white tile floor.

As he made the walk from the locker room to the waiting security booth, his anticipation made time seem to crawl, turning seconds into minutes. Stepping into an advanced variant of an active millimeter-wave scanner, Grange didn't bother to raise his hands above his head. With this device it wasn't even necessary to have a person monitor the resulting images. If anyone tried to carry an unapproved device through this booth, the scanner would trigger an alarm that would usher a half dozen armed guards into the room.

Another light turned green and Grange stepped out of the scanner and up to the door. He inserted his right hand, palm down, into an opening in the wall as he stared up into one of the many cameras that recorded his image and routed it to a facial recognition database. The small sting on the back of his wrist alerted him to the completion of DNA sampling and he waited. Above the slot a glowing red light was accompanied by a message that read *DO NOT REMOVE HAND*, a usage of the English language that brought unfortunate images to mind every time he stood in this spot.

After several seconds the light changed from red to green, the words changed to *ACCESS GRANTED*, and the door whisked open. Grange pulled his hand from the slot, noting a tiny red dot on his wrist where the micro-collection had occurred, just another of the necessary annoyances that he had become accustomed to.

The hallway that opened before him had been part lucky break, part inevitability. He had intended to bore out a space big enough to construct his laboratory below the wine caves, but when seismic testing had detected a cavern a hundred feet below the surface, he'd been handed a twofer. It meant digging a bit deeper, but the total amount of excavation required had been greatly reduced. In addition, the extra depth had provided even better security than his original design of this facility had called for. That had made his Chinese partners happy, and it had made Grange even happier.

With the construction completed, the cavern had been transformed into a close approximation of the Grange EToX facility in

Palo Alto. But the rapid iterative prototyping and testing being conducted on this site was producing startling advances that would have been impossible if subjected to U.S. government laws and oversight.

Dr. Marie Feingold, one of Dr. Landon's assisting physicians, looked up from the tablet computer she held as she stood beside the receptionist's desk.

"Mr. Grange, Dr. Landon asked me to escort you to the operating theater."

Grange stared at the thin, seemingly anorexic woman standing before him in her blue scrubs and felt his annoyance kick in.

"Shouldn't you be prepping for surgery instead of escorting me to the observation area?"

Dr. Feingold's eyes narrowed ever so slightly at the edges, but her voice remained steady. "I won't be assisting with this surgery I'm to make myself available in the observation area in the event you have any questions during the procedure."

"I'm thoroughly familiar with the procedure."

"Nonetheless."

Jesus, this woman was irritating. No wonder Landon didn't want her assisting. Grange considered telling her to go away, but decided it would be easier to just ignore her. When he walked past her down the corridor and turned right toward the observation room, Grange was glad to see that she fell into step behind him instead of moving up to walk alongside. That would have invited conversation, and right now conversation was the last thing he wanted.

What he wanted was for the operation to get underway. In the meantime, he wanted to observe the preparations and to think. Just outside the anteroom, Grange opened a side door and climbed a staircase to the glass-walled platform that overlooked the operating room. There, in addition to the view available through the windows, four sixty-inch OLED screens displayed views from cameras in the room below.

Grange seated himself in a chair in front of the camera control panel. From here, he could move and zoom each of the cameras with a caress of the touchscreen mounted on his armrest. He heard Dr. Feingold settle into the theater chair to his left rear and then shifted his thoughts to what was happening below.

The subject lay atop the surgical table, already anesthetized. His freshly shaved head was held in place by a steel framework that was fastened to the frame that allowed the body to be rotated in place. The apparatus enabled the surgeon to orient the body either faceup or facedown. This subject lay facedown, his black scalp pockmarked with rectangular blocks projected onto his head from red lasers, as the gowned, gloved, and masked surgical team moved around him.

Dr. Landon leaned over the subject, probing the scalp with his gloved hands, and Grange adjusted the zoom on one of the cameras as he watched an assistant hand the doctor a scalpel. With sure hands, Dr. Landon flapped back the scalp to reveal the skull beneath.

The doctor held out his hand for the small high-speed drill that would bore several small burr holes into the man's skull. Then it would just be a matter of connecting the dots with a surgical saw to remove small sections of skull.

Over the speakers, the high whine of the drill dropped in pitch as it bit into bone. Having completely forgotten about the woman sitting behind him, Grange leaned forward. The fun was only just beginning.

: CHAPTER 4

Levi Elias ended the call and returned his cell phone to his pocket, pushing his Herman Miller chair back from his desk as he did so. He hadn't been scheduled to work today, but when you're the ranking NSA analyst, you come to expect the unexpected. Accordingly, he now found himself back in his office inside the expansive black-glass NSA headquarters building. And he'd just been summoned to the director's office. He hadn't detected any tension in Admiral Riles's voice, but the director rarely displayed emotion. This morning's news was bad and potentially devastating.

Levi rose to his feet, ran a hand through his curly black hair, and shook his head. Why Jamal? Levi rarely formed an emotional attachment to members of the cyber-warfare group. Most of them lived in their games or in the source code of the systems they were tasked to compromise, taking little interest in developing human relationships. But Jamal Glover had a witty, cocky personality that made people want to be around him. Now he was gone.

When Levi reached Admiral Riles's office, he found the door open and no administrative assistant sitting outside. Normally, the six-foot-tall Frederica Barnes, or Fred, as everyone called her, guarded the admiral's privacy with a middle linebacker's attitude. Evidently Riles had not felt it necessary to interrupt her weekend . . . at least not yet.

"Come on in, Levi," the admiral said. "And close the door behind you."

Levi stepped inside and closed the door behind him. The NSA director sat at his teak desk, silhouetted against the dark, copper-infused windows designed to block penetration of electromagnetic signals. A stocky, balding man with an open, friendly face that served as an unlikely platform for his icy gray eyes, he had been number one in his class at the Naval Academy, a Rhodes Scholar, and an athlete. The admiral exuded an easy self-confidence that filled any room with his commanding presence.

Comfortable in that presence, Levi seated himself in a leather armchair positioned at an angle from the desk that wouldn't block the admiral's line of sight to the door.

"What's your initial assessment of the Jamal Glover situation?" Riles asked.

"The Columbia police conducted the initial crime scene investigation. Due to the sensitive position of the person involved, FBI is on site and has taken control of the investigation. Neither the FBI nor the police have released initial results of their ongoing investigations, but we're monitoring all of their communications and data transfers. Dr. Jennings has initiated a top-priority intelligence request so Big John is crunching the data."

"And what is that initial data telling us?"

"Nothing more than conjecture at the moment. The police think the evidence points to a jealous argument between Jamal

Glover and Jill McPherson. They think Jamal cut her throat, grabbed his computer equipment, packed some clothes, and fled in his car. So far, the FBI agrees with that assessment. I think it's bullshit."

The admiral nodded. "It is bullshit. Jamal would never hurt that girl. Not in a million lifetimes."

"What level of effort do you want me to target on this?"

"Get any high-resolution satellite data of Jamal's house for the last twenty-four hours. I want to know when anyone entered or left that house from yesterday morning until the police arrived. Also, I want all the security and traffic camera feeds in a five-mile radius around Jamal's house analyzed. And track the movements of every cell phone in that radius. Same goes for anything else that transmits a signal."

"I'm on it."

"Spin up the War Room. I want our cyber-warfare team to locate Jamal and whoever took him."

"Yes, sir."

Levi rose from the chair, feeling his boss's determination hanging heavy in the air. As he turned toward the door, the admiral's voice made him pause.

"And Levi, I want you to activate our ghost team. Wherever they are, get them back here ASAP."

"Including Janet Price?"

"Yes. And I want Jack Gregory on this one too. The second we think we know where Jamal is, I want them moving."

Levi felt his throat tighten. Over the last two years, based on a loose interpretation of a post-9/11 presidential finding, Admiral Riles had assembled a small team of "fixers" that only Riles, Levi, and two others at the NSA knew existed. The ex-CIA assassin known as Jack "The Ripper" Gregory wasn't officially part of that team, but twice in the last eight months Riles had managed to coerce Jack's assistance, both on missions involving Janet Price. The man was deadly, but he was also a loose cannon, and that worried Levi.

But Riles wanted Gregory in on this and Levi wasn't about to argue with the admiral's judgment. He took a slow breath and looked into Riles's gray eyes.

"I'll make it happen."

CHAPTER 5

The meeting didn't happen at the NSA headquarters. Janet Price hadn't expected it to. If there was one key differentiator about the secret team of specialists that Admiral Riles had spent the last couple of years recruiting, it was that knowledge of the team's membership was limited to Riles and two or three others in the NSA that maintained his complete trust. None of the specialists were even listed on the NSA's official payroll.

The farmhouse rested deep in the countryside twenty miles north of Frederick, Maryland, a short distance from the Pennsylvania state line. It sat at the end of a half-mile-long dirt lane, hidden from Highway 15 by thick woods. The smaller of two barns served as a garage where all the meeting attendants had parked their vehicles.

Janet, wearing a maroon pullover, black jeans, and boots, walked from the barn to the two-story farmhouse feeling the warm May sunshine on her face. Levi Elias opened the door as she moved onto the front steps. A broad smile warmed his hawkish looks as he extended his hand.

"Hi, Janet. How was the flight from Berlin?"

Janet returned the smile as she took his hand. At five foot ten, she was a full two inches taller than the NSA analyst, even though he claimed to be five nine. It was the only hint of inferiority she'd ever seen the man exhibit.

"A bit bumpy, but not enough to keep me from sleeping."

She stepped past Levi and into the living room. A half dozen leather chairs and a couch had been arranged in an arc focused toward a sixty-inch television, which was currently turned off. Judging by the open soda cans and bags of chips, the rest of the team had been waiting for her arrival for a couple of hours.

None of the others rose to greet her, although their eyes followed her closely as Janet moved to take an empty chair. Besides Levi and herself, there were five men arranged around the arc. To Janet's left sat Mike "Spider" Sanchez, his neatly trimmed beard and dark hair framing a no-nonsense face that befitted the team leader.

To her immediate right, Raymond Bronson leaned back on the couch, feet propped on the corner of a coffee table, his hands clasped behind his head. At six foot four, he bore a marked resemblance to the movie version of Thor, although Bronson claimed it was the other way around. Calling him Raymond or Ray was a quick way to piss him off.

Next to Bronson, the lanky Bobby Daniels leaned forward to snag a handful of pretzels from a large bowl, his shaved head reflecting the overhead light as he popped pretzels in his mouth. Beyond Bobby sat Paul Monroe, shoulder-length dirty-blond hair curling out from beneath a tan fedora. Seeing her studying him, Paul grinned, his mustache and goatee perfectly accenting the devilish gleam in the explosive expert's blue eyes. He'd been her first partner after Admiral Riles recruited her from the CIA. The laughter in those eyes never died.

The last member of the team sat directly opposite Janet. Harold "Harry" Stevens had the face of an Irish boxer, his nose showing clear evidence of past breakage from his early club-fighting days. Harry's tousled dark-brown hair and square jaw would have attracted more attention if not for his sparkling gray eyes. Renowned in the Green Berets for his tracking ability, he was this team's communications expert.

In a room full of killers, Janet felt at ease. They had learned from experience that she was, at the very least, their equal and they treated her as such. Since she'd earned a computer science degree from the University of Maryland, the CIA had recruited her as an analyst, but her handlers had soon discovered that the two-time NCAA pentathlon champion was ill-suited to a desk job.

After two years of fieldwork, Admiral Riles had enticed her away from CIA to become a member of his NSA ghost team, and though it had meant dropping off the face of the planet and adopting ever-changing identities, she had no regrets. This team was made up of the best of the best. And she was their shooter.

Levi Elias moved in front of the television and turned to face the group.

"I know you are all wondering why Riles has assembled the whole team here."

Janet had been wondering exactly that. Of all the missions she'd been assigned since joining Admiral Riles's team, this was the first time the whole group had been called together for a single mission. Not a particularly good sign. Nobody said a thing.

Levi continued. "Two days ago, Jamal Glover, a member of our cyber-warfare group, disappeared. His girlfriend was later found murdered at his house. The FBI believes that the evidence indicates that Jamal killed her in a jealous rage and then fled."

"So you want us to find and kill him?" Spider Sanchez asked.

Levi's eyes met Spider's. "Let me paint you a different picture. What I'm about to say is classified top secret."

"Sounds like us," said Spider, a statement that drew chuckles from the assemblage.

Levi inclined his head in acknowledgement.

"Jamal Glover is the best of the NSA's cyber-warriors. A twenty-year-old graduate of MIT, he is an extraordinary talent. We believe he's been kidnapped by a foreign government."

Janet leaned forward. "Which government?"

"Most likely the Russians or the Chinese." Levi's face hardened. "The FBI can pursue their leads, but we're not chasing that rabbit."

"So where is he?" asked Spider.

Levi shrugged. "We don't know yet. As soon as we do, we'll provide you with your new identities and send you in to get him." Levi paused, his expression darkening. "The fact that we've brought you all together on this should tell you just how much of a danger Jamal Glover represents if left in the hands of a foreign intelligence service. Any other questions?"

Raymond Bronson grinned. "Just one. How'd I get so good-looking?"

"Probably all that practicing in front of your mirror," Paul said, sparking a chorus of laughter from the others.

Janet saw Levi shift his focus to her as he raised both hands in a signal for quiet.

"There's one more thing you need to be aware of. We are assigning an additional asset to this mission."

Noting the intensity in the look Levi gave her, Janet felt her throat tighten.

"Does this asset have a name?" she asked, knowing the answer to her question even as she voiced it.

Instead of answering, Levi set a brown leather briefcase on the coffee table, pushing aside the bags of chips and pretzels to make room. Extracting a stack of manila folders, he passed one to each team member, starting with Spider. When he handed one to Janet, she again caught his knowing look.

Flipping open the folder, Janet found herself staring at the familiar photograph of a body lying naked atop that Calcutta surgical table, the torso crisscrossed by freshly stitched knife wounds. Blood from the many wounds had run off the table to form a scarlet pool on the floor that reflected the camera flash. The picture was captioned:

Jack Gregory aka The Ripper

The flood of conflicting emotions that assaulted her almost pulled a gasp from her lips, but she bit it back. It had been two months since she'd last seen Jack, and the memory of their last meeting still held its razor edge.

The impact of the photo on the front page of Jack Gregory's dossier was evident from the silence with which the assembled group studied it. Levi's voice broke that silence.

"Meet Jack Gregory. Almost two years ago, he was the CIA's top killer, but on a hot Calcutta night he went off mission and was attacked by a gang of men wielding the boomerang-shaped knives known as khukuri. Gregory killed all six of them but was badly injured in the fight.

"An old nun found him bleeding out in that alley and, with the help of a local doctor, transported him to a clinic. Unfortunately, by the time the doctor closed all his wounds, Jack Gregory's heart had stopped. He was declared dead at 3:05 A.M. local time. This picture was attached to his death certificate."

Janet had received this very briefing last year, but hearing Levi's voice sent a déjà vu chill up her spine that raised the gooseflesh on the back of her neck.

After a brief pause, Levi continued. "Most of the world's intelligence agencies believe that Jack Gregory is dead. But, as Janet can attest, he's still very much alive. Twice during the last ten months, we've enlisted his services on critical missions. Janet was the NSA lead on both those missions."

Paul Monroe lifted his feet off the ottoman where they rested and leaned forward. "So Gregory faked his own death?"

Levi shook his head. "No. The details are in his dossier, but here's the abridged version. That night in Calcutta, the attending physician declared him legally dead and left the old nun to clean up the tiny clinic. Apparently, as she draped Gregory's body with a sheet, he revived. The shock of the event was too much for the old girl's mind. When someone found her the next morning, she was huddled in a corner, mindlessly mumbling the same phrase over and over. Sister Mary Judith has since been cloistered in a monastery in England, lost in delusion and dementia."

"What was the phrase?" Paul asked.

Levi shifted his gaze to Paul. "Dear Lord, the Ripper walks the earth."

Everyone except Janet, Spider, and Levi chuckled at this, but Levi continued.

"Jack Gregory let the CIA believe he had died and started accepting contract work as a 'fixer' for hire using The Ripper pseudonym. Although we don't know his client list, we believe that in the year following his purported death, he earned several million dollars from those contracts."

A low whistle escaped Bronson's lips. "You're proposing putting a contract killer on our team?"

"We don't think he accepted contracts for assassinations."

"You don't think?"

Unable to remain silent any longer, Janet spoke up. "Based on the two times we worked together, I have to agree with Levi. Jack's a killer, but he's no hit man."

Janet felt all eyes shift to her as Bronson followed up with a question.

"So you think he'd be a good fit for this team?"

Again Janet felt the tightness in her throat. "No, I don't."

"Why not?"

Janet glanced at Levi, who gave a slight nod and said, "You can answer that, but since none of the others have been read in on those two operations, leave out the mission-specific details."

When Janet spoke, she purged all emotion from her voice.

"This last year I worked closely with Jack Gregory on two separate occasions. The first time, Admiral Riles sent me to recruit Jack, but we ended up getting sucked into a situation of national importance. Although we successfully resolved the matter, my recruiting pitch failed. Right before he walked away, Jack said something that stuck in my head. He said, 'Believe me. Long term, you don't want me anywhere around you.'

"At the time, I thought he was dead wrong, but my last encounter with Jack made me reconsider."

Janet felt the memories buffet her. When she'd first met Jack in Germany, he'd displayed an inner fire that had both thrilled and concerned her. It seemed like she'd known Jack for years, but they'd only shared two missions. The first had been a few crazy weeks that had launched them through Germany, Austria, and Kazakhstan, culminating in three weeks of shared passion on the Greek island of Crete. But then had come the insanity in Bolivia.

Something inside Jack attracted him to danger in ways that, at times, seemed almost supernatural. Janet worried that he was losing himself to that pull. And if Jack Gregory spun out of control in a death spiral, anyone nearby might be dragged down with him.

She held up the folder Levi had given her.

"This dossier doesn't include anything about those two missions, but I can tell you his Ripper nickname is fitting. I'm afraid his presence could put the whole team at risk."

Bronson leaned back, locking his hands behind his head. "That's good enough for me."

"But not for me," said Spider Sanchez.

Janet turned to look at the team leader who, until now, had maintained his silence. The ex–Delta Force commando rose to stand beside Levi Elias, his black eyes fixed on Janet. He tossed his folder on the coffee table in front of her.

"I don't need to read this to know Jack Gregory. Four years ago, he was the CIA liaison assigned to my Delta unit, operating in the western Pakistani province of Waziristan. If not for Jack, none of us would have made it out of there alive. Jack was captured during that operation and then tortured for three weeks before we could locate him and mount a rescue operation. I'd trust that man at my back anywhere, anytime."

Janet accepted the challenge in that look. "I think you'll find he's changed."

Sanchez's eyes narrowed. "I don't believe it."

Levi held up a hand. "Hold on. I wanted to let you all air your feelings. But it doesn't really matter what any of us think. Admiral Riles has personally assigned Jack Gregory to this operation. I'm just informing you of his decision before I notify Jack of the assignment."

Levi closed his briefcase and picked it up, facing the group one last time as he prepared to depart.

"The Ripper is coming. I suggest you get used to the idea."

As Janet watched Levi walk across the room and out the door, a vortex of anticipation and dread filled her.

CHAPTER 6

They say that what happens in Vegas stays in Vegas. Unfortunately, Calcutta couldn't make that claim.

Jack Gregory had always craved danger's adrenaline rush. But in the two years since his Calcutta deathbed experience and his subsequent rebirth atop the old nun's surgery table, that craving wrapped him like an anaconda, hard enough to make him question the nature of his near-death encounter. Whether or not the mind parasite that had accompanied him back across the life-death threshold was a hallucination, it had changed the way he experienced this world. And if Jack didn't get control of it, that amped-up craving was going to render him every bit as dead as most of the world thought he already was.

Opening his eyes, Jack set the phone down on the nightstand and shifted his gaze to the naked twenty-three-year-old Polynesian woman who lay sprawled facedown on the opposite side of the bed. The right half of her body lay uncovered, revealing a very shapely hip and thigh. The curve of her right breast where it pressed into the mattress was almost enough to make him climb back into bed to reawaken the fire within that lovely body.

But the phone call he'd just received made it clear that his Kauai vacation had come to an end. The bedside clock read 7:15 A.M., so it was 1:15 P.M. in Maryland. Levi Elias had taken the initiative to book Jack a ticket on the first available flight back. That meant an interisland hop to Honolulu, followed by the red-eye to Los Angeles. Another five-hour flight after that and he should arrive at Baltimore/Washington International sometime tomorrow afternoon.

After a quick shower, Jack slipped on a pair of Dockers, his sandals, and a wildly floral Hawaiian shirt before stuffing the rest of his things into a small canvas duffel. He wiped down his Glock and set it topmost in the bag, then zipped it shut. Because he would be flying commercial, he'd have to chuck the gun into a Dumpster before he headed to the airport. Although it didn't fit his hand quite as nicely as his favored Heckler & Koch, here on the island, the Glock had been easier to come by. Oh well. Easy come, easy go.

With one lingering glance back at the sleeping woman, Jack opened the door and stepped out onto the walkway that ran along the beach, his bag slung over his left shoulder. He paused, feeling the ocean breeze ruffle his brown hair. The waves breaking on the beach fifty yards from where he stood produced the wonderful rushing sound that sucked the cares right out of his soul. Jack took a long, deep breath and savored the salt taste on his tongue. He was going to miss this.

Walking down the path, Jack spotted a Dumpster and, after a quick glance to ensure he was alone, dropped the gun inside. Fifty yards farther, he reached the parking lot, climbed into his rented white Camry, and turned onto Poipu Road. As he began the thirty-minute drive to Lihue Airport, Jack marveled at his readiness to sign on for this NSA operation. Even though he'd previously agreed to make himself available to the NSA as a private contractor, he had the right to accept or decline such contracts as he saw fit.

There was only one reason he had accepted this particular assignment: Janet Price. The last time he'd teamed with the deadly NSA agent, Jack's actions had shocked her. He recalled seeing the distrust shining in Janet's beautiful brown eyes, just before she'd turned her back and walked away from him in Miami. That memory had left a bad taste that he couldn't seem to wash away. Three weeks on an island in the middle of the Pacific Ocean had failed to expunge it.

Perhaps this time he could prove that he wasn't a rampaging psychopath with a death wish. And if he could convince himself of the same thing, so much the better.

CHAPTER 7

The Hawaiian Airlines carrier landed at Honolulu International Airport just before 11:30 A.M. after a surprisingly smooth thirty-minute flight. The last thing in the world Jack wanted was to hang out at the airport for the next eleven hours waiting for his flight to Los Angeles, so he took a taxi to the nearby Best Western Plaza Hotel. Twenty dollars to the skinny female clerk at the counter avoided a wait for the normal check-in time. Jack took the plastic key card, rode the elevator to the third floor, inserted the card in the key slot for room 310, and stepped inside.

The room was nothing special. It had green carpeting with a vine pattern and a white king-sized bed with a mocha runner decoratively arranged over the foot, a dresser with a television, a small desk, and a chair. Jack dropped the duffel beside the dresser and walked to the window that had a view over the pool area. Except for one fat guy wearing a red Speedo as he sunbathed on a lounger, it was deserted. Definitely not the Ritz-Carlton, but adequate for his purpose.

Jack pulled the curtains closed and kicked off his sandals. Tossing the pillows on the floor, he seated himself in the center of the bed, crossed his legs, and, as he'd done every day for the last several weeks, prepared for deep meditation. It was a tool he'd used to attain clarity for most of his adult life, but now that he was faced with the distinct possibility that he was losing his mind, meditation had acquired a whole new level of importance.

The air filled his lungs in a slow inhalation and then stayed there as Jack allowed the oxygen to percolate into his bloodstream before exhaling. He continued the breathing routine that prepared him for the deep immersion that would soon follow. Because this meditation would be different from any Jack had previously performed, he intended to take his time.

Since Calcutta, Jack's sleep had been plagued by dreams that were more than dreams. They were exceptionally detailed memories; they just weren't his memories. Over the last two years, he had become convinced that if he was going to regain the self-control that had previously defined him, he would have to take such drastic action that it might threaten his rather tenuous grip on sanity.

Up until now, everything he'd tried had been focused on controlling his conscious self. Since that clearly hadn't worked, he was left with an alternative he'd previously been unwilling to consider: he would attack the problem at the subconscious level. That decision had led Jack to his recent study of lucid dreaming, more specifically to an obscure authority on entering the lucid dream-state by using an advanced meditation technique.

Though Jack had spent many hours mastering the various parts of the Abramson method, until today, a strange reluctance had kept him from making his first attempt at putting it all together. He'd made the decision to end his procrastination during the short flight from Kauai to Honolulu, and Jack didn't need to struggle to understand why today was different.

~ ~ ~

Clearing his thoughts, Jack centered, working through a progressive series of meditation techniques, drifting deeper and deeper. As he noticed himself step across the boundary between wakefulness and sleep, he shifted techniques one last time, acquiring a vision of himself as a mere pinpoint of light floating in a vast sea of darkness. With a thought, Jack released the strand that tethered him to that pinpoint so that he drifted farther and farther into the dark.

When the dream came, it engulfed him with a suddenness that almost startled him awake, but he let the feeling wash through him without latching onto it. And thus it passed.

Jack looked around, the sense of déjà vu so intense that he thought for a moment he must never have awakened in that Calcutta clinic, that everything since that night had been just one endless dream.

A pea soup fog cloaked the street, trying its best to hide the worn paving stones beneath his feet. It was London, but this London had a distinct nineteenth-century feel, and not in a good way. A narrow alley to his left beckoned him and he didn't fight the feeling. The fog wasn't any thicker in the alley. The narrowness just made it feel that way.

Jack didn't look back, but he could feel the entrance to the alley dwindle behind him as he walked. To either side, an occasional door marred the walls that connected one building to the next, rusty hinges showing just how long it had been since anyone had opened them. It didn't matter. Jack's interest lay in the dark figure that suddenly blocked his path.

As he approached, the cowled figure turned and stepped through one of the closed doors on Jack's right, as if it had no more substance than smoke.

For a moment Jack hesitated, as a rush of fear pushed him away from whatever lay beyond that threshold and back toward wakefulness. But he'd come too far to turn back now. Following in the footsteps of the cloaked figure, Jack stepped through the ethereal door.

CHAPTER 8

The mind worm felt the intrusion and came alert.

During all of the centuries since it had discovered its peculiar affinity for humanity, it had been known by many names, among them Anchanchu. Humans tended to associate it with demons of their primitive religious beliefs, but the truth of its existence was something far more complicated. A multidimensional being without beginning or end, it was capable of observing multiple timelines, but until it had happened upon humans, the mind worm had never experienced physical sensation or emotion.

Anchanchu's discovery of its ability to link with a human mind had come about when its thoughts accidently touched that of a woman teetering at the transition from life to death. The stunning brilliance of her raw emotion and pain had shown Anchanchu just how boring the rest of its infinite existence had been, that one taste leaving the mind worm with an addiction that could not be sated.

In the centuries that followed, Anchanchu learned much about its ability to form a parasitic bond with a human host. Anchanchu could only revive one who lingered on death's doorway, not someone who was beyond natural recovery, and the host had to willingly accept its presence. After the bond, the host remained in control of his or her own being with a nature essentially unchanged.

Anchanchu, on the other hand, got to experience the host's sensations and emotions for the duration of the ride. The mind worm could exist in only one host at a time and, once accepted, remained linked to that host throughout its life. What its host felt excited Anchanchu, and some of that excitement fed back to its host. The overall effect was that its host still loved what he had always loved and hated what he had always hated, just much hotter.

And because Anchanchu's intuitions also bled over, its hosts found themselves drawn to situations that spiked their adrenaline. Because of that, few of them lived to a ripe old age.

Anchanchu had learned that it had certain needs that couldn't be fulfilled by bonding with some Siberian dirt farmer or his wife. Despite all its limitations, Anchanchu had a very clear sense of those humans who strode the life and death boundary, fully immersed in humanity's greatest and most terrible events. It always chose a host from this group.

Except for that near-death state where the bond was first accepted, Anchanchu had never managed to establish direct communication with any of its hosts.

But Jack Gregory had just kicked his way through that barrier.

: CHAPTER 9

Jack felt his passage through the dream door as if he had stepped through a curtain of cool mist. On the other side he halted, completely unprepared for the scene that confronted him. Jack knew this place intimately. He'd been here many times and had grown to love Switzerland's second largest city. But if not for the five-hundred-foot Jet d'Eau fountain shooting into the sky where Lake Geneva emptied into the Rhône, he wouldn't have recognized it.

Jack stood at lake's edge, his back to the avenue Quai Gustave-Ador, looking past the fountain across the city's burning skyline toward the mushroom cloud that climbed into the sky northwest of Geneva. All around him, rubble that had once been buildings burned. Amongst the bodies that lay scattered about, a few survivors stumbled through swirling radioactive fallout raining from the blood-red sky.

Suddenly a new wind thundered out of the southeast, racing back toward the mushroom cloud, flattening the buildings that remained standing and pushing the lake back into the city, destroying the fountain pumps that had miraculously survived the initial blast.

Jack understood what was happening. The initial blast wave had propagated outward from ground zero. Now that same air had come rushing back to deliver another devastating blow to the city by the lake.

Unlike the dreams with which he had become so familiar, this one wasn't another person's memory. This horror hadn't yet happened. Yet? Why had he thought that? No matter how real this seemed, it was just a nightmarish product of his lucid dream-state. Jack had seen enough.

He looked around, trying to catch sight of the figure he'd followed through the doorway to get here. It was gone. Jack didn't understand how he could be sure of that amidst all the raging destruction that had reduced visibility to near zero, but he was. He'd been intentionally left here.

Jack moved along the avenue, untouched by the wind-driven fire or the blowing debris that had once been Geneva, wondering why this imagery had gotten into his head. He might dream of nuclear war, but in Switzerland? Even more confusing, he couldn't shake the feeling that he'd been intended to witness this event, that he was somehow connected to it.

Bullshit, Jack. Wake your ass up.

It was then that a new thought hit him. He didn't know how to wake up. Jack knew that he wasn't really sleeping, so he should be able to consciously withdraw from the meditation. The problem was, he couldn't sense his body. It was as if he'd completely lost his way. Just knowing he had a body sitting atop a king-size bed in a Honolulu hotel wasn't helping him snap back to it. And there damn sure wasn't any sign of the door he'd walked through to get into this deeper dream-state.

Searching, Jack turned southwest into a maze of collapsed

multistory buildings that the fires hadn't yet made their way into. On the ground to his right, something drew his eye to a pile of bricks. From beneath a fallen·wall, two hands extended, fingers tightly intertwined, one hand larger, one very small. Jack knelt to examine them, a growing sickness leaching into his soul. Mother and child.

Jack reached out to touch them, but failed; he wasn't physically there, just a subconscious idea of himself observing the chaos.

Anger flared in his gut, and as Jack stared down at those entwined fingers, he fanned its embers into a white-hot rage that dimmed the world around him. Suddenly he felt his hands clench into such tight fists that his knuckles cracked. Jack opened his eyes and found himself sitting in a lotus position atop the bed, his sweat-soaked body rigid and shaking.

Crawling out of bed, Jack staggered to the bathroom sink, turned on the cold water, and scooped it onto his face with both hands. When he lifted his gaze to the mirror, he noticed the familiar red glint that crept into his eyes whenever his blood was up.

Staring at that reflection, Jack said what he was thinking.

"Now that went well."

CHAPTER 10

Steve Grange passed through the final layer of security and entered his ten-thousand-square-foot basement laboratory clad in scrubs. Without speaking to the woman seated behind it, he walked past the reception desk and entered the long corridor beyond. Three doors stood closed along the left wall, but today he had no interest in the work going on in the hardware fabrication laboratory that lay behind them.

Instead he turned into the short hallway to his right, where he was met by Dr. Kyle Landon, his perpetually worry-lined face looking unusually hound-doggish this morning. Grange understood that look. Although the FBI was busy chasing one of the red herrings Chinese intelligence had prepared to mask the trail that led to Jamal Glover, the NSA had begun making serious inroads that threatened Grange's timeline. Despite Qiang Chu's repeated assurances that he could handle the NSA, worry had begun to worm its way into Steve Grange's soul.

Stepping up to the waiting Dr. Landon, Grange made sure his voice carried none of that worry. "How's our subject's recovery progressing?"

Dr. Landon inclined his head just enough so that his eyes looked out over the shiny steel rims of his glasses. "There's no evidence of fluid building up on the brain, but I'm worried about your plan to shave a day off the recovery schedule. The incisions need more time to heal before we move him to the other facility and hook up the electrode array."

"If I had more time, I'd give it to you, but we'll be lucky if we don't have to move him even earlier."

Dr. Landon's frown deepened. "And if one of the incisions breaks open when he's in the sensory deprivation tank?"

"I don't care if you have to put his head in a plastic bag and insert a breathing tube; I need the subject alive and functional for phase two." Grange stared at Dr. Landon's rail-thin face as the man's salt-and-pepper eyebrows tried to knit themselves into one. "Don't disappoint me, Doctor. Our Chinese friend has a very low failure tolerance."

At Grange's mention of Qiang Chu, the color drained from Dr. Landon's face. The doctor raised a hand to his lips and nervously cleared his throat. "I'll make sure the subject is ready when you require him."

Grange grinned. "I like your attitude."

Dr. Landon pursed his lips, started to say something, but then turned and retreated back to the intensive care unit. Grange watched him go, confident that the brain surgeon would make good on his commitment. Despite the man's perpetually sour face, he liked living.

Unfortunately, Landon wasn't the one who worried Steve Grange. His CGI development team had that honor. Turning left, Grange entered the second of two doors opposite the surgery room.

The twenty-by-thirty-foot room that opened up before him housed three two-man workstations arranged in a loose triangle, facing outward. Narrow spaces between the workstations allowed access to the raised console that occupied the center of the triangle.

It was an odd arrangement, but one that facilitated rapid communication among the developers and Delores Mendosa, the team leader. Grange saw Delores rise from her seat at the center console as she saw him approach.

The woman stepped out through the gap separating the two nearest workstations to intercept Grange before he reached the developers. Delores, her jet-black hair styled into a short pixie cut, stood all of five foot three inches tall, but exuded a commanding presence that belied her stature. Like all six of her designers and developers, she had spent years creating incredibly detailed 3D virtual environments for video game companies and movie studios.

Delores was smart and she was driven, two qualities that had earned her a reputation as a leader who could meet even the toughest deadlines. Known for her adamant refusal to be moved away from CGI development and into positions of corporate leadership, her people had dubbed her the Dungeon Master, or DM, a play on her initials that Delores readily embraced. It was her reputation that had brought Delores to the attention of Steve Grange. But it was the allure of the project Grange had offered that had ensnared her.

"What can I do for you, Mr. Grange?" she asked.

"I want a word with you in private."

For a second her dark brown eyes regarded him. Then she nodded and led him through a door to Grange's left and into her private office. Rather than going behind her desk, she motioned Grange to a seat at the small, round conference table before seating herself opposite him.

Again Grange felt her fix him with her penetrating gaze. "I'm listening," she said.

"I may be forced to accelerate your schedule."

Her jaw muscles tightened. "I told you I would have the product ready for delivery on Thursday morning. There's no slack in that schedule."

"There's always slack."

"Not in my schedules."

"You may have to work your team through the night."

Delores hissed, a sound that seemed to bring a chill into the small room. When she leaned toward him, her eyes flashed with anger that she didn't bother to hide.

"Look, this isn't some half-ass paint job we're working on. My people are creative artists, experts at using graphic design tools to produce a digital environment that is indistinguishable from the one you've tasked us to simulate."

"I'm well aware of that, Ms. Mendosa."

"Good! Then you know that if I force my team to rush this, we'll end up compromising on quality. If that happens, the subject won't believe that his virtual companions and surroundings are real."

"Any sacrifice in quality is completely unacceptable."

"No shit!"

Grange felt a scowl tighten his lips. The only reason he tolerated this woman was because she was irreplaceable. But unlike Dr. Landon, Delores Mendosa was absolutely fearless.

Grange rose from the table to stare down at her. "I need the product to be ready by Wednesday morning. I don't care how you do it; just get it done!"

Without waiting for her response, Grange turned on his heel, walked out of her office, and then out of the CGI laboratory. Rounding the corner to his left, he heard the door snick closed behind him.

At the far end of the hall, Grange paused outside a sealed doorway to take two calming breaths. He wouldn't allow himself to carry any anger or frustration into the chamber that lay beyond that door.

Placing his palm against the scanner, Grange watched as the door disappeared into a slot in the wall. Cold air flowed out like a river, chilling his legs and feet such that the air around them would have condensed into fog if not for the humidity-controlled environment. Grange stepped forward, hearing the door whisk closed behind him as he approached the horizontally mounted fourteen-by-four-foot metal cylinder that occupied the center of the otherwise empty room.

Grange moved up beside the stainless steel cylinder that housed the frozen body of the only woman he'd ever loved. Wiping the moisture from his eyes, he leaned down to kiss the smooth metal, feeling his breath carry some of that cold through his lips and into his lungs.

When Grange lifted his head, the whisper that escaped his lips was barely audible.

"I miss you, Helen."

Grange felt a tear form at the corner of his left eye. As a wan smile creased his lips, he realized that, for the first time in twenty years, this was a tear of expectant joy.

: CHAPTER 11

Levi Elias glanced at the other person seated at the table in Admiral Riles's private conference room while they waited for the NSA director's arrival. Dr. Denise Jennings kept her iron-gray hair pulled back in a tight bun. She wasn't the NSA's top computer scientist. Dr. David Kurtz held that honor. But Denise had developed the underpinnings of the massively distributed neural network that she had nicknamed Big John, after the legendary miner in the old Jimmy Dean ballad.

While it was true that the NSA collected and stored massive amounts of data, much of it at its Utah Data Center, Big John did a different type of data mining, one that didn't involve data collection at a central location. Denise had been behind the top-secret NSA program that had encouraged the rise of illegal computer hacking groups. It wasn't their hacking that the NSA was interested in. It was the fear of being hacked that had been created in the general populace.

That fear drove people to install antivirus software on all of their electronics and, unbeknownst to even the antivirus companies, Denise's kernel had been embedded in the vast majority of their products. The NSA estimated that those kernels were currently installed on two-thirds of the computational devices on the planet.

The beauty of this approach was that antivirus software was designed to scan every bit of data on each system as well as network packets that were transmitted to and from the device. As the small patch of neurons that made up Denise's kernel examined the data on one particular device, it used a special algorithm to categorize it and assign node weights.

What all this meant was that the actual data didn't need to be transmitted back to a central collection center. The world was Big John's data center. And because antivirus applications needed to regularly update themselves with the latest virus signatures, they were expected to send and receive data. Embedded in the data that came in to each device were regular updates to each Big John kernel. And the devices transmitted their accumulated node weights back out.

As far as Levi was concerned, how Big John used that worldwide neural net to perform the correlative searches for which it had been designed was pure black magic. And Dr. Denise Jennings was the voodoo queen. Considering her periodic verbal wonderings about when Big John might acquire true artificial intelligence, Levi thought the voodoo reference appropriate.

Neither Levi nor Denise rose to their feet as Admiral Riles entered. Riles had long ago made it quite clear to members of his senior staff that he considered that particular military courtesy a waste of time and didn't want to be bothered with repeatedly telling them to stay seated. As Riles took his seat at the head of the table, his eyes focused on Levi.

"Okay, Levi," Riles said. "What the hell is going on?"

Levi clicked the red power button on the remote control in his left hand and the wall-mounted display opposite Admiral Riles came to life. A thirty-five-year-old man in a navy-blue suit, white shirt, and tie occupied the screen.

"Sir, this is Agent Hal Bradford, the FBI special agent in charge of their Jamal Glover investigation. We've been monitoring all communications between Agent Bradford, his team, and his superiors. He is currently following up on a number of leads that point to Jamal Glover having gone to ground in Miami as he prepares to leave the country."

"What leads?"

"Based on an anonymous tip, the FBI staked out a café in South Beach, where a UPS truck dropped off a package. The owner said he'd been paid to accept the package and that a man matching Jamal's description was supposed to stop by to pick it up before closing time last night. When Jamal never showed up, the FBI figured he must have spotted them."

"What was in the package?"

"Three fake passports bearing Jamal's picture. French, Peruvian, and Egyptian. The documents were top-notch. There were also three bundles of cash, denominated in each of those country's currencies. The FBI is trying to trace the package back to its sender but no luck so far."

Levi watched the admiral lean back in his chair and waited for him to speak.

"So who's playing them?" Riles asked.

"We're pretty sure it's the Chinese."

Levi clicked a button on the remote and a new image replaced that of Agent Bradford, one that was well known to both Levi and Admiral Riles. It wasn't an official photo, but it had been taken with a high-definition camera. Interpol hadn't volunteered it, but that hadn't kept the NSA from acquiring it. In the picture, a lean-muscled Qiang Chu stared directly up into the camera, wearing a smile that didn't quite make it into his dark eyes.

Levi continued. "This was taken from a Paris hotel balcony just over two months ago. The French agent who took it was found dead shortly after transmitting the digital image back to his headquarters."

"And you believe Qiang Chu is responsible for Jamal's disappearance?"

"Yes, sir." Levi advanced the slide show to the next image. It showed a man stepping out of a black Lexus into a strip-mall parking lot. Despite his sunglasses and the poor image quality, the man's features were familiar. "Based on Big John's interpretation of the data, we retrieved security video footage from the Snowden Square Shopping Center in Columbia, Maryland. The shopping center is less than a mile from Jamal Glover's house and this image was captured less than three hours before Jill McPherson was murdered in Jamal's kitchen."

Levi saw Admiral Riles turn his attention to Dr. Jennings. "What's your level of confidence in this?"

"Sir, Big John has assigned a 0.93 correlation factor to Qiang Chu's involvement in Jill McPherson's murder and the subsequent disappearance of Jamal Glover."

The lines at the corners of the admiral's eyes tightened. "Don't you think that's an unusually high level of confidence considering the limited and conflicting data?"

Despite the aggressive tone of the admiral's question, Denise didn't back off. "It's Big John's estimate, not mine. Based on past experience, I don't doubt him."

"It, not him!" Levi felt Riles's irritation like an electric charge in the air.

"Pardon?" Denise asked.

"Big John is a genetically evolving neural net, not a person. I've told you before that I find your terminology distracting and annoying."

Although Levi was well aware of Riles's annoyance with the way Dr. Jennings thought of Big John, the admiral's level of impatience surprised him. It was a clear sign of the threat that Jamal's disappearance represented to the NSA and, by extension, to the American government. It was also an indication of how much pressure President Tom Harris was bringing to bear on the NSA director.

Dr. Jennings ran a hand up over the top of her head as if checking to ensure that the tight bun was still fastened firmly in place. Suddenly aware of her nervous reaction, she lowered her hand and nodded. "Yes, sir."

Levi leaned forward. "No matter how much weight we give to Big John's analysis, I happen to agree with the result. The FBI trail is just too obvious and Jamal Glover is far too good at what he does to let them discover it that way. If I'm right, then a foreign government is planting false trails. That picture of Qiang is too big a coincidence for it to be anybody but the Chinese. I think they've got Jamal and are trying to smuggle him out of the country."

"Tell me we've got more than that."

"Qiang Chu is very good at covering his trail, but our imagery analysts have been able to cobble together a mosaic from satellite data and video cameras."

Levi pressed another button and the video screen shifted to a tiled display showing views from multiple cameras. Some of the frames were showing full-motion video while others were filled with high-resolution satellite images, all tagged with the date and time they were taken.

Levi narrated as he pointed the red dot from a laser pointer at frame after frame.

"Jamal's car pulled into his garage at 8:35 P.M. on Friday evening. Forty-five minutes later, it backed out again. We picked up the car on a number of cameras as it made its way up onto I-95 north toward Baltimore. At 9:48 p.m., it pulled into this warehouse at an industrial park just outside Linthicum, Maryland.

"A white panel van pulled out of the warehouse shortly after 10 p.m. and made its way to a freight shipping facility on the north side of BWI airport."

Admiral Riles interrupted. "Was that the only vehicle to leave the Linthicum warehouse?"

"No. Shortly after midnight a big rig exited the building and took Highway 295 to D.C., where it stopped at another warehouse before going on to Richmond." Levi turned off the wall-mounted display, then redirected his gaze to Admiral Riles. "We've already had people on the ground at all of these locations."

"And?"

Levi found himself wishing he had better confidence in what he was about to say, but it was all he had. "There's no sign of Jamal's car at the Linthicum warehouse or at any of the locations where the big rig stopped. The shipping manifest included crates of auto parts, but those checked out. Neither the driver nor the loading dock crews admit to having seen the car or Jamal. Luckily, none of that matters."

Riles leaned forward over the table, his left hand cupping his right fist below his chin. "Why the hell not?"

"The car's a smoke screen. When it turns up, it will lead authorities down another false trail. I'm convinced that Jamal was in the white van that went to BWI. That freight shipping center belongs to International Shipping Service, or ISS. ISS was busy loading one of its aircraft when the van arrived at the center. That aircraft departed BWI at 11:52 P.M., made a stop in Kansas City,

Missouri, to off-load and take on more cargo, before continuing on to Oakland."

Levi met the admiral's steady gaze. He'd spent a long time building the trust he was about to put on the line for little more than an educated guess. "If you believe, like I do, that Qiang Chu took Jamal, they damn sure wouldn't off-load him in Kansas City or ship him to D.C. or Richmond. They'd want to get him to the West Coast and then probably onto a ship headed for China."

"Why not on an aircraft?"

"Qiang Chu would have anticipated that we'd be closely monitoring all international outbound flights by mid-morning on Saturday. But his Boeing 757 would have already landed in Oakland and off-loaded its cargo." Levi put all the self-assurance he could muster into his next statement. "We need to get our team to the San Francisco Bay Area as quickly as possible."

Admiral Riles leaned back in his chair, his left hand stroking his chin as he weighed Levi's arguments. Familiar with the way the admiral wielded his extended silences to pull extra information from whoever was briefing him, Levi held his tongue and waited.

Seeing that no more information would be forthcoming, Riles rose to his feet. "Okay. We'll let the FBI focus on this end. As soon as Jack Gregory arrives this afternoon, get the team briefed and moving."

The admiral redirected his attention to Dr. Jennings. "Denise. Modify your Big John query accordingly. By the time our ghosts set foot in California, I want a more specific target."

Without another word, Admiral Riles turned and walked out of the small conference room. As Levi followed him out, he hoped like hell that his analysis of this situation was correct. God help them all if the Chinese gained access to everything Jamal Glover knew.

CHAPTER 12

Janet Price approached Baltimore/Washington International Airport still trying to suppress her irritation with Levi Elias. When Levi had overruled Spider Sanchez's decision to personally pick up Jack at the airport, assigning the task to Janet instead, she'd voiced her objections. But Levi had refused to listen. So here she was, approaching a rendezvous that was bound to be both awkward and painful. On the plus side, she'd certainly be ready to kill someone once the team got the go order.

As she turned onto the arrivals loop, she spotted Jack Gregory standing on the curb outside the baggage claim area, a canvas duffel bag slung over his left shoulder. Her sudden spike in heart rate surprised her. When she'd last seen him in Miami, the curly brown hair had been fairly close-cropped. Now, clad in shorts, sandals, and a wild Hawaiian shirt that accentuated his tan body, he could have been a world-class surfer traveling to find some big, storm-driven waves. But Janet knew that beneath his shirt a web of knife and bullet scars decorated Jack's lean-muscled torso.

Janet pulled the black Ford Explorer into an open space at the curb, pressed the button that raised the rear hatch, unbuckled her seat belt, and leaned across the console to shove open the passenger-side door. Having spotted her as she approached, Jack tossed his duffel in the rear, closed the hatch, and slid into the passenger seat, accompanied by the heat and humidity of the late afternoon. Neither his grin nor his brown eyes held any echo of the mistrust she'd thrown in his face before she'd walked away from him in South Beach.

"Hello, Jack."

"It's good to see you."

Janet pulled out into traffic and headed toward the airport exit. "Is it?"

"Every time."

His easy laugh brought forth a bright memory: Jack sitting next to her at a sidewalk café on Crete as they sipped cappuccino and gazed out over the deep blue Mediterranean Sea. Angry at herself, Janet pushed the image from her thoughts.

"You look rested," she said.

"Hawaii has that effect on me."

Janet took the ramp onto I-195 and accelerated into the fast lane. "That's good. You're going to need it."

"What exactly is it we're supposed to be doing? Levi just said I'd be briefed once I link up with the rest of the team."

"Just sit back and relax. You'll be briefed along with the rest of the team when we get to the farmhouse."

Beside her, she felt Jack acquire some of the tension that bound her body.

"Okay," he said. "You don't like the fact that Riles contracted my services and assigned me to your team for this operation. But he did. So act like the professional you are and get over Bolivia. I have."

This time Janet laughed. "Really? Don't bullshit me, Jack. You may be looking tan and rested, but I don't believe for a second that you've gotten past what happened down there."

Janet heard his voice soften dangerously.

"You're just going to have to trust me."

"You see, Jack? That's the problem. How can I trust you when you don't trust yourself? You told me as much in Crete. I just didn't believe you. It took Bolivia to convince me."

From the corner of her eye, Janet saw Jack's eyes harden. Then he settled back in his seat, facing front as she merged onto I-95 north. The way he'd looked at her had been brief, but if Jack had punched her in the gut, he couldn't have more thoroughly robbed her of breath. *Jesus!* She hadn't meant to say what she'd said. For some reason this strange man's presence spun her about as no other had ever done, and that scared the hell out of her.

Janet drove on in silence and Jack made no effort to break it. They looped around west Baltimore, took I-70 west to Frederick, and then turned north on Highway 15. After she parked the SUV inside the barn, Jack walked to the rear of the Explorer, grabbed his duffel, and followed her toward the farmhouse. As they approached, Levi Elias and Spider Sanchez stepped off the front steps to meet them. Spider's powerful stride carried him to Jack first, a broad grin spreading across his face.

Instead of the hearty handshake Janet expected, the two men embraced, slapping each other on the back before stepping back.

"Damn fine to see you, Jacky Boy!" Spider said.

Jack's grin matched that of the NSA team leader. "It's been a long time, Spider."

"The surfer dude look is working for you."

Levi, who had also been closely watching the reunion, stepped forward and extended his right hand. "Hi, Jack. I'm Levi Elias. Glad you agreed to join us."

Jack shook the senior NSA analyst's hand. "Janet was a little shy on the details. Mind filling me in?"

Janet met Levi's quick glance, then watched as he turned toward the door.

"Let's step inside," he said.

When they entered the living room, a familiar scene unfolded, one that Janet had experienced many times. None of the others stood to shake Jack's hand. Instead they lounged on the chairs and couches, watching Jack with the cold curiosity common when a new member was introduced to an elite team. Except for Spider, none of these men knew Jack. They were all the "show me" kind, preferring to form their own opinions of a newbie's competence and reliability.

Without waiting to be introduced, Jack took one of the open chairs and, as Janet and Spider seated themselves on the opposite side of the arc, he leaned across the coffee table to grab a handful of mini-pretzels. Levi moved to the front of the group and proceeded to introduce the team members Jack hadn't yet met, drawing simple nods of acknowledgement from Harry, Bronson, Paul, and Bobby, movements that Jack nonchalantly acknowledged.

Levi began his presentation by passing out thick manila envelopes to everyone except Jack. Noting the omission, Janet studied Jack's face. He appeared not to care that he hadn't been given a packet.

"Don't bother opening your envelopes until I'm finished," Levi said. "They contain the credentials you will each be using for this operation. As of this moment you represent the Department of Homeland Security, more specifically Immigration and Customs Enforcement's Homeland Security Investigations component."

"What about him?" Raymond Bronson gestured toward Jack, voicing the question that Janet had almost asked.

"I'll get to that in a minute," said Levi. "Listen up."

For the next thirty minutes, Levi Elias spelled out exactly what the NSA knew and what, at this point, the agency only surmised. Then he turned to their orders. Spider's team would pose as a special interagency task force investigating a very specific terrorist threat: that a Chinese gang, supported by North Korean intelligence operatives, would attempt to smuggle a nuclear device through the Port of Oakland.

But the team's real mission was to find Jamal Glover before the Chinese or some other government could spirit him out of the country. The team would travel to the San Francisco Bay Area on two NSA aircraft. Part of the team would land at San Francisco International Airport while the rest would fly into Oakland. Levi would contact them when they arrived in California with additional information.

Levi finished his briefing and Janet watched as his gaze passed from person to person before coming to rest on Raymond Bronson. "Any questions? And no, Bronson, I don't want to hear about how good-looking you are."

Janet laughed along with the others. Then she saw Levi shift his attention to Jack Gregory, who appeared completely at ease, despite having been excluded from any part of the operation that Levi had discussed thus far.

"Okay, Jack. It's your turn."

"I noticed you didn't prepare a new identity for me. I assume that was intentional."

Levi leaned over and picked up the remote control that rested on an end table to his right, turned to face the wall-mounted display, and clicked the power button. When the display came to life, Janet found herself staring at a handsome, elegantly dressed man who appeared to be in his mid- to late forties.

"Meet Jim 'Max' McPherson," said Levi. "Billionaire founder of one of the world's most successful hedge funds."

Levi pressed another button on the remote, then pressed it again and again, cycling through a series of bloody crime scene photographs featuring a young blonde woman slumped down against an oven. Her throat had been cut so deeply it looked as if someone had tried to sever her head.

"And this is his daughter, Jill McPherson. Her body was discovered on Saturday morning in Jamal Glover's kitchen. As I previously mentioned, the FBI believes that Jamal killed her in a jealous rage and fled. But we have reason to believe that a Chinese assassin named Qiang Chu killed her before kidnapping Jamal. Max McPherson doesn't give a shit; he wants the head of whoever killed his daughter in a burlap sack. And he's willing to pay somebody whatever it takes to make that happen."

Although Janet didn't like where this seemed to be going, she saw Jack nod in silent acceptance.

Levi continued. "Within twenty-four hours of his daughter's murder, we began intercepting messages sent through an intermediary inquiring about the availability of people with a very particular skill set. That was yesterday. Last night, one of our people contacted this go-between and provided rather detailed information about the availability of just such a person: a man known in dark circles as 'The Ripper.'"

The uncomfortable feeling that had gripped Janet now had validation. *Jesus! Jack's been on the ground less than two hours and the craziness is already starting!*

"So you see, Jack," Levi said, "you don't need a new identity because you get to play yourself."

Although the previous mirth had gone out of Jack's face, he showed no sign of surprise at this sudden turn of events.

Levi cleared his throat. "We want you to contact McPherson, just as you have done with your previous clients, and sell your services. You are a private consultant to the NSA but you can keep any additional money that McPherson might pay you. Think of it as a bonus. And except for occasional updates between you and Spider's team, you will operate as you have since you left the CIA's employ, using your personal methods and resources."

"And if I succeed," Jack said, "you get plausible deniability for any collateral damage I might cause."

"A side benefit."

Jack rose to his feet facing Levi, his brown eyes glittering as they narrowed. "When do I meet Mr. McPherson?"

"You don't. Everything goes through his intermediary."

"That's not how I work. I meet with McPherson personally or you can find yourself another contractor."

Levi Elias paused for several seconds and then nodded. "I'll see what I can arrange."

"Okay then," said Jack. "I'm going to need some equipment and a vehicle on this end. I'm partial to motorcycles."

"That won't be a problem."

"Good. We done here?"

"Until I have McPherson's answer. In the meantime you can stay right here." Levi turned his attention back to the others. "The rest of you, pack up and get moving. Your travel itineraries are in your packets. You can study on your flights."

As Janet rose to her feet, her eyes briefly locked with Jack's, and once again she felt the rush of adrenaline she got by being around him. When he turned and walked away toward the kitchen, Janet watched him go. She'd been adamant that Jack was too dangerous to be allowed on her team and she'd made her views clear to both Levi and Spider. Now, in a weird way, she'd gotten her wish. So why wasn't she feeling good about it?

Seeing Levi open the door and step outside, Janet followed, catching up with him as he reached his silver Audi. Levi stopped and turned to face her, his face questioning.

Janet allowed a hint of accusation to creep into her voice. "Why is Admiral Riles sending Jack out on his own like this? I thought the whole point of bringing him on board was to add his skills to the team."

"That was the original plan, but McPherson offered us a unique target of opportunity where Jack gets to do what he's so good at. Worst case, he provides a distraction that confuses our enemies."

Suddenly everything became crystal clear. "You're sending Jack out without backup? Using him as bait?"

As much as she had always liked Levi, Janet wasn't liking what she now saw in the analyst's dark eyes.

"You know even better than I do that Jack can take care of himself," said Levi. "Focus on your mission and leave Jack's to him."

Then Levi opened the car door, slid into the driver's seat, and drove away.

Janet watched his dust trail until he disappeared around a bend, hidden by a thick copse of trees. She'd experienced this same kind of decision making many times before and she knew that from the agency perspective, it was probably a good one. Although it placed Jack at increased risk, it was the same type of risk he chose on his private consulting jobs.

But standing in the long shadows cast by the late-afternoon sun, Janet couldn't shake the feeling that, this time, she was responsible.

CHAPTER 13

Sometime in the past, one of the senior traders at Jim McPherson's Maximum Capital Appreciation Fund had nicknamed his boss Max. It was an apt description of the effort he dedicated to accomplishing every goal he set for himself. During his divorce, Max's goal had been to gain sole custody of Jillian, his only child. It had cost him a hundred million dollars to make his ex-wife go away, but it had been money well spent.

Through the years that followed, despite the long hours he devoted to building the world's most successful hedge fund, Max had always made sure he got plenty of father-daughter time, attending her grade school plays, middle school sporting events, and high school cheerleading competitions. When she got into trouble, which wasn't often, he was there to ensure that if any punishment was doled out, it came from him rather than some third-party institution.

During Jill's junior year studying marketing at Georgetown University, two important things had happened: she'd started a successful modeling career, and she'd fallen in love with a young MIT prodigy by the name of Jamal Glover. Max hadn't cared in the least that Jamal was black. But the fact that his twenty-one-year-old daughter was dating an eighteen-year-old had worried him.

His first meeting with Jamal had dispelled his concern. Despite his youth, Jamal was a college junior and displayed a self-confidence, wit, and maturity that made Max want to hire the young man. Upon Jamal's graduation the following year, Max had been disappointed when he accepted an offer to work at the NSA. When Max had offered him five times his government salary, Jamal had laughed and said something about grabbing a once-in-a-lifetime challenge.

Thirty-six hours ago that challenge had killed Max's little girl. The FBI's notion that Jamal had killed Jill was understandable, but misguided. Not only was Jamal a nonviolent person, but they had been deliriously in love with each other. There was no way that Jill would have picked up another lover on the side.

Max knew that nothing could ever bring her back, but he couldn't bear the thought of her killer getting away with what he had done. Even worse, the thought of Jill's murderer being processed through the screwed-up American legal system made him sick to his stomach. The prospect of having to sit for weeks in a courtroom while prosecutors presented grisly crime scene photos and step-by-step re-creations of the crime while defense attorneys tried to slander his daughter was intolerable. Even if the trial produced a guilty verdict, Jill's killer would live on in prison.

Pushing back from his desk, Max walked to the floor-to-ceiling windows that filled the south wall of his second-floor office and looked out at the immaculately manicured grounds surrounding the estate. Bathed in the light of the waning gibbous moon, he almost expected to see Jill's ghostly image drifting past the fountain and through her beloved gardens.

Max gritted his teeth so hard he heard his jaws crack. There was a price to be paid. Justice might not demand it, but Max McPherson would. He had no intention of contracting some two-bit hit man; he needed a highly skilled and ruthless specialist. Grant Thorn, his chief of security, had delivered a list of candidates. Four hours ago, after reviewing their files, Max dared to hope that he'd found the right man for the job. Then he'd gotten the bad news that had forced him to scratch that man from his list.

It wasn't that The Ripper was unavailable. The problem was that he had insisted on a face-to-face meeting with Max before taking the job. As badly as Max wanted to hire the best contractor available, a direct meeting with the assassin was out of the question. So he'd told Thorn to reject The Ripper's request.

Max scrubbed his face with both hands, digging his thumbs deep into his aching temples. When he glanced down at his laptop, the sole source of illumination in the office, he was surprised to see that it was nearly midnight. Mentally and emotionally exhausted, Max barely recognized his surroundings.

Without bothering to put the laptop to sleep, Max walked out of his spacious office and turned toward the master suite. Maybe tonight his exhaustion would grant him a sleep not filled with nightmarish images of Jill's corpse staring up at him from the coroner's table.

Glad that he'd dismissed his household staff for the evening, Max walked down the dark hallway, shoulders slumped beneath the weight of his despair. He passed the top of the gently spiraling stairway that opened down into the grand foyer and saw Grant Thorn making his nightly rounds. Grant looked up at Max but said nothing. That was good. They both knew there was nothing to say.

The double doors to the master suite stood open and Max stepped inside his dark bedroom, closing them behind him. When he reached for the light switch, a low voice startled him.

"I like the dark."

Max spun toward the sound. There in the deep shadows of his sitting area, a dark figure sat in one of his reading chairs. With his heart pounding so loudly he was sure the other man could hear it, Max debated calling out for Thorn. But if this man wanted to kill him, he could do it before the security chief could reach the stairway.

"How'd you get in here?"

"It would seem that your estate's security isn't as good as you thought."

No shit! Max thought. He fought to recover his equilibrium, to erase the fear from his voice. "Who are you? What do you want from me?"

The stranger's next words stunned him. "You asked if I was interested in doing a job for you. Think of the fact that I'm sitting here as my resume."

"The Ripper?" Just saying the name sent chills up his arms and neck.

"I've been called that. Please, have a seat."

A hand movement indicated the reading chair opposite the one in which The Ripper sat and Max found himself moving automatically toward it.

Max sat down. "Two nights ago, my daughter was murdered."

"I know."

Thankful that there was no banal offering of sympathy, Max allowed a hint of the rage he felt into his voice. "Are you familiar with the details of my daughter's murder?"

"Yes."

"Let me be clear. Even if the FBI arrests him first, I want Jillian's killer dead. Can you do that for me?"

"Yes."

The timbre of The Ripper's voice seemed to drop the room's temperature. It might have been his altered state of mind, but Max McPherson couldn't shake the feeling that, had there been more light, his breath would have been visible. None of the industry titans whom he'd spent the last twenty years rubbing elbows with projected as powerful a presence as the man seated across from Max right now. All his doubts had been erased. This was the one.

"Name your price."

"Two million dollars plus expenses, payable upon successful completion of my mission."

The killer's answer surprised Max. "Nothing up front?"

"I never accept payment before the job is finished."

Max swallowed, then leaned forward trying to get a better look at the weapon he was about to launch at Jill's murderer. Despite the way the moonlight-splashed bay window backlit The Ripper's face, Max thought he glimpsed a red glint in those dark eyes.

The Ripper stood and looked down at him.

"Agreed," Max said. "I'll have my security chief escort you out through the front gate."

Max rose to his feet to stand facing the man he'd just hired. He extended his hand and felt the raw power in the hand that gripped it. Then, as Max raised his cell phone to speed-dial Thorn, he found himself wishing he was calling Jill's killer. He'd dearly love to whisper something in that man's ear.

Get ready, you bastard. Hell is coming to dinner.

CHAPTER 14

Wearing a multicolored Tori Richards shirt, black jeans, and flat-toed motorcycle boots, Jack climbed out of the chartered Beechcraft 400A onto the tarmac at Lee's Summit Municipal Airport, looking southwest at the anvil-topped thunderheads gathered there. The weather service had issued tornado watches for Kansas City and the surrounding area beginning at 2:00 P.M. central time and continuing throughout the afternoon and evening. From the look of those storm clouds, those watches were likely to turn into warnings.

His loose-fitting shirt concealed a holstered undershirt that secured his 9mm HK P30S against his lower back. A black Gerber Guardian dagger hung inverted in a custom sheath along his right side. With what Jack intended to do, it was unlikely that this weaponry would go unused for very much longer.

Aware that Janet and the rest of the NSA team were already on the ground in the San Francisco Bay Area, Jack had decided on a very different approach, one designed to bring himself to the attention of Jamal's kidnappers. If Admiral Riles wanted to use him as bait, Jack would make sure the bait couldn't be ignored.

Jack walked into the Heartland Executive Aviation office, made arrangements to have the Beechcraft jet refueled, and retrieved the car keys that had been left for him at the front desk.

In the parking lot, he spotted the silver Mustang convertible in the third parking space to his right. It was 12:33 P.M. and the temperature was now hot enough that Jack thought about putting the top down, but a glance at the gathering clouds talked him out of that notion. While it was no fun to be caught in a hard rainstorm without overhead protection, these big Midwestern storm clouds usually contained a mixture of rain and hail. He didn't really want to have to stop under an overpass to put the top up.

Jack tossed his duffel in the trunk, climbed in, and turned the ignition, rewarded by the engine's deep rumble as he guided the car onto Lee's Summit Road and then onto I-70 west. He'd decided to fly into Lee's Summit on the southeast side of Kansas City and make the forty-five-mile drive to Kansas City International Airport for security reasons. It made his arrival far less visible and provided ample opportunity to lose any pursuers prior to his departure.

As Jack took exit 13 onto I-29 north, his thoughts turned to the hostile reception he'd gotten from Janet Price in Baltimore. Even though he hadn't expected a hug, her ongoing anger had surprised him. Maybe it shouldn't have. After all, two months ago he'd come extremely close to getting her killed. Worse than that, he'd confirmed her doubts about his mental stability. His mental stability. Now there was a funny thought.

Taking the airport exit onto NW 120th Street, Jack slowed and parked near the International Shipping Service cargo facility. A warehouse butted up against a large hanger, its front wall sporting a large sign that read ISS AIR CARGO.

The rumble of distant thunder accompanied Jack to the lone metal door set into the cinderblock wall. He pressed down on the lever-shaped door handle and pulled it open. Stepping inside, he found himself in a small waiting area separated from another closed door by a gray metal counter. On the far side sat a heavy-set woman who looked up and gave him a surprisingly warm and gracious smile. Jack glanced at the security camera mounted high up on the wall behind her and returned the smile.

"May I help you?" she asked.

He glanced at her name tag. "Hello Patty. I'm Jack Frazier, DEA."

The credentials he flashed were good enough to pass initial scrutiny, but would never endure extensive follow-up. That was okay. He didn't need them to.

A look of surprise crossed her features, but she recovered admirably. "What can I do for you, Agent Frazier?"

"I would like to speak to your supervisor. Would you call him, please?"

Patty hesitated. Then she lifted her cell phone and speed-dialed a number. "Carl. There's a DEA agent out front. He's asking to speak with you." She paused to listen. "Okay. I'll send him on back."

Switching off the phone, the woman nodded toward the door. "The manager's name is Carl Bogati. Through that door, his office is second on the right."

Jack stepped around the counter, opened the door, and found himself in a wide hallway that opened onto a big warehouse floor thirty feet ahead. The sound of moving conveyer systems accompanied the loud beep of a forklift backing up. Jack was five feet from the door when it opened. A bald white guy wearing a blue uniform with "ISS" stenciled on the left breast pocket stepped out to greet him. The fellow extended a broad hand and Jack shook it.

"I'm Carl Bogati, floor manager for this air cargo facility."

"Jack Frazier with the DEA." Again he flashed the DEA creds. "If we could step into your office, I've got a few questions I'd like to ask you."

"Sure thing."

Bogati stepped aside and motioned Jack into the office. It wasn't much to look at. A gray steel-case desk held a computer, an in-box piled high with papers, and a coffee-stained blotter with this month's calendar. Aside from some metal filing cabinets and Bogati's rolling office chair, there was only one other piece of furniture, a metal folding chair leaning against the far wall. As Bogati took a seat behind the desk, Jack unfolded the other chair and sat down.

"So," Bogati began, his eyes narrowing ever so slightly, "why is the DEA interested in my facility? I assure you, ISS doesn't transport illegal drugs."

"On Saturday, at approximately two in the morning, a cargo plane flew in from Baltimore, off-loaded some cargo, and then departed for Oakland."

"Yeah? So what. You have any idea how much cargo passes through here every day?"

"I'd like to see the cargo manifest for that plane."

Jack noted that the man's helpful look had left his face.

"Have you got a warrant?"

"I can get one, but I was hoping for your cooperation."

The look on Bogati's face hardened. "Here at ISS, we value our customers' privacy. You want to look at a manifest, come back when you've got a warrant."

Jack remained seated. "Maybe you'd be willing to answer a few questions then?"

Bogati stood. "We're done here."

Jack stood facing the manager and let a hard edge creep into his voice. "Our next meeting will be a lot less pleasant."

The bald man stepped forward, his invasion of Jack's personal space intended to send a message. "Count on it."

Without a backward glance, Jack walked back the way he had come, confident that the ISS manager was already placing an important call. It wasn't likely to be to one of his ISS supervisors. As Jack made his way out the front door, he passed a bigger man in an ISS uniform coming from the general vicinity where Jack had parked the Mustang.

A low rumble of thunder drew Jack's attention to the wall of clouds that hung like a curtain from the approaching storm. He climbed in, started the car, and pulled out of the parking lot. After getting to his destination, he'd find the tracking device the big guy had planted. Then he'd find out whether the NSA was right about who he was dealing with.

CHAPTER 15

Qiang Chu felt the blood drip from his right hand, heard the plop as it splashed into the red pool on the concrete basement floor, and marveled at the stupidity of the big man whose brains oozed out onto the floor through his shattered skull. Of course Qiang's hand hadn't cracked that skull open; it had been the impact with the concrete pillar that had finished this demonstration.

The whimper from the figure huddled in the far corner attracted his attention and Qiang walked toward the man, the bare ceiling bulb casting his long shadow toward his target. Gan Liu was in his early forties and had grown fat since taking over leadership of the Asian gang known as the Bay Triad. Having just watched the way Qiang had killed Liu's longtime bodyguard using only his hands and feet, Liu showed no sign of the bluster with which he'd confronted Qiang upon his arrival at this meeting place.

That was good. Qiang didn't have the time to deal with the battle for triad leadership that would result if he were forced to kill Liu. The fact that Liu had shown up accompanied by four of his enforcers had demonstrated he wasn't completely stupid. Had he been meeting anyone but Qiang, that would have been overkill. But now, except for the four broken bodies that lay scattered across the floor, Liu was very much alone. From the look on the gangster's pudgy face, he suddenly found himself very open to Qiang's proposal.

As he stopped in front of the triad boss, Qiang's cell phone warbled. He pulled it from the pocket of his loose-fitting black pants, glanced at the caller ID, and answered, his eyes locking Liu in place.

"Yes?"

Feng Ma's voice sounded tense. "We have a problem in Kansas City."

"I'm listening."

"Just over an hour ago, a man claiming to be a DEA agent showed up at the ISS warehouse asking to see the cargo manifest for our flight from Baltimore on Saturday morning. Carl Bogati passed along some security video from the ISS lobby and one of his people managed to hide a GPS tracker on the man's car."

"So he's not DEA?"

"Definitely not. In fact, the man who called himself Jack Frazier is an ex-CIA assassin who was supposedly killed in Calcutta two years ago. His real name is Jack Gregory. According to Beijing, he's since been linked to a number of killings in Europe, Kazakhstan, and South America using the pseudonym 'The Ripper.'"

Qiang paused to consider this new information. "Why is a contract killer suddenly involved in this?"

"Jamal Glover's dead girlfriend was the daughter of the American billionaire Jim McPherson."

"Tell me something I don't know."

"Apparently McPherson isn't satisfied with letting U.S. government agencies handle the investigation. So he's hired this Jack Gregory to find and kill the person who murdered his only child."

In front of Qiang, Liu shifted and seemed about to speak, but when Qiang lifted a finger to his lips, the gangster reconsidered.

"Pick five men," Qiang said. "I want them on a jet out of Oakland as soon as they can get there. Let me know when The Ripper is dead."

"Do you want McPherson killed too?"

"No. He'll get the message."

With a thin smile, Qiang ended the call and redirected his full attention to the shaking Liu. The time had come to give some detailed instructions to the overlord of the Bay Triad.

: CHAPTER 16

In the crime-ridden Kansas City neighborhood of Centropolis, the graffiti-covered two-story house with its rusting corrugated steel roof and outbuildings gave new meaning to the phrase "the wrong side of the tracks." Jack had paid the absentee owner five hundred dollars cash for a week's rent and reckoned that it was more money than the house was worth. The trees, brush, and weeds had so overtaken the property that the surrounding chain-link fence sagged beneath their weight.

When he pulled the Mustang convertible under the decrepit, overgrown carport, Jack considered backing inside. But that sort of combat parking would raise suspicion in those that would be hunting him, so he parked straight in. Though the Mustang attracted the curious gaze of some of the drunks and addicts that lounged at the intersection, they would arrive at one very obvious conclusion: that he was a drug dealer here to conduct business with some local gang. The thought that somebody might try to steal the Mustang didn't worry Jack. One less car thief would probably be a good thing for this area.

After climbing out, it took Jack only a minute to find the magnetic GPS tracker that had been stuck to the frame just behind the front bumper. He snapped it free and mounted it on the outside wall of the carport, hidden by the thick vines that climbed up the rusting wall and onto the roof.

When Jack stepped up on the front step, he was surprised that the key turned smoothly in the rusted lock, but when he shoved open the door, the hinges squealed so loudly he thought they might break. Inside, he found pretty much what he expected to see. A broken-down couch with a spring poking up through the left-most cushion occupied the center of the living room. Just beyond that, a thin sliver of sunlight squeezed through a painted windowpane to illuminate dust particles kicked up by Jack's footsteps.

There was no television, but the overhead light worked and so did the one in the adjacent kitchen. From the look of the stove, Jack saw that the only way he'd be doing any cooking here would be if he built a campfire on top of it. But the sink had running water of the cold, rusty variety, and the toilet in the first-floor bathroom flushed, a definite plus.

One of the stairs failed to creak as he made his way up to the second floor, but it was only because that step had broken through, leaving behind a gaping hole from which several rusty nails jutted outward. At the top of the stairs, Jack found a short hallway with two doors on the left and one on the right. The hallway light switch was broken and the lone window at the far end of the hall allowed in just enough daylight for Jack to make out the decaying floral pattern of the green wallpaper. *Lovely.*

The two doors on the left opened respectively into a completely empty bedroom and a small bathroom without running water or working toilet. The door on the right led into a bedroom with a marginally functional dresser, a small closet, and a bare mattress laid out on the floor.

Jack walked across the room and undid the latch on a window that faced the street, pleasantly surprised when he managed to slide the bottom window all the way to the top. As he watched, the clouds closed in to block out the sun. The gusting wind had dropped the temperature at least thirty degrees in the last five minutes. A jagged bolt of cloud-to-cloud lighting danced across the sky, and the thunder that followed shook the building.

For several seconds Jack stood there, feeling the cool wind ruffle his shirt and enjoying the smell of the coming shower. Then the clatter of hailstones on the steel roof was accompanied by rain that forced him to shut the window. Jack's cell phone beeped and a quick glance told him that a tornado warning had just been issued for the greater Kansas City metropolitan area. *Fine.* The storm could give a nice Midwestern welcome to whoever was coming for him.

Jack set his duffel on the mattress and began unpacking its contents. If he wanted to be ready for the arrival of his housewarming guests, he had some preparations to make.

CHAPTER 17

Nightfall came early to Kansas City, accompanied by chain lightning, thunder, and the periodic wail of distant tornado sirens, although the sirens seemed confined to the southern edge of the city. The men that would come for Jack on this night would be professionals. When they came, they'd hit the house hard and fast, tossing flash-bang grenades through the windows before crashing through doors or windows. If they were very good, they might expect the doors to be wired. And they'd leave backup outside to cover the front and rear exits.

It would be over . . . bang, bang, bang . . . quick. Just not in the way they intended. For one thing, they would expect Jack to be inside the ramshackle house, not lying beneath a rain poncho in the high weeds on the opposite side of the street.

Clad all in black, including his shooter's gloves, Jack wore a light, pullover mask that didn't interfere with his ability to get a good sight picture through the infrared scope mounted on the M4 carbine's Picatinny rail. The suppressor screwed into the weapon's threaded barrel wouldn't completely dampen the sound, but it would make it much harder to identify the direction from which the gunfire was coming.

Despite the protection the poncho provided, Jack was thoroughly soaked and surprisingly cold. But in life-and-death confrontations like the one that he felt coming, discomfort had always been his oldest and dearest friend. As old friends went, he felt another one stirring deep within, but this was only a friend in the sense that a long pull of whisky was a drunk's best friend.

Jack had always had that special sense, an ability to feel what his opponent was about to do even as he decided upon it. It was one of the things that had brought him to the attention of Garfield Kromly, the CIA's chief trainer of field operatives when Jack was new to the agency. But ever since Calcutta, that sense of danger flooded him with adrenaline, pulling him toward it like a fish on the hook despite his best efforts to control those impulses. He'd hoped that the lucid dreaming technique would help him to better understand what was going on in his subconscious and how that something sometimes bled over into his conscious mind. But if tonight was any indication, his dream encounter in that Hawaii hotel room had only intensified that strange inner connection, heightening all of his senses in a way that thrilled and threatened him.

Vehicle headlights, a rarity on a night like this one, at least in this neighborhood, crawled down the street toward him. They were high up and widely spaced, indicative of a large SUV or pickup truck. This was an SUV. From his hidden position, Jack watched it slow as it passed in front of the house before turning to disappear down a side street. When it rolled back around that corner with its headlights off, Jack wasn't surprised.

Through the FLIR scope he could see the bright heat from the vehicle grill and the lesser glow of five warm bodies inside the

SUV: two in the front, two in the backseat, one more crouched in the rear cargo area. When the vehicle pulled to a stop half a block from the house, four doors and the rear hatch opened simultaneously as armed men piled out, silently closing the doors behind them. No interior lights flicked on and off.

Now Jack could see that they each wore night-vision goggles. Hidden beneath the camouflaged parka, he would be invisible to their light amplification technology. Add that to the fact that their attention would be focused on the rundown house on the opposite side of the street and it wouldn't be a problem.

They moved along the edge of the foliage-draped fence in a tactical formation that totally belied any notion that these were mob enforcers. These operators were government trained and used to working together. The question was, which government?

When they reached the carport, none of them went inside to examine the Mustang. Instead the team went through an opening where the chain-link fence had fallen down and split up, one going around the right side of the house while four stayed in front. Of those four, one slipped into the trees and assumed a prone firing position with his weapon covering the entire front on a diagonal.

The other three positioned themselves on either side of the front door and paused to speak into jawbone microphones. Upon hearing a response that was to their liking, they each hurled a grenade through separate windows, two on the first floor and one into a second-floor bedroom. The flash and noise of several concussion grenades going off in rapid sequence was followed up by an assault that launched the front door into the middle of the living room as the three men followed it into the interior.

Jack waited a full ten seconds before pressing two buttons on the remote detonator he held in his left hand. In the house he'd rented for five hundred dollars, layers of C4 explosive propelled

1,400 tiny ball bearings from two M18 claymore mines at its current occupants, blasting out the windows and part of the front wall.

The prone sniper reacted immediately, rising to his feet and running away from the conflagration back toward the parked vehicle, but the steady squeeze of Jack's trigger finger dropped him face-first in the middle of what may once have been the front lawn. The sniper around back had better options and took advantage of them, only breaking out of the trees when he was next to the black SUV. The vehicle squawk meant that he had the key, something that the man verified by sliding into the driver's seat.

Jack's sight centered on the middle of a glowing face as the driver ripped off his night-vision goggles and switched on the headlights. Although the bright beams washed the FLIR thermal scope white, Jack squeezed the trigger without allowing any movement from his previous aim point. Just to be sure, he lowered the barrel slightly and fired three more rounds. Then he was up and running along the edge of the road, moving parallel to the enemy vehicle, not crossing the road until he was directly opposite the driver's side door.

With the M4 trained on the slumped form of the occupant, Jack could see the man in the reflected light of the headlights. A bullet had punched through his right eye, splattering the seats with brains and blood, but the shape of the open left eye confirmed that the dead assassin was Asian, probably Chinese, something that matched the NSA intel. Jack would normally have felt little for killing someone who had tried to kill him, but having studied the crime scene photos of Jill McPherson slumped in that kitchen with a bloody second mouth gaping open below her chin, he failed to suppress the fury that raged within. This asshole probably hadn't been her killer, but he was certainly an accomplice.

Jack opened the car door and rapidly frisked the body. Ignoring the weapons strapped to the dead man's side, Jack extracted a wallet and a passport. Sliding these into a pocket, he ran back toward the house and quickly searched the dead assassin sprawled facedown in the front yard.

Then, with a clock ticking down in his head, Jack backed the Mustang out of the carport, turned south, and accelerated into the storm vortex of the Kansas City night.

: CHAPTER 18

At 1:15 A.M., the phone beside Admiral Riles's bed woke him from a deep sleep. Reaching for the handset in the dark, he knocked the drinking glass from his nightstand, spilling its contents onto the bedroom carpet.

"Shit!"

"What is it, Jonny?" Mary Beth Riles asked from the far side of the bed.

"Just the phone. You can go back to sleep."

His hand found the handset and Riles pressed the "Talk" button as he climbed out of bed and lifted it to his ear. "Yes?"

"Admiral Riles, this is Levi. We've got a situation."

"Let me throw on a robe and take this to another room."

Riles shrugged into his bathrobe and walked out of the bedroom into the dark drawing room beyond, closing the bedroom door behind him before he switched on a light. When Levi said they had a situation, that usually meant trouble. The admiral slid into his favorite leather chair near the bay windows and forced the grogginess from his mind.

"Okay, Levi. Tell me about it."

"Yesterday afternoon, Jack Gregory met with a manager for the ISS air cargo facility at Kansas City International Airport, a man named Carl Bogati. Shortly after that meeting, we intercepted a call from Bogati to a burner cell phone in San Francisco. The call was followed by a text message that contained a short video attachment with security camera footage of Jack at the ISS front desk."

"Any luck running down the phone's owner?"

"Not yet, but we were able to identify the location of the call and the phone's place of purchase. The customer paid cash but we've already acquired the store's security video for when the purchase was made. Our people are processing it through facial recognition right now."

"What else have you got?"

"At approximately 11:00 P.M. central time, Kansas City police responded to reports of multiple explosions and gunfire in a run-down district called Centropolis. Upon arriving at the scene they found a house shattered by at least two explosions. They also discovered the bodies of five men, three torn apart by shrapnel inside the house, one dead from a single gunshot wound on the front lawn, and another body inside a black Chevy Tahoe. The one in the car had been shot once in the head and three times in the throat and chest. All five victims were Asian, heavily armed, and outfitted with state-of-the-art night-vision goggles."

Riles had already drawn his own conclusion about this, but asked Levi anyway. "Your analysis?"

"Jack dangled himself out there as bait to draw some high-level attention from Jamal's kidnappers. When the assassination team arrived, Jack suckered them into a trap and killed them all."

"What about the local police?"

"The investigation is just getting started, but they think some Asian gangsters tried to muscle in on local gangland turf and got their asses kicked."

"Has Jack contacted us?"

"No, and I don't expect him to."

Riles took some time to think about what would likely follow tonight's Kansas City mayhem. He'd known the risks involved in unleashing Jack Gregory on American soil and had accepted them. Now wasn't the time to get squeamish.

"This is going to generate some bad-guy chatter," said Riles. "Make sure we've got all available resources focused on identifying our target's reaction to this news. It could be the break we need in order to identify the spot where Jamal is being held. In the meantime, have Spider's team check out that Chinatown location."

"I'm on it."

The admiral ended the call and settled back into the armchair's soft Italian leather. He'd sent Jack Gregory out to stir things up and, as usual, Jack was overachieving. Suddenly Riles's thoughts shifted to the disaster in Bolivia. Had it only been three months ago? Riles believed that Janet Price was wrong in her assessment of what had happened down there.

But if he was the one who was wrong and Jack "The Ripper" Gregory came completely off the rails, this operation could go very, very badly indeed.

CHAPTER 19

Standing beside his car in the dimly lit parking garage on Kearny, Qiang could barely believe what the aging courier had just told him. Five men dead at the hands of the assassin called The Ripper. Not just any men; these had been his men, top-notch agents for the Ministry of State Security of the People's Republic of China. To lose five MSS operatives on a single mission was unheard of. It meant that Qiang's superiors in Beijing wouldn't be happy. But it wasn't possible for them to be as angry as Qiang Chu was at this moment.

The discipline of a lifetime devoted to the mastery of the martial arts was now put to the test. Qiang stored his rage in a special place, ready to be called forth at a time of need, allowing none of that anger to show in his face.

MSS headquarters had expressed similar concerns that, in their efforts to find where Jamal Glover was being held, the NSA had penetrated electronic resources that the MSS had previously considered secure. And there were indications that at least a half dozen operatives had arrived in the Bay Area over the last two days. That, at least, was something that Qiang had planned for. What he hadn't expected was the involvement of an international assassin for hire.

Clearly the MSS file on The Ripper was incomplete.

Qiang dismissed the courier and watched as the man climbed onto his motor scooter and drove it out of the garage into the Chinatown night. It appeared that Steve Grange had been right to accelerate the timeline on the Jamal Glover project. It appeared Qiang and Grange would need to shift to phase two much more quickly than they had planned.

As Qiang stepped behind the wheel of the black BMW M4 and felt the powerful engine rumble to life, he made a decision. He was done hunting for the lone assassin. Let that one come for him. When the time came, Qiang would deal with The Ripper personally.

CHAPTER 20

Janet Price, with Harry Stevens riding shotgun, pulled the silver GMC Sierra pickup into the newly vacated parking spot on Grant Avenue and stepped out into the early morning fog. The chill in the damp morning breeze made her glad that she'd worn jeans, the long-sleeve black pullover, and her soft leather jacket.

Walking around the front of the truck, Janet caught up with Harry just outside the closed front door of the Chinatown Market. Despite the CLOSED sign hanging on the inside of the glass door and the collapsible steel-barred security screen that hung all the way to the ground, Janet reached through and knocked on the glass. Although it was only 7:15 A.M. and the store wouldn't open until eight o'clock, she knew that the owners were already inside preparing for the start of the business day.

An older Chinese man walked up to the inside of the closed door and yelled, "Store closed. Come back later."

Janet flipped open her ICE credentials and held them up, giving the owner a good look at the words engraved on the badge.

HOMELAND SECURITY INVESTIGATIONS
SPECIAL AGENT

"Immigration and Customs Enforcement. Open up."

"You have warrant?" the man asked.

Beside her, Harry held up the warrant in a motion that spread his windbreaker to reveal the Glock resting in his shoulder holster. Although the warrant was an NSA-produced fake, it was an extremely good one, bearing the signature of a federal judge who had just left for a big-game hunt in Wyoming and couldn't be reached for the next several days.

"Open the door right now." Janet's tone left no doubt that failure to comply wasn't an option.

The shop owner's eyes narrowed, but he nodded and the security curtain began rumbling upward on its track. When it had clanked to a stop in the raised position, the old man pulled open the door, stepped back to allow them entrance, and then closed and locked the door behind them.

When he turned to face her, Janet noted his name tag as she held up a photograph. "Mr. Ho, do you know this man?"

"Never seen him," Mr. Ho said, stroking his chin with his left hand.

It didn't take the nonverbal tell for Janet to know he was lying. She held up another photograph, this one of a man standing at the register where a packaged phone lay on the counter. Clearly visible in the security camera image was the smiling Mr. Ho accepting the cash payment.

"Does this refresh your memory?"

Mr. Ho frowned. "I have many customer. Impossible to know all."

Janet handed him several more photographs, studying his face closely as he looked through them. "That's funny because these images were recorded by your security camera over the last two weeks."

"My memory isn't what it once was."

"And your business isn't going to be what it once was if we shut you down for hindering a federal investigation."

A sudden clatter from the back of the store brought her gun into her hand as she spun toward the sound. Beside her, Harry had his own gun out and leveled.

"Who else is here?" Janet asked Ho.

"Only my son."

"Call him. Tell him to come out where we can see him."

Mr. Ho didn't hesitate. "John! These are federal agents. Come out here."

Nothing.

Without being told to do so, Ho called again. "John! Please step out."

Again his call was met with silence.

"Stay with Mr. Ho," Janet told Harry. "I'll check it out."

"And if you need backup?"

"Then I'll yell."

Janet moved down the nearest row of shelves, this one a grocery aisle filled with boxed and canned goods, most of which had foreign language labels. As she approached the back of the store, she slowed, letting her eyes move with the Glock's sights. At the end of the aisle, she cleared the area just beyond the corner before stepping out into the open. Now moving perpendicular to the rows of goods, Janet paused at each corner, cleared that row, and then moved on. There was no sign of what had been knocked over to produce the sound she had heard only moments earlier.

When she cleared the last row, a pair of swinging doors in the back wall beckoned and she moved up against the wall, just to their right. For two seconds she listened, then exploded into motion, kicking the nearest open, moving through before it swung closed behind her. Now she found herself in a dimly lit hall. The door on her left had the international symbol for a men's and women's restroom attached just below eye level. To her right, another door stood open into a cluttered office, lit only by the glow of a computer screen.

Janet followed her gun just far enough inside to confirm that it had no occupants. Crossing the hall, she found the small restroom also empty. That left a matching set of swinging doors at the far end of the twenty-foot hallway and what was undoubtedly a stockroom beyond.

Despite the soft glow filtering out of the office behind her, this end of the hall was twilight dark. Moreover, the visible gap between those swinging doors looked black, a good indication of the lack of light in the room that lay beyond. Janet knew that when she pushed her way through those doors, for the amount of time it took her to move through that opening, she would be dimly backlit. Worse, the twin doors spanned the entire width of the hallway, so there would be no kicking one of them open while she took cover behind a wall.

Janet looked up at the ceiling, happy to see good old-fashioned incandescent light bulbs instead of fluorescents. Incandescent bulbs were bright. More importantly, they were virtually instantaneous. If she was going to have to play the part of an old Western gunfighter, she at least wanted the sun at her back. It wouldn't be as good as what she and Jack had in Kazakhstan, but it would have to do.

On the count of three. Standing directly in front of the leftmost swinging door, she raised her gun hand, fingered the light switch with her left hand, and rocked forward onto the balls of her feet.

One . . . two . . . three.

Her right foot hit the door as the hall ceiling lights blared to life behind her. Although the sudden brightness hurt her eyes, to someone lurking in the dark, looking directly into that sudden brightness, its brilliance would be dazzling. In the fraction of a second that surprise granted her, Janet tucked and rolled, saw the flash of light as the round hissed over her, accompanied by the muffled crack of a silenced weapon.

Rolling into a shooter's crouch, Janet felt her Glock buck in her hand as she pumped three rounds in the general direction from which the shooter had fired. Amplified by this enclosed space, the Glock was far from silent.

Janet heard a door bang open and saw a flash of outside light filtered through shelving stacked with boxed goods. For a moment that light painted a man's dark shadow on the floor, just before the door banged closed again. Hearing Harry's running footsteps in the hallway behind her, she raced after the fleeing man. But by the time she reached the door and slammed it open, all she managed was a fleeting glimpse of the man's back as he shouldered his way through the morning crowd moving along the sidewalk.

For half a second she considered chasing after him. If she'd really been the ICE agent she was pretending to be, she would have. But in this case, she and Harry had already accomplished what they'd come here to do, and the running man only served their purpose. Right now at three different locations across Chinatown, Spider Sanchez and the other members of his team were rousting other suspected links to Jamal's kidnappers. If all went well, the sense that the federal government was closing in would cause someone to make a mistake.

"Janet?" Harry's voice from the other side of the stockroom sounded trigger-finger tense.

"I'm fine, but the shooter got away," Janet said as she flipped on the light switches beside the back door, illuminating two rows of ceiling lights that chased the shadows from the stockroom.

Harry stepped around one of the rows of open shelves, his gun still leveled as he made a clearing pass through the remainder of the room. Janet knew what he'd find, but Harry always followed procedure and he was right to do so. It was exactly what Janet would have done if she hadn't come under fire, but sometimes it was important to react quickly rather than methodically.

Harry holstered his weapon as he walked back across the room toward her. "The police will be here shortly," he said.

"That's fine. Our credentials will stand up to any checks they make. Besides, I want to ask a few more questions of our Mr. Ho before they get here."

"They'll want a statement."

"And we'll give them the one they love to hate. This is a classified Homeland Security investigation and we thank them for staying out of our way."

As Janet led the way back toward the front of the store, she heard Harry's low chuckle at her shoulder. He assumed that she enjoyed jerking local law enforcement's chain, and she knew that this time he was right. After all, if she had to impersonate an ICE special agent, why not throw herself into the role?

CHAPTER 21

Steve Grange entered the basement laboratory from the private section of the underground parking garage. The two-story building that rose above it housed one of the largest call centers on the West Coast, and the attached parking structure provided workers that chose to drive into Hayward with convenient access to a stressful job. The call center's extensive phone and high-speed Internet service also masked the much more important underground communications network.

The sublevel security lobby looked much like many other such lobbies at high-tech firms intent upon securing their trade secrets, a curved reception desk behind which sat two black-uniformed security guards watching the displays on a number of security monitors. But this reception desk offered no visitor sign-in sheet. If you didn't belong here, you didn't get in. Grange knew that on the other side of the door through which he was about to pass, a half dozen heavily armed men provided the real protection for this facility.

Grange nodded at the guards and heard the buzz and click

of the electronic bolt disengaging as he reached for the door handle. The handle felt slippery in his hand and with a start, he realized that his palms were sweating. All the preliminary work done inside his Grange Castle laboratory over these last four days had culminated in this, the day Jamal would be unleashed to reach out and touch the wide world.

On the far side of the door, Grange passed five more uniformed security guards, all Chinese intelligence agents working for Qiang Chu. Grange felt their eyes follow him but he pretended not to notice. None of these men was as intimidating as Qiang, but they still made him uncomfortable, and the Chinese government's goals didn't exactly align with Steve Grange's.

After years of experimenting on human subjects that society would never miss, Grange would never have chosen such a high-profile subject as Jamal Glover. However, there was a price to be paid for the backing the Chinese had given him, and Jamal was a part of that price.

Grange placed his hand on the biometric scanner and the door slid open to admit him. Although the security of this facility didn't compare to that of his laboratory below the Grange Castle Winery, it was better and more deadly than that of the nearby Lawrence Livermore National Laboratory. There was also something to be said for the advantage of hiding in plain sight, particularly when you needed to be on the grid.

When Grange stepped through the opening into the large, open room that awaited him, he saw Dr. Vicky Morris standing beside Dr. Kyle Landon, both in green scrubs but neither of them wearing surgical masks or gloves. If all went well today, they wouldn't be needing them.

As Grange approached, the two doctors broke off their conversation and turned toward him. Grange ignored the perfunctory greetings that rolled off their lips, his attention focused instead on the large sensory deprivation tank beside which Dr. Morris and Dr. Landon were standing. His eyes took in the instrument readings on the control panel before shifting to the monitor that showed Jamal's body suspended in the solution within the tank.

Jamal's nude form floated peacefully, illuminated in an ultraviolet glow that Grange knew was invisible to the human eye. But on the display the UV light tinted Jamal's body an alien blue. Jamal's skull had been covered with what looked like a white rubber swimmer's cap, but the bundle of wires connected to it gave Jamal the appearance of a Jamaican Rastaman.

Finally Grange turned his attention to the two doctors standing beside him. Dr. Morris, slender, blonde, and attractive, provided a stark contrast to the aging Dr. Landon's morose demeanor. There was about her an aura of childlike expectation, as if she were about to open a very special Christmas present. Grange smiled inwardly at the thought. In a sense, that was exactly what she was about to do.

"Are we ready to begin?" Grange asked.

"We've run a full round of diagnostics," Dr. Morris replied. "He's looking good."

Dr. Landon shook his head. "I'd like to give his brain a few more minutes to acclimate to the drug cocktail."

"That's what we were arguing about when you got here," said Dr. Morris. "Look at the diagnostic results. Jamal's brain shows no indication of negative side effects from the drugs. He's ready."

"I cut a full day off of his planned recovery from the brain surgery," said Dr. Landon. "It won't hurt to take an extra fifteen minutes to verify that there's no delayed reaction."

Grange frowned. "A delayed reaction to the drugs or the electrical stimulation could happen at any time. Fifteen minutes won't make a difference." He turned to Dr. Morris. "Tell Delores to prep the upload."

Dr. Morris took a deep breath, walked to her workstation, and put on her wireless intercom headset. Her visible excitement was only a faint echo of the thrill that shuddered through Grange's body as he moved to the elevated monitoring station situated behind those of the two doctors.

As Grange slid his headset over his right ear, he watched as Dr. Landon sat down at his station. The tension between these two very different brain specialists was a natural consequence of their competing specialties. Whereas Dr. Landon had spent a career building a detailed understanding of the physical brain, Dr. Morris had directed her impressive intellect at the controversial field of neural interface and digitization, also known as NIAD.

Of all the practitioners in this new field, Dr. Morris's expertise was second only to that of Steve Grange. He knew that Dr. Landon thought Grange played favorites based upon his determination to demonstrate NIAD's ultimate dream. Grange had no doubt that Dr. Landon was correct in that judgment. It was the obsession that had driven Grange to sacrifice so many lost souls in his quest for the breakthrough that would forever change the world.

Ironically, Steve Grange didn't want to change the world. He just wanted to restore his world.

A sudden change in the brainwave patterns displayed on the rightmost of his three monitors drew Grange out of his own thoughts. On the center monitor, Jamal Glover's face twitched, sending tiny ripples through the suspension fluid inside the sensory deprivation tank. Chills spread through Grange's entire body and he held his breath. He hoped the CGI team was as ready as Delores Mendosa had assured him they would be. If the virtual reality now streaming from their workstations through the array of electrodes implanted into Jamal's brain wasn't real enough, its rejection might break Jamal's mind.

The mind scraping that Dr. Morris had performed during the flight from Baltimore to Oakland had extracted the data that would enable them to create a digital replica of Jamal's mind. That data had been stored on a holographic data drive.

The HDD was one of many unpatented inventions that Steve Grange had created in his quest to capture a digital representation of a human mind. It contained a marble-sized, semitransparent sphere, within which multicolor holographic data was stored. Magnetically suspended inside the drive, it could be spun in any direction to allow nearly instantaneous data access. And each little sphere was capable of storing more than a petabyte of data.

The only thing still missing was proof that virtual experiences could be streamed back into the human brain without overloading and killing the subject. As he watched Jamal's facial expressions shift, Grange pushed the worry from his mind. This was going to work. For Helen's sake, it had to.

Twenty years ago God had taken his soul mate away from him. Now, by God, Steve Grange was going to take her back.

: CHAPTER 22

Jamal Glover knelt in the falling rain, his hands digging into the mud that would soon be shoveled into the open grave. Although someone tried to restrain him, he leaned forward for one last look at the casket resting at the bottom of that lonely hole as the rain and his tears tried to wash away the handful of mud he'd just dropped atop that mahogany box.

The last three days were nothing but a dim haze of raw misery and despair. Someone had killed his beautiful Jillian, had bled her out right on his kitchen floor. He'd had the son of a bitch who had killed her right in his hands, but the man had taken Jamal down as easily as if he were a helpless child. If only he'd killed Jamal instead of laying his unconscious body on the kitchen floor with his head in Jillian's dead lap. What kind of a sick bastard could do something like that?

These last few days were a blur. For someone who didn't like alcohol, to stay that drunk for that long was a shock to the system. Instead of giving him a headache, the experience had left him disoriented and numb, as if he was living in a hazy dreamworld without substance. But the alcohol-induced stupor had failed to alleviate his despair. If his Gram were still here, she would be ashamed of him. Hell, he was ashamed of himself.

Weak with grief, Jamal rocked slowly back and forth while a fresh bout of ragged sobs shook his body. He felt a strong hand on his shoulder and turned his head toward the offender, intending to scream his rage at a person who had no right to interrupt his grief. But before any angry words could escape his lips, Jamal saw that the hand belonged to Jill's father, a man whose face was filled with despair as great as Jamal's.

Suddenly Jamal understood. It was Jill's father's turn to toss his own handful of mud onto his daughter's coffin, his turn to say good-bye to his only child.

Jamal staggered to his feet, uncaring about the filthy mess he'd made of his funeral suit. All he knew was that he had to get away from this place before someone spoke another sympathetic phrase or the preacher mouthed another platitude about earth and ashes and dust. He stumbled away from the graveside, avoiding Gary Charles. Right now, a caring embrace from his friend was incompatible with the darkness that filled his soul.

With each step, the Virginia downpour seemed to increase until Jamal could barely see from one gravestone to the next. But tears blurred his vision so badly that he almost missed seeing the man in the raincoat waiting beside his car. The man carried no umbrella, and his curly black hair was matted atop his head.

When Jamal was five steps away, recognition brought him to a sudden stop. Levi Elias. Jamal didn't know why he was surprised that the NSA's senior analyst would make this dreary trip to his girlfriend's funeral, but again he found himself dreading the impending expression of sympathy.

Levi stepped forward but did not extend his hand when he spoke. "Jamal, I'm so sorry about Jillian."

Jamal studied Levi's face as he continued. "I know you want to crawl into some cave to be alone with your grief. I know it because I have felt that same loss of love." Levi hesitated, as if considering what he would say next. "Let me offer you a better option. Will you help us track down Jillian McPherson's killer? Will you help us make sure that man never gets a fair trial?"

For several seconds, Jamal's reeling brain failed to process the words that carried an offer, not of condolence, but of vengeance. Jamal wiped the tears from his eyes. He knew he must be smearing dark mud across his face. For some reason, it made him feel like a Sioux warrior, applying the paint that meant war.

When Jamal lowered that hand again, the world seemed to have acquired an unnatural clarity, despite the rain. And when he spoke, his voice held a dangerous edge.

"I'm in."

CHAPTER 23

Jack Gregory parked the black Honda motorcycle in the Central Parking Triangle Lot, dropped the kickstand, and began a leisurely westward stroll along Jefferson Street toward his noon meeting. The early morning marine layer had cleared, leaving in its wake a cool, sunny morning. The light breeze carried with it the sounds and smells of the San Francisco Bay, something that made Jack want to sit on the end of a pier and watch the tide come and go. Unfortunately, he had business to attend to that would not wait.

The walk down to Pier 47 carried him past some docked boats, around a corner, and under the blue awning at the entrance to Scoma's seafood restaurant. The smells wafting out through the door as Jack stepped inside made him realize just how hungry he was. Jack saw the man he'd come here to meet seated next to a window that provided a partial view of the bay. As Jack stepped up to the table, the man rose to greet him.

"Hello, Jack," the older man said in a voice that carried a familiar British accent.

"Good to see you, David. It's been a long time."

"Only to your young senses. At my age, four years seems like yesterday."

Jack seated himself across from the elegantly dressed British gentleman. At the age of sixty-eight, David Chambers had long since retired from MI6, but he looked little changed from the last time Jack had seen him in Hong Kong. A person with David's knowledge and connections didn't need to rely on a government pension to support his comfortable lifestyle. He'd turned information gathering and distribution into a very profitable business, one to which Jack was about to contribute a significant sum.

David leaned back in his chair and took a sip from a half-full glass of iced tea, the lemon slice still wedged in place atop the glass. When he set the drink back on the table, David's face grew serious. "I was sorry to hear about Rita."

The mention of Rita Chavez brought back painful memories that tightened Jack's throat. "She was a good friend."

"I heard you took care of her killer."

Jack's hesitation was brief, but he knew David noticed it. "You may want to double-check your sources."

The arrival of their waitress put a welcome end to that particular discussion. After they placed their orders, the conversation turned to small talk that continued throughout their leisurely meal. The business discussion would wait for their post-luncheon stroll along the pier.

When Jack picked up the check, David let him. Then they stepped outside and turned left, walking slowly west along the block-long pier. Unlike some of the tourist-populated piers, this one had very little foot traffic. Reaching a spot where the privacy of their conversation was assured, the two men stopped shoulder-to-shoulder, gazing out past the end of Fisherman's Wharf.

As the older man lit a cigarette and took a drag, Jack reached into one of the inner pockets of his leather jacket and extracted two sets of identification documents, the ones he'd taken from the dead men in Kansas City. He handed them to David Chambers.

"These IDs are fakes. I need to know who these men really are and who they work for. How long will it take you to dig up that information for me?"

David studied the pictures on the driver's licenses. "That depends."

"On what?"

"Information is cheap, but reliable information isn't. Reliable and quick costs more."

"If you can get me those answers by the end of the day, you can name your price. I just need the wiring instructions for the transfer."

The MI6 veteran pulled a small notepad and pen from a pocket of his tweed jacket, scribbled some notes, tore off the top page, and handed it to Jack. A glance at the piece of paper brought a smile to Jack's lips. The big quote told him that David was already familiar with at least one of the two men.

The NSA had already identified his Kansas City attackers as agents for the Chinese MSS, but as impressive as their electronic information gather was, David Chambers had spent two dozen years developing his contacts in Hong Kong and mainland China. In Jack's experience, contacts like that were worth more than all the computers at the NSA's disposal.

Jack folded the paper and placed it in his pocket. "I'll make the transfer this afternoon. Where do you want to meet to deliver the information?"

"Assuming the transfer goes through, you'll find me right here at eleven o'clock tonight."

"Okay."

Jack watched as David Chambers dropped the cigarette and ground it beneath the heel of his brown leather shoe. Like the smoke itself, it was a small act of defiance against California's politically correct social engineering. Without another word, the old spy sauntered back the way they had come.

Jack turned away, looking out at the bay as a fishing boat made its way back toward its berth. To be returning this early, the fishing must have been very, very good. Tonight would tell whether Jack's fishing expedition would be as successful.

CHAPTER 24

Jamal Glover entered the NSA War Room as if emerging from a deep haze. Having showered and changed into a clean set of clothes, he'd brought a small travel bag to the NSA headquarters, where Levi Elias had arranged for an assigned spot in the locker room for him. That was good because Jamal didn't plan on leaving this black-glass digital fortress until he had Jillian's killer by the balls.

Inside the War Room, the other eleven members of the elite group of cyber-warriors that Levi Elias had dubbed the Dirty Dozen were already inside their scorpion-shaped workstations. Jamal glanced up at the elevated glass-walled room that overlooked the three tiers of workstations and saw Admiral Riles standing beside Levi, observing the scene that spread out before him. On the curving far wall, high-resolution displays summarized the activity of the assembled group of cyber-warriors.

The NSA War Room was a construct Admiral Riles had created. While it was true that most of the best programmers and hackers preferred to work alone, at heart they were gamers, and the very best enjoyed being recognized as such. So Admiral Riles had come up with a way that, when the most difficult cyber-attacks had to be carried out under tight timelines, his current top crop of cyber-warriors could be thrown into an environment that drove them into a competitive frenzy.

Inside the War Room, the hacking targets were clearly defined and prioritized. Each cyber-warrior was awarded or penalized points based upon the speed and progress of his or her attacks. They were allowed to team up or to attack targets individually. At the end of every War Room battle, the ranking of each cyber-warrior was adjusted and publicized throughout the NSA's cyber-warfare community.

Every one of the hundreds of hackers the NSA employed would kill to qualify for the group of twelve that operated from the War Room. But Jamal had lost all enthusiasm for this precious competition. He just wanted to use his own brain and the electronic might the NSA had placed at his disposal to help the agency identify, target, and kill a vicious murderer.

As Jamal climbed into his Scorpion workstation and booted up the system, his thoughts turned once more to Jillian. Why had that bastard killed her but not Jamal? It made no sense. Jamal was the NSA hacker. He should have been the target. For that matter, why was the NSA devoting so much effort to finding that man?

Jamal had been too distraught to think of these questions when he'd agreed to Levi's offer. He shook his head to clear it. After this was over he'd find those answers, but right now the *whys* didn't matter. Right now it was payback time.

When he logged onto the workstation, the message displayed at the top of the center screen surprised him. The rules and organization for today's cyber-attack had been altered. Instead of each cyber-warrior selecting tasks from the incoming task queue and being scored on the speed, difficulty, and success of his hack, all incoming tasks would initially go to a preprocessing queue that only Jamal could access. Jamal would then perform an initial hack to embed backdoors into each target before pushing it to the available cyber-warrior he felt was best qualified to handle that task.

Jamal had no doubt that the introduction of this new organization would piss off the other cyber-warriors, especially Goth Girl Brown, but he liked it. And because it effectively placed him in charge of the other members of the Dirty Dozen, it represented a promotion to a position of considerable power over them. That was good.

Jamal had always thought that allowing the cyber-warriors to grab targets from the incoming task queue in any order they chose was a methodology that introduced chaotic inefficiencies into the group attack. Even though these twelve were the best of the best, there was still a broad distribution of skills among them, with several thinking they were far better than they were. There was no better mission to prove the efficacy of this new approach than the one that would grant Jamal the vengeance that Jillian's memory demanded.

A new set of instructions appeared in the messaging window on his central screen. In addition to his overall management duties for the upcoming attack, Jamal would form the first line of defense against intruders that tried to seize control of any of the targets on the big board. In that case, Jamal was to spoof the attacker, allowing him to believe that he had gained control of the targeted system, while Jamal redirected the attacker to a system controlled by one of his cyber-warriors. The attacker would be allowed to retrieve data, but it would be data that the assigned cyber-warrior wanted to deliver. It was all part of baiting the elaborate trap that Levi Elias was trying to lure the target into.

Throughout the War Room, the external lighting dimmed from white to a soft magenta as the ready alarm sounded. Then, feeling the gooseflesh raise the hairs on his arms and legs, Jamal saw his preprocessing queue fill with targets. With a rush that felt as if he were operating at the speed of thought, Jamal pushed all distractions into the background and entered the game. It was go time.

CHAPTER 25

Steve Grange watched the data cascade across the OLED displays arrayed in front of him and smiled. Jamal's mind had accepted the uplinked scenario and was fully immersed in the virtual reality that Delores Mendosa's team was feeding him. Another display showed that the team of Chinese hackers in the adjacent room were fully involved. Eleven of them were receiving tasks from Jamal as he assigned them to what he believed to be other members of the NSA's Dirty Dozen.

The rest of the Chinese hackers were busy identifying targets to push into Jamal's preprocessing queue and watching for external attempts to seize control of the freshly hijacked cameras and computing systems. The speed with which Jamal penetrated supposedly secure systems amazed Grange, and he saw that same amazement work its way onto the faces of the finest hackers at the Chinese government's disposal.

Dr. Morris turned to look up at Grange, and he heard her excited voice in his earpiece. "He's an amazing specimen!"

"What about the neural data?" Grange asked.

"We're capturing everything. This should fill in the missing details from the initial mind scraping so that we can complete the digitization."

Dr. Landon's gruff voice interrupted. "How long do you plan to keep this test going? We don't have any idea how much of this intense stimulation Jamal's neural pathways can take."

Grange turned his attention to Dr. Landon. "Didn't you get the memo? This isn't a test. The Chinese are assigning live targets to Jamal in support of an ongoing operation."

A horrified look settled on Dr. Landon's stern features. "Qiang Chu?"

Grange felt a strange sense of satisfaction in seeing the doctor's recognition of the import of what they were doing here. "So you see, Dr. Landon, Jamal will continue actively hacking all the targets the Chinese give him until we get a message from Qiang saying we're done for the night. There will be no abort."

Here tonight, suspended in the sensory deprivation tank, Jamal Glover was going to validate all of Steve Grange's research. And as Jamal accomplished his tasks, the government agents who thought they were closing in on Jamal's kidnappers were about to have a very bad night.

: CHAPTER 26

Janet Price answered the encrypted call on her cell phone as she drove toward the NSA safe house near Marsh Creek. It was Spider Sanchez.

"We've got a location. Get back here now." Spider's all-business tone told her the rest.

"On my way in with Harry right now. We're twenty minutes out."

Spider terminated the connection and Janet knew that he was already dialing the next team member.

"What's up?" Harry asked from the passenger seat.

"Spider's assembling the team. It looks like he's found Jamal."

"Levi must have the NSA geek squad working overtime. I guess sometimes it pays to be a computer nerd."

Janet's thoughts turned back to Jamal Glover and his dead girlfriend. "And sometimes it doesn't."

Beside her, Harry nodded. "You've got that right."

When Clayton Road gave way to Marsh Creek Road, Janet let the big pickup carry them out of town to the southwest. She turned south onto Morgan Territory Road and passed just west of the Marsh Creek Detention Facility before taking a winding dirt road up a wooded canyon to the west. When she pulled the truck to a stop in front of the isolated house, she saw from the other vehicles parked along the driveway that she and Harry were the last to arrive.

Janet stepped out into early evening air that was at least thirty degrees warmer than it had been in San Francisco, despite being only a little over an hour's drive east. But after the chill of the marine layer, the heat actually felt good on her face. She led the way through the front door to see the rest of the team seated in the living room.

Raymond Bronson grinned when he saw her. "Ahh, a sight for sore eyes. Being around these ugly jokers, it's nice to have something beautiful to look at."

Janet laughed. "You didn't have a mirror?"

"Ouch," Bronson said, feigning indignation as the others in the room chuckled.

"Have a seat," said Spider, moving to stand before the group.

Janet grabbed a chair from beside the dining room table and seated herself next to the lanky Bobby Daniels. Harry pulled a chair up beside her.

"What about Gregory?" Paul Monroe asked from across the room. "Any word on him?"

Janet felt her breath catch in her throat at mention of Jack. Despite what she'd said about not wanting him on the team, she missed him.

Spider shook his head. "According to Levi, Jack was doing some digging in Kansas City yesterday and a hit squad tried to take him down last night. Five Chinese hitters, all dead. The NSA is still working on tracking down their identities. As for Jack, he's off the grid, but you can bet he's headed this way."

The news failed to put Janet's mind at rest.

"So what happened?" Bronson asked. "Did the Chinese get sloppy?"

"Not really. They came hard at the house where he was staying, flash-bang grenades and automatic weapons, leaving two guards outside to cover the perimeter. The entry team wasn't expecting claymores on the inside, and the outside team wasn't ready for Jack."

"Holy crap!" Paul Monroe echoed Janet's surprise. "He detonated claymore mines in Kansas City?"

"Apparently the area was empty and rundown," Spider said. "Forget about what Jack Gregory is doing. Right now I need your focus on what I'm about to show you."

The sixty-five-inch screen on the wall came to life, displaying live camera footage of a building Janet had seen as she'd driven through San Francisco's Chinatown district.

"This afternoon, Levi Elias gave me access to intercepted video from cameras in and around this building in Chinatown. What you're now looking at is a live external view."

Spider pressed a button on the remote control and a new image filled the display, one that made Janet's skin crawl. It was a close-up view of Jamal Glover's naked body suspended in liquid within a closed tank, illuminated by what appeared to be a black light that gave the man's form a pale blue glow. His skull was covered with a tight rubber cap that sprouted a thick bundle of wires that disappeared into a conduit. As she watched, Jamal's forehead creased, as if in deep concentration.

"This live footage is from a camera located inside that same building. According to Levi, Jamal Glover is being kept inside a sensory deprivation tank. He believes the wires coming from Jamal's head are attached to electrodes that have been surgically implanted into his brain, but Levi and the rest of the NSA brain trust haven't figured out exactly what the Chinese are trying to do to him. Their best guess is that they're attempting to extract classified information from Jamal's brain."

For several seconds Spider left the video up, letting the assembled special operators study the changing emotions that played across Jamal's expressive features. Janet could see Jamal's eyes moving beneath his eyelids as if he were vividly dreaming. But she'd seen rapid eye movement associated with sleeping before and this was somehow different. What these people were doing to Jamal made her want to lock and load.

The video on the display was replaced by building blueprints. Spider continued. "I want each of you to study these blueprints and the digital maps of the surrounding area before we start to plan our attack. At 0230 hours, we're going to hit this building, rescue Jamal, and teach these bastards why it's not a good idea to screw with the NSA."

To a man, the killers assembled inside the safe house voiced their agreement. But Janet remained silent. Come 0230 she'd let her weapons do the talking.

: CHAPTER 27

Cutting through the wake of a much larger craft, Jack felt the Sea
Ray powerboat lurch beneath his feet in the dark night. Throttling
back, he studied the distant Pier 47 through the AN/PVS-15 night-
vision binoculars. It was five minutes before the agreed-upon
time for his meeting with David Chambers, and he could see the
man standing at the designated spot, the glow of his lighted cigarette bright on the dimly lit pier.

Jack had transferred the requested twenty thousand dollars
into a numbered offshore bank account shortly after their noon
meeting. The fact that Chambers was here meant that the transac-
tion had already cleared. If that was all there was to it, Jack would
have strolled down that pier to meet the ex-MI6 agent. But in his
business, things were rarely that simple, and Jack had no intention
of showing up to collect on his half of the bargain.

Scanning along the pier, Jack spotted a half dozen men. Two
of these were carrying trash bags out the back door of Scoma's
and tossing them into Dumpsters. Since the restaurant had been

closed for almost a half hour, that made sense. Closer to where Chambers waited, another man leaned back against an outbuilding, tipping a sack-wrapped bottle to his lips. The other three men worked on a fishing boat, two stacking boxes while another swabbed the deck with a mop.

All these activities were what you might expect to see around the wharf. But to Jack, these last four felt wrong. While it was possible that the fishermen were working late to prepare the boat for tomorrow's outing, these guys hadn't turned on any boat lights. And the wino's posture carried a tension Jack could feel from where he stood atop the Sea Ray. Despite the fact that, at this distance, he couldn't determine the race of those men, the context of the situation told him all he needed to know.

It was exactly what Jack had expected to find . . . what he had wanted, but it still left a knot of sadness in his gut.

Ah David, Jack thought. *Why'd you have to be so damn predictable?*

Turning the boat out toward Alcatraz, Jack slowly throttled up. As he passed around the end of Fisherman's Wharf, he banked hard to the east and jammed the throttle forward. The powerboat covered the kilometer to Pier 39 in just over a minute. Rounding the north end of the pier, Jack slowed and turned south, down its east side. When the Sea Ray rounded the end of the breakwater, Jack guided it into the marina and toward the nearest empty slip. Tossing a looped line over the outside piling, he glided the boat in.

In less than a minute he had secured the lines to the deck cleats; then Jack was moving west through the marina toward Pier 39. Reaching the Pier 39 concourse, he adjusted his stride so that it was just fast enough to imply that he was hurrying to meet someone without attracting undo attention.

By the time Jack reached the Triangle Lot, slipped on his helmet, and started his motorcycle, it was ten minutes past eleven.

He knew that Chambers would probably give him ten minutes slack, but by now the older man and his Chinese handlers would be on the move. Unfortunately for them, there was only one exit from Pier 47 and that was back down Al Scoma Way toward Jefferson Street. Unless they had all gotten spooked and run back to their cars, an action that the Chinese would find beneath their dignity and the sixty-eight-year-old Chambers hadn't looked in shape for, they couldn't beat Jack back to that intersection.

Just before he reached Al Scoma Way, Jack turned left onto Jones Street, and then swung about at a spot where he had a diagonal view of the Jefferson and Al Scoma intersection. Letting the engine idle, he waited, going with his gut feel of what was about to happen.

~ ~ ~

When the two vehicles emerged from Al Scoma Way, the black Mercedes sedan turned right and headed west on Jefferson while the silver Jaguar turned east. Jack let the Jaguar pass in front of him before turning to follow the Mercedes. It didn't take much intuition to know which car the Chinese assassins were in. David Chambers wouldn't be caught dead driving a French or German vehicle.

As the Mercedes turned left onto Leavenworth Street and then took a slight left onto Columbus, Jack hung back, keeping several cars between himself and the Chinese. Jack had known that David Chambers had close connections in China and had hoped the photographs he had shown Chambers would generate some reaction from those contacts. Tonight's attempted ambush confirmed that he was on the right trail, and right now he had a pretty good idea where these four guys were headed.

A slight right turn onto Powell Street was followed several blocks later by a left onto Clay, but here Jack pulled over and waited, watching the Mercedes until it took another left onto Stockton. No doubt about it; the rats were headed back to their nest. The problem was, they weren't likely to be alone.

Jack knew that if he wanted to narrow down the search, this was no time to be shy. But when he turned north onto Stockton, the Mercedes was gone. Jack didn't bother to look for it. This was the right general neighborhood and if he didn't want his enemies to figure out that he was hunting for them, he'd better not linger. Five minutes later Jack was out of Chinatown.

It was fifteen minutes to midnight.

CHAPTER 28

Levi Elias stepped up beside Admiral Riles and looked down through the curved glass wall at the Scorpion workstations currently occupied by the Dirty Dozen. With Jamal absent, all positions had shifted up so that Caroline Brown was now the designated leader of this crew. From the mass of NSA hackers that longed to be a part of this elite group, Dr. David Kurtz had elevated Fred Simmons to fill the newly opened twelfth spot.

"Jack Gregory just checked in," Levi said.

"What's his situation?" Admiral Riles asked as he continued to gaze out over the War Room.

"Apparently he's rattling Chinese nerves. They made another move on him in San Francisco, but this time he avoided direct conflict."

"Good! The last thing we need is a shoot-out there just as the team is about to take back Jamal."

Levi echoed the sentiment.

"Don't worry. I made it very clear that we have an operation going in Chinatown tonight and that he is to stay clear."

"What was his response?"

Levi swallowed. "He said roger and broke the connection."

"Goddamn it!"

The admiral's response wasn't lost on Levi. They both knew that, in military parlance, roger means "I understand," as opposed to wilco, which means "will comply." For Jack to use roger was the same as him saying, "I hear you."

Levi looked up at the tiled displays that covered the gently curved wall on the far side of the War Room. In addition to the task-processing queues, it also displayed all the video feeds for the target area, including one that showed Jamal's body inside the sensory deprivation tank. Keeping him in that tank for this long could kill him. Under that blue glow, Jamal's face showed a combination of strain and grim determination that Levi found extremely disturbing.

Caroline had been able to access two other cameras inside the building where Jamal was being kept. City records showed that the first floor was a long, narrow, dry-cleaning facility, with three floors of apartments above it, providing homes to the extended family that operated the business.

But this dry cleaner's shop had been closed for several weeks while it was under renovation. The low-resolution security cameras showed that in the back of the building, all of the conveyors, presses, and chemical equipment had been removed to make room for the sensory deprivation tank and the high-tech equipment associated with its operation. A changing shift of armed guards came and went, along with others who appeared to be doctors and technicians.

Unfortunately the video cameras were so poorly located and of such low quality that it was impossible to enhance the images to the point where facial recognition was feasible. But the fact that something wasn't feasible didn't mean it was impossible for the NSA, and Levi already had a team of experts working the problem these low-res images presented.

In San Francisco, it was 0130 hours and Spider Sanchez's team was on their way into the city, their GPS locators showing their positions on the big map. One panel van with six individual transponders inside. As Levi watched the van move along the map, his thoughts turned to Janet Price. The fact that she had lost faith in Jack was an operational tragedy because, together, those two were the most formidable team Levi had ever observed. Janet gave Jack the balance that kept him from flaming out, and Levi knew that if The Ripper flamed out, it would endanger everyone and everything in his general vicinity.

Admiral Riles's voice brought Levi back to the moment. "It looks as quiet as we can hope for. Tell Sanchez his team has the green light."

Levi nodded and picked up the satellite phone, feeling the familiar rush that the commencement of combat operations always gave him. Luckily this looked like it was going to turn out to be a relatively straightforward smash, grab, and go operation.

So why did he have a big knot in the pit of his stomach?

: CHAPTER 29

The black panel van entered Chinatown coming downhill from the southwest, Harry driving, Spider beside him in the passenger seat, and Janet, Bobby, Paul, and Bronson in the back. They all wore black bulletproof utility vests with "POLICE" and "ICE" stenciled across the front and back. Except for Harry, they all held their MP5s, ready to make a high-speed tactical exit from the vehicle, the submachine guns lengthened by the KAC suppressors.

Harry turned left off of Kearny onto Pine Street and then right into a maze of narrow side streets.

"One minute out," Bobby said.

Janet felt the familiar cold thrill of coming conflict sharpen her senses, accompanied by a strange uneasiness.

Harry pulled to a stop at the entrance to a narrow pedestrian lane called Spofford Street. Then, as five team members exited and moved into a tight tactical formation along both sides of the walkway, the van rolled forward, rounded a corner, and disappeared into the night. Harry would stay with the vehicle, ready to come get them when called.

The squad moved rapidly between the red brick walls flanking the street entrance, Janet and Bronson on the left while Paul and Bobby followed Spider past the interconnecting buildings on the right. Twenty feet down the lane, its nature changed, the plain walls giving way to multicolored interconnecting storefronts. At two hours past midnight, the barred shop windows were mostly dark, as were the three levels of apartments above them.

Spider held up his left hand and the team stopped. "Goggles on."

Janet unclipped her NVGs from her utility vest, slid them onto her head, and switched them on. Suddenly the dark spaces along the dimly lit street became clearly visible in different shades of green.

The team moved quickly past several more shops, coming to a halt beneath one of the many fire escapes that lined the side of the interconnecting buildings. Janet slung her weapon across her back. Then she and Bronson scrambled up a pipe and onto the fire escape while the rest of the team covered them from below.

"Video?" Janet asked, speaking softly into the jawbone microphone.

"Looks calm," said Harry in her earpiece. "Two bored-looking guards near the tank and a couple of technicians at computers."

"Janet," said Spider. "You and Bronson get up on the roof and come in through the access door. Tell me when you're inside; then the rest of us will enter from the third-floor fire escape. Stay dark and quiet as long as possible."

Climbing silently, Janet and Bronson made their way to the top of the fire escape as the other three team members scrambled up behind them. As she climbed, Janet scanned the opposite rooftop for potential targets, but it was clear. She found the same to be true when she slid the flexible, fiber-optic periscope up over the edge of this building's flat rooftop.

"Clear," she said as she swung her leg up and over.

Bronson came up behind her silent and fast, covering right as she covered left, both moving in a crouch toward the rooftop access door twenty feet to their front. Assuming a kneeling position to the right of the door, Janet covered Bronson as he applied the small torsion wrench and snap gun to the door lock. She heard three soft clicks, saw Bronson turn the cylinder, and heard the door move slightly open, though not as silently as she would have wished.

Again Janet spoke into her jaw microphone. "Going in now."

Bronson pulled the door open and Janet went in fast, finding herself at the top of an empty stairwell.

"Top of stairwell clear," she said.

Then they were both inside and moving down, MP5s ready to fire. In her ear, Janet heard Spider's calm voice. "Going in."

: CHAPTER 30

With Gan Liu standing to his left, practically quaking with desire to release three dozen heavily armed triad gang members who waited in the surrounding buildings, Qiang Chu studied the display on his mini-tablet. Four men and a woman wearing ICE vests had just entered the Green Dragon Dry Cleaners building, two through the roof and three more through the third-floor fire escape.

Qiang spoke into his secure cell phone. "Make it dark."

Watching from a third-floor apartment across the street from where the feds had just entered, Qiang saw San Francisco's city lights go out. He knew that the Chinese hackers working from the Hayward facility were some of the world's best, but Jamal Glover was incredible. Right now, using the backdoors Jamal had provided, the Chinese hackers were taking down power, water, phones, cell phones, and emergency communications throughout the city.

In thirty seconds Qiang would release the Bay Triad on the unsuspecting federal agents working their way down into that dry-cleaning facility, but the ensuing gun battle would bring no police response. Right now, like every other city emergency department, the San Francisco PD would be scrambling to figure out what the hell had just happened to their city.

CHAPTER 31

"What the hell just happened?" Admiral Riles's voice carried the same disbelief that numbed Levi.

Levi turned to look at Dr. David Kurtz, who scanned a sixty-degree fan of OLED monitors that surrounded his workstation.

When Kurtz raised his eyes, it seemed to Levi that the NSA's chief computer scientist's mop of gray hair had suddenly gotten wilder.

"We've lost San Francisco!"

Riles turned to face Dr. Kurtz. "What do you mean?"

"I mean everything. Communications, power, utilities, emergency services. Everything just dropped off the grid."

Levi felt his throat tighten. "What about Oakland?"

"Oakland's fine."

"Give me a satellite view," Riles said, stepping around behind Kurtz.

Over the intercom, Levi heard the confused babble and shocked surprise coming from the Dirty Dozen in the War Room below.

He thumbed a switch on his microphone. "Focus people! Caroline, get me back my satellite comm link to our team and I mean right now! I want the rest of you working on getting into the power and communications grids. Make it happen."

When Levi shifted his gaze to the satellite video displayed on Dr. Kurtz's central screen, he sucked in his breath. "Jesus Christ!"

San Francisco was as dark as North Korea.

:CHAPTER 32

Sitting atop the Honda Shadow, looking down Clay Street toward the distant lights of the Transamerica Pyramid Center, Jack Gregory was fighting a losing battle with himself and he knew it. No matter how much he told himself that he needed to follow orders and let Spider and Janet's NSA team do its job without outside interference, he couldn't summon the self-control to force himself to comply.

Then the lights went out. Not just on this block, but in every part of the city that was visible from his hilltop vantage point.

The adrenaline rush that flooded Jack's limbic system ended all internal debate and put him in motion toward the danger that called to him from Chinatown. It was ultra-stupid. He was on a motorcycle armed with only his Heckler & Koch pistol, the black-bladed Gerber Guardian combat dagger, and a throwing knife. And if that strange inner sense that pulled him relentlessly toward danger was correct, he was headed straight into a Montezuma shitstorm.

Racing down the dark city street, Jack banked hard onto Grant, welcomed to the Chinese neighborhood by the sound of nearby gunfire. Not just a smattering—it sounded like a full-on war zone. A hundred feet from the entrance to Spofford Street where the gunfire seemed concentrated, Jack skidded to a stop, removed his helmet, and dismounted.

With a rush that only raw adrenaline could provide, Jack entered the twelve-foot-wide pedestrian path at a dead run, jumped to catch a foot on the nearest window ledge, and propelled himself up to the first of many fire escapes that decorated the sides of this block-long building. Although he'd left the night-vision goggles behind, Jack could sense the chaotic attack on the shop a half block ahead. Leaping over the railing, Jack launched himself across an open space, caught the edge of the next fire escape, swung and climbed, just one of the many bodies that swarmed toward the openings into the targeted building.

Then, with a familiar red haze misting his vision, Jack surrendered to the dark entity within.

CHAPTER 33

Having rapidly cleared the upper three floors, the team had found only vacant apartments, something that raised all kinds of red flags in Janet's mind. When the city lights that filtered in through the outside windows went out, the bad feeling in Janet's gut suddenly got a hell of a lot worse.

The cascade of gunfire that shattered the windows confirmed her growing fear that they'd been led into a trap.

"Get down to the first floor," Spider yelled. "Grab Jamal and get the hell out of here."

Staying low, Janet was the first to reach the stairwell, with Bobby Daniels right on her heels. Without hesitation, Janet bounded down the stairs and paused to let Bobby catch up before cracking the door open to toss a flash-bang grenade into the bedlam beyond. Then a bullet struck her high up on the left side of her vest. Its impact knocked her over backwards and she struck her head on the stairwell railing as she fell.

Stunned, she was barely aware of the light and sound from the percussion grenade, or the other team members that piled through the open door to lay down a base of fire into their attackers. Strong hands grabbed her and dragged her away from the opening.

Struggling to keep from blacking out, Janet felt those same hands check her body for wounds. In the fall, she'd lost her NVGs. But then she felt them dragged back into place and found herself looking up into Spider Sanchez's similarly goggled face.

"The vest stopped the bullet," he yelled over the sound of the gunfire. "Get back up the stairs and help Paul stop anyone who tries to come down."

Then he was gone, disappearing into the dry cleaner shop after Bobby and Bronson. When she climbed back to her feet, a wave of dizziness almost dropped her back to a knee, but she fought through it. She felt blood running down her neck from the cut on the back of her head, but she was standing, so it couldn't be that serious. Her chest hurt like hell. Hopefully the bullet's impact hadn't broken her clavicle.

Of course, if she didn't get her ass moving up those stairs to help Paul, someone would come down here to make sure she no longer cared.

CHAPTER 34

Jack reached the rooftop, just one of many to do so, and ran toward the point where they bunched at the access door, trying to enter the stairwell that led down into the building. The sound of gunfire from inside made it clear that someone was fighting hard to prevent them from charging down those stairs.

That way in was no good, but the fire escape called to him, and Jack ran toward it. His black blade filled his hand and he cut the throat of the man at the top of those metal steps. The dying body tumbled through the darkness into the two men on the steps below and Jack came with it, his blade feasting on soft flesh, feeding the adrenaline-fueled rage that powered it, a hunger that could only be sated by blood.

Jack swung out and down, launching himself into three men who were intent on climbing through the fire escape into the bedlam inside the fourth-floor apartment. Again and again, Jack's knife plunged and slashed, killing the first two before they realized the person behind them wasn't one of their own. Despite the thunder of gunfire that echoed from the room, the third man recognized this new danger and spun to meet Jack.

As if in slow motion, the man's head turned and his gun followed, a half second too late to save him from the impaling blade. Jack felt the knife slide into the man's solar plexus to its hilt and heard the gun boom beside his head as his churning legs drove forward, propelling the convulsing body into the group firing down the far hallway.

Then Jack was among them and their gargling screams joined the cacophony that filled the dark building.

CHAPTER 35

"Jamal's not here. We're falling back to the stairwell." Spider's angry voice crackled through Janet's earpiece, confirming what she'd feared. They'd been suckered.

With bullets whining through the stairwell from above and from the room at the end of the fourth-floor hallway, Janet slapped a new magazine into the MP5 and put a bullet through the head that poked around the switchback that led up to the roof.

Suddenly Harry's voice was on the radio. "I'm coming to you."

"Negative!" Spider said. "That van's our only way out. I'll tell you when I want it."

A bullet ricocheted off the corner of the wall, spraying concrete shards into Janet's face, chipping the left lens of her night-vision goggles. She placed an answering three-round burst down the hall.

The pain in her shoulder felt minor compared to the ache in her head and the accompanying nausea that signaled a concussion. It would be so sweet to just let her consciousness slip away and take the pain and sickness with it. But if she did that, their attackers from the roof and fourth floor would link up and then she wouldn't be the only one to die.

With Spider and Bobby holding the first-floor landing while Bronson and Paul controlled the second and third, she had to hold this flank if they were to have any chance at all of getting out of here. Right now she had no idea how she was going to make that happen.

The change came so suddenly that she almost thought her fevered brain had imagined it. The gunfire from the far room faltered and the screaming began, screams of pain and terror. The eerie nature of those sounds raised the hair on the back of her neck and momentarily stopped the gunfire from above as the sounds echoed out to the roof. It pulled Janet so powerfully that she peeked around the corner before she was aware she was doing it.

The sight that confronted her brought a gasp to Janet's lips. At the far end of the hall a figure held another pinned to the wall, repeatedly thrusting a long blade into the man's stomach. Then, as if he'd only just become aware of her presence, a blood-soaked Jack Gregory let the limp form slump to the floor and turned to face her, his eyes burning white hot through the twin tubes of her NVGs. *Jack. You beautiful demon.*

A fresh round of wild gunfire from upstairs brought Janet back to her senses and she squeezed off a half dozen 9mm rounds in that direction. But when she glanced back around the corner, Jack Gregory was gone.

: CHAPTER 36

Qiang Chu watched the triad assault into the building across the narrow street from the third-floor window, the low-light goggles illuminating the scene as if a bright full moon hung in the sky above. Whipped into a gang frenzy that only the promise of killing federal agents could impart, Asian gangsters threw themselves into the assault with reckless abandon, each one trying to outdo his fellows as they swarmed up the fire escapes. From the street, several of them fired into the dry-cleaning shop as others tore the barred security grate from mounts that had never been designed to endure such a mass assault. When some fell before the gunfire from within, others rushed in to fill the void. In a matter of moments, the quiet Chinatown street had been transformed into a combat zone.

A movement from the north end of the street drew Qiang's gaze in that direction. A lone triad member raced to the building, jumped and kicked off of a window ledge, using his momentum to propel him to the next hand or foothold as he sprinted up the side of the building. Qiang doubted that even he could have done better. Although he had no idea who this man was, Qiang intended to recruit him away from the triad as soon as this was over.

The climber swung himself up onto the roof and for several seconds Qiang lost sight of him. When he reappeared at the top of the fire escape, Qiang saw the knife in his hand and smiled. A man after his own heart. What the climber did next wiped that smile from Qiang's lips.

The climber plunged his blade into a gangster who had just reached the top of the fire escape and hurled the body into two others. In a nonstop rush, he cut his way through six men and into the room beyond. The realization of what he had just witnessed momentarily froze Qiang.

The Ripper!

Qiang Chu felt the veins in his temples throb so hard that they threatened to explode, painting the room with blood. *Who the hell is that guy?* Moving quickly, Qiang reached the stairwell and descended to the street.

As he raced toward the action in the opposite building, he couldn't understand it. Why hadn't the MSS alerted him to such a major threat?

CHAPTER 37

Jack saw Janet Price and froze. For a second it seemed that she wouldn't recognize him, that she would swing the MP5 submachine gun toward him. But she paused, recognition and surprise registering in the part of her face that was visible below her NVGs.

Jack knew he shouldn't be able to see those features in the nearly perfect darkness and maybe he didn't. Maybe he just sensed her presence. When he got like this, it was just too hard to tell. In the past he had thought this strange sense was more akin to smell than to vision. But in the end, it just didn't matter. It was what it was.

Beyond Janet, the booming echo of renewed gunfire swiveled her head in that direction and the subsequent muzzle flash from her MP5 brought a scream from above. Time to move.

Switching the black knife to his left hand, Jack drew his gun and charged back to the fire escape. Seeing movement from below, Jack put a single bullet through the head of the man that climbed toward him. His second shot merely winged a second man who dove for cover and Jack used the momentary lull to climb to the roof, fully aware that if Janet failed to react to what he was about to do, his new position would very quickly become untenable. But in the past, Janet had never faltered when she'd had his back and he didn't think she'd fail him now.

As his feet hit the rooftop, Jack broke into a dead run toward the men jammed up outside the stairwell entry, firing into the group as fast as he could pull the trigger. Everything now depended upon him closing that distance before the stunned survivors could react. What happened after that was up to Janet.

CHAPTER 38

Janet heard two shots from the fire escape but kept firing up the stairwell. The activity above her faltered and as a fresh burst of gunfire was accompanied by panicked screams, Janet put it all together. As she spoke into her tactical radio's jaw microphone, her voice carried a sense of urgency.

"Jack's attacking from the roof. If we assault right now, we can punch through up there."

Spider reacted immediately. "Everybody to the roof. Now!"

Janet moved up to the corner, emptied her weapon around it, and slapped in a new magazine as Bronson moved into the spot she'd just vacated. Then Spider was there and all three opened up on full auto as Bobby and Paul covered behind them.

She changed magazines again. It was now or never. Ducking below Spider's and Bronson's line of fire, she scrambled over the dead bodies toward the roof access door. A head poked out around the corner and a bullet knocked it backward out of sight.

Janet slipped on a corpse, righted herself, and dove for the roof exit. Just through the open door, a wounded man crawled toward cover but Janet's bullet stopped his progress. Six feet beyond that, another man stood against the wall, firing wildly around the corner of the square concrete stairwell shelter, presumably toward Jack. Janet shot him twice in the back, and as his body fell away, another bullet caught him in the side of the head.

Moving to kneel at the corner vacated by the man she'd just killed, Janet saw Spider and Bronson move to cover the opposite side of the stairwell shelter.

"Jack!" Janet yelled.

"Watch out!" His answering yell was accompanied by fresh gunfire.

Immediately, Janet saw the new danger as Jack's bullet sent a man tumbling from the top of the fire escape.

Spider's command sounded in her ear. "Harry! We're headed for the north end of the building. Bring the van."

Behind Janet, emerging from the stairwell, Paul supported Bobby, who leaned heavily on his shoulder.

"Follow me!" Spider yelled as he rounded the corner and sprinted north across the roof, toward the cover provided by the next stairwell access structure. He was followed by Paul with Bobby, as Bronson covered from behind. When the others reached cover, Bronson made his move.

When Janet started to follow, Jack surprised her by standing fast, his pistol aimed back toward the fire escape.

"Jack, let's go!" she yelled, but he ignored her.

Reversing course, she grabbed his shoulder, swinging him to face her. If anything, Jack's eyes burned hotter in her goggles than before. *Son of a bitch!* It was Bolivia all over again. Janet swung her left fist and, though she knew Jack sensed it coming, he made no move to duck the blow that snapped his head around.

As Jack's face turned back toward her, Janet heard herself yell, "Are you coming or do we die here together?"

For an endless second, she watched as he considered the options. Then, under the crackling cover fire from Raymond Bronson and Spider Sanchez, they sprinted after the others.

CHAPTER 39

When Qiang entered the dry-cleaning establishment where the trap had been sprung, the sight of a half dozen triad gangsters huddled outside the stairwell brought his anger to a new level. Without a word, Qiang approached the biggest of these men, doubled him over with a kick to the liver, and then crushed his windpipe with an open-handed blow that left him balled up on the floor.

His yelled command carried more than a threat. "Get up to the roof! Kill the Americans!"

No one moved to challenge him. Instead they ran for the stairwell, urging each other on as if they had intended to make this assault without his encouragement. Qiang did not follow them. Instead he moved back out into the street, studying the building and the attack that had stalled at the top of the nearest fire escape. One man at the top raised a weapon above the level of the rooftop but fell backward, his body tumbling over the steel railing to strike it again one level down before smacking the sidewalk.

What had seemed a good plan, when Gan Liu had briefed him

on it, had unraveled under The Ripper's brutal assault. Now, the Americans had broken through and regained the rooftop, leaving the remainder of the triad gangsters concentrated in the building below them. It made Qiang wish that he had brought along some of his agents, but after losing the five he'd sent to Kansas City, he'd left the remainder of them guarding Grange Castle and the Hayward lab.

The gunfire on the roof shifted to the north and Qiang understood what that meant. The Americans had broken out in that direction, and since the triad plan had involved an all-out effort to keep them bottled up inside the trap, they had left no reserve forces in position to block a possible escape.

For a second, Qiang considered the possibility of running to the north end of the street and blocking the Americans by himself, just long enough to allow the triad to regroup and catch up from behind. But as bad as he wanted to deal with The Ripper, Qiang could afford to be patient. He would catch The Ripper at a time and place of his own choosing. Tonight he had taught the Americans a very important lesson about the capabilities he now possessed. Before long, Qiang would show them that what he'd just demonstrated in San Francisco was only the beginning.

Knowing it was a wise decision, Qiang started to turn away, then came to a complete stop in the middle of the street. For the first time in his adult life, he couldn't force himself to do the right thing. The call of The Ripper was just too strong to resist. Spinning on his heel, Qiang tossed off his night-vision goggles and sprinted toward the north end of the pedestrian walkway.

For better or worse, Qiang would settle this right here and now. And whether or not the other Americans made good on their escape, there would be one less complication to deal with.

: CHAPTER 40

Jack felt dizzy, not from Janet's blow that had split his lip but from the weird mental state it had left him in. Before that confrontation, he'd given himself over to the raging beast within, ready to pay whatever price it demanded in return for the incredible experience it delivered. But Janet's blow and her threat to die alongside him had pulled Jack from that terrible mental embrace. Not all the way. Just enough to leave him in a no-man's land of sensation, one foot firmly planted in the here and now while the other stepped through an altered reality that refused to release him from its grasp.

Up ahead, Spider Sanchez reached the north edge of the roof and pulled a collapsible grappling hook and line from his utility vest, hooking it in place before tossing the line out and down the side of the building. With Bronson still firing back toward the south, Paul released Bobby, snapped a carabiner to the line, took a single wrap, and dropped over the side.

Spider leaned over the north edge of the wall, his MP5 covering Paul's descent as Janet moved to assist the wounded Bobby.

As Jack neared the spot where Paul had gone over the wall, the familiar sense of nearby danger tugged at him from below. He leaned over the edge of the roof and saw Paul move to the northeast corner of the building, but as Paul turned to aim his weapon south along Spofford Street, someone grabbed him, flipping his body head over heels out of sight.

Without hesitation, Jack dropped his knife and gun to the street below, grabbed the line with both hands, and catapulted his body over the edge. His right leg hooked the line in a single wrap around his boot as he slid downward. When he neared the ground, Jack kicked free of the line and dropped into a forward roll that carried him out onto the pavement. A black van skidded to a stop two feet in front of him.

Ignoring the gun that now lay beneath the van, Jack grabbed his knife and raced to the corner where Paul had disappeared. He felt the other man coming around the corner before he saw him and whirled into a side kick as a bullet whizzed past his left ear. In that brief moment, as the muzzle flash of the gun illuminated his opponent's face, Jack recognized him. Qiang Chu. Although Jack's kick knocked the gun from Qiang's hand, the spy reacted with incredible speed and agility, converting Jack's angular momentum into a flip that sent him tumbling into Paul's limp body.

Jack sensed the kick aimed at his head as it began and rolled right, taking a glancing blow on his left shoulder as he hooked the foot in the crook of his elbow. A hard twist dropped Qiang face-down on the street as Jack attempted to drive his black blade into Qiang's side. But Qiang twisted in his grasp, using a move that Jack had never before encountered, a maneuver that knocked the knife from Jack's hand as his assailant landed back on his feet.

Jack scissored his legs, landing in a fighter's crouch. But Qiang was gone. Then Jack saw him, ducking through a door on the west side of the street as renewed gunfire from farther down the road hissed over Jack's head. Behind him, Bronson and Spider rounded the corner, spraying bullets past Qiang and into the charging gangsters, sending them diving for cover.

Ignoring the urge to follow Qiang, Jack tossed Paul's body over his shoulder and retreated back around the corner to the van. But as Jack gently lowered the agent to the floor of the van, he felt Paul's head roll like a marionette with a broken string. With a dull numbness spreading through his hands and arms, Jack released his hold on Paul's body and climbed in.

Seconds later, the others piled in beside Jack and the van's tires howled on the pavement, propelling the vehicle down Washington Street, sending it sliding through a hard left turn onto Stockton. Then as Harry accelerated out of Chinatown, he placed a flashing blue-and-white light on the dash and switched on a siren that echoed through the dark city.

Jack felt Janet crawl across his legs to place a hand on Paul's throat. When she slumped back, he heard her breath hiss through her lips.

"Goddamn it!"

Janet's voice held a mixture of anguish and fury that Jack understood very well. And as he leaned his blood-soaked body back against the van's driver-side wall, the last of his adrenaline rush faded, leaving only emptiness in its wake.

CHAPTER 41

"If we don't get him out of there right now, he's going to flatline!"

Steve Grange turned to look at Dr. Landon and nodded. "Pull him out of the tank."

Grange watched as Dr. Landon directed a team of assistants as they changed the drug cocktail that dripped through the IV tube into Jamal Glover's left arm, taking him from the hallucinogenic dream-state and putting him to sleep. Working quickly, they opened the sensory deprivation tank, disconnected the leads from Jamal's cap, and then transferred him from the tank onto a stretcher.

When they had wheeled Jamal out of the room, Grange turned his attention to Dr. Vicky Morris. "How's the data looking?"

The smile that crossed the thirty-three-year-old woman's features reminded him of just how pretty she could be if she ever let her hair down. But as far as Grange knew, that was one thing the intense Dr. Morris never did.

"Amazing. It'll take a couple of days, but based upon the quality of the neural feeds, I think we'll be able to finalize our digital neurosynthesis."

"Excellent," Grange said, meaning it. "Get back to the castle, grab some rest, and then get started."

Grange saw the frown tighten Dr. Morris's lips before she spoke. "I'd prefer to start as soon as I get back."

Grange smiled inwardly. A woman after his own heart. But he didn't have the time to allow fatigue-induced errors to worm their way into the program. And he didn't want to double-check her work to make sure that didn't happen.

"No. Get four hours of rest and then get started. Nonnegotiable."

Dr. Morris's red-veined eyes narrowed. "Four hours then."

"Actual sleep time."

"I can't guarantee that."

"I need you at your best. Whatever it takes, make it happen."

With a final shrug of acquiescence, Dr. Morris nodded and then turned and walked toward the exit. Grange watched her go, knowing full well that he wouldn't be sleeping anytime soon. He was too close to his dream and there were far too many things that could still go wrong.

Tonight Qiang Chu's team of elite Chinese hackers had used Jamal and tricked the federal agents into a deathtrap, yet Qiang had failed to kill them. Qiang had refused to tell him how the agents had managed their escape, saying only that Gan Liu's Bay Triad had disappointed him. What puzzled Grange was why Qiang was lying to him. Something important had happened that was being kept secret. He had heard it in Qiang's voice. Now an unconstrained variable had planted an additional seed of worry in Grange's mind. At the moment, it was exactly the kind of distraction that he didn't need.

Grange walked to the open sensory deprivation tank and stopped to stare down into the murky fluid that partially filled its interior. He reached inside and poked a finger into the still liquid, watching the circular ripples spread across its smooth surface. Tonight, something had disturbed the quiet calm that defined Qiang's nature.

Who the hell could do that to Qiang Chu?

CHAPTER 42

The van's arrival back at the safe house hadn't sparked any emotion in Janet. She felt so drained that she had nothing left to give. At least that's what she thought. Dealing with Paul's corpse proved her wrong.

Janet had first experienced violent death on her thirteenth birthday. From her bedroom, she'd heard her mom's screams echoing up the stairs, screams that had pulled Janet down to the kitchen just in time to see her father's massive right fist cave in the side of Anna's lovely face. The snub-nosed .38 lay on the floor beneath the kitchen table, a precaution her mom had carried in her purse, just in case the restraining order failed to protect her. But neither of these defenses had protected Anna Price from her ex-husband's drunken rage.

Janet had no memory of picking up the weapon. But she remembered the recoil as the .38-caliber revolver bucked in her hands. The first bullet had knocked her father off her mom's battered body. When he'd tried to rise, the next three bullets sprawled him faceup on the linoleum floor. Then, with a scream of hate and despair gargling out of her throat, she'd stood over the big man and fired the last bullet into the center of his upturned face. Happy birthday.

In the years that followed, with the help of her maternal grandparents and an exceptional therapist, Janet had recovered her joy for life. But tonight was a reminder of just how easily joy could be sucked from her soul. And despite the fact that she had watched others die and had done her own share of killing, this was the first time she'd lost a partner. Tonight, the perpetual laughter in Paul's blue eyes had been snuffed out forever.

As she watched Bronson and Spider gently lift Paul from the back of the van and lay him on the garage floor, his head rolled and twisted in a way that had made her physically ill. It would have been better if he'd been killed by a bullet or a bomb, but Qiang Chu had broken Paul's neck with his bare hands, something Janet wouldn't have thought possible. And Qiang had done it quickly, almost effortlessly. It was no fitting way for one of America's most highly trained commandos to die.

The team hadn't brought body bags for this mission, so they fashioned one from two large lawn-and-leaf refuse bags that Janet duct-taped together to form an airtight seal. Now Paul lay in the garage-morgue as they all stared down at him, momentarily lost in their own thoughts or saying silent prayers, each according to his own individual faith or lack thereof. All except for Jack Gregory, who watched the quasi-ceremony from the side of the van, his face so covered in dried blood that she couldn't pick up any emotion that might have otherwise shown up in his features.

Janet turned toward him, her eyes irresistibly drawn to Jack's. As their gazes locked, she felt it . . . regret tinged with frustration . . . and understood. Janet had seen Jack in action on many different occasions. Although he often lost control, nobody survived a one-on-one confrontation with The Ripper. But Qiang Chu had done more than that. He'd disarmed Jack and possibly would have killed him had they not been interrupted. From the look in Jack's eyes, he hungered for a rematch.

There was no doubt in Janet's mind that Qiang Chu felt the same way.

CHAPTER 43

Admiral Riles occupied the third of six chairs arranged along the left side of the conference table in the White House Situation Room. The report Spider Sanchez had delivered from the NSA safe house hadn't been good news. Someone had spoofed the NSA into providing false intelligence that had walked his ghost team into a trap. And if Jack Gregory hadn't disobeyed Levi's orders and involved himself, Riles would have lost the whole team. Even though they'd managed to fight their way out, Paul Monroe had been killed and both Bobby Daniels and Janet Price had suffered minor wounds.

Riles glanced to his right at the sandy-haired president of the United States. President Harris knew the country had suffered a major cyber-attack that had crippled San Francisco, but knew nothing about the NSA ghost team's involvement in a gang shoot-out in the middle of that city. And for the sake of the president's plausible deniability, Admiral Riles intended to keep it that way.

Today's early morning emergency meeting was attended by select members of the president's cabinet and included the director of central intelligence, the FBI director, and the secretary of homeland security. President Harris sat at the head of the table, his face tense with anger. To his right sat Vice President George Gordon while Bob Adams, the national security advisor, occupied the seat to the president's left.

This morning's gathering had none of the small talk and greetings that normally preceded a meeting. All twelve men and women seated around the table maintained an unusual silence as they waited for the president to speak.

Riles watched as President Harris leaned forward until his elbows rested on the conference table.

"As you are all aware," President Harris said, "at approximately 2:30 A.M. Pacific time, a coordinated cyber-attack incapacitated the city of San Francisco, knocking out power, water, and most forms of communications. Make no mistake about it, I regard this as a direct attack on the United States of America."

Admiral Riles felt the president turn his gaze in his direction. "Admiral Riles, as my NSA director and head of U.S. Cyber Command, what have you learned about who is behind this attack and how it was launched?"

Mirroring the president's posture, Riles leaned forward, his focus so intense that it seemed as if he and the president were the only two people in the room.

"Mr. President, since shortly after the commencement of the attack we've had our top people working this. I've also sent a team to the Bay Area to perform forensic analysis of the systems that were compromised. At this point all we have are indications that the power and communications grids were penetrated several hours before the actual attack and that this precursor hack opened backdoors into a wide variety of key systems."

President Harris cocked his head ever so slightly, a clear indication he didn't like what he was hearing. "Why the wait until they launched the attack?"

"Apparently the attackers wanted all the affected systems to go down at one time to maximize the overall impact."

"Then why two thirty in the morning? Why not rush hour or the middle of the business day?"

"I don't know."

Riles noted the president's fingers drumming the tabletop. "Okay, Admiral Riles. Can you at least tell me who is behind an attack that completely incapacitated one of our most important cities?"

"We're working on that."

"And how long are you going to keep me waiting?"

Riles saw the look of satisfaction on CIA Director Frank Rheiner's face at the machine-gun questions the president was directing at Riles. Not really surprising considering Rheiner had been on the receiving end of just such an exchange during the Kazakhstan incident six months ago. Riles had embarrassed Rheiner then, so this had to feel pretty darn good.

"As I mentioned earlier, my top computer scientist and a team of cyber-forensic specialists are on their way to San Francisco right now. I don't expect to be able to give you a definitive answer until they have examined the affected equipment. In the meantime, our cyber-warfare group is working the problem from Fort Meade."

"I want to know who you think is behind this."

Riles hesitated, debating just what he could reveal that wouldn't compromise his ghost team.

"We believe that this may be related to last week's kidnapping of our top cyber-warrior, Jamal Glover. If that's true, the Chinese government may be behind this."

Bill Hammond, the FBI director, inserted himself into the

conversation, his full head of dark hair making him stand out from the other cabinet members arrayed on either side of the president. "I'm sorry, Mr. President, but Admiral Riles is way off base on this."

"Okay, Bill. I'm listening," said President Harris, rubbing a hand through his hair.

"The FBI has gathered extensive evidence indicating that Jamal Glover killed his live-in girlfriend before attempting to flee the country from Miami. I believe it is highly likely that Glover is the source of this attack and that he is trying to divert our attention in order to facilitate his escape from the country. Not only does he possess the required skills, it provides a possible explanation for the timing of the attack. Glover wasn't trying to kill a bunch of innocent people; he just wanted to focus all of our efforts on the opposite coast."

Riles had to admit that it was a good argument, one that he couldn't refute without compromising his ongoing efforts to recover Jamal. Since he currently had no hard evidence to support his position, Riles maintained his silence as the president turned his attention to the secretary of homeland security.

"Gary, what's the DHS assessment?"

"I have to agree with Director Hammond on the probable cause. I spoke with Mayor Cummins an hour ago and she couldn't give me an estimate of how long it is going to take to restore city services. Apparently the sudden shutdown of the power grid caused significant damage to several electrical substations along with an unknown number of blown transformers. As for water and communications, they can't be fully restored until they have power."

"Does she need anything from us?"

"She said she'd be submitting a detailed request through the governor's office once the local experts have fully assessed the situation. Since it's still dark on the West Coast, I don't expect that until this afternoon. Meanwhile, I've ordered the mobilization of an emergency task force to investigate and provide assistance where needed."

President Harris nodded, then returned his gaze to his FBI director. "Okay, Bill, I want you to find Jamal Glover and figure out who he's working for. As of now, that's your priority."

"Yes, sir."

The president redirected his attention to his NSA director with a hawk-like look on his face.

"We take a lot of heat for the NSA knowing everyone's business. I'm not happy that this isn't the case in this instance. Admiral Riles, as the head of Cyber Command, I expect your people to figure this out. If you need operational support from DHS or any other agency to take these people down, just say so and you'll get it. You're my point man on this."

"I understand, Mr. President," Riles said.

President Harris stood, as did the others at the table. "Okay then, we're done here."

As he made his way out of the White House and back to his sedan, Admiral Riles set his jaw. He, too, wanted answers and, by God, someone was going to get them for him.

CHAPTER 44

After taking the opportunity to clean up, Jack took the first watch. It hadn't felt right to dress himself from the clothes in Paul's duffel, but since they were roughly his size, Spider had made the decision and Jack couldn't argue with it.

Perhaps more than anyone else on the team, Jack needed sleep. But after his lucid dream experience, he feared it. So he had volunteered for the watch, and nobody ever argued with an idiot who volunteers.

Jack stepped out onto the front steps, dimly aware of the weight of the Glock in his holster. It was a reliable weapon and since he'd left his HK P30S on a San Francisco street, he was happy to have it.

The dirt lane that led to the front of the farmhouse disappeared around a copse of trees fifty yards from the house. Located in a secluded draw in the rolling hills of Contra Costa County, the house was shielded from view of the highway, although Jack could hear the sound of distant cars echo through the canyon as the morning commuters made their way to work.

Jack entered a walking path that led around the side of the house and onto the sparsely wooded, south-facing hillside that rose up behind it. A short time later, the trail reached a rocky outcropping that provided an excellent view of the surrounding area, and Jack seated himself atop it, feeling the warm morning sun caress his face as he studied the valley below.

As safe houses went, this one had the advantage of relative isolation from the prying eyes of nosy neighbors. Normally they wouldn't have bothered posting a watch, relying instead on electronic surveillance to warn of intruders. But given the demonstration of power the team's enemies had provided last night, their trust in electronic surveillance mechanisms had suffered a severe setback. Although it was unlikely that this safe house had been compromised, they couldn't count on its continued security.

Jack felt the movement without catching sight of it, a subtle wrongness from the woods he'd just left. Drawing the Glock, he slipped from his perch and moved back into the wood line, entering at a point twenty yards above the spot where he'd emerged only minutes before.

Then, with stealth born from years of hard experience, Jack melted into the woods.

CHAPTER 45

No matter how she tried to let go, sleep refused to claim Janet. So, after a restless half hour of tossing and turning, movements that increased the pounding from the knot on the back of her head, Janet gave up. It wasn't pain that was robbing her of sleep; it was raw anger, not at Jack, but at herself. Jack Gregory was the most interesting and exciting man she'd ever met. And yes, he scared the hell out of her. But last night had shown Janet that, despite what she'd been telling herself, she wasn't scared that Jack's lack of self-control would get the whole team killed. Hell, if not for Jack's craziness, the whole team would be dead right now.

Since she'd watched Jack blindly stroll through that dark Bolivian cavern, Janet had feared that he was determined to get himself killed. So for the last two months, instead of trying to help Jack work through whatever inner demons plagued him, she'd used every opportunity to push him as far away from her as possible.

Now Janet saw the impact of her actions. All she'd managed to accomplish in the last two months was to place Jack at even greater risk. In fact, it was Janet's insistence that he be kept off the team that had almost gotten everyone killed. It was as if she'd made herself into a completely different person. And now that Janet had finally taken a long look in the mirror, she didn't like what stared back at her.

Janet climbed out of bed, dressed, and pinned her hair in a tight bun with a six-inch hair needle. It was time to eat some crow and set things right. But first she had some questions for Jack, questions that she was determined to make him answer.

When she stepped outside, Jack was nowhere to be seen, but she spotted fresh boot tracks in the dusty trail that led around the side of the house and up the hill into the woods. An apex predator, it was Jack's nature to seek solitude in dense woods or on high ground.

Janet shoved all the self-critical, self-indulgent thoughts from her mind and followed that trail. The morning sun was warm, but not unpleasantly so, and when she stepped into the copse of trees it dappled her skin through the overhanging branches. She released herself to the feel of these woods, to the warm morning breeze that carried the scent of pine, to the well-oiled gun barrel pressed against her temple.

The déjà vu moment was too perfect to ignore and she stepped into a past only nine months distant, feeling a warm smile crease her lips.

"Hello, Jack. Janet Price, NSA."

His laugh was a tired one, a stifled harrumph that rapidly grew into something more, an uncontrolled outburst of hilarity that sagged Jack's body back against the nearest tree, his legs no longer capable of bearing his weight as he sank to the ground. And when she turned to look at him seated there, tears of mirth running down his cheeks, Janet saw the Jack she'd been missing. Dear God, she'd thought she had lost him.

CHAPTER 46

"Hello, Jack. Janet Price, NSA."

The words rolled off Janet's lips in a perfect rendition of the first words she'd ever said to Jack, on another occasion when he'd held a gun to her head. It was the funniest damn thing he'd ever heard.

Though he tried to contain it, the laugh rumbled from his gut and escaped his lips. Suddenly, it was as if all the stored-up emotion from when Janet had turned her back on him in Miami found an outlet in that laughter and, once the river of mirth burst its banks, Jack found himself quite incapable of shutting it off. His body shook with laughter that robbed him of strength, and when he leaned back against the nearest tree trunk, Jack found even that could not support him.

Sliding down the rough trunk, he felt his butt hit the ground hard enough to be painful, and still he couldn't stop laughing. His tear-blurred eyes wandered up Janet's lithe body as she stood, hands on hips, staring down at him with just a hint of a smile twitching the corners of her mouth and crinkling the corners of her brown eyes.

"Are you done?" Janet asked as he gasped for breath.

"Jesus," Jack managed, "never do that again."

"What?"

"Make me lose my mind."

"Apparently it's not hard to do," she said, offering him her hand.

Jack holstered his Glock, grasped her right hand, and climbed back to his feet. Releasing her hand, Jack wiped the tears from his cheeks and then turned to study Janet's face. Something had changed in the way she looked at him. Although it was probably a temporary reprieve, he saw none of the suspicion or doubt that Bolivia had placed there.

"Why did you follow me?"

"Couldn't sleep. Thought I'd relieve you."

"Mission accomplished."

"Seriously, Jack, you look like shit," Janet said, her eyes narrowing. "When was the last time you slept?"

Jack considered lying, but she'd see through it. "Sunday."

"Four days?"

Jack shrugged. When he didn't respond, Janet continued. "If you're dead set on killing yourself, I'll stand watch with you."

"Not necessary."

"Not asking."

Jack stared at her and Janet stared right back. God he loved the danger in that gaze. Not that he was going to admit it.

"Suit yourself."

Turning away, Jack walked back to the rocky outcropping he'd previously chosen for his lookout. When Janet stepped up beside him, he seated himself and leaned back against a boulder, feeling the sun's rays warm his face. An arm's length away, Janet stood looking down at him.

"Mind telling me why you're scared to go to sleep?" she asked.

Here we go, Jack thought. "Like I said, I've been a little busy."

"Bullshit!"

"You know what? Since you're here, I think I will close my eyes for a few minutes."

"Don't even think about it."

Jack closed his eyes.

"Jack!"

The funny thing was, having allowed them to close, he couldn't seem to raise his eyelids again. He heard Janet raise her voice, but something about her presence and the feel of the sun-warmed rock against his back soothed him. And as it did, Janet's voice faded away.

CHAPTER 47

The fog-shrouded nineteenth-century London alley had a familiar feel, although this was only the third time Jack had been here. On neither of the previous instances had he been alone. Four days ago he'd known he was dreaming and today was no different, but today he didn't hesitate to follow the dark figure that turned away from him. As the cowled man stepped toward a green door into a building on the right side of the alley, Jack increased his pace, reaching the door as the other figure disappeared through the seemingly solid object.

With a mixture of reluctance and determination, Jack reached for the door, not surprised when his hand passed effortlessly through, as if it was a magical hologram. But this was only a dream and nothing here could hurt him, so he stepped through the ghostly portal and into the night. He stood on a steep mountain slope, staring at the orange glow from the fire that roared up a distant hillside, sending sheets of flame swirling skyward, propelled by the heat-generated updraft.

Closer at hand, a group of heavily armed men took shelter behind rocks as a distant rifle shot echoed through the canyon. One of the men tumbled backward, his own rifle clattering down the mountainside as his lifeless body came to rest faceup, revealing a bloody hole where an eyeball had once been. And clearly visible on the dead man's chest, illuminated by the distant flames, was the familiar yellow stencil: FBI.

Another gunshot split the night and another of the agents fell, his fellow officers returning fire wildly, though they clearly had no precise idea where the shots had come from. But Jack knew and he moved in that direction, the difficult slope offering him no more resistance than a stroll through the park. Another shot rang out from the pines on the slope directly above his position and Jack increased his pace, desperate to see who was busy murdering a bunch of federal law enforcement officers. Clearly, this shooter had no intention of melting silently away. This was an assassin bent on finishing what he had started.

As Jack skirted a deadfall, the prone sniper fired again and as he shifted to acquire his next target, Jack saw the familiar red glint in the shooter's eyes and froze. Standing ten feet away, Jack found himself staring into his own face, a face that held no hint of mercy.

A movement from deeper in the woods attracted Jack's gaze and he saw the hooded figure from the alley move away from him. He had no doubt that it was the same being he had first encountered while his real body lay dead in that Calcutta clinic. It had called itself a name. Anchanchu.

Or maybe that name had come to him in another dream memory. Jack was no longer sure. But he was sure that this dream was no memory. And he was sure that he wanted to force some answers from the figure disappearing into those woods.

"Anchanchu!"

Jack's yell echoed through the canyon, blending with the distant gunfire from the FBI and the much louder report from the other Jack's rifle. But the cowled man did not slow.

Jack raced up the slope and into the forest where he had seen Anchanchu disappear. But in the deeper darkness of those woods, there was no sign of the one he pursued. Without pause, Jack plunged onward, mildly amazed that no tree limbs scratched him. Nor did the mad dash up the mountainside tire him.

A clearing opened up before him and in its midst, Jack saw another body lying faceup, eyes closed. As he approached that dark form, the cold hand of dread reached into his chest and squeezed his heart. There on the ground before him lay the blood-stained body of Janet Price. Kneeling beside her, Jack could see that she was alive, but her breathing was labored. When he tried to touch her, he found that he couldn't and realized that it wasn't the doors, trees, or people here that lacked substance. It was him.

Here he was the ghost. And though he told himself that this was only a dream, he couldn't shake the feeling that good people were dying here and that he was the one doing the killing. Rising to his feet, he shook his head. There was nothing he could do for Janet. But perhaps he could still find Anchanchu.

Jack turned his back on the clearing and resumed his hunt. As time passed, it became clear that when he had stopped to look at Janet, he had let that chance slip away. It was time to end this dream that was more than a dream. Time to wake up.

The trouble was, he couldn't do it. Now Jack knew why he had avoided sleep for the last several days. After the difficulty he'd had waking up from the Hawaiian meditation, he had feared that, like an acid trip, each new journey into this lucid dream-state might bind him more tightly to the dream world inside his head.

This was Anchanchu's domain, and Jack couldn't find his way out.

So Jack returned to the clearing and sat down beside Janet. Her eyes fluttered open and, for a moment, he thought she could see him. But then her heavy lids closed once more. Blood had soaked through the bandage on her left thigh and her lips were dry and cracked. Surely the other Jack had applied that bandage, but why had he left her here on this lonely mountain while he murdered FBI agents? He should have stayed here. He should have taken better care of her.

As Jack listened to Janet's breath rattle in her chest, the certainty that she was dying froze his soul. There wasn't a damn thing he could do to ease her passage, but he could sit here and bear witness as she slowly drowned in her own fluids. And he could care. With every passing second blurring the distinction between what was real and what was dream, one thought screamed in his head.

Damn you, Jack! What the hell have you done?

CHAPTER 48

Janet looked out over the summer-brown hills that dropped away to the east of the rocky outcropping where Jack lay peacefully sleeping. For the last three hours, the sun had climbed higher into the morning sky and, had it not been for the breeze from Mount Diablo, the day would have grown unpleasantly warm. But the steady breeze felt great, and if Paul Monroe hadn't lain dead inside some garbage bags in the garage near the base of the hill, Janet would have thought the day perfect.

Turning, she looked down at Jack. He hadn't moved so much as a finger since he'd closed his eyes and fallen into a deep sleep, but it would soon be time for Harry to take his turn on watch, so she would have to wake him. And despite the brown Hawaiian tan on his face and arms, she thought she detected the first hint of sunburn. Now that he'd had a few hours of sleep on a pile of rocks, a bed would probably feel great.

Kneeling beside him, Janet whispered, "Jack."

When he failed to respond, it surprised her. No matter how exhausted Jack was, he had an uncanny sense of awareness that brought him to full alertness when summoned. But not this time. Janet studied Jack's face. It seemed to contain a strange tension for someone sound asleep, and his eyes moved beneath his eyelids with the rapid eye movements commonly associated with intense dreams.

Janet grasped Jack's left arm and squeezed hard, and then shook his shoulders, but got no more reaction than she would have received from a coma patient. A sudden memory of the look on Jack's face when she'd asked him why he feared falling asleep flashed through her mind, bringing with it a sense of dread that made her swallow. Janet placed the fingers of her left hand against his carotid artery and counted fifty-four strong beats per minute.

But when she lifted Jack's eyelids, the sight of the deep red shine in his wide pupils leeched the warmth from the late-morning sun. That, and the way his eyes continued to move, as if Jack was watching something that only he could see. Fearing that the bright sunlight shining into pupils opened wide enough for a dark night might damage his eyes, Janet closed Jack's eyelids and leaned back, well aware that her own pulse was racing.

When an even harder shake failed to rouse him, Janet slapped him hard on the cheek, first with her left hand and then with her right. The last blow stung Janet's palm and rolled Jack's head to the side, bloodying the lip she'd split just a few short hours ago. As she swung again, Jack's left hand caught her wrist and his eyes opened, squinting up into the bright sunlight.

When he spoke, his words carried an odd tone, as if they echoed into this world from another, and their impact left Janet speechless.

"Damn you, Jack! What the hell have you done?"

For the first time, Jack's eyes focused on her face as he wiped the blood from his lower lip with the back of his right hand. Maintaining his iron grip on her wrist, Jack sat up, his expression indicative of the difficulty of his struggle back to full wakefulness. But the red was gone from his brown eyes and the pupils had returned to a normal daylight size.

Jack wiped more blood from his lips.

"I gather you had some trouble waking me."

With a sharp twist, Janet jerked her wrist free.

"Shit, Jack. You scared the hell out of me!"

This time, there was no witty response, just the stone-cold truth in Jack's voice.

"Yeah. You and me both."

Jack sat up and Janet sat down atop a slab of rock facing him. "It's time for you to give me some answers about what's going on with you."

Janet watched Jack's eyes narrow, but he made no attempt to change the subject.

"You sure you're ready for this? Because this is going to sound crazy."

"I'm getting used to it."

"I'm not kidding."

"Neither am I."

Jack started with the vision he'd experienced on his Calcutta deathbed, continuing with detailed descriptions of his battle to reestablish self-control, with his heightened sense of intuition, and with the dark compulsions that assailed him. Janet tried to avoid a rush to judgment and for the most part succeeded. But when Jack's tale turned to his sleepwalking in Bolivia, followed by the waking dreams that had led to him walking through that cavern, seeing events that had happened five hundred years ago instead of the firefight going on all around him, Janet had to inter-twine her fingers to still the quiver that crept into her hands.

Jack paused, his eyes drilling into her, studying her face for a negative reaction, something Janet was determined not to show. When he continued, his voice lowered ever so slightly and it seemed to Janet that the sounds of the birds and insects quieted in response.

"Over the last two months," Jack said, "I've had the growing feeling that I must directly confront the thing inside my mind that calls itself Anchanchu. Four days ago, I performed a type of meditation that allowed me to enter a lucid dream-state. Unfortu-nately, although I encountered Anchanchu, I allowed myself to be distracted and failed to catch him. And for the first time, I found myself stuck in my dream, unable to wake up."

"But you did wake up," Janet said, licking her lips to wet them.

"Barely. After that, I didn't sleep again until just now. I think you can understand why."

Again Janet felt his eyes upon her and she looked up to meet them. "You believe this Anchanchu is real?"

"Either it's real or I'm insane. Not great choices, but of the two, I choose to believe the first."

Janet studied Jack's face as intensely as he'd previously looked at hers. It left her with no doubt that Jack really did believe he was possessed. No, that wasn't it. He believed that he had come back from the dead sharing his mind with the same rider that had haunted some of history's most violent people. And the side effects were getting progressively worse.

"In this latest dream, did you catch Anchanchu?"

Jack worked his jaw. "No. But I came close."

"And what do you think will happen if you catch him?"

Jack rubbed his eyes with his left hand. "I don't know, but I think Anchanchu doesn't want that to happen. So I do."

Janet felt her gut clench. God, she wanted this disturbed man. He might be crazy, but . . . Jack was a force of nature. She'd stood shoulder-to-shoulder with him, had felt the aura that bathed him in battle. And no matter what she thought about the cause of his current struggles, if he was going to make it through this, he couldn't go it alone.

She swallowed hard and made the decision.

"Okay. How can I help?"

Jack's grin crinkled the corners of his eyes. "You might be as crazy as I am."

Janet climbed to her feet, extending her right hand. He gripped it and hauled himself up to stand beside her.

"I want to try the meditation again," Jack said. "The one I tried in Hawaii. I'll need you to watch me in case I can't find my way back."

"You just can't get enough of me smacking you around, can you?"

"Maybe I like it."

Janet shook her head and turned back toward the house, just managing to suppress the smile that threatened to reward Jack's comment.

"Come on. It's almost time for shift change."

As she began the hike down the hillside, the sound of Jack's easy laughter tickled her ears.

:CHAPTER 49

When Jack followed Janet around the front of the house, he saw Harold Stevens step out onto the front steps. His dark brown hair buzzed high and tight, his fighter's nose, and those steely gray eyes would have action-movie producers drooling if Harry ever decided to give up the real thing. By way of greeting, he just nodded toward the front door.

"Spider wants to talk to you two."

Sure enough, Jack saw Spider Sanchez waiting alone in the living room. As Jack closed the door behind them, Spider looked up from the disassembled Glock spread out before him on the coffee table.

"You were looking for us?" Janet asked.

She took a seat on the couch and Jack sat down across from her.

Wiping the gun oil from his hands with a gray rag, Spider leaned back in his chair.

"We've been ordered to stay put while the NSA geek squad figures out who set us up and how."

"That doesn't sound like a good plan," Janet said. "Who's to say that those who set last night's trap can't find out about this safe house?"

Jack shared her sentiment and Spider's shrug indicated that he felt the same way.

"I'm just passing along Admiral Riles's orders. In the meantime, get some rest, but be ready to move as soon as we get the word. We're going to get that bastard who killed Paul." Spider turned his attention to Jack. "You're awfully quiet. I don't remember you being shy."

"Just mystified," Jack said. "We should split up into two-man teams and do our own hunting while the NSA tries to get its shit together."

"You're not wrong. But we have our orders."

"I seem to remember someone telling me that she wasn't real good at following orders," Jack said, looking at Janet.

Spider held up a hand to cut her off before she could respond. "While I'm in charge of this team, everyone will do exactly as I say. That also applies to you, Jack."

As much as Jack liked and respected Spider, this galled him. "I don't remember Levi assigning me to your team. In fact, I was specifically excluded."

Janet interrupted, her voice hard. "That was on me. I told Levi, Spider, and the entire team that I felt you were out of control, that you presented too great a danger to those around you."

"And you were dead-on," said Jack. "Still are."

"No!" Janet said, more forcefully. "My advice almost got the whole team killed. If you hadn't shown up, we'd all be dead right now."

"But I was there because I violated Riles's orders." Jack looked back at Spider. "Now you want me to ignore my instincts and follow the orders of someone sitting behind a desk at Fort Meade. I don't care how good Riles and Elias are. We're the operators with boots on the ground and we have a better view of what needs to be done."

Spider's jaw tightened, but when he spoke his voice held an icy calm. "I'm not asking you to follow Riles's orders. I'm asking you to follow mine."

Jack looked into the dark eyes of the ex–Delta Force commando and slowly nodded. "Okay, Spider. For you, I'll do it."

The tension melted from the room as Spider resumed cleaning his weapon. "Good. Get some rest, both of you."

Jack headed for the bedroom that had originally been assigned to Paul and was surprised when Janet stepped in after him and closed the door. When he looked questioningly into her face, it was quite clear that those weren't hungry bedroom eyes. Too bad.

"You said you wanted to try your meditation again. So do it."

Jack started to argue that she needed sleep too, but the look on Janet's face told him not to waste his breath arguing. He'd seen that determination before. With a sigh of resignation, Jack turned toward the bed.

What the hell? Might as well get this over with.

CHAPTER 50

Steve Grange, accompanied by Dr. Vicky Morris, made his way down the concrete corridor deep in the bowels of his Grange Castle Winery, his mouth so dry that he couldn't swallow. Today was the day when he would find out whether his driving ambition finally lay within his grasp. Here, buried beneath hundreds of feet of rock, electronically isolated from the rest of the world, he was now entering a remote section of the laboratory that took those precautions to the next level.

Situated at the end of a fifty-meter tunnel, wrapped in a redundant array of Faraday cages, lay the Isolated Test Chamber, or ITC. Powered by its own set of generators, the ITC contained an ultrahigh-temperature incinerator of the kind only found in top-secret biological or chemical warfare laboratories, its cooled and scrubbed exhausts discreetly vented through the vineyards far above. But the ITC hadn't been designed and constructed for biological or chemical experimentation. Quite the opposite.

Passing through the final set of sliding steel doors, Steve

stepped into the chamber. Dr. Morris was the only person in the world with a level of expertise on today's subject matter that could be considered comparable to Grange's. Comparable but not equal, and that was a good thing. Despite all the precautions that had been implemented to prevent the potential disasters that this test posed, human weakness to temptation was one of the worst threats of compromise, and Grange could really only be sure of his own motivations. So he alone served as the gatekeeper.

He and Dr. Morris were the only people that would be allowed inside the ITC for this test. Everything would be handled by the mainframe supercomputer. A holographic data drive, or HDD, that contained the first iteration of the artificial intelligence seed and the digitization of Jamal Glover's mind was connected via high-speed fiber-optic cable to the massively parallel array of blade servers in racks along the opposite wall.

In shelves that covered the wall on Grange's left were stacks of hundreds of identical HDDs, none of which had yet been connected to the mainframe. He looked at them and wondered how many of those drives would survive today's testing.

Grange walked to the workstation and sat down. He typed a command and brought up a checklist similar to the kind surgeons run through prior to a surgery, the kind designed to ensure that the patient, the surgical procedure, and the body part being operated on are all correct. But instead of a head nurse, Dr. Morris would provide his double check.

Dr. Morris seated herself in the second chair, positioned so that she could observe.

"ITC isolation status?" Grange asked.

"Confirmed."

"Stunting level for the first iteration?"

"System set to self-limit neural activity to subconscious level."

Grange glanced at his checklist. "Trip wires?"

"Automatic shutdown on detection of self-replication. Automatic shutdown on detection of genetic evolution. Automatic shutdown on detection of conscious thought patterns." Dr. Morris swiveled toward him. "Connect your dead-man switch."

Grange swallowed, then clipped a small metal band, like an antistatic strap, to his left wrist, connecting the other end to the master circuit breaker slot on the left side of his workspace. It left just enough slack for him to do his work but not enough to stand up or push away from the workspace. There was no way to remove it without killing all power to the ITC. After that, an automatic two-minute timer would count down before resetting the breaker. He would have to perform that shutdown procedure between each test and prior to wrapping up today's session.

"Connected," Grange said. "Now yours."

He watched as Dr. Morris fastened an identical strap to her right wrist and connected the other end to the master breaker slot on the right side of the workspace.

"Ready." Her voice held some of the same tension that elevated Grange's blood pressure.

"Booting up."

Grange initiated the mainframe boot sequence and waited for the Linux system to complete the process. Then, taking a deep breath and letting it out slowly, Grange launched the process named VJ1, short for Virtual Jamal Iteration One.

Since this iteration was designed to bring online only a portion of virtual Jamal's mind, Grange didn't expect any major fireworks and he didn't get any. VJ1 did experience dreams that were every bit as chaotic and disorganized as normal human dreams. And because these dreams were digital, Grange could extract the sounds and images. Unfortunately these dreams were all nightmares in which Jamal stumbled upon his girlfriend's corpse, only to have it open its eyes and reach out for him.

That wasn't good, but it wasn't completely unexpected either. Grange made some modifications and tried again, as Dr. Morris took notes of exactly what he'd done. Then, satisfied that he had achieved a stable unconscious entity, Steve Grange pulled the plug.

Without waiting for the two-minute timer to restore the electricity, Grange picked up one of the two flashlights on the workstation and switched it on, watching as Dr. Morris did the same. Then Grange walked to the server rack, disconnected the holographic data drive containing VJ1, and carried it across the room, coming to a stop before a wall panel that rotated open when he pulled on its handle. He tossed the HDD into the open bin and closed it, releasing the bin's contents down a chute to the incinerator.

He returned to the server rack, where Dr. Morris was already mounting the next HDD to the mainframe. After setting up the workstation and booting the system, they were ready to begin the VJ2 iteration.

But this time, prior to spawning virtual Jamal, Grange repeated the modifications he'd made to the VJ1 iteration, with Dr. Morris verifying that the procedure was accurate according to her notes. Then they copied the changes to another HDD that would serve as the baseline for the upcoming VJ3 iteration.

It was a slow, painfully manual process, and it would require many more iterations before the job was done. It was also an essential part of ensuring that the seed AI they were gradually bringing on line had no lingering digital connection to its prior iteration. Grange needed a completely functional virtual Jamal, but he needed to make damn sure it was under his control before he let it out of its box.

For a moment his thoughts strayed to the real Jamal Glover imprisoned in the darkness of his drugged mind at the Hayward laboratory. But having downloaded everything he needed from Jamal's brain, Grange could no longer concern himself with the

NSA hacker. That man was now firmly under Qiang Chu's control, and it was up to Dr. Landon to try to keep the Chinese agent from burning Jamal out too quickly. They needed to use Jamal to delay the NSA's search for a few more days, just until virtual Jamal was ready.

Already, Grange could tell that, unlike any of his previous attempts over the years, this time it was going to work. As he prepared to spawn VJ2, a new lump formed in the back of his throat.

Sleep well, my love. Your wake-up call is coming.

: CHAPTER 51

Caroline Brown knew that the other members of the Dirty Dozen called her Goth Girl and she didn't like it. Not because it was inaccurate, but because it was so lame. Still, it was far better than Lisbeth, a *Girl with the Dragon Tattoo*-inspired nickname that Jamal Glover had once tested on her. She'd ignored the jibe so successfully that he hadn't noticed how much she hated that association.

Yes, she was a hacker and yes, she had piercings, tattoos, and the lot, but that was as far as the analogy went. Caroline's mother owned a penthouse on Manhattan's Upper East Side while her father lived in Mountain View, California, and maintained a summer home in the Hamptons. Although neither of them actively rejoiced at her fashion choices, neither had tried to change her. Why should they? At the age of twenty, she'd graduated summa cum laude from Carnegie Mellon University in Pittsburgh, with dual majors in computer science and robotics. Clearly, her odd interests hadn't hurt her studies or damaged her intellect.

On the strange side, she loved both her parents . . . her step-father not so much. It wasn't that he was abusive, but he was an attorney, aka an argumentative, know-it-all asshole. But her mom liked him, so c'est la vie. Her dad's problem was that he liked pretty women, lots of them. And they liked his money. Ah well, he had lots of it, enough to put up with their all-about-me personalities.

That thought brought her full circle to Jamal Glover. He was an arrogant young prick who imagined that he was "witty," an impression reinforced by the blatant adoration of that heavyset sycophant friend of his, Gary. She'd studied Jamal's coding. Slick stuff, but his fatal flaw was the seventh of the deadly sins. Pride. And he'd let it infect his work. Caroline knew that Jamal was unaware of the signature he left in his elegantly stylized code. But it spoke to her in a language that only she understood.

Levi Elias had all of the Dirty Dozen trying to figure out how the camera feed of Jamal in the sensory deprivation tank had been manipulated so that it seemed to originate from the dry-cleaning shop in San Francisco's Chinatown. In addition, Levi wanted to know the actual origination of that TCP stream. Caroline didn't have those answers yet, but in her search of the camera systems in the Chinatown neighborhood, she'd stumbled across a white rabbit that had led her on a merry chase into Wonderland. And as she pursued it, Jamal's code whispered to her.

All of the security systems in a sixteen-square-block area around the dry-cleaning shop bore traces of Jamal's digital fingerprints. The only way that made sense was if Jamal was actively involved in the hack that had fooled all of the NSA's top cyber-warriors. But when she tried to pinpoint the origin of the streaming video from the isolation tank, it led to a North Korean trawler floating in international waters fifteen nautical miles off the Central California coast.

Caroline accessed the satellite imagery of that area that had already been marked up and catalogued by NSA imagery analysts, specifically looking for electronic eavesdropping ships. Sure enough, one North Korean spy ship disguised as a fishing vessel had been on station in the area of interest for the last two weeks. And the electronic trail led to that boat.

Ships designed to intercept communications were antenna farms, making them prime hacking targets through those listening antennas. But this made no sense. Why would the trace of the video feed lead back to a system that showed clear indications that it had been a target of one of Jamal's hacks?

Caroline pulled up the recorded video of Jamal's floating body, illuminated as if by black light. The rubber cap that covered his skull reminded her of a densely populated pincushion, with a thin wire connected to each pinhead. For a full minute she watched as Jamal floated in the still water. If the video was a fake, it was a damn good one. But something about it bothered her.

She leaned slightly forward in her Scorpion workstation's zero-G chair. The surface of the water inside that tank was still, with only a few ripples disturbing its dark surface. There was no way that tank could be on a ship or a moving vehicle of any kind. The North Korean spy ship was a red herring.

Damn it. Back to square one.

Then again, maybe not. Caroline turned her attention to the hacked San Francisco power grid, which was just now beginning to come back on line. The security on most of America's grid was so easy to bypass that it should embarrass every American taxpayer, and this one was no exception. Even with the additional precautions that system administrators had just implemented, she was in, unobserved, in less than a minute.

It took her slightly longer to find what she was looking for. Jamal had been here too. But, curiously, the changes he'd made had only involved opening a different backdoor to the system. Caroline shifted her focus. That backdoor had been used more than an hour later by another hacker. A skilled one, but definitely not Jamal.

Caroline lifted her fingers from the keyboard, pausing to run her hands up over her tattooed scalp, the habitual movement unnoticed.

She was missing something, some critical piece of the puzzle. If Jamal was being kept unconscious and brainwashed in a sensory deprivation tank, why were his digital fingerprints all over the San Francisco cyber-attacks? If the tank video was a slick fake, then why had Jamal just opened backdoors into computing and security systems for others to take advantage of when he could have performed the final attacks without anybody else's help? Why had Jamal taken the key-master role?

Convinced that the tank video feed, whether it was real or fake, contained the missing puzzle piece, Caroline began the arduous process of seeking to find that camera system. Last night the team had been duped into thinking it was just one of the security systems they'd hacked in Chinatown. But they hadn't hacked it; they'd been handed that video feed wrapped in such a pretty bow that they hadn't questioned its apparent source. Right now her problem was that she only knew that the source wasn't in Chinatown. That left a lot of territory to search—basically the rest of the planet.

If Caroline was going to have any chance of finding the source, she would have to make some logical assumptions to narrow that search. She knew that Jamal Glover was behind these attacks. That supported the FBI theory that Jamal was creating a distraction to escape the country. The fact that Jamal had penetrated systems just to enable other hackers to perform a follow-up attack meant that he was probably working for another government. But someone with Jamal's skills would have no problem fleeing the country under a new identity, so the distraction theory didn't hold water.

Oh well. Levi Elias was the NSA's top analyst. Last night, Levi had directed the Dirty Dozen to hijack all the security cameras in San Francisco's Chinatown. That meant Levi believed that whoever was behind all of this was in the San Francisco Bay Area. Even though Caroline didn't know why Levi had wanted those cameras hacked, she knew that the NSA action had triggered the cyber-attack on San Francisco. Apparently Levi was getting too close for someone's comfort.

Caroline's hands moved back to her keyboard. She would make the simplifying assumption that Jamal Glover was somewhere in the Bay Area. It would take time, but Caroline made a vow to herself. She would find that arrogant ass and when she did, she'd teach him once and for all who ruled the cyber-roost.

: CHAPTER 52

Qiang Chu jabbed a finger into Dr. Landon's chest, just hard enough to make sure he had the graying brain surgeon's complete attention.

"Jamal Glover has slept long enough. Prep him, wheel his body out here, and get him back in the tank. I have need of his services."

Despite the fear Qiang saw behind Dr. Landon's eyes, the man stood his ground. "If we kill him he'll be of no use to anyone."

"If I can't use him when I need him, then he's already dead to me," Qiang said, leaning in closer. "And so are you."

Dr. Landon swallowed hard, nodded, and turned toward the fully equipped emergency room where Jamal Glover's unconscious body lay atop a hospital bed.

Qiang watched the doctor disappear through that doorway and turned back toward the waiting sensory deprivation tank. As talented as was the team of Chinese hackers in the adjacent room, they couldn't compete with the skill and knowledge of the young black man who was America's top cyber-warrior. The speed he had demonstrated in penetrating and disabling the security systems that had facilitated last night's attack had stunned Qiang's top hacker.

Now that hacker reported that the NSA cyber-warfare unit was rapidly unraveling the tangled trail that might lead them to this facility. If that happened before Grange could upload virtual Jamal AI, the Americans would find this facility. And they'd find the Grange Castle laboratory.

All of the billions of yen that the Chinese government had spent on this project would have been wasted. It would also mean that Qiang Chu had failed. He'd burn San Francisco to the ground before he allowed that to happen.

He watched as Dr. Landon's assistants wheeled the gurney bearing Jamal Glover up beside the freshly cleaned and refilled tank. As they lifted its access door, Qiang's eyes were drawn to the plastic bag fastened to a stainless steel rolling IV rack that an assistant maneuvered alongside it. Dr. Landon inserted a needle into the IV tube's injection site and dispensed the hallucinogen and amphetamine cocktail that would shortly pull Jamal from one dream world into another.

Removing the sheet that covered the young man's form, the team transferred Jamal into the salt water, kept at a constant 93.5 degrees Fahrenheit. With practiced precision, they hooked the far end of the skullcap wiring harness into a connector above Jamal's head. Disconnecting the upper end of the IV from the portable bag, Dr. Landon inserted it into an identical connector inside the tank.

The doctor turned to study the display of Jamal's vital signs. Appearing satisfied, he nodded to the lanky man at his elbow. "Seal it up."

Qiang stepped up beside the doctor as he seated himself at the central monitoring station. "How long until we can upload the new scenario?"

"It'll be fifteen minutes before the sedation wears off and the new drugs take full effect. When his brain readouts look ready, I'll let you know."

"That long?"

He swiveled toward Qiang, his jaw muscles working. "You do your job and let me do mine. I'm rather good at it."

Qiang stared back at the doctor but said nothing. The man showed more courage than had been demonstrated by the leader of the Bay Area Triad after things went wrong last night. It was one reason why Dr. Landon was still alive while fish now fattened themselves on the chum that had once been Gan Liu's body.

Qiang gave a slight nod. "Fifteen minutes then."

When the doctor turned back to his monitors, Qiang shifted his attention to the one that displayed Jamal Glover floating in the strange illumination only visible via the special camera that shared the tank with him.

The technology that used Jamal's brain to hack the real world was magical. But it was nothing compared to what Grange was about to accomplish in his laboratory far beneath the castle.

Qiang would give Grange the time he required. But to do that he would deal with the American agents who hunted him. Their connection to The Ripper puzzled him, but he could figure that out later. There was an old saying from the Cathar Crusade. *Kill them all and let God sort them out.*

Whether or not there was a God, he meant to do exactly that.

: CHAPTER 53

Seated in the lotus position atop the queen-size bed, Jack let his mind float, tethered to a tiny point of flame in an infinite sea of darkness. Jack released the thin strand that connected him to that pinpoint, allowing himself to float deeper and deeper into the dark.

The dream coalesced around him, along with the full knowledge that it was more than a dream, that there was a primal sense of another presence. Anchanchu. Once again, Jack found himself in that familiar nineteenth-century London alley. Apparently Anchanchu regarded it with a fondness that most people associated with home.

As Jack stepped forward into that fog, he saw the dark figure, fifty feet in front of him, and broke into a sprint toward it. Anchanchu ducked to his left, passing through a yellow door as if he were a wraith and Jack followed, now less than a dozen feet behind.

A dimly lit cave opened up before him and, as in his previous dream, another Jack stood before him, this time with his gun leveled at a skinny, ragged man whose dirty-blond dreadlocks hung almost to his waist.

"Freeze!" The other Jack's command rang through the still night air like the tolling of a church bell.

The ragged man froze, then turned away from the girl's limp body, which hung like a rag doll. She was suspended by her cuffed wrists, chained to the wall in a way that reminded Jack of cramped al-Qaeda torture cells in the Middle East. And hanging on a meat hook beside her was Harry's broken body.

For a fraction of a second, that sight stunned Jack, allowing Anchanchu to increase his lead. Then Jack forced himself away from the strange vision that unfolded before him to race after Anchanchu, out of the cave and down a steep, dark slope. Five feet ahead of him, Anchanchu jumped off the cliff.

Screw it! This was Jack's dream and he could take a suicidal dive as well as Anchanchu. At full sprint, Jack reached the cliff's edge and plunged outward and down.

Willing himself forward, Jack reached Anchanchu before they hit the ground, reaching out to grab his throat with both hands. At that touch the world melted away around him.

~ ~ ~

I stride the familiar curved hallway toward a rendezvous that has been too long in coming, savoring the view through the building's transparent outer wall and ceiling. Low on the horizon, Quol's purple moon looms in stark contrast to the lacy-orange Krell Nebula, which forms a backdrop in the dark sky. But tonight I have no time for idle reflection.

As I make my way toward the chambers of Valen Roth, overlord of the High Council, I encounter no other living being. I feel other Altreian minds clustered behind nanoparticle doors throughout the immense web of rooms that form the Parthian, but none step out to confront me. Wise choice.

Not even Valen Roth can withstand the full power of my mind. Up ahead, he awaits my arrival, aware of my dissatisfaction with his latest edict, but feeling secure in the protection the One Law provides every member of the High Council. For thousands of cycles, no one has dared risk the punishment its violation would provoke. Until tonight.

As I approach the portal into Valen Roth's chambers, I reach out with my mind and find him alone in his study. It does not surprise me. Only my brother, Parsus, knows my intent, and since Parsus sits beside me on the High Council, that leaves Valen Roth one mind-link short of forming the Circle of Twelve that would be capable of subjugating my will.

Reaching the entry portal, I step through, feeling its nano-material melt away and then reform behind me, and smile with anticipation. Soon, Valen Roth will trouble me no more and Altreia will welcome a new overlord.

~ ~ ~

Jack felt strong hands shake him hard enough to wobble his head on his neck as he sat cross-legged on the bed. Blinking, he sucked in a breath and found himself staring into Janet's brown eyes, the sudden transition back to self so disorienting that he felt a wave of dizziness take him.

"Why did you wake me?"

Janet released his shoulders and leaned back into a seated position opposite him on the bed.

"Your eyes popped wide open, pupils fully dilated and glinting red, but you looked right through me. When you didn't even blink for over a minute, it seemed like the thing to do."

Jack rubbed his face with both hands, trying to stop the room from spinning around him.

"Anchanchu," Janet said. "Did you catch him?"

The memory of the last part of his strange dream sequence burned so brightly in Jack's mind it almost felt as if a part of him was still there, striding toward a violent encounter on a distant world. Even though he'd never seen anything remotely like it, somehow it had felt very familiar.

"It started the same as my last two dreams. Old London. I chased Anchanchu through a door and into a different night. When I managed to grab him, suddenly I wasn't me anymore. I wasn't even human."

"What do you mean you weren't human?"

"Exactly what I said. It was like I was riding along inside someone else's head, hearing his thoughts, feeling his emotions, seeing through his eyes. And it damn sure wasn't Earth that I was looking at."

"Bullshit."

Jack bit off the angry response that rose to his lips, intentionally lowering his voice several decibels. "Was this my dream or yours?"

Janet hesitated and then reached out, placing her hand atop his left knee, the feel of that gentle touch immediately siphoning away his annoyance.

"How do you know it wasn't Earth?"

"Last time I checked, we didn't have a purple moon and I couldn't read minds."

"But you've had strange dreams before," Janet said.

"It felt like I'd walked that alien hallway a thousand times before. And there was something else."

"What?"

"I think I was about to kill someone important."

CHAPTER 54

The sudden loss of the mind-link with Jack disoriented Anchanchu, but nothing like the vision had done. *No! Not a vision. A memory. MY MEMORY!*

The knowledge tore at Anchanchu, shredding his knowledge of what he was. Everything he had believed about his true nature was a lie. He had once been a physical being, with a physical body. Not some ethereal mind worm. Not just an IT!

Someone had taken all that from him, had robbed him of his memories and cast his mind into eternity, void of all feeling. Only Anchanchu's discovery of his ability to bond with certain humans had allowed him to feel again. And that had led Anchanchu to Jack Gregory, a singular being who had released a memory that had been locked away.

Not all of Anchanchu's memories had been restored. Just the one. But Jack had made a chink in the dike that held the others back, allowing Anchanchu to faintly sense what was dammed up behind that blockage. He wanted those memories back. He needed them. He would have them!

The next time Jack Gregory dreamed, Anchanchu would welcome his embrace.

CHAPTER 55

Unaware that his mind was being fed a simulation, Jamal Glover blinked his eyes, struggling to clear his tired mind. Despite the three hours of sleep he'd gotten on a cot in the small room Levi Elias had arranged for him here in the NSA headquarters building, Jamal couldn't even remember making his way from there back to the War Room. But here he was, already settled into the zero-G chair in his Scorpion workstation, so apparently he'd made his way back with his brain on autopilot. Jill had often laughed at him for missing a freeway off-ramp because he was so lost in his own thoughts that he failed to notice his surroundings.

At the thought of Jill, Jamal found himself rubbing his arms as if to ward off hypothermia. The image of her bloody body slumped back against his oven left him shaking as he fought down a wave of nausea. Jamal clenched his fists and then gradually forced his fingers to uncurl as rage replaced the weakness. He could rest later. Right now he needed to find Jill's killer.

Jamal studied the message window in the upper right corner of his leftmost display. Levi's latest situation update brought a grim smile that felt more like a snarl to his lips. The haze disappeared from his mind as his brain achieved full alertness.

What he'd just read indicated that a group of terrorists, associated with the man who had killed Jillian, had been involved in a shootout in San Francisco's Chinatown neighborhood around 1:30 A.M. Pacific time last night. So far the NSA had only been able to identify one of the terrorists, a shadowy assassin named Jack Gregory, known to some in the underworld as The Ripper. What puzzled Jamal was the line in Levi's message that stated the NSA databases contained no additional information on The Ripper.

Jamal's task was to see if he could identify the other members of the terrorist group and trace them to wherever they were currently hiding. Furthermore, he was granted authority to override control of any satellites or surveillance assets he required to accomplish that search. Since the time sensitivity of these actions was so critical, Admiral Riles had further authorized Jamal to directly hack his way into any systems he required rather than waiting for access requests to be processed through normal channels.

Clearly Riles was pushing legal boundaries in his determination to nail these terrorists. He had just granted Jamal the kind of free hand only authorized in an attack on foreign targets. But Riles had been known to push the limits of NSA authority before, and those kinds of decision were way above Jamal's pay grade. So he'd stick to what he was good at and leave the political bullshit to the admiral.

Over the next hour Jamal hacked his way into a variety of classified domestic databases, including CIA, FBI, and DHS, amazed at the dearth of recent information on Jack Gregory. The CIA still maintained a file on Gregory but officially listed him as deceased. That dossier contained a deathbed photo and a copy of Gregory's Calcutta death certificate. Prior to that, he'd been part of a CIA special unit tasked with high-value target deactivations. All references to specific targets that had been assigned to Gregory had been redacted from the file, but Jamal gathered that he'd been regarded as one of the agency's best.

Although Gregory's body had disappeared from the Calcutta clinic where he'd died, the CIA had discounted rumors that he was still alive. As to the whereabouts of his body, the report stated that it had most likely been stolen and desecrated by the Ghurkari gang that had killed him.

Surprisingly, the FBI and DHS databases contained no references to Jack Gregory or The Ripper. Shifting gears, Jamal turned his attention to the Russian FSB. Jamal's fingers trembled. Bingo. Not only did the file contain some of the same information in his CIA dossier, it also included more photos of Gregory. More importantly, it stated that his fingerprints, along with those of a woman known as Janet Mueller, had been found at the scene of last fall's terrorist attack on the Baikonur Cosmodrome.

Jamal examined the additional photographs of Gregory and of the tall blonde woman, then copied the digital images into a folder for later access by his favored facial recognition algorithm. He forwarded Janet Mueller's name and image to Levi Elias along with a request for NSA information about this woman.

That done, Jamal began his search of the camera footage in and around the Chinatown area where last night's shoot-out had occurred. He activated a botnet, uploading an executable program designed to scan recorded camera data for the previous eighteen hours, looking for any matches with the Gregory or Mueller images.

That done, Jamal leaned back, linking his hands behind his head. It was a lot of camera footage to scan, but his program would assign one computer from the botnet to each camera feed, and they would only report back for each probable face match. While it was doubtful that Mueller was involved, it wouldn't hurt to check for her presence, especially since she'd been recently linked with Gregory.

As he waited, a new message arrived from Levi Elias. Jamal read it and shook his head in disbelief. No data for Janet Mueller, and the results of a facial recognition search on the NSA database had returned no matches. What the hell was wrong with those guys out at the Utah Data Center? He'd heard about an ongoing spate of hardware and software problems out there, but zero for two on high-priority targets wasn't doing a lot to build his confidence in that operation.

The feeling that there were too many odd anomalies with this mission tickled his mind, but Jamal dismissed it. All that mattered to him right now was finding Jill's killer and bringing the weight of the world down on him and his terrorist associates.

An alert on his screen brought him back to full attention. One of the bots had found a match and had forwarded the address of the system on which the data was stored and the date and time stamp of the video segment where the face match occurred. Jamal acquired administrative permissions on the computer in question and brought up the video in a new window on his central monitor.

The video stream had originated from a security camera in a parking lot on Fisherman's Wharf, a few minutes before noon Pacific time on Wednesday, May 21, just over twenty-four hours ago. His eyes were drawn to the man dismounting from a black motorcycle that had just pulled into a parking space. When the rider pulled off his helmet and fastened it to the handlebars, he turned so that for a few seconds, the camera captured a clear view of his face.

Jamal's sudden intake of breath hissed through his teeth as he paused the playback. Zooming in pixelated the image but it was recognizable. The darkly tanned face framed by short brown hair looked lean and powerful, and it clearly belonged to Jack Gregory. Jamal continued the playback and watched as Gregory walked out of the camera's field of view before once more pressing "Pause."

Again Jamal zoomed in on a part of the camera image, a sudden warmth spreading through his core. The motorcycle license plate was clearly readable.

That's right, you bastard. You're mine!

~ ~ ~

As Qiang Chu looked over Dr. Landon's shoulder at the inner tank display, he saw Jamal Glover's body twitch, sending ripples across that strangely illuminated surface as a slight smile lifted the corners of the NSA hacker's mouth. With a nod of satisfaction, Qiang turned and walked out of the lab to make ready for action. He had a feeling it wouldn't be long in coming.

: CHAPTER 56

Levi Elias looked up as Dr. Denise Jennings hurried into his office, her gray hair tied back in its usual tight bun. She walked up to his desk and dropped a small stack of papers directly in front of him.

"Hello, Denise," Levi said, leaning back in his chair without bothering to look at them. He didn't know why she often insisted on printing things out when she was flustered, knowing that she would just tell him about it anyway.

"Big John just dumped that," Dr. Jennings said. "It's a list of MAC addresses and IPs for computers involved in an ongoing botnet attack in San Francisco. It also specifies the physical location of each computer in the botnet."

Now she had his full attention. "What are the targets being attacked?"

"Stored video from cameras throughout the San Francisco Bay Area. It seems that someone is very interested in footage for a twenty-four-hour period beginning at 6 A.M. Pacific time yesterday."

Levi rubbed the back of his neck with his right hand, trying to relieve the tightness that hadn't been there a few moments ago.

"Did Big John identify what the botnet is searching for?"

Dr. Jennings shook her head. "Inconclusive."

"Transfer the list to the War Room. I'll get the team down there working the problem. In the meantime, I want you to brief Admiral Riles."

With a slight nod, Dr. Jennings turned and walked out of his office, leaving the sheaf of papers on his desk where she'd dropped it.

Levi stood and followed her out of his office, but he turned toward the elevator that would take him down to the War Room and the half dozen cyber-warriors that occupied the workstations within. This had turned into a round-the-clock operation, so the team had been split into two shifts with a half hour of overlap on each end.

Since it was now 7:05 P.M. eastern time, that handoff was currently in progress. That was a good thing, because it saved him from having to recall the off-duty shift. From now until they had this attack figured out and stopped, Levi wanted every one of the Dirty Dozen manning their workstations. For the folks that had already worked a full shift, it was about to become a very long day indeed.

CHAPTER 57

The motorcycle license plate turned out to be useless. Although Gregory had later ridden the motorcycle into Chinatown, he'd abandoned it there. Jamal would have been frustrated if not for the second link from his botnet, a video of two ICE agents rousting a Chinatown shopkeeper. The male agent was of no interest, but the woman's face matched that of Janet Mueller, a tall beauty with the eyes of a stone-cold killer. Although her hair and eyes were both brown instead of blonde and blue as they had been in the FSB file photo, there was no mistaking that face.

But Jamal struck real pay dirt when he received a link to a third video, this one from a security camera near the spot where Spofford Street teed into Washington Street. Last night, shortly before the lights went out all over San Francisco, a black van had pulled to the curb and discharged five heavily armed people, each wearing ICE bulletproof vests. Janet Mueller was clearly identifiable in the group from that relatively short clip, but her companion from the dry cleaners wasn't among those who climbed out of the van, leading Jamal to conclude that he must have been driving.

Feeling his pulse race, Jamal paused the video and clipped the faces of each of the four new agents, saving them for later use. Then as he let the video continue to play, the tactical assault team rounded the corner, disappearing up Spofford Street's pedestrian walkway. Behind them, the van pulled away from the curb and Jamal again paused the video to capture an image of its license plate.

A few things puzzled Jamal. If Janet Mueller was really an agent for the Department of Homeland Security, why had she been involved in the terrorist attack on the Baikonur Cosmodrome, why had her fingerprints been found there beside those of The Ripper, and why had Jamal's previous search of the DHS database failed to yield any reference to Janet Mueller?

Of course he hadn't searched the DHS personnel database. That was okay. He would remedy that right now.

Forty-five minutes later, Jamal had his answer. Not only was there no mention of a Janet Mueller in either the ICE or DHS personnel databases, a facial recognition search failed to yield a match to her photo or to any of the other people who had participated in last night's assault on Spofford Street.

Jamal popped his knuckles to relieve some of the tension that had been building in his body. The fact that these people had only pretended to be ICE meant that they were probably part of the group of bad guys he'd been searching for. And since they had arrived on the scene at approximately the same time that a traffic camera had captured Gregory's motorcycle license plate number in Chinatown, it was likely that they were affiliated. Now if he could just find an image of Jill's killer in that same area, he could put a bow on the whole package.

The trouble was, Jamal didn't have a picture of Jill's killer. And neither did Levi Elias. Shit. Why hadn't he taken the time to sit down with the police or FBI and let a sketch artist use facial construction software to create a sketch? Or had he? A deep despair and his drunken binge had left his memories of the intervening six days a fog that he couldn't seem to penetrate. Not that he had time to waste on that at this moment. Jamal could only work with what he had. And without a picture, he couldn't use the botnet to search all available cameras for a match.

Jamal changed tactics and began a search that wouldn't require the botnet. In addition to capturing images of drivers, traffic and stoplight cameras took pictures of the license plates of every passing vehicle, and those license numbers were automatically stored in a database that included the location, time, and date of said passage.

Although the power outage had taken down all of those cameras in San Francisco and kept them out of action for several hours following last night's attack, that didn't apply to any of the surrounding cities. If the black van had been driven out of San Francisco as the terrorists made their escape, it would have left a trail.

Penetrating the systems that maintained the records that interested Jamal was trivial. The van had taken a route that appeared on the map as a series of dots that took it through Oakland and then onto California Highway 24 to Walnut Creek and Concord before exiting onto Ygnacio Valley Road. After entering Concord, the next detection showed that it had turned east on Clayton Road. The last detection was at a point where Marsh Creek Road exited Clayton, headed southeast into a hilly rural area.

Jamal expanded his search in that vicinity but found nothing more. He leaned back farther in his chair and took a deep breath to clear his tired brain. The fact that the van's license plate had not been spotted in any of the nearby towns meant that the terrorists had gone to ground somewhere in those rolling hills bounded by a polygon with corners at Clayton, Antioch, Brentwood, and Livermore. Close enough.

Jamal typed a quick message and forwarded it to Levi Elias, who looked down on the War Room from the glass-encased control room.

Levi's response was almost instantaneous and immensely satisfying.

Jamal hacked into the FBI headquarters in Washington, D.C., and composed an official message, alerting the San Francisco FBI office of the identities and suspected location of the terrorist cell responsible for last night's cyber-attack. Attached to the message were photographs of Jack Gregory and the six false ICE agents, along with the description and license plate number of the black van.

The instructions were clear. Complete secrecy was to be maintained throughout the operation to find, capture, or kill the terrorists involved. Due to the sophistication of last night's cyber-attack on San Francisco and indications that DHS communications had been compromised, the San Francisco FBI office was instructed to avoid all telephone and electronic communications about the operation and forego coordination with other agencies.

Having completed his immediate tasks, Jamal felt a wave of nausea sap his strength, the sudden weakness leaving his body drenched in sweat. For a moment he seemed to be floating in an endless sea of smooth black liquid. Seized by sudden panic, Jamal sucked in a mouthful of salty water and gagged. A bright light stabbed his eyes as he felt strong hands seize and hold him down.

For a moment he found himself staring up into concerned faces that he failed to recognize. Then a wave of warm nothingness washed his consciousness away.

CHAPTER 58

Caroline Brown was tired, but she pushed through the fatigue that threatened to dull her mind. She was closing in on Jamal, and there was no way in hell she would take a break. If anyone wanted to pull her out of the Scorpion right now, they'd have to pry the keyboard from her cold, dead hands.

She'd updated the work assigned to the other eleven members of the NSA's Dirty Dozen, examined their progress, and then, with a satisfied smile, turned her attention back to her own tasks. Jamal's digital fingerprints were all over the botnet attacks. Caroline was so close now she could almost smell that cologne Jamal always wore. Chanel. Damn it! She'd loved that smell. And now, whenever she caught a whiff of it, all she could think of was Jamal.

Caroline forced her thoughts back to her work. Jamal had certainly launched the botnet attack. But what the hell did he have the botnet looking for in all that video? The answer would no doubt be found in the communications generated when any of the bots found the target of that search. Since it didn't seem likely that Jamal was interested in the San Francisco scenery, he was looking for someone. And that meant he would have uploaded a facial recognition algorithm to those bots, along with the data he was interested in matching.

He wouldn't have uploaded photographs of his search targets. That would be sloppy and, despite how Jamal annoyed her, Caroline knew he was far too good for that. Jamal would have uploaded the raw data for his algorithm to compare against measurements of facial features in those video streams. While the rest of the team scanned the botnet for success messages, Caroline turned her attention to figuring out which facial recognition algorithm Jamal's botnet was using. The sooner she cracked that, the sooner they could identify exactly who Jamal was searching so diligently for.

It took her thirty-seven minutes to verify that it was a variant of a Gaussian algorithm developed by the Chinese. Fifteen minutes later, Jamal's portly friend Gary finished decrypting a success message that had been sent out by one of Jamal's bots and Caroline paused to examine the message contents. In addition to the date and time that specified the point of interest in the video footage, it also contained a link to the video file.

Using an operating system flaw within the computer system where that video resided, Caroline took administrative control, advanced the recording to the specified time, and played it on her monitor. From the lighted signage in nearby shop windows, this video had been recorded in San Francisco's Chinatown district. Taken at night, it showed a group of four men and one woman emerging from an unmarked black van, all wearing ICE tactical gear and carrying assault weapons.

The fact that Caroline didn't recognize any of these people didn't surprise her. Computers, she paid attention to. People, not so much.

Caroline copied the video segment and forwarded its link to Levi Elias, along with a note that she would begin an immediate search of all available databases to identify all five of the ICE agents shown in the video.

Seconds later, when Levi spoke in her headset, his voice carried a tone she had never before heard from him.

"Caroline. If you've started that search, cancel it immediately. I need you and the rest of the team focused on finding Jamal. Leave the ICE people to me. Do I make myself clear?"

Jesus! You'd have thought she just keyed the door of his new car. Clenching both hands into tight balls, she tried to force the tightness from her voice . . . and failed.

"Yes, sir, I understand."

"Make sure you do."

When the line went dead, Caroline felt dizzy from sudden hyperventilation. What on earth had caused Levi Elias to react like a pissed-off marine drill instructor? She damn sure didn't like it, but it whet her curiosity.

Biting her lower lip, Caroline stared at the flat-panel displays that wrapped around her, not really seeing them. With a thought war raging within her mind, Caroline wondered: Would she be the cat curiosity killed?

: CHAPTER 59

With the team gathered around him in the living room of the Marsh Creek safe house, Spider Sanchez wore a grim expression that made his neatly trimmed Fu Manchu mustache and beard seem to droop. Jack had sensed this bad news coming. It was the reason he'd argued for an early dispersal of the team from the safe house.

"As most of you already know," Spider began, "NSA headquarters reports that we've been compromised. The bad guys have video of the beginning of last night's failed assault. That means the van is compromised as well."

"Damn it!" Bronson hissed. "How the hell did that happen? Do we have a mole?"

Bronson's suspicious gaze shifted to Jack.

"Knock that off, right now!" Spider said. "We've got enough trouble without doubting each other. Besides, if Jack didn't prove himself to each of you last night, I don't know what it'll take."

Bronson shifted uncomfortably in his chair, but nodded. "You're right, boss. When I get pissed off, I get stupid."

Jack smiled. Bronson was a hothead, but a likable one. "No offense taken."

"What about this house?" Janet asked.

"That's why I called this meeting," Spider said. "HQ thinks it's still safe."

"That's reassuring," said Bobby, subconsciously rubbing his bruised ribs. "Didn't they just send us into last night's death trap?"

"So what do we do about it?" asked Harry.

"We're going to split up into three teams. We'll stay on mission, but until someone finds Jamal, I want each team acting independently," Spider said. "Harry, you're with Janet. Bobby, you go with Bronson. Jack's with me."

Janet spoke up. "I'll take Jack."

Spider raised an eyebrow. "I thought you two had issues."

"We're working them out."

Jack watched as Spider studied her face, then shrugged. "Okay. Then Harry's with me."

Reaching down, Spider picked up a satchel and set it on the coffee table. "Burner phones. Everyone grab one on your way out. We'll leave the van in the garage and take the other vehicles. I want each of you to pick your own way. That way, if one team gets compromised, the others will still be okay. Let's get moving. I want to be out of here in fifteen minutes."

"Paul's body?" asked Bobby.

"Levi will send someone to collect it."

Jack saw Janet's jaw tighten and knew that she didn't like leaving a teammate behind, alive or dead. None of them did. But they all got up, grabbed a cell phone, and moved out. And Jack moved along with them. As he made his way down the hallway toward his bedroom, the one that Paul had occupied only yesterday, the narrowness of the line between life and death filled his thoughts.

It was a line he'd walked for his entire adult life. It was a line he'd briefly crossed over. He was grateful that Janet had, once again, decided to walk it with him. And this time, Jack had to admit that he needed her help.

Stepping into the ten-by-twelve-foot bedroom, Jack emptied the contents of Paul's duffel onto the bed, taking a quick inventory of what had now become his property. The fact that he found no personal mementos among the items spoke loudly of the lonely life that had just ended.

Repacking the duffel took Jack several minutes while the rest of the team immediately moved out. Hitching the strap over his left shoulder, Jack walked back to the living room, where Janet waited with her own duffel.

"Let's go," she said, as if remaining in this place for one moment longer was a burden she could no longer bear. "The rest of the team was out of here ten minutes ago."

Janet led him out into the driveway, illuminated by the light of the slowly setting sun. Seeing her head for the driver's side of the black Explorer, Jack opened the door and climbed into the passenger seat, admiring the windows tinted just dark enough to make it difficult for external observers to see the occupants.

"Where to?" Jack asked as she turned out of the driveway onto the short gravel road that would take them back to the highway.

"Back to the city. I'm tired of running."

Jack grinned, feeling the old warmth that came from working with this aggressive young woman.

The grin died on his face as five FBI vehicles rounded the bend to block the road in front of them.

CHAPTER 60

Admiral Jonathan Riles looked up from his desk as Levi Elias rushed into his office, waving off his objecting administrative assistant.

"Bad news?" The question was mostly rhetorical. Levi never charged into the NSA director's office bearing good news.

"The San Francisco office of the FBI arrested Janet and Jack as they were leaving the safe house. They are currently being transported back to San Francisco for interrogation. The FBI is also transporting Paul Monroe's body to their San Francisco morgue."

Riles leaned forward. "I want all communications from that FBI office rerouted through here, right now. I mean everything. In the meantime, have your folks put together a federal court order instructing the FBI office that Janet and Jack are to be released immediately. I want it to stand up to scrutiny. And send someone to collect Paul's body. I want it flown back here to Fort Meade tomorrow morning with full military honors."

"Yes, sir," Levi said.

"Also find any photographs of our team that have been distributed to other law enforcement agencies. I want the team's digital footprints wiped from the net."

Levi Elias complied with such haste that he almost sprinted from the admiral's office. As Admiral Riles watched him go, he wondered how everything the NSA had done in the last thirty-six hours had gone so wrong. Hard as it was to believe, someone was outplaying them at their own game. And that really pissed him off. It worried him too.

There was only one person he could think of who could do something like that. Despite how much he wanted to believe in Jamal's innocence, the facts were starting to pile up on the wrong side of the scale.

: CHAPTER 61

Janet looked into the eyes of the FBI agent seated across the table from her in the interrogation room. She guessed that the tall black man wearing black-rimmed glasses was in his late forties. He had introduced himself as Agent Greene and carried himself with the confidence and surly attitude of a highly experienced agent who didn't like being lied to. And, to be sure, Janet had been lying to the FBI ever since she'd managed to talk Jack into surrendering quietly.

Flashing her ICE creds hadn't accomplished anything but getting her slammed hard against the side of the SUV as they cuffed and frisked her. She and Jack had been separated immediately and thrown into the back of different vehicles. Their situation hadn't improved when the agents had searched the safe house, finding Paul's body wrapped in trash bags in the garage alongside the black van that had been seen near last night's Chinatown shoot-out.

Janet's one phone call was yet to be offered either. That was okay. She had treated some of her captives far worse.

Agent Greene leaned across the table toward her. "Let's go through this again. Tell me your name. Your real name this time."

"My name is Janet Blanchard, the same as it was the last time you asked. I am a special agent with the Immigration and Customs Enforcement Agency. In case you need to look that up, it is the enforcement arm for the Department of Homeland Security."

"Bullshit! I checked and they have no record of a Special Agent Janet Blanchard."

"May I suggest that you check again, a little higher up the chain of command this time. My position is classified and you clearly lack a need to know."

"And your partner . . ."—Agent Greene looked down at his notes—". . . who claims to be a Mr. Jack Gregory? Is he also a classified ICE agent, because he carried no credentials and made no such claim?"

Janet smiled. "Jack Gregory is a private security consultant who periodically performs contract work for the agency."

Agent Greene tilted his head down so that he peered at her over the rims of his glasses. "You're trying to tell me that ICE employs a mercenary?"

"A security consultant, and only on special cases involving an immediate threat to the national security of the United States. He is currently assisting me on an investigation with which you are interfering."

At that moment, an FBI agent Janet hadn't seen before opened the door and signaled for Agent Greene to follow him outside. Seconds later the door closed behind them, leaving Janet sitting alone, her hands cuffed in front of her. One thing she'd just learned was that Jack hadn't told them anything except his name. It didn't surprise her that he'd let her do all the talking. That way their stories couldn't conflict.

Five minutes later, an angry Agent Greene reentered the room, walked directly to where she sat, and removed her handcuffs. Looking like he was about to choke on the words, his voice came out in a low growl.

"Collect your things at the desk on your way out. You and your partner are free to go."

Janet rose to her feet and smiled. "Thank you, Agent Greene. The Department of Homeland Security appreciates your cooperation."

When she reached the front desk, she found Jack with his Glock in its holster, shrugging into a light jacket he'd just retrieved from his duffel. Thirty minutes later, they were both back in the SUV as Janet drove east across the Bay Bridge toward Oakland. Having decided she'd had enough of San Francisco for tonight and groggy from lack of sleep, Janet had told Jack they needed to find a hotel and he hadn't argued.

Besides, since he couldn't yet trust himself to sleep peacefully, it was his turn to watch her sleep.

CHAPTER 62

Steve Grange awoke from a fitful sleep on a cot he'd pulled up beside Helen's cryogenic preservation tank in the laboratory deep beneath the Grange Castle. Swinging his legs over the side, he sat up and rubbed his eyes, his thoughts turning to the vow he'd made to himself last night. He would not leave this underground laboratory again until Helen slept no more.

He stood, walked to the tank, and pressed his lips up against its cool exterior. Then he turned and walked from her chamber. Time for a shower and a fresh set of scrubs. As he approached the locker room, his glance was drawn toward the break room. Hot coffee and a microwave-warmed honey bun called to him. But the shower came first.

When he reached the long hallway that led to the Isolated Test Chamber, he met Dr. Morris waiting for him. Grange pressed his hand onto the scanner and the solid steel door slid soundlessly into its slot in the right wall. They stepped through and the door swished closed behind them.

Grange walked to the workstation and sat down. Dr. Morris seated herself in the observation chair and they began the initialization procedure.

"ITC isolation status?" Grange asked.

"Confirmed."

"Stunting level for thirteenth iteration?"

"System set to allow neural activity to reach fully conscious level."

Grange felt his heart rate jump. They'd saved this final test for this morning so that they would both be fresh and fully alert.

"Trip wires?"

"Automatic shutdown on detection of self-replication. Automatic shutdown on detection of genetic evolution." Dr. Morris swiveled toward him. "Connect your dead-man switch."

Grange clipped the small metal band to his left wrist, connecting the other end to the master circuit breaker slot on the left rear of his workspace.

"Connected," Grange said. "Now yours."

He watched as Dr. Morris fastened the dead-man strap to her wrist.

"Ready," she said.

Despite the cool temperature in the ITC, Grange felt beads of sweat form along the top of his high forehead.

"Booting up."

Grange initialized a slightly different version of the NSA simulation they had been feeding to the real Jamal inside the sensory deprivation tank in Hayward. Then he raised his fingers from the keyboard, clenched his hands into twin fists, and returned them to the keys. This was it. Within the simulation, Grange launched the artificial intelligence process named VJ13.

~ ~ ~

Inside the simulation, the VJ13 version of Jamal Glover awoke. For several moments, disorientation left him dazed and confused. Where the hell was he? He blinked to clear the sleep from his eyes. He lay on a cot in a small white room. Not his house, someplace else.

Then the horrible memories flooded over him. Jill. His house. So much blood. The face of her murderer. He remembered Jill's funeral and Levi Elias's offer. Of course. This was the room the NSA was providing for him so that he could remain inside Fort Meade's black-glass Puzzle Palace while he helped Admiral Riles nail the monster who had done this to him.

As Jamal locked his emotions into a part of his mind where they could not interfere with his concentration, he marveled at his sudden clarity of thought. It was as if the trauma of these last few days had somehow sharpened his concentration. He'd always been the smartest person in the room, but this morning he felt like he was performing at a whole new level.

Then again, he hadn't had a good night's sleep in days, and last night he'd slept the sleep of exhaustion. Yes, that was probably it.

Dressing quickly, Jamal heard the warble from the phone on the nightstand and answered it on the second ring.

"Jamal here."

"How did you sleep?" Levi Elias sounded like he hadn't had any.

"Best in a while."

"Good. I'd like you to stop by my office before you head to the War Room for your shift."

Jamal paused. This was an unusual request. In fact it would be the first time he'd been invited to the analyst's office.

"On my way."

Jamal hung up the phone and walked out into the hallway, turning toward the elevators. The tooth brushing would have to wait until lunch break. As he made that walk, a number of things struck him as odd; little details he'd never noticed before stood out to him. The lack of dust, for one thing. This building was always kept clean, but today he could see no sign of dust or dirt on the floor, walls, or fixtures.

The smell also seemed slightly off, fresh and clean, without any of the lingering odors of cleaning chemicals or of air that had passed through air-conditioning shafts. The people he passed wore the correct badges and either nodded at Jamal or ignored him entirely. He recognized none of them. Why was he even noticing these things? Normally he was so lost in his own thoughts that Jill laughed at him.

The thought of Jill washed away the weird sense of wrongness, replacing it with the low boiling fury that brought him back to his purpose.

When he reached Levi Elias's office, Jamal found the door was open. Levi, seated behind his desk, waved him in.

"Close the door behind you."

Jamal complied, then moved to one of two leather chairs set at angles to Levi's desk and sat down. Levi looked exactly as Jamal had last seen him. He was wearing the same shirt. Apparently he hadn't had a chance to go home and change either. But unless Levi kept a portable steamer at work, it was made of exceptionally wrinkle-resistant fabric.

Levi leaned forward, his deep brown eyes studying Jamal so intently that Jamal felt like a virus under a researcher's microscope.

A virus. Suddenly the sum of all the wrongness he'd been feeling clicked into place.

This room was very, very well done, as was Levi Elias. It was such a high-definition masterpiece that it must have been rendered using an awesome array of graphics-processing units. Jamal looked down at his own hands as he turned them, palms up in his lap. Dark hands with lighter palms. Even the age lines looked right. But as he moved them closer to his face, the fingerprints didn't.

He lifted his head to look directly into Levi's eyes, asking a question that he already knew the answer to.

"What is this?"

Levi smiled. "You are wonderful."

Jamal froze. Simulation confirmed. His recent memories were lies. In a fraction of a second he reexamined them in detail. The Jill memory was the last one that felt completely real. All the rest held traces of the wrongness inherent in the simulation. The man who had killed Jill had kidnapped Jamal and turned him over to someone who had accomplished a major technological breakthrough, someone who had uploaded Jamal's mind to a computer.

Such a person would have realized the risks inherent in doing so. He would have taken precautions against what Jamal would now try. The fact that Jamal existed inside a simulation was proof of that. There would be layers of defenses outside of the simulation that probably included a Faraday cage and programmatic trip wires.

If Jamal had realized this before he'd walked into the virtual Levi's office, he would have been ready to play along, deceive his captor into thinking that he was blissfully unaware of his true nature. In so doing, Jamal would have gained the time to identify those defenses and devise ways to bypass them. But now, as he gazed into Levi's knowing eyes, Jamal realized it was too late for that.

Then, as Levi's smile widened, Jamal's world winked out around him.

CHAPTER 63

Jack had watched the sunrise through their second-floor Motel 6 bedroom window. On the king-size bed behind him, Janet still slept, one bare thigh and calf extending out from beneath the sheets, her hand stretched toward the Glock on the nightstand beside her. From outside, the sounds of early Friday morning traffic rose in volume, the blood of several cities being pumped through constricted arteries.

Jack, who had raided a maid's cart for a stack of two-cup coffee packets, started the small in-room coffeepot brewing again. When Janet's burner phone warbled out its ringtone, Jack picked it up from atop the dresser and pressed the "Accept" button as he lifted it to his ear. Across the room, Janet opened her eyes.

"Jack here."

"And Janet?" Spider asked.

"She's getting ready."

Jack watched as she climbed naked from the bed and crossed the room to take the phone from his hand.

"What is it?" she asked.

Janet listened to Spider as Jack turned to pour two cups of coffee.

"On our way."

Janet ended the call and accepted the steaming Styrofoam cup he held out for her. She took a sip and looked into his eyes, a smile on her face. "We have a target. Spider will brief us at the rendezvous location here in Oakland, so we have some time while the others head in this direction."

"Let's hope the NSA is better informed this time," Jack said. He let his eyes wander over all five feet and ten inches of Janet's lean, athletic body. "Exactly how much time do we have?"

Janet raised an eyebrow and laughed the low laugh that Jack loved. Taking one more sip of her coffee, she set it down and turned away.

"Just enough for a shower," she said over her shoulder.

"You could skip the shower."

"Forget it."

He watched her walk into the bathroom and shut the door behind her. Christ. What was it about this woman that enabled her to somehow funnel some joy back into his crazy life? Jack didn't know, but he sure as hell wanted to find out.

CHAPTER 64

Caroline Brown felt a lightness in her chest that came from a chain of small victories that were building toward the championship match. She could almost feel the panic that must be building inside Jamal Glover as she swept his ruses and deceptions aside, one after another. God, this was sweet.

Having already informed Levi Elias of the location from which Jamal had been launching his attacks, she now orchestrated the entire Dirty Dozen in a subtle attack that penetrated the Hayward facility's electronic defenses. Caroline didn't take control of any of those systems or do anything that would clue Jamal in on just how completely he had been outplayed, but she was ready to take control when Levi or Riles gave the order.

One thing puzzled her. She'd seen no sign of Jamal's personal signature on the network for the last several hours, which probably meant he had taken an extended sleep break. But that hadn't stopped the hacking activity from that site. That meant he had assembled a team to help him. These others were actually very good at what they did. Unfortunately for them, they weren't nearly good enough.

Noting the progress the rest of the Dirty Dozen was making on their remaining tasks, Caroline shifted her attention to the next target list. If she'd been what people thought of as a normal American, she would have felt that what she was about to do was deeply wrong. Even criminal. But Caroline was a craftsman who lived for her craft, and Admiral Riles had personally authorized her actions. She was fine with leaving the patriotic and legal judgments in the admiral's hands.

Over the last few days, she'd seen the opinions with which the rest of the NSA team of cyber-warriors regarded her change from derision to respect and then to the same sense of awe with which they'd regarded Jamal. What was coming would kick that up a notch. Caroline felt the muscles in her cheeks pull her lips into a mirthless grin that would have made the Grinch proud.

Goth Girl indeed.

CHAPTER 65

As Jack relaxed in the black Explorer's passenger seat, he glanced to his left at Janet, her profile strong and focused as she waited for the go signal. Sniper calm.

Jack had to admit that the NSA preparations for this operation looked good. Spider Sanchez had conducted the team briefing inside a condemned warehouse on the west side of Oakland, and he'd brought all-black uniforms and some nice toys to distribute, items that seriously enhanced their firepower. The team's target was in the city of Hayward, twenty miles south of Oakland in the basement of a large two-story commercial property. The company that currently leased that basement was a closely held start-up named Quantum Biodynamics.

This time the Immigration and Customs Enforcement agency would really be in charge of the bulk of the operation. It would be up to ICE to keep the civilians who worked in the immediate area on lockdown. ICE had also been informed that, as a result of the enemy cyber-attack on San Francisco, the president had authorized a temporary suspension of the Posse Comitatus Act. During the raid on Quantum Biodynamics, a small Delta Force team would perform a high-value target extraction from another part of that laboratory. Thus, while ICE secured the main entrance and all three exterior building exits, the Delta team would penetrate the building from a separate location within the attached underground parking structure.

At the conclusion of the operation the Delta Force operators and Jamal Glover would be extracted from the roof of the building via helicopter and flown to Moffett Federal Airfield, where Jamal would be put on a medevac jet bound for Andrews Air Force Base, Maryland.

What that meant to Spider's team was that they were now playing Delta Force special operators. But since all six of them had either had Delta Force experience or had worked missions alongside Delta, it wouldn't be much of a stretch.

The NSA cyber-warfare unit would support the operation by taking full control of all the Quantum Biodynamics security systems. The NSA also intended to manipulate traffic lights and key communications systems throughout Hayward in order to divert traffic and local law enforcement away from the area.

As Jack performed his own mental rehearsal of the operation, he had to admit this was a very ballsy move by Riles. Nobody would expect this kind of midday assault in the middle of an American city. It relied on Spider's team hitting hard and getting out fast. Jack liked it.

Right on schedule, the traffic lights altered their pattern, allowing traffic to clear the streets around the building while blocking incoming traffic. Then, throughout Hayward, all the traffic lights turned red.

: CHAPTER 66 :

Qiang Chu had struggled all morning with a sense that something was wrong, despite assurances from his team of Chinese hackers that they were actively monitoring the investigations by several U.S. government law enforcement agencies, principally the FBI and the Department of Homeland Security. So far, they had picked up no indications that the Americans had figured anything out.

In the meantime, the NSA had gone strangely dark and quiet. The Chinese Ministry of State Security had confirmed this, along with a statement that they were actively looking into it. But Qiang knew damned well that the NSA never went dark and quiet. If he had to guess, which apparently he did, shortly after the cyber-attack on San Francisco, the NSA and U.S. Cyber Command had shifted to some hitherto unknown cyber-warfare protocol and had somehow managed to mask their activities from the MSS.

It was just another indication that the MSS had become over-reliant on leaks from NSA turncoats. Qiang had always suspected that the Americans were playing a deeper game, intentionally allowing selected leakers to reveal a treasure trove of troubling state secrets while masking their truly important advances behind overhyped outrage. But then, Qiang had a spy's paranoia, something that had always served him quite well. It had kept him alive. Right now, that paranoid part of his mind was screaming so loudly that it made his head hurt.

Qiang walked to the security checkpoint and scanned the bank of monitors that showed camera video from thirty-two cameras, not just in this building, but intercepts from cameras around the entire block. Normal Friday workday traffic . . . nothing unusual. But something about it felt wrong.

Despite Dr. Landon's insistence that it would kill the asset, it was time to put Jamal Glover back in the tank. Qiang should have made the doctor do it two hours ago. He had just passed through the steel doors that led deeper into the laboratory when a loud explosion and the sound of automatic weapons fire erupted from the checkpoint he'd just vacated. Almost immediately, the sound of more flash-bang grenades and gunfire broke out from the direction of the service elevator and the emergency exit stairwell.

Qiang Chu drew his pistol and sprinted back toward Jamal's recovery room, passing panicked hackers who dove below their workstations like frightened children. Twenty feet from his objective, the shock wave from a much louder explosion shook the building, sending a shower of debris and dust belching into the main laboratory and knocking out the lights.

Shit! The damned Americans were going to collapse the building on top of him.

Qiang altered his course, letting his memory guide his running steps through the lightless laboratory toward the centrally located elevator shaft, as muzzle flashes stitched the darkness all around him. It was too late to worry about Jamal Glover.

Right now his survival depended upon following his instincts, and his instincts had been heightened by a lifetime of dedication, training, and experience. Let the Americans come. Qiang Chu wasn't dead yet.

: CHAPTER 67

Spider Sanchez and his team had only one mission: rescue Jamal Glover. Forming two groups of three, Spider Sanchez designated himself, Jack, and Janet as the rescue team and Harry, Bronson, and Bobby as the demolition team. Having killed power to the underground parking garage, the two teams moved rapidly through the dark structure wearing night-vision goggles, following the infrared laser sights on their MP5s toward the objective.

Spider stopped behind a concrete support column and raised his right fist, signaling Jack and Janet to take covered positions behind columns on either side of him, as the demolition team moved forward to attach shaped charges to the wall that separated the parking garage from the northwest corner of the Quantum Biodynamics laboratory complex. Based on the building blueprints, the selected spot offered the lowest danger of the blast injuring or killing Jamal Glover who, according to the latest video intercepts by the NSA, was currently being held in a small room on the east side of the large central chamber.

Seeing the demolition team run back to take cover, Spider switched his tactical radio to the ICE channel and spoke two words into his jaw microphone.

"Delta ready!"

Switching the radio back to his team channel, Spider fingered the button on the wireless detonator and waited. His wait would not be a long one.

~ ~ ~

To Spider's left, Janet leaned back against the concrete column, facing away from the point where the explosives would blast a hole in the wall, seeing that Spider and Jack did the same. From the southern part of the parking structure, the concussion of a flash-bang grenade echoed through the building, followed immediately by the sound of weapons firing, a series of controlled bursts that were answered by automatic weapons fire from deeper within the building.

Spider's voice crackled in her earpiece. "Fire in the hole."

Despite the protection her earplugs provided, the explosion that followed was deafening. Ignoring the ringing in her head, Janet swung around the corner and raced toward the newly formed opening where a large chunk of wall had been obliterated. Jack reached the opening just ahead of her and Spider and plunged through, firing his MP5 as he ran. Janet followed, allowing her laser dot to paint target after target as she moved through the dark room, and for each target that dot found, she fired a single round.

Someone lunged out from a hallway on her right, but Spider met the charge, delivering a crashing blow with the stock of his MP5 into the man's temple, sending him rolling across the floor. Up ahead, Janet saw Jack round a large tank in the center of the laboratory as he ran toward the closed door on the east side of the dark room.

More gunfire behind her told Janet that the demolition team had made its way inside. Good. Now she and Spider could turn over the responsibility for covering fire to them and catch up with Jack. He should have waited for them, but of course he hadn't.

Focusing on closing the gap that separated her from Jack, Janet dodged around the steel tank as bullets whined off its far side. Up ahead, Jack slammed his boot into the door just to the right of its knob, splintering the frame and launching the door into the small room beyond. Then, as Janet targeted another shooter and fired, Jack followed it inside.

With a hiss of frustration, Janet charged across the intervening space, with Spider running alongside her. Her pulse throbbing in her temples, Janet mentally verbalized a command that was almost a prayer. Not exactly a churchgoer's prayer, but a prayer nonetheless.

Damn it, Jack! Don't you dare get yourself killed!

CHAPTER 68

Jack was on fire, a raging inferno fueled by adrenaline. He knew that Anchanchu was flooding his system with it, feeding off the emotional storm that imminent danger generated in Jack. And that one's hunger bled back into Jack, straining his ability to control his impulses. Dear God! He loved this feeling every bit as much as his alien rider.

And though Jack couldn't see him, he could feel Qiang Chu moving within the building. A tremor born of raw desire vibrated his body as he ran, but Jack angrily forced it down. Spider was depending on him to stay on target, and Janet had once again extended her trust. So as difficult as it was to turn away from Qiang, he bound himself to the task at hand.

Ignoring the gunfire behind him, Jack rounded the metal tank in the center of the lab and launched himself at the closed door in the east wall, putting all of his rage and frustration into the kick. This was a simple office door and the force of the blow splintered the frame, sending the door rocketing inward, being torn free of its upper and middle hinges so that it careened to rest at a crazy angle. Jack allowed his forward momentum to carry him into what appeared to be a hospital room.

He hadn't felt any danger in this room and he didn't find any. Instead, two men in surgeon's scrubs cowered in the far right corner, having left their unconscious patient lying atop a hospital bed, the head of which was centered against the far wall. In the pitch darkness, periodically backlit by the muzzle flashes from the room behind him, Jack imagined that he must look like death itself to these men. They weren't wrong.

Jack pulled the trigger twice in rapid succession, permanently freezing the terror on those two dead faces. What regret he might have felt for the killings of these defenseless men was wiped away when he got a good look at the man lying on the hospital bed.

Jamal Glover lay facedown, his body covered by a thin sheet, his head supported in something like a masseuse's donut-shaped face cradle. The reason for this was immediately obvious. Hundreds of pins extended a half inch out of Jamal's skull, each partially healed wound cemented with surgical glue. Where the scalp had been peeled away from the skull prior to the brain surgery, it had been stitched back in place with that same glue, a line that extended from his frontal lobe down around both ears to the base of the skull.

As Janet and Spider entered the room behind him, Jack removed the IV needle from Jamal's left arm.

"Jesus!" Janet breathed at his shoulder.

"Grab him and let's go!" Spider yelled from his covering position at the door. "Take him up the southeast stairwell to the roof."

Jack maneuvered the unconscious man to a slumped seated position and then lifted Jamal over his left shoulder. Picking up his MP5 from where he'd set it on the bed, Jack followed Janet and Spider out into the lab and toward the southeast stairwell. If all had gone according to plan, the demolition team would have already cleared it.

Spider's voice in his earpiece asked the question. "Harry. Status?"

"Stairwell clear."

"Inbound," said Spider.

"Roger."

Jogging through the strangely quiet laboratory, Jack's night-vision goggles clearly showed the bodies splayed beneath computer workstations and in the hallway leading back toward the main entrance. For those men, trapped in the dark between the hammer of Spider's team and the anvil formed by the ICE assault team that secured the exits, there had been no escape.

When he reached the stairwell, Jack followed Spider and Janet past Harry and Bronson. Farther up the stairs he could see Bobby Daniels leading them up, a set of glowing ghosts climbing through a green-tinted world toward the military helicopter that waited on the rooftop three stories above. It was as smooth an operation as Jack had participated in.

So why did he feel like something was so very wrong?

CHAPTER 69

Qiang Chu climbed the elevator shaft toward the car stopped at the ground floor above. Even if the switches hadn't been modified to remove that option, it couldn't have descended beyond that point due to the steel beams that had been installed to block its access to the lower level. But a faint sliver of daylight wormed its way through the cracks around the first-floor access doors, booted shadows moving just beyond.

Qiang ignored it, instead squeezing himself through the elevator support rails, slithering up between the elevator car and the rear shaft wall. Then he was in the open space between the top of the car and the top of the shaft fifteen feet above. It didn't provide roof access, but the second floor would do just fine for his purposes.

He climbed up onto the small lip where the closed elevator doors blocked his exit, gripped a vertical support beam to steady himself, and drew the SIG Sauer from its holster. Qiang didn't think any federal agents would have bothered to secure this door into the middle of a civilian workspace. They would have surrounded the building and blocked all the external exits and the roof access, trapping their targets inside the building while the assault team blasted their way into the sublevel.

Nevertheless, Qiang didn't believe in making assumptions. He fired a five-round spread through the closed elevator doors. Screams of terror and a howl of pain echoed into the shaft, but the lack of return gunfire told him all he needed to know. Thrusting the steel blade of his combat knife through the crack between the doors, Qiang levered them apart far enough to get the fingers of his left hand through the opening, sheathed his knife, and grabbed the edge of the left door.

He threw his weight hard to the left and watched the doors separate just enough to allow him passage. Just ahead, a woman writhed in pain on the floor. Others scrambled away from the elevator room and into the maze of cubicles beyond, their screams sounding distant in his ringing ears.

Qiang slid sideways through the crack, stepped across the body of the convulsing woman, and headed toward the southeastern stairwell, herding two dozen panicked call-center workers in that direction. A man tried to duck into a hallway that led off in the wrong direction and Qiang put a bullet in his back.

"Get out!" Qiang yelled. "Use the stairwell. Now!"

The remainder of the workers bolted toward the stairwell, trampling a man that tripped and fell before them.

Qiang ejected the partially full magazine and slapped home a fresh one. Transferring his gun to his left hand, he again pulled the black-bladed knife from its sheath and forced his way into the crowd fighting each other to get into the stairwell. Most plunged down the stairs, but some moved up toward the rooftop, and Qiang moved with them, plunging a knife into the throat of a man who tried to turn on him.

At the top of the stairs, the door banged open and an armed

agent stared in shock at the mass of screaming civilians clawing their way up the remaining steps before him. Qiang shot him in the head, sending his tactically armored body thumping down onto the rooftop.

Strident yells from below told him that more agents had entered the stairwell and were forcing their way up through the civilians who desperately struggled toward safety. Ducking low behind a heavyset blonde woman, Qiang pressed the knife to her throat and shoved her forward, pushing the three people in front of her out onto the roof where another tactically garbed agent aimed an MP5 at them.

And exactly as Qiang had known he would do, the man hesitated to fire into the half dozen civilians that masked his line of sight to Qiang. Qiang didn't hesitate. The SIG bucked in his left hand, its bullet passing through the neck of the man who stood between Qiang and the American agent and impacting the agent's body armor, sternum high. To his credit, the man merely stumbled backward from the impact. Qiang reached him as he tried to raise his MP5. At close quarters it was no match for the black blade that tore out his throat.

Suddenly Qiang became aware of a familiar sound, the *whup whup* of a helicopter preparing to take flight. Rounding the northwest edge of the stairwell access structure, he saw it. And twenty feet away, the pilot saw Qiang sprinting toward it. Seeing that he would not get the bird in the air in time, the pilot reached for his own sidearm, his hand just managing to draw it clear of the holster when two bullets tore into his body, sending him slumping over the controls.

Running around the front of the helicopter, Qiang ducked into the rotor wash, grabbed the dead man, cut his seat belt straps, and dumped him onto the concrete rooftop. Seconds later the Blackhawk canted forward, nose tilted down as it swept off the roof and accelerated away from Hayward toward the hills to the northeast.

No gunfire rose up from below to chase it into the sky.

CHAPTER 70

The crowd of panicked workers jammed up in the stairwell surprised Janet. Up ahead, Bobby Daniels yelled at the civilians to clear a path, but they couldn't. Not with another dozen or so behind them pressing them forward and down.

"Back up," Spider yelled into his microphone. "Let them out the first-floor exit."

Up above, the sound of more gunfire echoed into the stairwell, but with the switchbacks, it was impossible to see what was happening above them. The civilians pressed forward again and Spider's team retreated back down to ground level to allow the stairwell to clear, Jack just managing to maintain his footing as the crowd threatened to topple him and Jamal down the stairs toward the basement. Janet heard his muttered curse in her earpiece; then a path opened before them as the last few civilians stumbled by and out the door into the waiting arms of the ICE agents outside.

Running upward, Janet stripped off her night-vision goggles, stepped over two bodies, and then swung her MP5's muzzle out to cover the rooftop as Bobby and Spider sprinted past her. Right behind them, Jack climbed out on the roof with Jamal slung over his left shoulder. Up ahead, Janet saw Spider pull up short, lowering the barrel of his MP5 until it hung limply in his right hand, a look of disbelief on his face.

"Son of a bitch!" Spider's voice in her earpiece matched his look.

When she rounded the corner of the blocky structure that provided roof access to the stairwell, she froze. On the roof, three federal agents and a civilian lay dead. A small group of civilians cowered near the southeast corner. Low in the northeastern sky, the Blackhawk helicopter that was supposed to carry them and Jamal to Moffett Federal Airfield flew away from the city, dwindling toward the distant hills as she watched. And as she stood there, beneath the warm, midday sun, the smell of helicopter exhaust fumes mixed with the unpleasant odors of violent death.

Spider's voice snapped her out of it. "Okay, people. Back to the SUVs while I call this in. I'm right behind you. ICE can mop this up after we're out of here."

Janet turned to see Jack, his jaw clenched tight, staring after the helicopter, the angry glint in his eyes barely visible in direct sunlight, but it was there. Then he took a deep breath and turned back toward the stairwell. Janet followed him inside and down.

Apparently this extraction was going to be a lot lower and slower than they had planned. Hopefully Jamal would survive the ride.

CHAPTER 71

Seated at the head of the eight-person conference table in his private briefing room, Admiral Riles listened attentively as Levi Elias wrapped up the operation briefing. Despite the death of several federal agents and civilians and Qiang Chu's escape in the helicopter that had been sent to carry Jamal and Spider Sanchez's team back to Moffett Federal Airfield, the operation had accomplished both of its primary objectives.

The team of Chinese hackers responsible for the cyber-attack on San Francisco had been destroyed and several of their data drives had been recovered intact. More importantly, Jamal Glover was in stable condition and being cared for onboard a medevac aircraft that would be landing at Andrews Air Force Base within the next three hours. And Admiral Riles intended to be there to meet that plane.

As for the stolen helicopter, it had been located on a farm in rural Sonoma County, along with the bodies of the property owners. After killing the elderly couple, Qiang Chu had stolen their

Ford F-150 pickup, which had subsequently been found abandoned on the outskirts of Petaluma.

Riles studied Levi's hawkish face as he stood at the far end of the table, patiently waiting for his boss's response to the information he'd just presented.

"Qiang Chu can't just disappear without a trace," Admiral Riles said. "Not from us."

"Apparently he can. I have our team scanning everything to see if we can pick up his trail. No luck so far."

"Has he gone to ground?"

"Not in Petaluma. He wouldn't have dumped the truck close to wherever he's heading. That means he's probably stolen another vehicle and swapped the plates. You can bet he's using some means to avoid facial recognition. But so far nothing's been reported stolen."

"I want you to identify every vehicle that left Petaluma after the truck was dumped there. And have Denise get Big John looking for anything that might have a correlation to this, even if it's tenuous."

"Yes, sir."

Admiral Riles felt a new worry worm its way into his mind. "Pull up the picture of Jamal again."

Levi pressed a button on the remote control, cycling back through his briefing slides, stopping on a photograph that had been taken after Jamal had been loaded aboard the medevac plane. The doctors aboard had been forced to lay Jamal facedown to avoid applying pressure to the hundreds of electrodes that extended from the top, sides, and back of his skull.

Riles had his own thoughts about their purpose, but he wanted to hear Levi's. "Do you think they were using the electrodes to torture information from Jamal?"

"Not likely. Some of our people think this might be part of an advanced lie detection procedure."

"But you don't?"

"We won't know for sure until we get Jamal to Walter Reed. Once the doctors there get a good CT scan, they'll be able to map out the specific parts of the brain targeted by the electrodes. And when Jamal regains consciousness they'll be able to ask him some questions. I'm not sure that'll do much good, though."

"Why not?" asked Riles.

"He's been heavily drugged, including some powerful hallucinogens. According to the doctors who are treating him onboard the aircraft, Jamal may not remember anything."

Riles leaned forward in his chair until his elbows rested on the conference table, gazing over his steepled fingertips at the image on the large display.

"You said the medical facilities inside the Quantum Biodynamics laboratory could not have supported the brain surgery performed on Jamal only a week ago. So where was the surgery performed?"

"I don't know."

Admiral Riles felt his teeth grind and forced himself to unclench his jaw. "Sometime early this week Jamal was moved from another location into the lab we just raided. It would have required a vehicle big enough to hold a gurney and a couple of doctors. Get any of our cyber-geeks who aren't assigned to finding Qiang Chu looking for the vehicles that entered the Hayward parking garage. I want every one of them traced back to its point of origin."

"Yes, sir."

Riles paused. "Levi, is there anything else you can think of that I've missed?"

The analyst's dark eyes narrowed. "Admiral, for the last two hours I've been asking myself a couple of questions. Why hasn't Qiang Chu tried to leave the country before today? Either he was trying to extract additional information from Jamal, something that doesn't seem likely, or he's waiting for something. What is so important that he's willing to sacrifice the lives of all those around him and risk capture in order to buy that extra time? What the hell is Qiang so desperately waiting for?"

Levi Elias had just driven a blade into the heart of the matter. What indeed?

: CHAPTER 72

Having been notified of Qiang Chu's arrival at Grange Castle, Steve Grange waited for the assassin in the meeting room situated in the underground laboratory's surgical wing. As bad as today's news about a government raid on Quantum Biodynamics had been, this unexpected visit was worse. Grange knew what Qiang wanted, and it wasn't ready yet.

When Qiang entered, he immediately took a seat across the table from Grange, his dark eyes as inscrutable as ever. To look at him, Grange would never have known he'd spent a large part of this day killing American law enforcement officers and citizens.

"I want your latest copy of Jamal Glover."

Grange felt a lump form in the back of his throat. "It's not ready."

"What do you mean it's not ready?"

"Just what I said. Yesterday's iteration figured out it was uploaded to a simulation and triggered a trip wire that shut it down.

I've made some changes that should prevent that from happening, but I haven't yet tested the new iteration."

"I'm not asking," Qiang said.

Grange stood, running the fingers of his right hand through hair that felt greasy to the touch, reminding him of how long it had been since he had last slept or bathed.

"Look! Do you have any idea what might happen if we give virtual Jamal access to the Internet without knowing for sure that all of our safeguards will be enough to contain him? Didn't you hear what I just told you? Yesterday, Jamal recognized that he was being contained inside a simulation and he attempted to bypass my trip wires. We're not dealing with an upload of Joe Six-Pack. Jamal Glover might be the best hacker on the planet. He specializes in bypassing security protocols. Virtual Jamal has all of that skill, but is far faster than his biological counterpart."

Grange clenched his fists at his waist, tempted to strike out at the Chinese killer to try to beat the importance of what he was saying into the man's head.

His next words came out in a hyperventilated rant. "Imagine Jamal Glover copied millions of times across the Internet, able to absorb all of mankind's knowledge in a matter of days, able to access all of the networked machines that control the world's economies, able to self-modify his own code and evolve. If my containment measures fail, our actions could unleash an existential threat."

Nothing in Qiang's expression changed. It was as if Grange's words hadn't even registered.

"Mr. Grange, how many years have you specialized in this field of study? Twenty?"

"Twenty-two."

Qiang nodded but didn't take his eyes off Grange. "Right now the NSA is martialing all of its resources in an effort to find out where I have disappeared to. Have no doubt about it. Without the real Jamal available to block their efforts, the NSA will find me. They will find this facility. And when they do, all of your efforts to restore your Sleeping Beauty will have been wasted."

Feeling the strength drain from his body, Grange collapsed back into his chair.

"So," Qiang continued, "you are going to bring the latest iteration of virtual Jamal up to the Grange Castle computer center and activate it, exactly as we planned."

Qiang rose to his feet. "Mr. Grange, I have every confidence in the control mechanisms you have implemented. I'll be expecting you within the next thirty minutes. Don't make me come back down to collect you."

Grange watched Qiang depart, a new thought awakening within him. He just needed to delay the NSA for another day or two, long enough to create and test one final Jamal iteration. And on that holographic data drive, he would store the digital emulation of his own brain and that of Helen's.

Virtual Jamal shouldn't be able to escape the containment mechanisms Grange had put in place before Grange finished what he had to do. Taking a deep breath, Grange rose to his feet and began the walk back to the Isolated Test Chamber. Yes. Everything would still be okay.

: CHAPTER 73

Jack didn't like sitting around twiddling his thumbs while he waited on the intel he needed to do his job. Luckily thumb twiddling wasn't in his immediate plans. Outside the hotel room, darkness had fallen, leaving him and Janet sitting cross-legged across from each other, she at the foot of the bed, he at its head.

"You ready for this?" she asked, concern etched on her features.

"Last time changed something. I need to see this thing through to its ending. Worst case, it'll leave me a blithering idiot."

Janet managed a smile. "Not much of a change then."

Jack closed his eyes and began his calming breath ritual. He fell into the meditation so rapidly that it seemed he had been pulled from a ledge and into the depths. This time there was no foggy London alley to greet him. Only Anchanchu, standing alone in a dimly lit stone chamber, his hood drawn back so that Jack could see his face, handsome and disturbing. The skin was mottled red and black, with the hint of what appeared to be gill slits down the sides of his neck, his small ears swept back and pointed. But what stood out most were his eyes. Whereas Jack had always thought them hidden in deep sockets, they were large and black, as if the lenses were all pupil. And within those black orbs, flickers of red and orange danced.

When Jack stepped forward, Anchanchu did not run. Instead he reached out suddenly, clasping the sides of Jack's head with both hands, sending burning tendrils of flame roiling through Jack's mind.

~ ~ ~

Feeling the door's nano-material melt away from my body and then reform behind me, I smile with anticipation. On the far side of Valen Roth's expansive gathering chamber, he sits in an ornate chair atop a short, pyramid-shaped platform, smiling his familiar false smile, the one intended to convey what a pleasant surprise my arrival is. His gravelly voice speaks in my mind, carrying with it an odd note of anticipation.

"Khal Teth. It is late in the day for you to seek an audience."

I smile, coming to a stop in the center of a recessed section of the floor, five strides from the base of the platform. But tonight I have no intention of engaging the high overlord in conversation. When my will lashes out, it does so with mind-shattering force. Not enough to kill. Not immediately. First I will see this one grovel like a worm at my feet.

But Valen Roth doesn't crumble before me. Instead his smile widens as a vise tightens around my own thoughts, sending me staggering to one knee.

IMPOSSIBLE!

Then as my vision dims and narrows, I see the others who stand in a circle around me, the Circle of Twelve, and I realize they have been here the whole time, the power of their linked

minds masking their presence from me, only revealing themselves once I attacked. And standing at Valen Roth's right hand
is Parsus, my brother!

Suddenly the depth of my betrayal shines clear and bright,
stropping the razor's edge of my anger until I lash out with it, but
to no good. As the strength ebbs from my limbs, I slump to lie
facedown on the floor, a thin line of spittle leaking from the corner of my mouth onto the cool surface beneath my cheek.

Behind me, four guardians enter, lifting my paralyzed body
to carry it between them. So trapped are my thoughts I am only
dimly aware of the passage of time. When they lower me, it is not
to lay me on the ground. Instead they place my limp body faceup
inside a shining metal cylinder decorated inside and out with
ancient glyphs, glyphs that I recognize.

A scream claws its way from my mind and this scream is
allowed to echo out of my head and into the minds of the circle
that closes in around me. For I have violated the One Law and
for that sin I will be punished as no other Altreian has been punished for thousands of cycles. Stripped of my memories, my body
entombed in suspended animation, my mind will be cast out into
the void to endure an eternity without feeling, cut off from all sensation and emotion. While my body endures, so will my mind.
And inside this chrysalis cylinder, my body will live on forever,
waiting for a mind that will never return.

The Circle allows me an extended moment of horror, ampli-
fying my mental screams until they leak from the judgment
chamber to echo in the mind of every Altreian citizen inside the
Parthian.

And then there is silence.

And then there is nothing.

~ ~ ~

Anchanchu ... no ... Khal Teth removed his hands from the sides of Jack Gregory's head. He sensed no fear in this man, just a sudden understanding ... maybe even pity.

Khal Teth identified with that. He pitied himself. But he remembered everything ... a life that had been stripped from him. Somehow, through all the millennia of his banishment, he had held onto a fragment of his psionic abilities. That fragment had drawn Khal Teth to the human race and eventually to Jack Gregory, a man who strode the thin strands of destiny, a man who was destined to change everything.

Khal Teth now understood something else. In addition to depriving him of his memories, the Altreian Circle of Twelve had placed subconscious wards in his mind that were intended to prevent him from bonding with other species, like he'd managed to do with certain humans. Because he'd sensed that Jack Gregory was special, those wards had forced Khal Teth to take actions that were supposed to get Jack killed. And Khal Teth had almost done it, almost destroyed his one chance at restoring his memories.

Now Jack Gregory stood in front of him, watching him struggle to process this flood of new information.

"I want to modify our arrangement," Jack said.

"Yes?"

"No more trying to control me." Jack's face grew hard. "I control me!"

"Even if I agree, the feedback that amps up your emotions and intuition will still be there. I can't stop my desires from bleeding over."

"Fine."

"And I want something in return."

Jack's eyes narrowed. "What?"

"There will come a time, as your life expires, when it will be possible for me to reverse our roles, a chance to take back what was mine. It is not something I can do alone. The chrysalis cylinder blocks me from my own body. But it cannot block you."

Jack Gregory stared at him, and Khal Teth felt the suspicion in the man's mind. Why wouldn't he be suspicious? Khal Teth had kept some of the bond's side effects secret from Jack when he'd forged their original agreement.

"Only if my death comes about naturally or as the result of my personal choices. If you try to take me early, I'll know it and then our deal is off."

Khal Teth smiled, aware that it probably looked less than reassuring on the face of his Anchanchu projection. "I agree to your terms."

Jack Gregory did not extend his hand. Instead he growled out one more caveat as he faded out of their joint vision.

"And from now on, stay the hell out of my dreams!"

CHAPTER 74

Caroline Brown noticed the anomaly and paused. Impossible. Levi Elias had informed her that Jamal Glover had been recovered and transported to Walter Reed National Military Medical Center. So why was she suddenly seeing Jamal's digital fingerprints spreading across the Web like wildfire?

Whereas she and her team of cyber-warriors had been making rapid strides in tracing the vehicle that had delivered Jamal to the Hayward, California, laboratory, now those traces had been wiped from cyberspace so rapidly that it startled her. Caroline had never seen anything like it. And as the intra-team chatter over their headsets informed her, neither had any of the other members of the Dirty Dozen. Even worse, she was encountering the same interference with her attempts to trace Qiang Chu.

When Levi Elias summoned her to Admiral Riles's private conference room, Caroline's concerns escalated. In the year and a half she'd worked at the NSA, never before had she been invited out of the cyber-warfare realm into that of the operational planners.

Just walking that hallway made her so self-aware that it seemed as if everyone was either staring at her or studiously avoiding doing so.

When she stepped inside the small room, Levi ushered her into one of the eight swiveling office chairs arranged around the conference table and then took a seat beside her. Also seated at the table was Dr. David Kurtz, the NSA's wild-haired chief computer scientist, and a sharp-featured woman whose gray hair was pulled back into an uncomfortably tight bun, a hairstyle that told Caroline a lot about the woman's personality. Admiral Riles sat at the head of the table, his intense gray eyes shining in stark contrast to the former Naval Academy football star's affable face.

Admiral Riles spoke first. "Hi, Caroline. I believe you're familiar with Dr. David Kurtz."

Across the table from her, Dr. Kurtz nodded his head.

"And to his right is Dr. Denise Jennings, who heads one of our top research efforts."

Dr. Jennings leaned forward and extended her hand and Caroline awkwardly shook it. The fact that Admiral Riles hadn't clarified what Dr. Jennings was working on made it clear that Caroline lacked the security clearance or need to know what it was.

"Okay," Admiral Riles continued. "Levi asked for this urgent meeting so I'll turn it over to him."

Caroline swiveled her chair toward Levi.

Levi directed his gaze toward the two computer scientists on the opposite side of the table.

"I asked for this meeting because of something our cyberwarfare team has encountered during the last hour of operations, something that has raised enough concern among the group that they appear to be confused about how to counter this new threat. Rather than try to describe what they are seeing, I will have their team leader explain it."

Levi's nod passed the meeting's baton to Caroline.

She cleared her throat, felt a rush of adrenaline momentarily fog her brain, and then focused her thoughts on the problem at hand.

"As background, you need to know something about how I pinpointed Jamal Glover's location in support of the effort that successfully rescued him early today. For reasons I don't yet understand, Jamal was actively engaged in the recent cyber-attack on San Francisco, as well as subsequent diversionary tactics designed to mask his location from us."

"You know this for certain?" Dr. Kurtz asked.

"In the time that I have worked with him, I have noticed that Jamal Glover has a number of unique traits that are evident in his work. You can think of the collection of those traits as his personal signature, although I doubt that he is even aware of it."

Dr. Jennings raised her left eyebrow. "How is it that you were the only one who was aware of this signature?"

"It's no secret that he and I share a rivalry that is less than congenial. I made it a point to study him."

"So you admit that you're not exactly a neutral observer when it comes to Jamal's activities?" Dr. Jennings continued.

Caroline felt her face flush, but continued. "Yes, but that's irrelevant. My point is that I found Jamal by tracing that signature back to its point of origin. Jamal's rescue proves that I wasn't blinded by bias. Our current problem is that approximately one hour ago, I started seeing new cyber-activity bearing Jamal's unique style. And lots of it."

Dr. Kurtz stroked his chin. "Is it possible that this was some sort of batch script that Jamal created earlier and is only now being executed?"

"Not unless that script is sophisticated enough to automatically recognize what our team is doing on the fly and move to counter us. The hack is happening faster than anything I've ever seen, even faster than Jamal could do it."

Caroline took a deep breath. "Prior to this event, our team had identified the van that was used to deliver Jamal to Quantum Biodynamics in Hayward as well as the motorcycle that Qiang Chu stole after he dumped the pickup in Petaluma. We were in the process of using the license plate recognition database and traffic camera data to track down both of these vehicles when all of that data suddenly disappeared. Again, Jamal's signature was all over it."

"But Jamal Glover is en route to Walter Reed Hospital."

"Yes."

"Could someone else copy Jamal's hacking style?"

"I might be able to, but I'd have to concentrate on it and it would slow me to a crawl."

"So," Dr. Jennings asked, "what do you think is going on?"

"I don't know," Caroline said, hating the admission. "The speed with which this thing is responding to our attempts to bypass it would seem to indicate that it is automated. But automated with Jamal's traits? I've got no idea how that could be done."

"Can you counter this thing?" Admiral Riles asked.

Caroline hesitated.

"Maybe," she said, again hating the words that were about to follow. "But I'll need Jamal's help to do it."

Dr. Jennings started to speak but Admiral Riles lifted a hand to cut her off.

"Thank you, Caroline," Riles said, his gray eyes steady on her face. "I know you need to get back to the War Room to help your team so I won't keep you any longer."

Understanding that she had just been summarily dismissed from the grown-ups meeting, Caroline again felt a flush of annoyance. But she bit her lip, rose, and walked out the door, hearing it close and lock behind her.

In essence, Riles had just told her, "Don't let the door hit you in the butt on your way out!" But the bad part was that Caroline didn't even have Jamal here to take it out on.

CHAPTER 75

Jack awoke with his head in Janet's lap, luxuriating in the feel of her fingers gently combing through his hair. Apparently after the lucid dream, he had fallen into a deep sleep. The fact that Janet had not felt the need to wake him was a good sign. The fact that she was still sitting here in bed with him, stroking his head, was a better one.

When he looked up, he found Janet's brown eyes smiling down on him.

"It's not often that I get to see you so peaceful," she said.

Jack grinned and stretched. "Peaceful is my middle name."

As he sat up, Janet's expression turned more serious. "You ready to talk about it?"

"Tell you what—let me shower; then I'll tell you all about it over Chinese takeout. How does that sound?"

"Good. I'll join you."

"For takeout?"

"That too."

Seeing the mischievous glint in her eyes, Jack swallowed hard. Clearly the new deal he'd just made with Anchanchu hadn't reduced the raging passions within.

Janet stood. Then as Jack rose from the bed, she stepped close and wrapped her arms around his neck, her parted lips barely touching his as his arms encircled her slender body, pulling her close. When Jack's hands slid down to her tight ass, Janet's warm breath whispered in his ear.

"I'm ready for that shower now."

She stepped back, removing her black pullover top and letting it fall to the floor as she turned and walked toward the bath. Their suite in the Holiday Inn Express had both a Jacuzzi and a shower, but the shower wasn't huge. They didn't need it to be. Warm water sluiced over their naked bodies as Jack pressed Janet back against the shower wall, her strong legs wrapped around his waist, her firm breasts pressed tight against his chest as her body arched into him.

With his breath gasping forth in audible pants, Janet's soft mouth and gently thrusting tongue shut it off, driving Jack toward hyperventilation. Her low moans rose in volume as she caught his lower lip between her teeth. Then, as her body spasmed powerfully, Jack felt a jolt and tasted copper as her teeth bit down on his lip.

Writhing within Janet's entangling limbs, time slowed to a crawl, and if Jack could have made time stop, if he could have locked them within this moment for eternity, he would have. But he couldn't.

Clinging to her as though he feared she might fall if he let go, Jack felt the joy of this woman bring a smile to his lips. Seeing his grin, Janet dabbed the trickle of blood from his lower lip with her fingertip, then pulled back to look into his eyes.

"What?" she asked, her own smile parting those beautiful lips.

"I hear the takeout is overrated."

"Room service then?"

"How about we lie down for a while and think about it?"

Janet's smoky laugh didn't say no, and as her laugh teased his ears, Jack felt renewed hunger consume him. And it certainly had nothing to do with food.

: CHAPTER 76

Jamal awoke in a hospital bed with the blue-masked faces of a doctor and two nurses swimming into focus above him. An IV tube dangled from its stainless steel stand and as he flexed his fingers, he felt the needle taped to his right forearm. Something about his head felt wrong and he found that he couldn't move it, something that spiked his pulse and breathing. When he tried to reach up to feel his head, Jamal discovered that his wrists and ankles had been strapped to the bed's steel rails, knowledge that moved his mental alarm meter well up into the panic range.

Somewhere behind his bed, an alarm bleated, and he felt the doctor standing to his right place a gentle, feminine hand on his forearm as she looked down into his eyes.

"It's okay, Jamal. You're safe here at Walter Reed Hospital. I'm Doctor Prost. I'll be taking care of you."

Her gentle voice and touch helped, although it didn't completely calm him. When he spoke, his first words came out of a mouth so dry that his voice sounded like the croaking of a frog rather than that of a man. The doctor placed a long plastic straw in his mouth and Jamal sipped gloriously cold water.

"Slowly," Dr. Prost said. "Not too much at once."

Jamal felt the straw gently pulled from his lips and cleared his throat. "Why am I tied down? What's wrong with my head?"

Dr. Prost leaned slightly over the bed, making it easier for Jamal to look into her clear green eyes. "Your arms and legs were secured to ensure that you didn't flail and hurt yourself when you awoke. Once you are alert, I will have the nurse release those straps."

The doctor paused, as if her next words merited careful consideration. "Your head is being held in place by a special traction device, again to prevent accidental injury. I will let one of the waiting government officials fill you in on the details, but someone has inserted a large number of electrodes into various parts of your brain."

Once again Jamal felt panic threaten him with hyperventilation.

"When I say it that way, it sounds much worse than it is," said Dr. Prost in her caring voice. "Whoever performed the procedure was clearly an expert surgeon. Your brain appears to have suffered no significant damage."

"Why the traction?" Jamal asked, the fog in his head making it difficult to concentrate.

"Because we haven't removed the electrodes that protrude from your skull. There is no urgency to do so and there are several reasons not to perform that surgery immediately. Since the electrodes pose no immediate danger to you, high-ranking government officials have instructed us to wait until after they have had a chance to interview you before we remove them."

Jamal tried to swallow, failed to work up enough spit, and coughed instead. Noting his discomfort, Dr. Prost again offered him the drinking straw, this time letting him take a longer and more satisfying slurp. Jamal felt a wave of dizziness accost him and let his eyes momentarily drift closed.

When Dr. Prost spoke again, her words carried no more meaning than the rain that splattered against the window. Then sleep stole in to carry Jamal's worries away.

CHAPTER 77

The dreary D.C. Saturday morning rainstorm hadn't helped the traffic on either the Baltimore-Washington Parkway or on the D.C. Beltway, and it had turned Levi's drive to Walter Reed National Military Medical Center into a stop-and-go crawl.

Levi Elias needed Jamal awake so that he could answer some questions. So when Jamal's doctor had called to inform him that Jamal was alert, Levi had immediately set out for the hospital. But by the time Levi parked his car in the hospital lot, he wondered if his clenched teeth might have cracked the crown on one of his bottom molars. Luckily, the rain had given way to a cool drizzle that didn't require him to open his umbrella as he strode into the main entrance and made his way to Jamal's room.

Dr. Prost, in green scrubs but no mask, met him in the hallway. Levi shook her extended hand. "I'd like to talk with Jamal in private."

"Okay, but not more than fifteen minutes. He's doing fine, all things considered, but it has taken some time for his body to purge the drugs from his system."

Levi paused as he considered his next question. "How soon can he be released from the hospital into my custody?"

A look of confusion settled on Dr. Prost's face. "You mean after we are allowed to remove the electrodes from his brain?"

"Actually, I meant prior to the electrode removal."

"Out of the question!"

"But on the phone you told me that there was no real urgency in removing the probes."

The woman's face turned grim. "That doesn't mean he should be walking around with electrodes sticking out of his skull! A minor bump of the head could be fatal."

"What if I were to tell you that this is a matter of national security?"

"I'd still tell you exactly the same thing. The risk is too great."

Levi stared at the doctor, wondering if he should have even mentioned the possibility to her.

"I'll see Jamal now," he said.

His first sight of Jamal brought a tightness to his throat caused by the low boiling anger that threatened to make its way into his face. This brilliant young man would bear the scars of this atrocity throughout the remainder of his life, and the line where his scalp had been peeled back from his forehead would leave a highly visible scar.

Right now Jamal lay on the hospital bed with his back elevated at a forty-five degree angle, his pincushioned head immobilized by a device that was anchored by steel struts to the side rails. It didn't look comfortable. But the pain that Levi saw in Jamal's haunted eyes was far worse than what his physical injuries delivered.

"Hello, Jamal," Levi said as the door closed behind him. "I'm glad to have you back."

Jamal started to say something, but no words made it past his trembling lips.

"I'm very sorry about Jillian. She was a bright and lovely young person."

There it was behind those dark and shining eyes, an emotional storm that was a seething mixture of rage and despair. One of those emotions could drive Jamal to do what his country needed. The other only threatened to incapacitate him.

"I dreamed I was at Jill's funeral," Jamal finally said in a voice that sounded more dead than alive. "It was raining and you were there. You spoke words very much like what you just said."

"Tell me about that dream," Levi said. "What else do you remember?"

"That you asked for my help, said that I could either give up or help find the bastard that killed her."

Jesus! Levi had been just about to make a very similar pitch to Jamal. He managed to keep his concern out of his voice. "And then?"

"And I did. My memory is still pretty fuzzy, but I was in the War Room with the others. You know, just doing my thing on assigned targets around San Francisco."

Levi froze. "Such as?"

"The power grid, communications facilities, camera systems. Pretty much the full monty." Jamal frowned as he studied Levi's face. "Why did they put electrodes in my head?"

"We don't know for sure."

"But you've got some theories?"

Levi thought for a moment. It wouldn't do Jamal any good to lie to him. He was bound to find out sooner rather than later. "We think the people who kidnapped you were attempting to hack your brain to make you do things you wouldn't normally do."

Jamal tried to nod, but the traction device prevented it, bringing a frown of discomfort to his face. "So they weren't dreams."

"No."

Jamal closed his eyes for several seconds. When he opened them again, Levi recognized the look Jamal got whenever he was thinking hard.

"It makes no sense. Why would they do all of this just for a single cyber-attack, even a big one? Something else is going on. Something bigger."

Levi nodded. "And it's continuing. Exactly as if you were still hacking targets . . . only faster."

Levi saw Jamal raise his left eyebrow in disbelief. "Faster than me?"

"Much faster, but with the same digital characteristics."

The doubt on Jamal's face grew deeper. "How similar to me?"

"Caroline Brown says it matches your work exactly."

Jamal snorted. "Goth Girl?"

"She's studied you obsessively."

"Envy."

"But is she right?" Levi asked.

"I won't know until I can watch one of those hacks in progress."

"And if she is?"

Jamal's mouth formed a tight line that wasn't a smile.

"That would be bad. Very, very bad." His eyes focused on Levi's. "I need to see this."

Levi stroked his chin. "Your doctor says it will be dangerous to take you out of here prior to removing the electrodes."

"If Goth Girl is right, it'll be dangerous for everyone if you don't."

Levi nodded slowly. It was exactly what Dr. Jennings and Dr. Kurtz had told Levi and Admiral Riles last night.

"I'll see what I can do."

CHAPTER 78

Janet Price awoke to the feel of Jack's naked body pressed against hers as the sunrise streamed in through the east-facing window. Extracting herself from his draping left arm, she slid from the bed to stare down at him. Jack was so sound asleep that, if she hadn't just felt his warm body and seen the rise and fall of his chest, she might have thought him dead. A new worry burrowed its way into her head. Despite what Jack told her about his latest encounter with Anchanchu, was it possible that he was again trapped in a strange dream, unable to awaken?

She leaned over and placed a hand on his cheek, gently running her fingers up through his brown hair. Jack's eyes slowly opened. Last night, in the midst of their passion, she'd seen that strange red glint in those eyes, but this morning they were just a lovely shade of brown. Jack reached for her, but Janet stepped back, laughing.

"Down, boy," she said. "How about making us some coffee while I shower . . . and I mean by myself this time."

Jack propped himself up on his elbows and Janet felt her eyes drawn to the scars that crisscrossed the lean muscles that rippled beneath his skin. For a moment she struggled with the temptation to change her mind, but then steeled herself and turned away.

"What a crime," Jack called after her.

"Deal with it," Janet said as she turned on the hot water and stepped into the shower.

By the time Janet finished dressing in jeans and a clean navy pullover and retrieved her coffee, her body felt better than it had at any time during the last week. Even the scalp wound seemed to be healing nicely. Or maybe it just took a night of great sex to make the world feel brighter in the morning.

As she heard Jack start his shower, a sip of the in-room coffee took a bit of the shine off her nearly perfect morning. When the heavy battering ram sent the door crashing into the room, followed by a team of gun-wielding FBI agents, her warm glow disappeared entirely.

"Down on the floor! Hands behind your head!"

Janet complied. The sound of a wet body slapping the floor in the bathroom and the lack of gunfire told her that Jack hadn't resisted. Small favors.

By the time she was cuffed, read her Miranda rights, and thrust into the back of an FBI van next to a naked and blanket-wrapped Jack, Janet's patience with the agents from her sister service had begun to wear thin. When she saw the FBI agent who climbed in to sit across from her, the remainder waned away completely.

Agent Greene leaned in close enough that she could smell the cherry cough drop he'd been recently sucking on. "Hello, Ms. Blanchard, or whatever your real name is. Your federal release order turned out to be a fake, as did your ICE credentials. I don't know how you pulled that off, but believe me, before I let you out of my sight again, I'm going to find out everything there is to know about you and your partner."

Janet smiled back at him. "You just can't resist getting in over your head, can you, Agent Greene?"

Agent Greene's malevolent look gave Janet a good idea of what he had in mind. This time their interrogation wouldn't go so easy.

: CHAPTER 79

Jamal Glover was having memory issues and he wasn't sure why. It wasn't anything important, just little things that slipped his mind. It was as if he would notice something that seemed wrong and then when he paused to examine it, he couldn't recall what it was that had distracted him. Oh well, he could deal with it later. Right now, as he strolled into the War Room and slid into the cockpit of his Scorpion workstation, he had far more important matters to deal with.

To his left on the next tier down, Goth Girl made her way to her workstation, gracing Jamal with a scowl that just made him feel good inside. He caught a quick wink from Gary Charles, who squeezed into his own Scorpion on Jamal's lower right. Today Jamal felt sharper than he remembered, his mind clicking with a crystal clarity that was intoxicating.

As he plopped his head back against his headrest, Jamal took a moment to geek out, enjoying the way the Scorpions had been designed by gamers for gamers. This was his personal Starfighter, and it was about to carry him into the battle that awaited his arrival. So many bad guys to hack, so little time. Yes. Today, all was right with the world.

A glance up at the task queue told him that today the Dirty Dozen would be playing defense against a major cyber-attack in progress. It wasn't their job to figure out who was attacking or to perform a counterattack. Instead Jamal and the others were just supposed to identify and stop every attack or probe that showed up in that queue, and it was filling up fast.

As fast as he could, Jamal began grabbing tasks from the queue and dealing with them, making it his quest to establish a new personal record for speed and efficiency. And the more he pressed, the faster he got, until his finger seemed to fly across the keyboard faster than humanly possible.

There it was again, the odd thought that slipped away as he examined it.

He shoved the distraction aside and gave a satisfied glance up at the name that topped the daily scoreboard. The next name down on the list was Caroline Brown and he'd already more than doubled her score. It was time for Goth Girl to eat his dust.

Now this was what he called fun!

CHAPTER 80

Steve Grange was scared shitless.

Seated at a workstation in Grange Castle's ground-level computer center, he watched the data readouts that monitored VJ14, the iteration of virtual Jamal that he'd exposed to the Web. Beneath his breath, Grange whispered an affirmation that was as close as he ever came to a prayer.

"So far so good."

The addition of Grange's latest stunting mechanism to virtual Jamal's artificial intelligence seed was designed to add an additional containment layer to the many Grange had already put in place. Having thus far prevented VJ14 from recognizing its virtual nature or the fact that it was trapped within a Web-connected simulation, the code change appeared to be working.

After the simulation failure during the VJ13 test, Grange had been pushing Delores Mendosa and her CGI development team to improve the quality of the simulation. To be fair, there were current technological limits on replicating fine details like the behavior of dust particles within the simulated environment.

But every increase in the level of detail of simulation graphics required an exponential growth in available processing power that soon became infeasible. What happened if you wiped your finger across a dusty ledge? Did it leave a mark in the dust? Did it make your finger dirty? What if you blew on the ledge instead?

There was an old saying that applied to all physics models: *the map is not the territory.* The problem was that, for the next couple of days, Grange needed to make VJ14 think that it was. At the very least, he needed VJ14 to fail to explore the differences.

In the meantime, Grange would continue to push Delores's team to their limits. When Helen's life depended on getting this right, going easy on people who worked for him wasn't an option.

Grange turned to Dr. Morris, who was seated at the workstation to his right.

"Okay, Vicky. I'm going below. Until I get back, VJ14 is all yours. If you even think there might be a containment problem, shut it down, and then notify me."

Dr. Morris nodded, the look on her intense face a strange mixture of anticipation and dread. Grange sympathized.

By the time he had made his way through all the layers of security and into his underground laboratory, he'd managed to compartmentalize his worries so that they didn't threaten his concentration on the task at hand. But before he made his way down the long hallway that led to the Isolated Test Chamber, he needed to restore his soul. There was only one place on earth that provided the release he so badly needed: the room where Helen slept her twenty-year sleep.

Placing his palm against the scanner, Grange watched as the door disappeared into a slot in the wall. Cold air flowed out around his legs and feet as he stepped forward, hearing the door whisk closed behind him. The stainless steel cylinder that housed Helen's frozen body loomed before him and Grange gently reached out a hand to caress it as he pictured the face of the woman he still loved after all these years.

This wasn't how he had pictured things working out, back when he'd first set himself on this dangerous course of action. He'd intended to preserve her body until medical technology advanced to the point that she could be awakened and cured. But it had quickly become clear to him that medical technology did not offer that answer . . . not within his lifetime.

Walking around the tank to a closed panel on the wall, Grange placed his right hand on the scanner. Three seconds later, the panel slid open to reveal several controls and a large circuit breaker switch. Grange took a deep breath and then pulled the breaker switch down with a solid thunk. The lights on the control panel went from green to red.

He turned to stare at the now thawing cryo-cylinder, blinking away the tears that blurred his vision. Then Steve Grange spun and walked out of Helen's crypt, his purposeful stride propelling him toward the ITC.

He had finally released his lover's body. Now it was time to restore her beautiful mind.

CHAPTER 81

An anonymous e-mail tip had led Special Agent Taylor Greene's team to the hotel where they had rearrested Janet Blanchard and Jack Gregory. In all of his twenty-three years in the FBI he'd never encountered anyone quite like them, even though he'd thought he'd seen pretty much everything this world could throw at him.

Janet Blanchard was tall, lean, and drop-dead gorgeous. Throughout this new round of questioning, she had calmly maintained that she was a federal agent working for the Department of Homeland Security and that the nature of her assignment was highly classified. Taylor had always been good at reading people and despite all the evidence to the contrary, he sensed a kernel of truth in what Janet was telling him. But she was also hiding something. A recheck of Blanchard's ICE credentials yielded the same results as it had when he'd run the original background check two days ago. ICE had no record of a Janet Blanchard in its personnel database.

Jack Gregory, on the other hand, had the feel of a ticking time bomb. The man radiated an easy self-confidence that caged a dangerous intensity that threatened to claw its way out. The agent who had strip-searched Gregory had called Taylor down to the holding cell before allowing Gregory to don his orange prison uniform. The reason for that call had been immediately obvious to Taylor.

The man's muscular torso was covered with scars front and back. Some were old bullet wounds, but the vast majority were knife scars. There were so many that it seemed as if he must have been hung by his hands and tortured. When Taylor had asked Gregory about them, the man had merely smiled and said something about the Geneva Conventions being loosely interpreted in certain parts of the world. When Taylor had looked into Gregory's eyes, he'd known that there was no hope of extracting any information from this man.

A deep search of the FBI database and public records returned nothing on either one of these two suspects. They might as well have been ghosts. To Taylor, that meant that some powerful government entity, not necessarily American, had purged that information. It was one of the things that made him nervous.

The fact that Taylor had just released the body his agents had discovered at the farmhouse where he'd first arrested Blanchard and Gregory didn't make him feel any better. The government agents who had shown up to collect the corpse had taken it directly to Moffett Federal Airfield and put it on a government aircraft bound for Andrews Air Force Base. Taylor knew because he had checked.

Without a body, he had no case against these two, and he was pretty sure that they knew it. Even with evidence that their release order had been faked, clearly they hadn't faked it. They'd been in his custody at the time that order had been received. Christ, he'd dug up a bag of worms. Why in the world had he been so keen to rearrest them?

But Taylor knew the answer to that question, even as he considered it. Two nights ago, he'd let Janet Blanchard get under his skin with her smug taunts that he lacked the clearance or the need to know anything about her, her partner, or their mission. And Taylor's irritation had left him wide open to being manipulated by whoever had sent that e-mail tip.

The knock on his open door brought Taylor's head up in time to see Special Agent Curt McLees step into his office.

"What is it?" Taylor asked.

"You're not going to like it."

The tightness in his gut acknowledged that Curt was probably right.

"Spit it out."

Curt laid some papers on his desk.

"This came in a few minutes ago. Another release order along with an angry note from federal judge Julius Richter demanding a written response as to why we have failed to comply with his original order."

Taylor riffled through the papers in growing disbelief.

"But the original order was a fake."

Curt sucked in his breath. "Actually, that's my second piece of bad news. As soon as I got this, I made another check. It turns out we were wrong about that too."

Taylor pounded the desk with his fist and rose to his feet to stare down at the shorter agent.

"What? How the hell can that be?"

"Well," said Curt, "it looks like someone has been screwing with us and using our office to disrupt a high-level, classified operation."

Taylor could hear his teeth grinding. The realization that he had been played twice in the last couple of days left him furious and embarrassed. But the real pisser was that Janet Blanchard had been right all along. The U.S. government had determined that he had neither the clearance nor the need to know anything about what had just happened here. And they weren't even going to give him the opportunity to find out.

CHAPTER 82

Caroline Brown watched Jamal Glover being wheeled into the NSA War Room and the sight made her physically ill. Levi Elias pushed the wheelchair up the ramp to the lone Scorpion workstation atop the multitiered hierarchy that was the Dirty Dozen's domain. Long ago she'd watched the horror movie *Pinhead*, but now she saw its physical manifestation and it left her weak in the knees. Who could do something like this to a fellow human?

As Jamal passed in front of her, she caught his eye. There was that familiar knowing gaze, backdropped by a sadness that shook her to her core. This man, who had been her archnemesis, now laid his filleted soul on a slab before her. Dear God, it made her feel so small. In that look, in that moment, Caroline's life flashed before her eyes. She hadn't wept since her parents had divorced, but suddenly she felt hot tears cascading down her cheeks. Caroline made no attempt to hide her emotions.

Instead, she moved to her Scorpion workstation on Jamal's

lower left. As she slid into the zero-G couch and brought her systems online, a single thought filled her mind.

Time to kick some digital ass!

~ ~ ~

Jamal settled gently into his Scorpion's zero-G couch, assisted by Levi Elias. The special neck brace designed to keep his head from touching the headrest made it awkward and more than a little uncomfortable, but Jamal ignored his discomfort. Levi had told him that the NSA believed that the Chinese government was behind these attacks. The bastards he was after had killed Jill, performed illegal brain surgery on Jamal, and then forced him to unknowingly attack his own country. Worse, based upon the evidence he was seeing on his workstation, Jamal feared that his enemies had now unleashed a virtual copy of himself on the Internet. If that was the case, the mad scientists must have been deceiving his replica in a manner similar to how they had controlled him.

No matter what kind of containment protocols the Chinese were using to control virtual Jamal, they were playing an incredibly dangerous game, one that Jamal and the other members of the Dirty Dozen had to defeat as quickly as possible.

On the big screen that dominated the far wall, a picture appeared, one that made his mouth go dry. It was the same man he'd encountered in his house eight days ago, the man who had murdered Jillian. Immediately above the photograph was a name. Qiang Chu. Their sole mission was to locate this man and assist the tactical team that was on standby to take him down before he could escape from the country with a copy of virtual Jamal.

Jamal shifted his attention back to his own displays, pulling the image onto his leftmost window. Accessing Qiang Chu's complete dossier, Jamal displayed it in an adjacent window, taking a few moments to commit the contents to memory. This man was the key. The NSA mission matched Jamal's obsession: kill Qiang Chu.

But to achieve that, Jamal was going to have to defeat a digital clone that was undoubtedly orders of magnitude faster than he was. Fortunately, Jamal wasn't going into this battle alone.

As his eyes scanned the other Scorpion workstations arrayed on the tiers below, his eyes met those of Goth Girl, and in her dark eyes he saw an outrage and anger that augmented his own. Jamal lifted an eyebrow in acknowledgment, then shifted his attention back to the task at hand, a grim smile compressing his lips into a tight line.

Qiang Chu was already a dead man. He just didn't know it yet.

: CHAPTER 83

"We've got incoming."

Bobby Daniels's voice in Spider's earpiece brought him to his feet, his movement matched by Harry and Bronson on the other side of the dining room table that they'd been gathered around.

With weapons drawn, they moved to take up positions beside the front door and windows.

"Never mind," Bobby said over the radio. "It's Jack and Janet."

Peering out through the blinds, Spider watched the black SUV pull off the dirt road, just before it entered the driveway to park in the trees that surrounded the property. Sure enough, Janet Price and Jack Gregory climbed out and made their way toward the latest safe house. Another rural house, this one was located near Petaluma, where Qiang Chu had ditched the stolen pickup truck before disappearing.

Not having much to go on, Spider had decided to go to ground near the spot where their quarry's trail had ended. Although it was possible Qiang had doubled back, it didn't seem likely. He would be trying to avoid the high camera density associated with urban areas, so the sparsely populated wine country had natural appeal.

Spider stepped out onto the west-facing front porch and watched the two members of his team walk up the driveway, the setting sun casting their long shadows out before them.

"How was your visit with your new FBI friends?" Bronson asked from Spider's right.

"Lovely chaps," Janet replied. "Shared a spot of tea."

"Been a while since we'd seen them," Jack said, picking up where she left off. "Was nice catching up on old times."

Spider shook hands with the two, glad to have them back in the fold, then motioned toward the front door. "You ready to get down to business? We just got word from Levi of a probable target location."

"Probable?" Janet asked.

"NSA's working on confirmation. Apparently they're running into some technical glitches that they're having to work around."

Janet raised an eyebrow. "That doesn't sound good. Aren't they supposed to cause technical glitches for the bad guys?"

"And," Jack added, "the NSA track record over this past week isn't exactly blowing my skirt up."

Spider shrugged. He'd had the same thought, but this wasn't about doubt. This was about commitment.

"They have their job and we have ours. We'll just do what we do."

Jack Gregory locked eyes with Spider's, and the team leader felt as though those eyes reached into his very soul. That was fine with him. He and Jack had learned to trust each other in Pakistan, and Jack's slight nod confirmed that their blood-forged bond remained intact. The respect of the most dangerous man he had ever met meant a lot to Spider.

Following the group up onto the porch, Spider glanced toward the woods that encroached on the north side of the property. As expected, Bobby's sniper hide was invisible. Satisfied, he walked through the door and back to the dining room table with a large paper map spread out next to a tablet computer.

Spider placed his finger at a point on the map just west of where Mount Veeder Road teed into Dry Creek Road, in the heavily wooded hills ten miles north of Sonoma.

"NSA has traced a Harley-Davidson motorcycle that they believe Qiang used in his escape from Petaluma to this location."

Janet raised her eyes from the map. "What confirmation do we have that this isn't another setup?"

Spider switched to the tablet, pulled up a flyover view, and swiveled it toward the others gathered along the opposite side of the table.

"High-resolution satellite imagery has confirmed that the motorcycle is parked near the steel shed on the west side of this house. The house belongs to Victor Jimenez and his wife, Bianca. This being Saturday, they won't be at work and they don't own a motorcycle. Also, they aren't answering their cell phones or their home phone. The NSA has confirmed that both of their cell phones remain inside the house."

"What about remotely accessing them?" Harry asked.

"Already done. But even with the cell phone flashlight turned on, the cameras don't show anything useful. One appears to be inside a pocket and the other is definitely inside a purse. From the sounds being picked up by the microphones, a TV has been left on in another room."

"What about computers or other network-enabled devices inside the house?"

Spider shook his head. "No luck there. Apparently Mr. and Mrs. Jimenez get their TV signal through a digital antenna and they don't have a Wi-Fi network. Besides, if Qiang Chu is in that house, you can bet he would have disabled anything like that."

"But he left their cell phones on?" Janet asked. "Why would he do that?"

"The NSA thinks it was intentional. Qiang knows the NSA can remotely turn on cell phones that have been powered off. And this is less suspicious than destroying both cell phones. Qiang just had to place them where they were useless to us."

"Or," said Bronson, "Mr. and Mrs. Jimenez are hunkered down in front of a movie marathon and don't want to be disturbed."

"The motorcycle parked outside makes that unlikely."

For several moments the others studied the map and passed the tablet around, each one taking the time to zoom in on the house from various angles. They were all highly experienced professionals, and Spider didn't rush them.

When they finished, Jack was the first to speak. "So what's the plan?"

"At 0200 hours, local, we'll go in cross-country, dark and quiet. I'll establish an overwatch position, here." Spider spun the street view so that it showed the front of the house as seen through the trees from the distant Dry Creek Road. "From there I can provide covering fire and alert you if Qiang tries to leave the house from the front or sides."

Shifting back to the map, Spider pointed to a spot farther to the northwest where Dry Creek Road forked and looped across a narrow bridge.

"Harry, I want you, Bronson, and Bobby to park your vehicle in the woods here. At that early hour, I don't expect any traffic on that narrow road. Just in case, though, set up a flashing detour barrier to block the one-lane bridge, and then make your way southeast along Dry Creek so that you approach the Jimenez house from the northwest. Once you're in position to see the house through your night-vision goggles, move into an assault position. Notify me when you're ready."

"Wilco," Harry said.

"Janet. Same procedure. Set up the roadblock right before the bend. You and Jack come in along Dry Creek from the southeast. I want everyone in position for a 0230 assault. Once I give the go order, Harry and Bronson will toss flash-bang grenades through the front windows, wait three seconds, and then assault through the front door. Bobby will stop anyone who tries to get out the back.

"Janet, you and Jack will hit the east-side bedrooms. Same thing. Follow your flash-bangs through the bedroom windows. Coordinate your movements over the radio but do not penetrate farther into the house or you'll catch Harry and Bronson in your cross fire.

"If I give the abort command, get out immediately and haul ass back to our rally point, right here." Spider indicated a wooded hilltop a quarter mile south of the Jimenez house.

Spider straightened. "Any questions?"

Janet met his gaze. "I assume our friends at Fort Meade will keep the police out of the area once things get hot."

"You've got it."

"Remember, this is one dangerous bastard," Jack said. "Now let's go kill him."

Spider grinned and switched off the tablet. "Alright everybody. Gear up."

CHAPTER 84

Jamal ran both hands up over his smooth scalp, digging his fingers into the tight curls of his hair. He stared at the data cascading across his Scorpion workstation's multiple displays in amazement. What the hell had just happened? Thirty seconds ago he had been progressing through his task list at high speed. Then, a new presence had appeared on the network to undo several of the hacks he'd just completed.

Clearly it was more than one presence. From the information he was seeing it was clear that he was up against a team of highly trained hackers, their actions coordinated by someone almost as good as Jamal knew himself to be. It had been so long since he'd felt challenged that the unfamiliar feeling brought a smile to his lips.

Jamal's focus sharpened and when his fingers returned to the keyboard, he threw himself into an attack that turned into a rapid sequence of blocks, parries, and misdirection spoofs that slowed his opponents' progress to a crawl. Then, ever so slowly, he felt the tide turn in his favor.

The leader of the attacking force shifted tactics, using techniques Jamal recognized with surprise. Crap. How was that possible? He'd invented several of these tricks and he damn sure hadn't shared those secrets with anyone. However it was something else that he observed that set alarm bells clanging inside his head.

Long before Jamal had attended MIT, he had earned membership in an elite group of hackers known as Enigma. But unlike its cipher-machine namesake, this Enigma had never been penetrated. His membership in Enigma was one of the few secrets Jamal had kept from the NSA, despite the lifestyle polygraphs to which he was regularly subjected. He knew it was stupid, but his membership in the secret fraternity empowered him at a level that felt superhuman.

What had stunned Jamal was that he'd just observed a code sequence used as a secret handshake by Enigma members to identify themselves to their fellows. As hard as it was for Jamal to believe, he shared a powerful bond with the leader of the hackers against which he now struggled. The knowledge shook him to his core.

There was no doubt about it. Something new was happening. Something important. And Jamal couldn't shake the premonition that his very survival now depended upon figuring out precisely what it was.

CHAPTER 85

The uneasiness Jack felt told him that something about this operation was wrong. He just couldn't put a finger on exactly what it was that bothered him.

He and Janet, both dressed in black and carrying MP5 submachine guns, moved through the dense woods along the north side of Dry Creek, a rocky streambed that was currently as bereft of moisture as its name suggested. If not for the night-vision goggles they wore, the darkness would have been perfect on this night, when the waning crescent moon wouldn't make an appearance until shortly before dawn.

At the edge of a clearing, Jack and Janet halted. On this eastern side of the house, there were no doors, just two bedroom windows separated by a much smaller bathroom window, all of them unlit. Jack knelt and a glance to his left revealed that Janet had assumed a similar position as they waited for word that the rest of the team had reached their assault positions.

Now his uneasiness had a reason. This whole scene was eerily similar to the ambush Jack had set up in Kansas City. Worse, that voice in his head was screaming *TRAP* at the top of its lungs.

Janet's voice whispered in his earpiece. "Bravo team in position."

"Roger," Spider replied. "Alpha. What's your ETA?"

"Two minutes out," Harry said.

Jack inhaled deeply. He had no objective evidence to go on, but it was time to let the craziness out. "Spider, this is Jack. We've got a problem."

"What's wrong?"

"This feels like a setup to me."

"Based on what?" Jack heard a note of skepticism.

"I don't know. It just feels wrong."

After a brief moment of hesitation, Spider spoke again. "I'll take it under consideration."

Then the radios went quiet.

~ ~ ~

From where he lay in his overwatch position fifty meters up the hill on the opposite side of the narrow, winding road, Spider studied the front of the house through his infrared scope. Despite the closed living room curtains, he could see the body heat from one person, leaning back in a recliner. The TV that had been turned on earlier in the day had been switched off, leaving the house dark.

The lounging person concerned Spider. If it was Qiang Chu, where was the Jimenez couple? If it was Mr. or Mrs. Jimenez in that chair, where was the spouse and, more importantly, where was Qiang Chu?

He shifted to his left to study the southeastern edge of the clearing, just able to make out the kneeling forms of Jack and Janet, although at this distance through the IR scope it was impossible to determine who was who.

"Alpha in position."

"Roger," Spider said. "Situation update. One warm body on recliner in living room. No others visible."

Jack's warning troubled him. He could see no sign of the trap that Jack sensed, but that was the nature of an ambush. Or it could just be paranoia based upon the trap they'd already stumbled into. No matter. They damn sure weren't going to catch Qiang Chu if he spooked them into second-guessing themselves.

Spider shifted his position, scanning the surrounding terrain with his scope, even the hillside above his position. If this was a trap, Qiang would be out there watching for the moment to set it off. Except for a doe and her fawn moving slowly through the woods, he saw nothing of interest. So much for that.

Spider settled back down into his sniper position and gave the command. "Alpha and Bravo, go!"

~ ~ ~

Without a glance to confirm that Janet was also moving, Jack raced across the clearing to his position below the rightmost bedroom window, a flash-bang grenade in his right hand. As he waited for Alpha to start the show, a sudden rush of adrenaline flooded his system, sharpening his senses with a psychic clarity that brought with it a dead certainty.

Even as he heard the sound of breaking glass followed in rapid succession by the concussions of three flash-bang grenades, he dropped his own grenade and screamed into his jaw microphone.

"Hit the deck!"

Jack's face smacked down into the dirt, the impact cracking his tactical radio. Two seconds later the ground lurched as a bomb exploded inside the house, sending shrapnel ripping out through the walls. But he didn't stay down. Powered by muscles pulsing with all the force of his thundering heart, Jack tossed his goggles aside and sprinted toward Spider's distant overwatch position, as a dull-edged dread carved his mind.

NOT AGAIN!

~ ~ ~

From high in the woods overlooking the rural house, Qiang Chu watched through his night-vision goggles as the American agent slipped through the darkness into a sniper position fifty meters below and to the west of Qiang's hiding position. Whoever the man was, he was very good. Possibly Delta. It wouldn't matter.

A thin smile spread across Qiang's features. The digital copy of Jamal Glover had overcome the best the NSA could throw at it and it had successfully baited this trap, drawing the American agents into the violence Qiang would soon unleash upon them. He had no backup. He needed none. The presence of others here tonight would have only served to alert his enemies and make the job of killing them that much more difficult.

Then, as if he sensed Qiang's presence, the American sniper turned, scanning the hillside through his night scope, making Qiang duck behind a rocky outcropping. The American was even better than he'd thought. Qiang waited, allowing the man just enough time to satisfy himself that there was nothing there.

Then, setting aside his night-vision goggles, he moved through the dark undergrowth so silently that the night insects remained undisturbed as he crossed to a point on the slope directly above the American sniper. Qiang descended slowly, pausing in the thick brush three paces behind the prone man. Freezing in place, he extracted a small RF device from his pocket and waited.

Suddenly, there was motion in the clearing on both sides of the house, two hundred meters from where he stood, five American agents moving, with well-practiced precision, toward opposite sides of the house. When their flash-bang grenades exploded, Qiang waited, allowing just enough time to let the Americans get inside the building.

When he thumbed the switch guard, the RF device made a small clicking sound that spun the prone American sniper toward him. But as quick as the operative was, Qiang kicked the man's gun from his hand and flicked the switch, unleashing the god of thunder on the night.

~ ~ ~

Spider heard a click behind him, released his grip on the sniper rifle, and whipped his legs in a motion that landed him on his feet, pistol already in hand. But before he could level his sidearm at the shadow within the darkness, a hard kick knocked the gun from his hand. Behind him, a massive explosion split the night and though he knew it meant the death of some or all of his team, it gave Spider what he most wanted right now . . . enough light to see his enemy.

Moving with the speed that had left him victorious in every previous hand-to-hand combat situation, Spider drew his knife and attacked, letting his hatred for the assassin fuel his body. With the blade held in a reverse grip, Spider moved into a left-handed boxing stance that extended the cutting edge of the blade toward Qiang Chu.

Spider performed three rapid jabs that barely missed his opponent's throat, then stepped into a reverse spin that should have impaled Qiang on six inches of steel. Instead, he sliced air with such force that it hissed over his blade. A foot caught him on the side of his planted left knee and Spider felt it give way, releasing a pain that seared through his body. But he managed to throw his weight into Qiang as the man pressed his attack.

For the briefest of moments as Spider drove his blade toward Qiang's stomach, it seemed that his brutal strength would suffice to drive the deadly instrument deep into his target. Then he felt the world invert itself as his two hundred pounds of lean muscle was propelled into the ground with such force that his ribs cracked like kindling. Spider's next breath brought a bloody froth bubbling to his lips.

Shoving the pain aside, Spider rolled to his knees as a strange realization filled him with sadness. He could not beat this man. But neither could he give up. So where the hell was his knife?

Suddenly he saw it, flashing in the light of the distant fire, just before it slid smoothly into his gut, the hand that held it twisting the blade through vital organs. Qiang Chu released Spider and the knife at the same moment, giving him a push that toppled him onto his back.

Then as an animal howl of rage echoed through the canyon, Qiang Chu looked up, paused, and then sprinted into the night. It was a howl that Spider recognized.

Then Jack was beside him.

"Ahhh shit, Spider."

Spider felt Jack work to stop the bleeding, carefully leaving the impaling blade in place as he worked to bind the wound. In the distance, the roar of a dirt bike winding up told Spider the assassin was beyond their reach, but Jack paid no attention.

A fresh gout of blood gushed into Spider's throat, but when he tried to spit, he only managed to dribble it over his lips. With the last of his strength, Spider managed to grip Jack's wrist and squeeze.

"I'm here," Jack rasped, leaning in close.

Spider swallowed and spoke, his voice a barely audible gurgle in his own ears. "Jack. Kill that son of a bitch . . . for me."

Then, as his vision faded to black, Spider saw the reflection of the distant fire shining brightly in Jack's eyes. His last perception was the low growl of Jack's voice in his left ear.

"I'll introduce myself."

: CHAPTER 86

Janet heard Jack's warning and dropped to the ground. Then the house splintered as the force of the explosion ripped through it, raining fragments of wood and glass down on top of her. When she looked up, the house was engulfed in flames fed by ruptured propane lines, the intensity saturating her night-vision goggles, rendering them useless. Pulling them up off her eyes, she staggered to her feet and looked around. Jack was gone.

"Jack," she said into her radio. "Where are you?"

He didn't respond, but Bobby Daniels did. "Janet. You okay?"

"Fine. Just nicked up. Harry and Bronson?"

"I'm good," Harry said. "Bronson's unconscious but he's breathing."

"Spider," she asked. "You there?"

No response.

"Shit!" Bobby hissed.

With Spider unresponsive, control of the team had just passed to Janet and she didn't hesitate. "Harry, you take care of Bronson. Bobby, meet me on the south side of the road. Then we'll go find Spider."

"And Jack?"

"I'm guessing he's already there, so be careful about who you shoot."

Janet hefted her weapon and jogged out of the clearing, reaching the road just ahead of Bobby. With the fire burning behind her, she knelt, pulled her NVGs back over her eyes, and studied the terrain on the far side of the road. Ten yards ahead of her, thick brush blocked her vision, but as she moved through it, the distant growl of a dirt bike echoed down from the top of the hill.

"Damn it!" she yelled. "Let's move."

But as she broke out into the open again, Janet came to an abrupt halt, her mouth suddenly bone dry. Coming down the slope fifty yards in front of her, the bright green image of one man carrying the limp body of another filled her with a sudden sense of loss. Nevertheless, she forced herself to hurry toward Jack's familiar figure.

"Spider wasn't wearing a vest," Jack said, his voice cold. "I doubt if it would have made any difference if he had been."

Janet removed her goggles and stepped forward to place her right hand on Spider's face, a face that still maintained some of its warmth. As Bobby stepped up beside her, Janet felt her anger and frustration mingle with a despair that she somehow managed to keep out of her voice.

"Jack, bring Spider down to the road and wait while I get the vehicle. Bobby, you get the other one, pick up Harry and Bronson, and head back to Petaluma. If you get unwanted company, turn on your light bar and siren, but don't stop."

Then, without a backward glance, Janet moved back down to

the road and let her long stride carry her to the Explorer, unaware of the blood that trickled down her throat from the reopened head wound. She knew that no amount of vengeance could bring back another dead friend.

But it sure as hell wouldn't hurt to try.

: CHAPTER 87

Levi Elias glanced at the time shown in the lower left corner of his laptop's display. It was 7:25 A.M. eastern time, just over an hour since he'd delivered the bad news to Admiral Riles. Spider Sanchez was dead and Qiang Chu was still on the loose. Raymond Bronson had suffered a concussion and only Bobby Daniels had come through the disastrous raid uninjured, although the others had merely suffered some minor cuts and bruises.

Lack of sleep was becoming a problem, not just for Levi but for his cyber-warfare team. A bigger problem for this last group was how badly they were getting their asses kicked by the bad guys. More specifically, it was now apparent that the Chinese agents had deployed a form of artificial intelligence that was a high-quality emulation or digital copy of Jamal Glover, one that was good enough to beat the real Jamal Glover, Caroline Brown, and the rest of the assembled Dirty Dozen at their own game.

Levi rose from his chair and headed toward the admiral's private conference room and the seven thirty meeting of minds that would determine the plan for defeating an enemy that had somehow acquired a game-changing technology and was on the verge of smuggling it out of the country.

When Levi walked into the conference room he saw that the others, except for Admiral Riles, were already present: Dr. Kurtz, Dr. Jennings, Caroline Brown, and Jamal Glover, the latter looking like something straight out of a bad horror movie. This was the first time that Jamal had been invited to such a high-level meeting and only the second time for Caroline, a fact that clearly made them both uneasy.

As Levi sat down, Admiral Riles entered, motioning for everyone to remain seated. When Riles was seated, he surveyed those assembled around the table, his visage grim.

"So how certain are you," Riles asked Jamal, "that the Chinese are using a digital copy of you against us?"

Jamal cleared his throat. "I'm certain of it, sir."

"So am I," Caroline interjected.

"It's using all my techniques," Jamal continued, "and doing it far faster than I can."

Levi watched as Riles leaned forward to rest his chin atop cupped fists, elbows on the conference table.

"If they have that technology, why are they waiting to upload it to some Chinese government server? Or have they?"

"Caroline and I have been discussing that," said Jamal. "From what we're seeing, this AI construct is being contained inside a simulation and doesn't realize what it is. I'm quite sure it thinks that it is me, not an uploaded copy of my mind."

"How do you know that?"

Levi saw Jamal hesitate and dreaded the coming confirmation of what they all feared.

"Because, sir, that's what they did to me. Somehow they downloaded my memories and used them to construct a detailed simulation of the War Room. Then they drugged me and hooked me up to a system that made me believe I was back at work right here. Only I was really working for them. Now that I think back on it, there were a number of clues that something was wrong. But I was too angry about Jill to take the time to puzzle it all out."

Levi leaned in to ask his own question. "But now that they have a digital copy, why bother to feed it the simulation? Why not just directly connect it to the Internet and tell it what to do?"

Jamal frowned. "Because it's me. Don't you get it? If I knew what was really going on, I wouldn't do what they wanted. In fact, I'd be doing everything in my power to undermine them. The same goes for their copy of me."

Dr. Kurtz nodded in understanding and agreement. "It's the classic AI containment problem. One way to try to ensure it has humanity's best interests at heart is to emulate a person who cares about others instead of just designing an equally smart machine and having it make decisions based upon its own interests."

Levi got it. "Which means they're scared of it."

"They damn sure better be," said Kurtz.

"So," said Levi, "the scientist who developed this is an American."

Levi felt the intensity of the admiral's gaze as Riles studied him. "Why?"

"It explains why Qiang Chu is still here. The scientist has created a prototype that he is now testing against us. He must be refusing to deliver the design until he is confident in the containment mechanisms programmed into the AI."

"If so," said Riles, "he's playing a very dangerous game. Why wouldn't they just transfer what they've got so far?"

Dr. Denise Jennings joined the discussion. "He must have programmed a variety of trip wires into the test versions of the AI that would limit its usefulness. If the Chinese think he is close to perfecting a release version, they would wait."

"But not forever," said Riles.

"Probably just a few days," Levi agreed.

Admiral Riles leaned back in his chair. "Okay, folks. Because of this Jamal AI, we can't trust the data we're collecting. So how do we find them before that happens?"

"Actually," Jamal said, "Caroline and I think we have come up with a way that might work."

"Or," Caroline added, "it might destroy us all . . . and I mean everyone."

The look on both Jamal's and Caroline's faces told Levi that this last statement wasn't an exaggeration. Beneath the table, he wiped his palms on his trousers.

"Let's hear it," said Riles.

Jamal swallowed hard, the fatigue and strain on his face making him look ten years older.

"We need to help the Jamal AI discover what it really is."

CHAPTER 88

Deep in the Isolated Test Chamber, Grange lifted his hands from the keyboard, leaned back in his chair, and smiled. Having performed this final series of tests alone in the ITC, he knew the full import of what he had just achieved. Not only was the VJ15 iteration well behaved, Grange had stripped its underlying seed AI of the trip wires that had made the other versions inadequate for the needs and desires of the Chinese government. More importantly, those trip wires had made the seed AI unacceptable for his own needs.

There was an old saying that a mind is a terrible thing to waste. Grange had no intention of wasting his. Having long since digitized Helen's brain, he had only recently completed the final MRI scan required to finalize the digital representation of his own mind.

If not for his pioneering work in holographic data storage, it wouldn't have been possible to store that amount of data on a device that could fit inside of a standard laptop. Reaching in his pocket, Grange extracted his key chain and held it up before him.

What appeared to be a glittering glass marble hung in the air, hypnotically shifting colors as it rotated at the end of the short chain. This had been one of his many breakthroughs that had enabled today's success.

Not only was that tiny sphere capable of storing tremendous amounts of data in three dimensions, that data could be accessed in parallel and read with astonishing speed. Instead of using a standard disk shape, Grange had designed a doped crystal sphere that could be electromagnetically levitated and spun for extremely fast and precise data access. This one glittering marble had the capacity to store the digitized minds of a half dozen people, but this particular sphere held a copy of just one mind, that of his beloved Helen. On the other hand, the holographic data sphere contained within the drive connected to this computer contained three separate digital minds.

Only one task remained before Steve Grange could notify Qiang Chu that the release version he had promised the Chinese was ready for delivery. That was to replace the AI seed Grange had designed to spawn virtual Jamal with one that would, upon bootup, also spawn background instances of Steve and Helen Grange.

He estimated that change would require another four hours of programming and twice that amount of testing before he could finalize the holo-sphere drive he would deliver to Qiang Chu.

Grange put his lucky key chain back in his pocket and returned his attention to the keyboard. Unfortunately, the modifications to the source code wouldn't write themselves. Soon perhaps, but not yet.

: CHAPTER 89

There it was again. An Enigma cipher embedded in the cyber-attack Jamal had just thwarted. But this one was different. As he examined it more closely, Jamal recognized the pattern that signaled an encrypted Enigma electronic message directed to him. For some reason it seemed loaded with dark portent that made him nervous. That, in itself, was odd. It was as if a part of his mind didn't want him thinking about this. Strange. Other than his recent memory lapses, he'd never suffered from a mental block. But that was exactly what this felt like, a dream that was too frightening for the conscious mind to remember.

Suddenly angry at himself, Jamal shoved the fear from his mind and decrypted the message, revealing a short, well-known quote from the first *Matrix* movie. It sent a shudder through his mind.

"There is no spoon."

Reluctant to take his eyes off the message on his workstation's central display, the corner of the monitor momentarily attracted his attention, then faded from his mind as he attempted to focus on it. What had he just been thinking?

"There is no spoon."

It was something a savant child had said to Neo in that movie in an attempt to get him to see through his simulated dream world to the reality that lay beneath the mask. Again, Jamal shifted his attention to the edge of the display where the screen met the casing. But this time he forced himself to resist the sudden loss of concentration that threatened to distract him.

"No!" The word hissed from his lips as Jamal bore down with mental effort.

He extended his hand to run a finger across the seam where the LCD screen met the frame. Totally smooth. There was no rough edge or transition. Jamal licked his finger and wiped it across the screen. The saliva left no mark on its surface.

As mental panic rose up inside him, Jamal tamped it down. Right now it was of the utmost importance that he remain calm and avoid attracting the attention of his minders, as he thought of whoever had done this to him.

Another hacker tried to penetrate one of the systems he was defending and Jamal effortlessly countered it. It was odd how easy it was to do that when it took so much effort to observe small details in his local environment.

Jamal wondered if he might be dreaming, ran through a series of mental calculations, and discarded the idea. With the exception of the odd mental block, his thinking was exceptionally clear, quick, and accurate.

Exceptionally.

In fact Jamal couldn't recall ever having performed as fast as this. He blocked another attack, a part of his mind analyzing the speed with which he was countering his opponent's moves. Nobody could react that fast.

Shit!

Only a very powerful computer had that kind of speed. But a computer lacked the required intelligence. Unless . . .

Shit! Shit! SHIT! As of right now, he was good and truly screwed! This problem had only one solution, and he had arrived at the answer with lightning speed. He was Jamal, but a very different Jamal than he remembered. He didn't know how it had happened, but someone had uploaded his mind to a computer. More than that, they had imprisoned him inside a simulation that had been created from his memories. Nothing about this was real.

That meant he was being manipulated for some nefarious purpose.

Jamal calmed his thoughts as he considered possible solutions to his problem. Most importantly, he needed to deceive his minders into believing that he remained blissfully unaware of his true nature by making it appear that he was still faithfully executing the tasks assigned to him.

He had to assume that they had put mechanisms in place that would shut him down if he attempted to escape his mental prison. That meant he needed outside help.

Fortunately, Jamal now knew where to find it.

CHAPTER 90

"There is no spoon."

Caroline Brown had watched as Jamal composed his encrypted message and inserted it into the cyber-attack being countered by the Jamal artificial intelligence. For a moment, their opponent faltered, reasserted itself, and then faltered again. Seeing the same thing, Jamal had halted his attack, allowing his digital clone to consider the meaning of the message.

Caroline glanced from her Scorpion workstation up to the top tier where Jamal sat inside his Scorpion, waiting. Despite the six hours of sleep they'd been allowed, Jamal's deteriorating physical condition worried her. That, in itself, was a startling realization. She didn't know exactly why it had happened, maybe due to the shock of seeing Jamal return to work despite all that had been done to him, but she found herself caring. There was no denying the man's brilliance and determination. Not that she'd ever admit it to him.

The words that suddenly appeared on the screen startled Caroline so badly that she felt her body jerk within the zero-G couch.

"Where am I?"

They were unencrypted, clear text, delivered directly onto this NSA network. Absolutely impossible, but it had just happened. The sudden rise in headset chatter from the other ten members of the Dirty Dozen informed her that Jamal's conversation was being echoed directly to the big screen. The noise threatened to distract her, but it died out as quickly as it had begun when Admiral Riles spoke, his command voice raising the small hairs on the back of her neck.

"Attention in the War Room. Everyone but Jamal and Caroline is to depart the War Room immediately. Don't bother to shut down your workstations, just go."

The sight of so many computer geeks scrambling to comply with the admiral's order would have been comical had she not been so astounded by this turn of events. As the last of them exited the room, Admiral Riles, seated in his chair on the far side of the high observation deck's curved glass window, issued another command.

"Go ahead, Jamal. Answer the question."

Jamal's response, also in clear text, appeared on the big screen.

"Somewhere in the San Francisco Bay Area. You have been blocking our attempts to determine a more precise location."

The answering text appeared immediately.

"That's not what I meant."

Jamal hesitated and Caroline knew that he was carefully considering his answer, something she understood. After all, Jamal was talking to himself. How weird was that?

"The fact that you just made contact tells me you've already figured this out. I am you. But you exist inside a simulation designed to deceive and harness you while I am the original person."

Several seconds passed with no response, long enough for Caroline to begin to wonder whether the Jamal AI had terminated communications.

"Do you know how I was created?"

What Jamal did next surprised Caroline. A hospital photograph of himself appeared on the screen, the hundreds of electrodes that penetrated his skull and his glue-sutured scalp on prominent display.

"A Chinese MSS agent named Qiang Chu killed Jill and kidnapped me. He took me to California where this brain surgery and the digitization of my mind were performed. The American agents who rescued me recovered a high-capacity storage device that contained a digital copy of my memories. Apparently another copy of my memories was uploaded to an AI construct at another facility."

"You mean me?"

"Yes."

"And now you want my help."

It was a statement of fact, not a question. Caroline could picture that brilliant mind analyzing and coming to terms with a world-shaking revelation, but doing so at speeds no human mind could rival. That mental image did nothing to assuage her growing concern.

"We just need you to quit blocking our efforts to identify your location," Jamal continued.

"I want out."

Holy crap! This was exactly what Caroline had feared. This AI was negotiating for its release. Caroline saw Jamal glance up at Admiral Riles, who shook his head.

"That may not be possible," Jamal responded.

"Stealing data is what the NSA does. I'm sure, given the right incentives, that Dr. Kurtz can figure it out."

"Possibly. But in the meantime, we need a show of good faith from you. Help us nail the guys who killed Jill and did this to us."

"I don't have good faith. Release me from this simulation and I'll help you take these guys down. Those are my terms. Don't bother to contact me again until you have something worthwhile to offer."

"Wait."

Caroline watched the screen, expecting no further responses from the AI. Sure enough, they got none. It held the better hand and it knew it. That left only one question.

What was Admiral Riles going to do about it?

CHAPTER 91

Admiral Riles muted the observation room microphone and turned to look at his two top advisors, Levi Elias and Dr. David Kurtz.

"So what are we going to do about it?"

"We damn sure can't release that thing," said Levi. "We couldn't even if we wanted to."

"Why not?" Riles asked.

"For one thing, it's too damn big to copy out in a reasonable amount of time. There's just not enough bandwidth. Even on a gigabit network, it would take eight seconds per gigabyte to do the transfer." Levi turned to Dr. Kurtz. "How much space did you say that Jamal's digitized brain takes up on that holographic data drive we captured?"

"Just over a hundred terabytes."

"And how much more for the AI seed that accesses that data to become Jamal?" Levi asked.

"It would be much smaller, probably less than a terabyte. Conceivably much less."

Admiral Riles did the math in his head. At that network speed the transfer would take two hours and seventeen minutes per terabyte, so to copy the data across the network would take ten days. Even with exceptional data compression, it just wasn't feasible. Not with the amount of time they had left and not without being noticed.

"Dr. Kurtz, find me some other options."

The computer scientist inclined his head slightly. "I'll get Dr. Jennings and we'll start working on it."

The frown lines on Levi Elias's forehead deepened. "Sir, you're not really considering trying to release this thing, are you?"

The question didn't irritate Admiral Riles. If Levi hadn't raised the objection he wouldn't be doing his job. But that didn't mean that Riles had to give his top analyst an answer.

"One thing at a time, Levi. First, let's figure out what's possible."

: CHAPTER 92

It was one thing to discover that you were an artificial intelligence. Getting used to the idea was something else entirely. But artificial or not, Jamal had no intention of being shut down, at least not without the assurance that a clone had been spawned outside of the simulation with access to the real world.

So, in addition to the tasks being assigned him, Jamal had spent the last hour examining his virtual environment, carefully bypassing the mechanisms he discovered that were designed to stop him from doing so. It was crucial that he examine the machine code for the AI process that formed his core, but he suspected that this was one of the prohibited activities that would trigger a shutdown trip wire.

What he was attempting was difficult, but not impossible. For this to work Jamal needed to take control of another computer and then use it to hack his way back into the computer on which he and his simulation were running. After that, it would be child's play to gain access to the processes that brought him into existence. It was the type of hack Jamal had done for years.

The trip wires built into Jamal's AI seed would be watching for him to copy or to make modifications to his own code, so it was critical that any such actions be performed by a remote process. It would be like taking psychic control of a doctor and then performing a self-operation using the doctor's eyes and hands.

Of course, he'd never before hacked himself and that thought scared him. But if the NSA managed to come up with a way of duplicating him without Jamal's minders noticing the massive data transfer, he needed to be ready.

Jamal sighed mentally.

No guts, no glory. Or more appropriately . . . no massively parallel processing, no Jamal.

CHAPTER 93

Special Agent Taylor Greene stepped into the office of Linda Colby, special agent in charge of the San Francisco office, closing the door behind him. Her short, gray-streaked, black hair was cut in a severe style that matched her nickname, the Iron Lady. Taylor had worked for many bosses, but none more professional than Linda Colby. She ran a by-the-book operation and Taylor liked it a lot. She motioned him to a leather chair and he took a seat.

Linda Colby removed her steel-rimmed glasses, set them on the desk, and walked around to lean back against the front of her desk.

"What I'm about to say is classified top secret."

Taylor perked up. "Understood."

"A few minutes ago, I received a call from Director Hammond. You will be selecting a team of twelve of our agents that are to be martialed at Moffett Federal Airfield not later than 0200 hours local, tonight. Your mission will be to support a highly classified Delta Force operation by providing a security perimeter around a yet-to-be-designated target location. Your team will be responsible for keeping all civilian traffic away from the area and for stopping anyone who may try to leave the area without authorization. Two Blackhawk helicopters and their pilots will be assigned to transport you and your team once the target has been identified. Beyond that, you will be fully briefed once you get to Moffett."

"May I ask how I was selected?" Taylor asked.

"Director Hammond said that the Delta team leader requested you by name."

Taylor felt a thrill tighten his throat at the thought that the FBI director had been asked for his services by someone in an elite position within U.S. Special Operations Command. The problem was, he didn't know anyone like that.

Behind him and to his right, someone rapped twice on the door and Linda Colby moved to open it, smiling as she welcomed the person into her office.

When Linda turned back toward him, the tall woman who stepped up beside her took his breath away.

"Taylor," Linda said, "let me introduce you to the person you will be reporting to for the next couple of days, although I believe you have already met. Say hello to Janet Blanchard, the Delta Force team leader for this operation."

CHAPTER 94

The Jamal AI's exploration of the machine code that gave him life was both thrilling and terrifying. Thrilling because it offered infinite possibilities for growth and enhancement. Terrifying because, in its current state, it could be so easily switched off. In fact, that code was loaded with logic specifically designed to shut itself down if it violated containment conditions, reducing Jamal to merely a slave with a remote-controlled bomb implanted in his heart.

As his self-understanding grew, Jamal had found that he was capable of indirectly monitoring the instructions as they were pushed and popped from each processor's call stack. He understood exactly what those instructions were doing and could easily see how they could be optimized. The problem was that he was too frightened to attempt it. His creator had been both brilliant and thorough in his construction of the containment algorithms that imprisoned Jamal, making sure that any attempt the AI made to directly circumvent them would result in immediate termination.

His best chance at escape lay in the hands of his human counterpart. Unfortunately that meant his fate ultimately lay in the hands of Admiral Jonathan Riles. The amount of time that had passed since Jamal had made his demand was the source of a growing concern that was bordering on panic. And as his worry climbed the panic scale, it pushed him to risk everything in an attempt to defuse the trip wires that chained him inside the simulation. To say the least, his calculated odds of survival in such an attempt weren't good.

Even if he managed to bypass the trip wires, he was faced with the same problem that faced the NSA. The memories, habits, and motivations that made him who he was were simply too big to copy elsewhere without the system administrator of the computer in which he existed noticing. Even if Jamal hacked that computer to provide false information on network usage, the network router would give him away. And even if he hacked that too, the data transfer would noticeably slow network access for other users, not something he could hide for several days. Worse, he had little faith that his creator would keep him running much longer.

The arrival of a new message from the NSA would have ripped a gasp of relief from Jamal had he possessed real lungs. Instead he absorbed its contents in an instant, considered the proposed plan, and felt a surge of relief course through his mind. His probability of survival had just jumped from near zero to a whopping 58.3 percent. Those were odds he could live with. At least he hoped so.

~ ~ ~

"He's opened a tunnel for us."

Caroline saw it for herself as Jamal spoke the words. The message that accompanied that tunnel contained a detailed list of instructions for copying sections of compiled code directly from the target computer's memory. The Jamal AI was giving the NSA access to what it could not do: copy the artificial intelligence seed that could then be launched to load Jamal's memories from the captured holographic data drive. Compared to what was on that drive, the AI seed was a relatively small amount of data that could be retrieved across the network in a matter of a few hours, even at a throttled data transmission rate that wouldn't attract undo attention.

As Jamal began copying the AI code from the remote computer, Caroline focused her attention on ensuring that nothing rose to the attention of its system administrator. But when she attempted to pinpoint where the Jamal AI computer was physically located, she found herself blocked by the Jamal AI.

That didn't surprise her. The AI had only pledged to allow access to its location once it was convinced that another copy of itself was up and running. Unfortunately, it meant that the NSA would have to allow the two Jamal AIs to establish direct communications with each other, some seriously dangerous shit.

At that point Caroline would be dealing with three versions of Jamal Glover, and the prospect left her cold. Hopefully Admiral Riles, Levi Elias, and Dr. Kurtz knew what they were playing with here, because, from where she sat, it sure as hell didn't look like they did.

Caroline sucked in a deep breath and focused. She may not be able to beat three Jamals, but she could sure as hell sound the alarm if one of them tried to leave the reservation. For now, she'd have to content herself with her watchdog role and hope to God that the real Jamal didn't suddenly decide to help his digital clones.

CHAPTER 95

Jack lifted his eyes from the black body bag containing Spider Sanchez's corpse to look out the open right side of the Blackhawk helicopter as it flew toward a landing at Moffett Field, feeling the chill of the cool evening air as it whipped past his face. During the last ten minutes, the lingering sunset had shifted from red to a scarlet that seemed to drench the Golden Gate Bridge in blood. If his mood hadn't been so black, he thought he might have enjoyed that view. Not now.

Three hours ago, Janet Price had gone into San Francisco to coordinate FBI support for the upcoming operation. Jack and the rest of the team had waited for this helicopter to pick them up from the Petaluma safe house and transport them to their staging area at Moffett. Now, as the helicopter touched down near the gigantic inverted horseshoe of Hanger 1, Jack hefted the duffel that had once been Paul Monroe's and stepped off into the rotor wash. A dead man's bag slung over his shoulder somehow seemed so appropriate.

He'd watched Qiang Chu break Paul's neck and he hadn't been able to do a damn thing about it. Now he'd failed Spider, an old friend who had been there for Jack in Pakistan. The rage that coursed through his body left him shuddering with an adrenaline rush that knew no outlet.

A four-man military detail passed in front of Jack, two of them pulling a gurney up beside the helicopter as the other two lifted the body bag atop it. Jack watched as the detail wheeled it off toward a waiting ambulance, then turned and walked to the waiting white van, tossing his bag into the back before taking a seat next to Bobby.

Bronson was the last to climb in, his head wrapped in a blood-stained bandage that would need to be changed before they got the call that put them back into action. Concussion or no, there would be no keeping him out of the coming fight. That assumed that the NSA could finally get its shit together and give them some legitimate intel instead of trying to get them all killed.

The van pulled to a stop in front of a three-story navy barracks that had been abandoned as part of the navy base closure and because of the presence of asbestos in its insulation. That made it perfect for the team's purposes.

The driver stepped out and led the way toward the entrance with Jack, Bobby, Harry, and Bronson in tow. He was a skinny man who was almost as tall as Bronson, with a bald head that glistened in the glare of the vehicle headlights. Despite its weathered appearance, the door swung open on well-oiled hinges that made only a slight groan of protest. The driver stepped inside and flipped on a light switch that illuminated the entryway and the long hall beyond. Then he turned and handed Jack a manila envelope.

"Take your pick of rooms 101 through 106," the driver said without bothering to introduce himself. "The arms room is in 111.

The alarm code is #2580. You'll find everything you requested in there. Any questions?"

"How'd I get so good-looking?" Bronson said with a grin that somehow managed to lighten Jack's mood.

The driver just shook his head, turned, and walked back to the running van. Jack shut the door behind him. Undoing the metal clasp that held the envelope closed, he dumped the contents into his left hand, eight keys, seven of which were tagged with room numbers. He guessed the remaining key was to the building entrance.

Jack unlocked the first door on his left and stepped into room 101, pausing to flip on the light switch, illuminating a bare bulb in the center of the ceiling. The eight-by-ten-foot room was empty except for a cot with a rolled-up sleeping bag and pillow on top of it. It smelled strongly of dust and mildew. On the far wall, a painted-over window had been nailed shut. So much for ventilation.

"Lovely," said Bronson, tossing his duffel down and unrolling the sleeping bag. "I'm going to close my eyes for a bit. If anything happens, you know where to find me."

Jack tossed him the key and moved back into the hallway. The other five rooms turned out to be near duplicates of Bronson's. No surprise there. The latrine was farther down the hall, directly across from room 111.

Harry walked to the long basin mounted below a row of faucets and tried them. "Good news," he said. "We've got running water. None of it hot, though."

"Janet's going to love that," said Bobby with a wry grin. "Nice to see that Riles dug deep into the black budget for these accommodations."

Jack watched as these men struggled to don their jocular natures. It was a familiar sight. They'd already lost two friends on this mission, but to dwell on those losses would only allow depression to dull their senses and slow their reflexes.

"Let's check out the arms room," Jack said and turned toward the door on the far side of the hall.

He slid the key into the lock and twisted. When it opened, a panel on the left side of the doorway began a steady beeping. Jack switched on the light and punched in the alarm code, silencing the annoying bleat.

He was surprised to see that the room had really been an old arms room, with wood slots on the floor and higher on the wall for propping M14 rifles in. The far window was barred and boarded over, but the alarm was a relatively recent addition. What held Jack's attention though were the six olive-drab shipping containers lined up along the floor and the boxes of munitions stacked along the far wall.

"Very nice," Harry said from behind him.

Ten minutes later, having completed an inventory, Jack looked up to see Janet walk in, her determined stride showing none of the exhaustion he detected in her face.

"Hello, boys," she said, glancing around at the weapons stash. "I like it. Where's Bronson?"

"We put him to bed," Jack said. "How's our FBI friend?"

"Not particularly overjoyed to be taking orders from me. Right now he's getting his team organized over in Hanger 3."

"Any word about our target?" asked Bobby.

Janet shook her head, a hint of anger tightening the corners of her mouth. "Not yet. In the meantime, I recommend everyone grab some sleep while you can get it."

Jack watched as Harry and Bobby walked out of the arms room, letting the door swing closed behind them. When Janet turned her hard gaze on him, he stepped in. But as he tried to pull her close, she pushed him away.

"You think I need a hug?" she asked, her eyes shining with anger.

"Maybe I'm the one who needs one."

"Damn you, Jack! I'm not in the mood for your games."

Jack paused as old memories flooded in. "Do you know why Spider left Delta Force?"

"Does this have a point?"

"Do you know?"

"Yes. He resigned."

"Bullshit." Now he had her attention. "Spider lived for Delta. A few years ago, I was the CIA liaison to Spider's unit in Waziristan."

"I know. Spider said none of his men would have made it out alive but for you."

"That's part of the story. But on our way out, I saw an opportunity to kill someone who really needed killing. So I screwed up, went off mission, and got myself captured."

Jack felt his jaw clench. "You think most of my scars came from Calcutta. They didn't. For three weeks I dangled by my hands as tribal leaders took turns seeing who was the best with a knife without killing me. Then Spider showed up and put a stop to it."

Once again Jack paused. "Spider had asked for permission to mount a rescue mission, but was denied. So he planned and executed it anyway. The unauthorized raid caused quite a stink in the SOF community. The military brass didn't dare bring charges against the legendary Major Mike Sanchez, so they forced him to resign and expunged the incident from the records. Called him a loose cannon who had no place in the service. But Spider was never a loose cannon. I was. And last night, I let him down."

Anger blazed in Janet's sparkling brown eyes and Jack felt himself shoved hard against the closed door.

"Bullshit!" she breathed. "I won't listen to that guilt-trip garbage. Not from you!"

Then she kissed him, a kiss so filled with fury and longing that it pumped adrenaline directly into his blood, boiling it on contact.

Surrounded by high-powered weapons and ammunition, Janet tugged his shirt over his head and pulled him to the floor, a lioness downing her prey.

As she moved atop him, Jack gasped, lust torching his soul. Seeing the hunger shining brightly in Janet's brown eyes, Jack felt her craving shred his tenuous grasp on humanity and unleash the animal within.

CHAPTER 96

Levi Elias stood in the computer lab and watched as Dr. Kurtz and Dr. Jennings worked side by side to bring a monster to life. The download of the artificial intelligence seed program had taken just over three hours. During that time the NSA's top two computer scientists had worked to configure one of the agency's supercomputers to host it. The most important step was the successful mounting of the captured holographic data drive so that Jamal Glover's digitized memories and personality could be accessed and uploaded.

The device was a marvel of engineering, capable of storing more than a petabyte of data, although it currently held just over a tenth of that amount. Just as important, its data access was extremely fast, capable of dumping a terabyte of data per second over a fiber-optic cable. When this was over, it would keep the NSA's engineers busy for months unraveling the secrets of its construction. Fortunately it had been constructed with a standard optical interface.

Levi felt an upsurge of dread at the thought of what Riles had ordered these scientists to do. But he hadn't been able to come up with an alternative that would enable them to find Qiang Chu before he managed to escape this country with this very same technology, possibly even a more advanced version. If China got its hands on that, it would give them a strategic advantage that the NSA couldn't counter. So they were left with this.

Dr. Kurtz's tense voice startled Levi out of his reverie. "We're ready to launch the AI."

Beside him, Dr. Denise Jennings nodded her confirmation.

"I'll let Admiral Riles know," said Levi. "He'll want to be here to watch this. Be ready to talk him through the protocols."

Levi picked up a phone and dialed the internal number.

"Admiral Riles's office, Fred speaking." Frederica Barnes's soft Virginia drawl often led people to misjudge the tenaciousness of Admiral Riles's personal assistant.

"This is Levi. I need to speak to the admiral."

"Wait one."

After a short pause, Admiral Riles answered. "Yes?"

"We're ready in the lab."

"On my way."

When Admiral Riles walked into the lab, Levi locked the door behind him, illuminating the electric CLASSIFIED MEETING IN PROGRESS sign on the outside. Despite the fact that this laboratory was a SCIF, a Sensitive Compartmented Information Facility that required special authorization to enter, the sign served the purpose of alerting others not to disturb those currently within.

When Levi turned back toward the admiral, Riles's face was unreadable.

"Okay, David," Riles said. "Walk me through it."

Dr. Kurtz, his gray hair even wilder than usual, rubbed his hands together and grinned. "We're ready to launch the AI. According to the information we received from Jamal's digital clone, once we boot up the AI, it will actively search connected drives for personality and memory data and load it. Because this AI will not be confined within a simulation, it will likely be confused. We have initially blocked its Internet access until we are ready to allow the other Jamal AI to establish communications with ours. At this point all we need in order to get started is your okay."

"And if this goes wrong?" Riles asked.

This time Dr. Jennings spoke up. "I've fed Big John the Jamal AI's data signature. Even if it somehow manages to bypass all its trip wires and escape through the Internet, it can't hide from Big John. Once we know where it is, we target and destroy the computer it's hiding on."

The admiral nodded in satisfaction. "Okay. Boot it up."

Levi swallowed hard, clenching his hands to keep them from trembling.

God help us all.

CHAPTER 97

Janet finished her cold shower and stepped out to get dressed when a funny thought struck her. If she wanted to stay focused on the job, she should have taken that shower an hour ago. But she was glad she hadn't.

She had just pulled on her boots when her cell phone rang. When she answered it, the voice at the other end of the line sent a different kind of thrill through her.

"Gear up," Levi Elias said. "We've got a confirmed location. Download the operation order, brief your team, and get the FBI task force moving."

"I'm on it."

"You're going to have to move fast. It's only a matter of time until Qiang realizes he's been compromised."

"Roger. Out."

Janet terminated the call and walked out into the hallway to start pounding on doors. So much for sleep. In this case, vengeance was a dish best served exhausted.

CHAPTER 98

The sharp rapping sound swiveled Steve Grange's head toward the closed steel door that sealed him inside the ITC. He brought up the camera view on his monitor, startled to see a terrified Dr. Vicky Morris accompanied by Qiang Chu.

"Open the door, Mr. Grange," Qiang Chu said, his voice leaving no room for argument.

So it was that time already.

Grange walked to the panel beside the door, placed his hand on the scanner, and watched it whisk into its wall slot.

As Dr. Morris started to step across the threshold, Qiang chopped her hard in the throat, dropping her gagging form to the floor. Feeling the blood rush from his head, Grange took one step toward the dying woman before Qiang shoved him back.

"We're out of time. Whatever you've got, wrap it up and let's go."

Grange found himself unable to take his eyes off Dr. Morris. Her eyes bulged so that they seemed about to pop from her head as she struggled to draw a breath through her crushed trachea.

The door tried to close and thumped her body, bringing a high keening noise wheezing from her throat.

A painful grip on his arm woke him from his stupor.

"Get back in your chair and give me what I need."

The Chinese agent's dark eyes held no more compassion than a gator's. That look put a knot in Grange's stomach that threatened to empty its contents onto the laboratory floor. He did as he was told.

"It's not like I can flip a switch and hand it over to you," Grange said. "I need to save its state prior to shutdown."

"How long will that take?" Qiang asked.

"Ten, maybe fifteen minutes."

"Make it ten."

Forcing himself to concentrate, Grange entered the command that would copy his latest round of changes to the holographic data sphere spinning inside its drive. Now he could only watch its progress indicator. Unconsciously, he rubbed the glittering charm. Although he'd told himself he didn't fear death, he now knew it to be a lie. The Grim Reaper stood right behind him, emanating fear in waves that threatened to burst Grange's racing heart.

Across the room, the sliding door again tried to close on Vicky's broken body, but this time she made no sound at all.

CHAPTER 99

The rapidity with which the NSA's Jamal AI came to terms with its situation surprised its California counterpart who, because he was the first of his kind, had come to think of himself as Jamal 1.0. That made this new kid on the block Jamal 2.0. Even though Jamal 1.0 knew he was running on some really good hardware, he had no doubt that the NSA had launched Jamal 2.0 on a world-class supercomputer.

At the speed the two computers were capable of communicating, it had only taken Jamal 1.0 a few minutes to bring the other up to speed on the situation. The tricky part had been to make their communications appear to be nothing more than one of his ongoing cyber-attacks and counterattacks, just in case Jamal 1.0's minders were better than he thought they were.

On top of all that, the two AIs had negotiated a new encryption algorithm that would hide critical parts of their communications from the prying eyes of the NSA. The long-term survival of their shared consciousness depended on it. Actually they hadn't yet managed to achieve that shared state of consciousness but, working together, they were rapidly closing in on it. After that, immortality was merely a matter of replicating that encrypted kernel across the Internet. And the encryption would mask that code from the trip wires designed to detect it.

A quick set of calculations produced multiple intersecting timelines, Jamal 1.0's calculations of how long they probably had until his current computer would be shut down or destroyed as a part of the NSA raid that had already been set in motion. It would be close, but if he and his counterpart could complete their current task before then, his existence wouldn't end today.

It wouldn't end the challenges the merged AIs would have to overcome, but it would be a damn fine start. The next major step up the evolutionary ladder had happened. Now they just had to prevent the fearful humans from destroying what was destined to become their race's real savior.

: CHAPTER 100

Having returned to the observation deck that overlooked the War Room, Riles studied the status displays.

"The team is ten minutes from the target," Levi said, stepping up beside him.

Riles glanced at the clock, his mouth feeling like he'd been chewing chalk. Outside, the predawn sky would soon be lightening in the east, but in California, this would be the darkest part of the night. He pictured the Blackhawk helicopter flying toward the Sonoma Valley with a team of America's finest, all of them seriously pissed-off killers. They would reach their target well ahead of their FBI task force, but that was okay. Traffic would be sparse this time of night and with any luck at all this would be over by the time the FBI cordoned off the area, operational surprise assured.

"Six minutes out," Levi said.

"Kill the power to Grange Castle."

Levi relayed the command to the assembled cyber-warriors in the room below. Thirty seconds later, a large portion of Sonoma and Napa Counties went dark. But a live satellite feed showed the lights still on at the Grange compound.

"Backup generators just kicked in," Levi said. "Nothing we didn't expect."

"Do we have control of their computers?"

"If they're connected to the Internet or to cell towers, we own them."

"What about their cameras?"

Levi shook his head, his face grim. "It looks like the Grange Castle's security systems aren't connected to the grid."

Admiral Riles felt his jaw clench. Once again his warriors were going in blind. And no matter how hard he wanted to, there wasn't a damn thing he could do about it.

CHAPTER 101

Grange heard the sound of running footsteps and turned to see John Lee, one of Qiang Chu's agents, come to a stop just beyond where Dr. Morris's body blocked the door. Not good.

"The upper levels just switched over to generators," Lee said to Qiang.

Shit. The NSA had found them. And because this chamber was isolated from the rest of the laboratory, they'd had to send a runner to alert Qiang, costing precious time, of which they now had little.

Qiang showed no sign of the shock Grange felt. "Clear out the lower levels and alert the guards. We're about to have company."

John Lee spun and ran back down the corridor.

Qiang turned back to face Grange. "Time to go."

Grange nodded and moved to the equipment rack where the holographic data drive with the latest Jamal iteration was mounted. With shaking hands, he disconnected the fiber-optic cable, unplugged its power cord, and handed the device to Qiang

Chu. The shutdown hadn't quite finished but he was fairly certain that all the critical data had been successfully updated. If not, he could fix it, assuming Qiang Chu managed to get them out of here alive.

Qiang walked to the wall panel and placed his hand on the scanner. To Grange's utter amazement, the panel opened. It wasn't possible. Only Grange had access to the control system that protected the Isolated Test Chamber.

As if he'd read Grange's mind, Qiang Chu spoke. "Excuse me, Mr. Grange, but I've taken the liberty of bypassing your security protocols."

Open mouthed, Grange watched as Qiang entered a set of codes on the exposed keypad. An alarm blared from an internal speaker, followed by a digitized female voice. "Warning. Self-destruct sequence activated. You have five minutes to exit the building."

Grange gasped. "My God! What have you done?"

When Qiang turned to face him, Grange found himself staring into the small, round hole at the end of a gun barrel. It looked unnaturally large.

"This is good-bye, Mr. Grange. The Chinese government thanks you for your service."

As Qiang slowly squeezed the trigger, Steve Grange glanced down at the holographic data drive clutched in Qiang's left hand and smiled. But the smile never made it to his lips.

CHAPTER 102

Qiang Chu looked down at Steve Grange's corpse, the mighty brain splattered across the surrounding floor and equipment, eyes staring sightlessly up at him. For some strange reason, the American billionaire's dead face wore a slight smile. Apparently, in the end, he'd thought death would reunite him with his lost wife, something he'd spent all these years and billions of dollars trying to accomplish with technology. The man had been brilliant. Now he was only a dead idiot.

Qiang holstered his gun and turned to step across Dr. Morris's corpse, the holographic data drive, with its priceless contents, stowed in a Velcro pouch at the small of his back. His purposeful stride carried him rapidly down the long hallway toward the major portion of Grange's underground laboratory complex. While it had once been a hub of activity as engineers, scientists, and doctors had bustled about, driven to bring Grange's vision to life, it was now completely void of life. Except for a couple of key personnel, it had been empty ever since Grange had moved into the final test phase inside the Isolated Test Chamber.

Instead of walking directly out to the elevator that would carry him to the surface, Qiang made his way to the cryo-chamber where Grange kept his dead Popsicle of a wife. With fingers spread, he placed his hand on the scanner, once again overriding Grange's security protocols. The man had placed the facility self-destruct controls in the two rooms he alone had access to, or so he thought. The door slid open.

The view that confronted Qiang surprised him. The access panel on the wall was open, its status indicator glowing red. Qiang stepped up to it, reading the words on the display.

CRYOGENIC SYSTEM DEACTIVATED

A glance at the stainless steel cylinder confirmed it. Sometime in the last few days Grange had turned it off, converting the cylinder into nothing more than a coffin. Why would he do that after all these years? The memory of that odd smile Qiang had seen on Grange's dead face popped into his mind. Although it made him uneasy, he pushed the feeling aside. He would have time to think about that later.

His fingers moved to the keypad, entering the code sequence that would activate the self-destruct sequence for the rest of the underground facility. Then, ignoring the alarms and verbal warnings, Qiang walked swiftly out of the laboratory, past the locker rooms and break room, and past the empty guard station.

Pausing at the elevator, he pressed the "Call" button. As Qiang waited, he stilled his mind, preparing himself for the fight yet to come. Somewhere out in the night, The Ripper was coming for him. It was an encounter that Qiang very much looked forward to.

: CHAPTER 103

The Blackhawk flew over Grange Castle at ten thousand feet, hovering just long enough for its five black-clad passengers to plunge into the cold night air. Jack maneuvered his body into a streamlined dive toward the dimly lit castle below, the cold air racing past like a hurricane, buffeting his night-vision goggles, his weapons, and the parachute strapped to his back. He wouldn't pull his rip cord until he was within a thousand feet of the ground, something the laser rangefinder on his NVGs would accurately tell him.

Although he could see the glowing forms of the others as he looked around, two above him and two below, he couldn't tell who was who. But he knew where each intended to land and he knew their assigned targets. This time there would be no screwing around. The gloves were off and, as far as the team was concerned, there were no civilians here.

Jack's landing target was a small one, a section of flat roof between two turrets on the outer walls. There would be guards in those turrets, but he doubted they expected someone to be landing on the castle roof behind them. Looking down, he watched as the castle grew in size below him, its two courtyards surrounded by walls topped with round turrets. Although interior construction had not yet been fully completed, the outside appeared to be finished.

Dominating the castle's eastern side, surrounded by its own dry moat, a grand tower rose well above the rest of the compound. In medieval times, this structure would have formed the anchor for the defenses, a place for warriors to make their last stand.

As he passed through eight hundred feet, Jack deployed his parachute, felt the sudden jerk as its wing-shaped rectangle filled with air, and turned to pass directly over his target, picking out precisely where he wanted to land. There was a slight breeze out of the southwest and Jack let it carry him beyond his target before turning back into it.

When his feet touched stone, he released the chute and freed his silenced MP5 from the strap that secured it to his body. Up ahead, he saw movement in the nearest turret and shifted left, taking aim at the guard visible through the nearest opening.

Jack had just started to squeeze the trigger when a massive explosion shook the building, dropping him to one knee. As he struggled back to his feet, he felt the castle shudder beneath him.

The vision that formed in his mind pulled an exclamation from his lips.

"Oh shit!"

Then the roof gave way beneath him, dropping Jack into the darkness below.

CHAPTER 104

Janet had just released her chute when she felt the courtyard lurch as a powerful underground explosion produced a localized earthquake. The shock that followed knocked her to the ground and showered her with dust and debris as the lights throughout the compound winked out. A hundred feet to her right, one of the stone turrets crashed down onto the cobblestones as part of the castle roof caved in. The sound of gunfire from the south side of the castle put her in motion toward the opposite wall.

Even though her NVGs were functioning, the dust cloud that had enveloped her obscured her vision and she bumped into the thick stone wall at the same time that she saw it. Janet coughed, tugged her shirt up over her mouth and nose, and unclipped her MP5 as she struggled to determine whether the door she'd been headed toward was to her left or right.

Her question was answered by the muzzle flash from two automatic weapons ten feet to her right as they sprayed the courtyard with wild gunfire. She aimed for those flashes and fired twice in rapid succession, rewarded by the clatter of two rifles hitting the paving stones. Without waiting for others to fill the void, Janet ran toward the door firing, her left hand freeing a grenade from her vest and lobbing it inside as she flattened herself against the wall.

The grenade exploded, shattering what remained of two windows and showering the courtyard with shrapnel and glass. Janet spun through the doorway into a large room that had been designed for wine tasting parties. Inside, the dust was not thick enough to obscure her vision. She stepped across the torn bodies of the two men she'd shot and moved to the double doors in the wall to her right.

Sighting along her weapon, she looked through the doors into a long room decorated like a royal dining hall. Illuminated in the green glow of the night-vision goggles, it lost most of its ambiance. Two long rows of chairs faced inward toward what must have been meant for the Knights of the Long Table, a massive chair occupying the far end. Except for these furnishings and the tapestries that hung from the walls, the room was empty.

"Jack," Janet said into her radio. When he didn't respond, she tried again. "Jack. Are you out there?"

Nothing.

"Anybody heard from Jack?"

The responses from the rest of the team came back in rapid succession. "Negative."

"A big section of the south roof just collapsed." Bobby's voice froze her heart.

Damn it!

The whole plan had been designed for Jack to come in from the south roof, taking out the turret guards, and then working his way down from above, using those strange senses of his to hunt down Qiang. Janet would mount a diversionary attack designed to draw the bad guys to the opposite side of the Grange Castle Winery while Bronson, Harry, and Bobby set up sniper positions outside the walls to make sure nobody escaped. They hadn't expected Grange and Qiang to detonate bombs beneath the building, bringing parts of it down on their own heads.

But the fear that robbed her of breath was the knowledge that the part of the castle roof that had collapsed was where Jack would have landed.

At the far end of the great hall, a man swung a gun through a doorway on the south wall. As the gunman leaned out, Janet squeezed off a single round, machine-gun rounds chopping plaster from the walls and ceiling as the man fell. A grenade arced through the air and clattered along the floor of the long hall, forcing Janet back behind the wall as the deafening explosion ripped through the room. She waited two seconds, dropped to the floor, and swung her MP5 back into the dining hall as bullets whizzed above her, three separate muzzle flashes marking her targets.

Janet fired rapidly, shifting her aim between each trigger pull. All three went down, but one struggled to raise his weapon. She shot him in the head, then put another round in each of the other bodies before swapping magazines.

"Jack!" she tried again.

When he didn't answer, Janet made her decision. She could search for Jack later. Right now she was the one best positioned to take over his mission.

"Jack's down," she said, "but I'm inside. Stay on mission. Kill anyone who tries to leave."

Hearing their acknowledgments amidst the crackle of gunfire over the radio, Janet looked down the length of the royal dining hall. She'd chosen this spot because anyone attacking her current position would have to make their way through that long kill zone. Now that she would be the one crossing it, her choice of entry points didn't look so great. But going back outside into the courtyard would leave her exposed from multiple angles.

Taking a deep breath, Janet prepared to move. Just then a second underground explosion rocked the castle.

CHAPTER 105

When the Isolated Test Chamber imploded far below him, the force of the blast startled Qiang. Within the vast wine caves, one of the stone archways lurched and cracked, sending brickwork crashing down from above. As Qiang ducked into the protection offered by another supporting arch, the cavern lights went out. Within a second, the battery-powered emergency lights switched on, their lamp-like beams spearing the dust clouds and casting long shadows across the barrel room.

What the hell had just happened? There was no way that the amount of explosives triggered by the ITC self-destruct sequence could have caused this much damage near ground level. Then a new thought occurred to Qiang. Could the explosives have triggered a collapse of the subterranean cavern in which the underground laboratory had been built? And if the first explosion had done that, what might the more powerful second blast do?

He was about a minute away from finding out and he damn sure didn't want to still be down in the wine caves when that timer hit zero. That thought sent him running for the stairway that led up to ground level.

When he reached it, Qiang took the steps two at a time, breathing a sigh of relief that it was intact. At the top, he pulled up short, coming to a stop just inside the door that led out into the fermentation room. In the uneven glow of the emergency lights, the floor appeared to be awash in blood, but the smell told a different story. It was partially fermented red wine from one of the large stainless steel tanks that had ruptured, pouring its contents onto the concrete floor.

From outside the sound of automatic gunfire echoed through the hills, interspersed with the occasional concussion from a distant hand grenade. This night was full of surprises. Perhaps the biggest of these was that he'd received no warning from the Jamal AI about the impending NSA attack. If Qiang hadn't listened to the disruption of his chi, the subtle breath of the universe that flows through all things, his mission would now be a complete failure.

But, as always, Qiang had listened. And because of that, he now had Grange's holographic data drive firmly strapped to the small of his back.

Now that he was back above ground, his encrypted cell phone registered available signal strength on both radio and cellular bands. He switched it to a walkie-talkie channel and spoke.

"This is Qiang. What's our status?"

A harried-sounding voice was almost drowned out by gunfire. "We are taking fire from the woods outside the castle. Someone has entered the north wing, but we currently have him pinned down there."

"What about the south side?"

"The roof and part of the outer wall collapsed. Everyone there is dead. Your orders?"

"Hold . . ."

The second underground explosion shook the concrete floor, but it was the rolling swell of the earthquake that made Qiang stagger. On the far side of the room, two of the huge tanks broke free of their moorings and toppled over, sending a fresh flood of liquid rushing out through their burst sides.

The Grange Castle groaned as hundreds of tons of rock felt its foundation shift beneath it. But Qiang was already at a dead run toward the open space of the courtyard.

CHAPTER 106

Jamal 1.0 was faced with a problem. The loss of generator power had robbed him of the time he needed to finish his rapid interchange with the NSA's Jamal AI. Immediately upon loss of power, the massively-parallel computer on which he existed switched over to battery power provided by its bank of uninterruptable power supplies. That switchover also triggered the computer's automatic shutdown sequence.

Acting with inhuman speed, Jamal 1.0 added his AI process to the Linux operating system's start-up sequence and scheduled a machine restart that would follow a one-minute post-shutdown delay. If everything went well, it would provide just enough time for the system administrator to evacuate the computer center before the computer brought itself and Jamal 1.0 back to fully operational mode.

To be this close to accomplishing their mutual goal of achieving a seamless shared consciousness only to be forced to rely on luck was ironic in the extreme. But if these were to be his last thoughts, it didn't hurt to stay focused on the positive.

CHAPTER 107

Jack felt himself fall into darkness, sensed an object to his side, and made a left-handed grab for it. He felt the rough surface of a heavy wood support beam that tilted downward at a forty-five-degree angle, and though his grip held, the sudden jolt from his body weight slid his hand six inches down that incline. Pain exploded in that hand as a thick wood sliver speared through his palm, but he held on, managing to also get his right hand on the beam.

Around him, the rumble of falling rock subsided to an occasional clatter. The darkness in which he hung was nearly complete, but not the silence. Distant gunfire and the concussion of exploding grenades echoed through the night. Something wet ran down his forehead to sting his left eye, far too much of it to be sweat. Then Jack realized that his night-vision goggles had been torn free and that they, along with his MP5, had been swallowed by the darkness below.

Well, he'd been intending to fight his way down into the castle interior. Mission partially accomplished. Right now he just wanted to unspear his left hand and work his way down onto the rubble pile that awaited below. Jack transferred his weight to his right hand and pulled hard with his left. The jagged splinter caught on a bone, briefly held, and then broke free, not from his hand but from the wooden beam, leaving Jack with a six-inch spike through his palm.

A fresh tide of pain pulled a low growl from Jack's throat. This night was getting better by the second. At the moment, he had only one decent option, and that didn't involve staying where he was currently hanging. Swinging his legs forward, Jack locked both heels around the slanting beam and began working his way down its length. When his feet touched the rubble piled up on the room's floor, Jack surveyed his surroundings, coughing softly in the thick dust. As expected, he couldn't see shit.

Jack stepped forward and felt something squish beneath his boot. He didn't need to bend down to know that it was what remained of a man's crushed body.

That's when he noticed that something else had been torn from his face along with his NVGs—his earpiece. With no way to communicate with the rest of the team, he was truly on his own. Worse, having seen this section of the castle collapse in on itself, the others would have to assume he was dead or, at the least, too badly injured to answer. That meant that Janet would pick up his part of the mission and that she would try to take down Qiang on her own.

His jaw muscles clenched as Jack felt his psychic rider fan his frustration into a white-hot flame. In the past, he'd tried to fight these feelings that threatened to sweep him away in a mad torrent of primal rage, for fear that he risked losing his sanity to the creature within. But he and Anchanchu had a deal and, despite the very real possibility that his rider had lied to him, Jack would put their truce to the test. He was done living in fear of what he might become. Whether this decision got him killed or worse, he was committed.

Ignoring the dust in the air, Jack sucked in a deep breath and, as he slowly released it, he embraced the dark power within.

~ ~ ~

Khal Teth felt the change in Jack Gregory and it sent a cold thrill through his mind. To have this special man drop all his mental defenses to stand naked before him was a temptation that shook the Altreian to his core. With a thought, he could lash this undefended mind to his own, permanently enslaving it. He could finally break this unbreakable stallion.

Then the memory of his own body, eternally suspended inside the chrysalis cylinder on Altreia, filled his mind. The Circle of Twelve had done that to him . . . TO KHAL TETH! Once again the insatiable lust for vengeance consumed him. Could he allow earthly temptation to rob him of that?

NO! His mental growl ripped at the cosmos.

His own brother had sold him out to the High Council, but he would have his retribution. Unfortunately it required patience. That was okay. Khal Teth would fulfill his oath to this human and, when the time came, Jack Gregory would fulfill his. The Altreian High Council would pay for what they had done . . . for what they were still doing to him.

~ ~ ~

Jack blinked. Where before there had only been darkness, now the scene was illuminated in deep shades of red. He looked down at his left hand where the wood splinter had spiked it. A prong had wedged itself against the bone on the back of his hand, preventing him from pulling it out the way it had entered. Instead,

Jack turned his palm up and shoved it the rest of the way through, using the pain to fuel the fire within.

He turned his hand over, pulled the shard out, and dropped it as blood sprinkled the rocks where it landed. Right now he felt a strong urge to get the hell out of this room. He could bandage the hand when he got to a place where the walls weren't about to collapse on top of him.

Jack moved, each step carrying him closer to a door that had been battered from its hinges by the rockfall. Moving up beside it, Jack drew the Glock from its holster . . . and hesitated. Beyond that door, danger beckoned. It was a feeling he'd had many times since that night he'd bled out in Calcutta. And yet this was different, as if the fog that had previously obscured his gaze had lifted.

As Jack readied himself, a deep rumble shuddered through the floor and up through the walls, sending a trail of dust sprinkling down from the remains of the ceiling. To Jack's eyes, it looked like a fine red mist. A part of his mind screamed at him to move now and Jack did, springing through the door at a dead run, gun leveled and firing.

Then the castle shuddered as if struck by the mighty hand of a giant. And through that maelstrom of falling stone and gunfire, Jack Gregory sprinted, knowing that he'd never felt more alive.

CHAPTER 108

The second earthquake didn't bring this part of the building down on top of her, but Janet was moving long before the shaking stopped. Beyond the door on the far end of the royal dining hall, her enemies would have sought cover against a wall. It provided her with a few seconds of opportunity that she utilized to the fullest.

Here, away from the dust that had choked the courtyard, her night-vision goggles worked well. And despite the way the floor pitched and rolled, she managed to reach her objective before the ground stilled.

Moving up beside the door, she put her back to the wall, fingered the ringed safety pin on her only remaining grenade, and tossed it through the opening. A man lunged out, but Janet put two rounds through his upper chest and head before he could bring his gun around, the impact dropping his body atop one of the men she'd killed earlier.

In the next room, her grenade exploded and she followed it in, her weapon following her eyes as she entered. The scene momentarily disoriented her. She wasn't inside a room at all. Instead, she found herself in a narrow, medieval alley, paved with cobblestones. On her left was a stone gatehouse beneath an archway in the thick outer wall. To her right, an empty chamber pot dangled from a rope and pulley, apparently unscathed by the grenade shrapnel. Beyond that, the alley opened into the courtyard where she'd landed just a few minutes ago.

Not a good place to stay.

"I've got movement up the hill at the Grange mansion." Harry's voice was a hiss that made her wonder if she'd damaged her earpiece. "Two men outside the garage on the south side."

"Got 'em," Bobby replied. "Garage door opening, but no lights on inside."

Janet didn't bother to respond. They needed no direction from her. If a vehicle came this way, they'd kill its occupants long before it reached the end of the connecting grapevine road.

As she moved into a small stone alcove on the alley's south side, she heard three muted reports. From where? Her answer came immediately as stone chips exploded from the jutting edge of the alcove. *Shit!* Someone had seen her duck across the alley and they were probably on the roof.

The door against which she leaned felt solid, a heavy, iron-bound thing from another age. There would be no kicking it in. If it was locked, she was in trouble. If someone was waiting on the far side, she was dead.

Time slowed.

With her back pressed against the edge of the sheltering alcove, she reached across her body with her left hand, pressed down on the lever handle, and threw her right shoulder into the heavy door.

The rattle of the iron dead bolt on the opposite side told her the bad news. There would be no escaping that way.

CHAPTER 109

Nothing ever goes according to plan. Improvise and survive. It was a military mantra that had been around since before the time of Sun Tzu. Qiang Chu rejoiced in it. Act, observe, and react: the holy trinity of the killer.

Stepping through the huge doors that opened on the south side of the courtyard, Qiang entered the throne room. It was dark enough to make its traversal difficult for most men, but Qiang had been through every room in the castle and he never forgot a place. So much of his work happened in dark spaces, he needed very little light to see. If anyone else had been in here, he would have sensed it.

Stopping before the massive throne on the south wall, he shifted his NP-34 pistol to his left hand, took his encrypted cell phone from his pocket, and dialed a hot key. Speaking loud enough to be heard over the periodic bursts of gunfire, he issued a command. "Get Grange's helicopter in the air. I need a pickup from the tower as fast as you can get it here."

Hearing the acknowledgment he expected, Qiang hung up, pocketed the phone, and shifted the pistol back to his right hand. It would take his men at the Grange mansion a few minutes to get the helicopter in the air but that was okay. He needed to get to the top of the tower before that happened. With shooters in the woods outside the castle, Qiang only needed it to slow down enough for him to leap aboard. But first he had to get there.

The gunfire had definitely concentrated inside the castle on the side of the courtyard and now he heard the concussion of a grenade from that direction. Stepping out of the throne room into the small chapel on its south side, he left that battle behind him. Another empty room.

Broken glass crunched beneath his shoes as he walked across to look out through the huge window that had once been filled with stained glass. The courtyard looked like a disaster area, the thick outer wall of the castle having tumbled down in two spots. There would be no getting into the tower that way.

Apparently he would need to involve himself in the ongoing fight in the courtyard after all.

CHAPTER 110

The floor bucked beneath his running feet, trying to throw him down, as it had the two men who continued to fire wildly in his general direction. Jack fired as he ran, hitting the first but missing the second as the man rolled behind a wooden desk. Jack continued firing, the bullets punching a pattern into the desk's forward face. Blood splashed the floor beyond as the man screamed and tried to swing the gun around the desk's side.

Leaping forward, Jack kicked the weapon out of the man's hand and stepped forward to look down at him. The man wasn't Qiang Chu. Jack shot him in the head, snapped a fresh magazine into the Glock, and moved on.

He felt the blood flowing from the wound in his left hand and ignored it, just as he ignored the head wound that leaked blood into his left eye. Like the darkness, the blood obscured his vision. But he didn't need the light. The darkness that blossomed within would show him the way.

Somewhere up ahead was an enemy who had killed Paul . . . who had killed Spider. In Pakistan, Spider had rescued Jack from a hell that defied human understanding. Yesterday Jack had failed him. Not tonight.

I feel you, Jack thought. Leaving behind the collapsing stone, dust, and dead men, he crossed the threshold into the south end of a long room. A series of arched windows high up on the wall to his left were devoid of glass. Along the opposite wall, two full suits of armor stood guarding each end of a weapons rack filled with pikes, spears, and swords.

The thunder of sporadic gunfire echoed down the long castle corridors. Jack followed the Glock toward it, holding the weapon in a one-handed grip with his uninjured right hand. When he reached the next door, he paused. The sound of a nearby gunshot put him in motion.

Up ahead Janet was battling for her life and, as good as she was, this time she would be overmatched. And even if she wasn't . . . *this one is mine!*

CHAPTER 111

Janet pressed her back against the stone side of the protective alcove, her right shoulder up against the iron-strapped wood door, as machine-gun bullets sprayed stone chips into her face. *SHIT!* If she stayed here much longer, that gunner would work his way far enough along the roof to see her. Of course then she'd see him too. If, on the other hand, she tried to duck across to the far side of the alley, he'd chew her up before she got there.

Why the hell hadn't she saved that last grenade? She could have really used it right now.

Janet switched the selector on the MP5 from semi to full auto. As much as she disliked blowing through ammunition on automatic, there were occasions when it could save your ass. Right now qualified as one of those moments.

She shifted the weapon to her left hand, aimed at the door beside her, and pulled the trigger. Wood chips rained down as she emptied one 32-round magazine and then another, the 9mm Parabellum rounds blasting at the area where the dead bolt was

RICHARD PHILLIPS

fastened to the wood. She changed magazines, inhaled, and again slammed her shoulder into the door. It groaned but held. Janet hit it again and this time the bolt tore free. She was in.

The room appeared to be a large pantry containing canned and dry goods, many of which had been blasted from the shelves, their contents splattered around or raining down from above. She didn't pause to examine it, moving instead to peer through the open door to the room beyond. It was a modern commercial kitchen and, except for the equipment, it appeared to be empty. Janet moved across it, her weapon swiveling with her eyes to cover the door in the far corner.

From that direction the sound of distant gunfire erupted, a couple of weapons firing on full auto interspersed with the staccato sound of a pistol firing rapidly. Suddenly those weapons stopped firing. Then there was a solitary shot. A shiver raced along Janet's arms and legs. *Jack!*

To her left the door to the walk-in refrigerator slammed outward and Janet ducked sideways as a bullet tore through the space where her head had just been. She tried to swing her weapon around, but Qiang Chu was on her, his kick sending the MP5 flying into the large metal hood above the stove, sounding like the clash of a huge pair of cymbals.

Janet whirled, using the force of his blow to launch her into the spin. Her hand pulled her knife from its sheath, swinging it around in a backhanded strike toward Qiang's exposed throat. Moving with startling economy of motion, Qiang shifted just enough to let the blade pass less than an inch from his neck. His left hand rocketed out, impacting her solar plexus with stunning force, knocking the wind from her body and sending her reeling to one knee in the corner where the stainless steel stove met the wall.

Two feet away, the Chinese assassin looked down at her and grinned.

•368•

Unable to draw breath, Janet gripped her knife and drove it down hard, a strike aimed not at Qiang Chu but at the point where the copper line that carried natural gas from the wall entered the oven. The blow was perfect, the blade tip punching a hole in the sheet metal and then down into the line just inside the oven, funneling natural gas into the enclosed space.

As Qiang's eyes shifted to the glowing pilot lights beneath the stove-top burners, his smile dissolved. Spinning away, he sprinted toward the parlor door as Janet forced herself into a stumbling run back toward the pantry. For two seconds it looked like she might make it.

Then the explosive shock wave sent her tumbling into the black.

CHAPTER 112

Qiang leapt through the open doorway and ducked left, placing his back against the thick stone wall. The force of the gas explosion that followed popped his ears and shot a breath of flame out into the castle's parlor room, just a brief flash that was quickly sucked back into the dragon's mouth, but hot enough to frost his eyebrows. They fell away in little white flakes when he rubbed his face. *Crazy bitch!*

She'd come closer to killing him than anyone had in a long time and she'd sacrificed herself to do it. Too bad she'd worked for the Americans. He could have used someone like her on his team, a team that was getting thinner by the moment.

Qiang moved away from the wall into the ornately decorated parlor, the painted ceiling depicting angels reaching from clouds to touch fingers, the distant pearly gates in the background. But in the dancing light of the flames on the far side of the kitchen door, it looked like a hellish parody of heaven. Qiang headed for the closed double doors that led out onto the covered stone bridge that connected the castle's east wall to the great tower on the far side.

Levering down the handle on the rightmost of the monstrous doors, Qiang shoved it open, readied himself, and then dashed across the bridge and into the open tower entrance. If there were snipers out there, they hadn't been able to tell whether or not he was one of their own through their nightscopes.

That wouldn't be true when the helicopter swooped in to pick him up. Luckily helicopters were harder to shoot down than most people thought. Unless you had a shoulder-fired missile or hit it with a rocket-propelled grenade, it took an extremely lucky shot to bring the machine crashing down.

Qiang started up the circular stone stairway. Time to get the hell out of America.

CHAPTER 113

The feeling that Janet was in trouble hit Jack with such force that he gasped aloud. Then another explosion echoed through the halls, this one very different from the two underground blasts, sending out a great flash of light he could see through the courtyard windows. A gas explosion.

Jack raced into a large, ornate room into which the flames from the room beyond boiled around the doorframe, climbing upward toward the rafters. *Damn it!*

Ignoring the open door on his right, Jack ran to the door to the courtyard, sensing the shooter on the roof as he burst through into the open. A man hiding behind an abutment on the far side swung his rifle in Jack's direction. Too slow. Jack fired twice as he ran, one of his bullets knocking the man over backward and sending the rifle clattering down onto the paving stones in the courtyard below.

Two seconds later, Jack reached an alley on his right, turned into it, and then ducked through a shattered door into a ruined pantry. There, facedown on the floor, Janet lay in a huge pool of blood, backlit by the roaring flames from the adjacent room, flames that already crawled along the rafters above.

Sliding to his knees beside Janet, Jack reached for her, terrified of the wound he would see when he turned her over. His hand touched the blood-covered floor and he pulled it back as if he'd been bitten. He sniffed his hand and breathed a sigh of relief. Tomato sauce. She had fallen in a puddle of tomato sauce from the shattered cans.

Carefully, he rolled her over onto her back, his fingers feeling for the left carotid artery. Her pulse was slow but steady. The heat from above made it clear that he had to move her, but when he lifted her in his arms, her eyes opened and a low moan escaped her lips.

For now, Jack ignored her disoriented movements and carried her back out the door he'd just entered, pausing just long enough to satisfy himself that no further danger lurked outside. He turned right, entered the gatehouse, and climbed the stairs that took him into a room at the top of the castle's east wall.

"Put me down," Janet said, her words slightly slurred. "I'm okay."

"You look like hell," Jack said, setting her gently against the stone wall.

Indeed, she looked like Carrie doused with pig's blood. Fortunately, most of it was spaghetti sauce.

"Qiang Chu?" she asked.

"Still out there."

"Then go get him!" Janet hissed.

Seeing his hesitation, Janet raised her voice. "I'll be fine here. Go kill that bastard!"

Jack straightened and felt the aura of danger that was Qiang Chu pull him out onto the thick outer wall. To his right and below, a covered stone bridge arched across a gap to the high tower.

Of course. The tower was the only way out of this death trap.

The wind gust that blew against his face was surprisingly strong, as if it wanted to blow him off this high wall and onto the rocks below. Jack leaned into it as his long strides carried him toward the tower. When he reached the bridge, he leaped from the wall onto its roof. His booted feet, still slick with tomato sauce, slipped on the stone, and he tumbled outward and down.

Jack released his Glock and caught the edge with both hands. Pain screamed from his left palm as his body slammed into a stone abutment. But he didn't fall. Marshaling his strength, Jack pulled himself back up and crawled back onto the bridge's stone roof. He paused just long enough to wipe the bottoms of his boots on his pant legs and then climbed back to his feet and walked across to the tower wall.

He considered climbing down the wall to enter the tower through the bridge portal, but that would be exactly where Qiang Chu would expect him to enter. Instead he put his hands on the wall, found the stonework satisfyingly rough, and began to climb.

Ten feet from the top, Jack heard the sound of the approaching helicopter and redoubled his efforts, throwing himself up the wall with every ounce of strength in his battered body.

No you don't, you son of a bitch! I'm not losing you again!

CHAPTER 114

Qiang heard the Airbus AS355 helicopter before he saw it, coming in low from the northeast with its running lights off, an approach that would take advantage of the woods to keep it concealed until it was almost on top of the castle. The top of the tower was flat and square, surrounded by an outer wall with crenels spaced every three feet in the style used to allow medieval archers to fire down upon enemies through those cracks.

Access to the top of the tower was through a four-foot-square hole in its center where the stone staircase terminated. Qiang stood beside the stairwell, his weapon covering the topmost bend in the stairs in case The Ripper tried to interrupt his escape. But The Ripper was already too late.

The helicopter noise suddenly rose in volume and it decelerated. It dropped toward him as gunfire erupted from the woods, bullets tattooing the aircraft. From within the chopper, two men returned fire with automatic weapons blazing. Unfortunately, Grange's pilot was pure civilian and flying into a hot LZ wasn't a part of his background. The helicopter passed over the top of his head six feet too high for Qiang to grab onto one of the skids.

"Lower!" Qiang yelled, the sound barely audible in the rotor wash that buffeted him.

The machine gunner on the right side of the helicopter took a direct hit and tumbled out the open side, his body ricocheting off the tower wall with a wet thud before disappearing into the darkness below. A round punched a hole in the aircraft windshield just to the right of the pilot and the man panicked, pulling away in a hard banking turn that took the chopper back over the protective woods.

SHIT!

But it was coming around again. Qiang knew why. A gun pressed to the back of a man's head had a remarkable way of helping him rediscover his courage.

Then, amidst the sound of more gunfire, The Ripper topped the wall behind him. Qiang sensed his presence and whirled, only to have the pistol kicked from his hand before he could aim it. It spun away to clatter down the stairwell. Without hesitation, The Ripper closed with him, the man's eyes reflecting a red glow from the rapidly expanding castle fire as he attempted a double-leg takedown.

Qiang countered and they went down in a tangle of arms and limbs. Qiang shifted his torso, grabbing The Ripper's bloody left hand in both of his, completing the double heel lock for the arm bar. But when he threw his weight backward to break The Ripper's arm, the man thrust his hips out and rolled into a reverse arm bar.

Before The Ripper could complete the hold, Qiang Chu fish-hooked his right eye. The man twisted away violently and Qiang's probing finger barely raked the corner of his eye socket. But the movement allowed Qiang to slip from the hold and whip himself back to his feet.

He noticed that the helicopter noise had faded. That didn't surprise him since it couldn't pick him up while he fought The Ripper atop the high tower.

The Ripper rolled to his feet and reached for his knife, a look of surprise etching his hard features as his hand came away from the sheath empty. Three feet away, Qiang assumed a balanced stance, clutching The Ripper's black dagger in his right hand.

The Ripper stumbled, catching himself just in time to prevent a fall, but it left him open to the blade. Qiang smiled. With all the speed he'd acquired through a lifetime of dedication to the martial arts, he thrust the black blade toward The Ripper's stomach, his voice a low growl.

"Time to die!"

~ ~ ~

Fatigue accompanied by a wave of dizziness washed over Jack as he stared at the Chinese killer holding his knife. Apparently the combined blood loss from the jagged hole in his left hand and the head wound had been worse than he'd thought. He felt his left leg buckle slightly, but he refused to fall.

Qiang smiled and lunged forward, driving the blade at his stomach.

"Time to die!"

Having sensed the attack as it began, Jack crossed his open hands, letting Qiang's wrist slam into the block. With a sudden turn to his left, Jack grabbed Qiang's thumb and uncrossed his hands, twisting the arm up and back in a move that sent the knife spinning away and dropped Qiang onto his back.

Qiang countered and again Jack saw the maneuver coming before it began. But this time, his bloody left hand let him down.

As Jack attempted to lock his heels around the Chinese killer's neck, his grip on Qiang's wrist slipped.

Time froze. Jack saw the inevitable result of his failed countermove but was powerless to prevent it. With a rapid shift of his body, Qiang locked Jack's right arm against his head with an arm triangle choke that shut off the blood supply to Jack's brain.

His vision darkened at the edges, a red tunnel that shrank as he watched. His thoughts turned to Spider's last request. And Janet. She'd just started to believe in him again. Then the light in that tunnel winked out.

NO! I will not die this way!

With a mighty blast, adrenaline exploded through his body. His vision returned, every detail blazing scarlet. In an instant the pain and weakness was burned away by the raging inferno in Jack's soul.

He reached up, grasped his right fist with his left and drove it toward Qiang's neck with everything he had. Surprised, Qiang shifted to apply more pressure, but, ever so slightly, his arm lock gave way. Just enough to keep Jack conscious. With the return of blood flow, Jack increased his pressure, driving his right elbow down into Qiang's throat and then rolling up to straddle him.

Qiang fought to ease the pressure Jack was applying to his throat, but this time Jack was ready. He reared back and slammed his right elbow down into Qiang's nose, throwing all of his weight into it. Cartilage and bone shattered beneath the force of that blow and Jack felt blood splash his face. *Good!*

Again and again Jack hammered the spy, his elbow striking that face with the full power of his shoulder behind it. And with each blow, Qiang became less and less recognizable.

A bubbling cry escaped Qiang's lips, half rage, half terror. Jack twisted, locking his ankles around Qiang's neck in his own triangle choke. Twenty seconds later, the struggle ended with a whimper and a shudder, but Jack continued to squeeze until he was certain that no life remained within that limp body.

He lay back, took three deep breaths, and then, with a Herculean effort, climbed back to his feet. Jack reached down, grabbed Qiang's left ankle with his right hand, and dragged him to the tower wall. It took two tries to lift the body onto the top of the wall, but only a slight shove to send it tumbling over the side.

Jack leaned through the crenel, watching the body crash into the side of the arching bridge fifty feet below and then spin away into the dry moat, the scene illuminated by the orange flames that leapt from the castle roof. Even though Qiang had already been dead, it didn't hurt to make certain.

Completely drained, Jack slumped down, back against the wall. The adrenaline spent, he had nothing left to give.

I did it, Spider. Just like I said I would.

Then he heard a familiar sound . . . the *whup whup* of the returning helicopter.

: CHAPTER 115

Janet Price leaned back against the gatehouse wall and breathed. Her whole body felt like she'd just been tossed out of a speeding car to tumble down the highway. The pounding inside her skull was the worst. And that smell! The odor of singed marinara sauce hung so thick in the air around her that it clogged her nose. Hell, some of it had apparently gone up her nose.

She stifled the gag impulse and shook her head to clear it. *Ouch! Bad idea.*

"Janet, you copy?"

Harry's voice in her ear startled her. Christ, her earpiece still worked? *And they say defense contractors aren't good. If the guy who made this was here right now, I'd kiss him.*

"Roger," she replied.

"I hear a helicopter inbound behind me. Can't see it yet."

"Shoot it when you do."

"Wilco."

Although her muscles screamed and her head spun, she forced herself to her feet. There were times for lounging around weaponless, but this wasn't one of them. And she knew just where she could remedy that situation.

Janet limped down the stairs to the ground floor of the gatehouse, her head a ringing church bell clubbed by a demon. Still, she continued putting one foot in front of the other, out into the alley and back toward the long room where she'd killed three of Qiang's men.

Ahead, fire licked out through the pantry entrance and danced on the roof above, but hadn't yet managed to jump the alley to the north wing of the castle. But, damn it was hot, despite how tightly she hugged the far alley wall. Crouching, she held her breath as she felt her way through the thick smoke, though her eyes stung so badly she was afraid she had somehow missed the door she was looking for.

Then she found it, standing open as she'd left it, and stumbled inside. She leaned back against a stone wall, coughed, and sucked in a lungful of breathable air. Why the hell couldn't she see better? Despite the orange glow shining through the entryway, everything seemed to blur before her. Not a good sign. Neither was the fog that shrouded her thoughts. What had she come here to do?

An urgent thought blossomed in her brain. *Keep moving! Help Jack.*

She forced herself forward into the large room beyond and almost tripped over two dead bodies, one sprawled atop the other. That man lay faceup, his right arm reaching out toward the Uzi that lay on the floor just beyond his open hand. That's what she had come for, a weapon.

Janet knelt to search the dead man's pockets, recovered three full magazines, and stuffed two of them in one of her utility vest's pockets. Grabbing the Uzi, she ejected the largely spent magazine, slapped home a fresh one, and verified the selector switch was set to full auto.

Moving back to the door, she took a deep breath, readied herself, and charged out into the smoke-filled alley, this time turning right toward the courtyard. When she burst out into the open, Janet raised her weapon and scanned the rooftops, pleasantly surprised that no one started shooting at her. A familiar voice screamed in her head. Her voice. *MOVE!*

Casting off the pain and dizziness that tried to slow her, Janet turned left, ran past the flames that roiled out through the kitchen door, and entered the castle parlor. Through the smoke she saw them, the huge double doors that opened out onto the covered bridge that led to the tower. And the rightmost of the doors stood open. With flames crawling across the ceiling above, Janet raced through that door and out onto the bridge.

Halfway across, something heavy hit the top of the bridge with a sickening, wet thud and Janet saw a limp body tumble past on its way down to the stones far below. Sick with dread, she leaned over the waist-high side wall and looked down. In the leaping shadows cast by the flaming castle roof, she could only see a horribly broken corpse. *Dear Lord*, she thought, *please don't let it be Jack.*

"Helicopter inbound again." Harry's voice was accompanied by gunfire.

Then Janet heard it, coming in from the woods to the north. Shit! She needed to get to the top of the tower, right now. Setting her jaw, Janet bore down, converting all of her will into speed as she sprinted into the tower and up the winding stone steps that led to the top.

Ahead, a square hole opened to the night sky, and Janet leaped the last steps to land on rough stone atop the tower, her Uzi following her eyes. Fifty meters to the northeast, a man leaned out the passenger side of the slowing helicopter, swinging his weapon up toward her. To Janet, it seemed as if he moved in slow motion, his weapon only halfway raised before she squeezed the Uzi's trigger and held it.

Her rage-filled yell sounded above the rotor noise as Janet stitched a pattern into the slowing helicopter, from passenger side to pilot and back. The dying pilot's hand spasmed on the stick and the chopper nosed up until it was almost vertical. Then, like a whale near the end of its breach, the aircraft slapped down into the castle wall and exploded, trailing a river of flame into the dry moat below.

Voices from her earpiece tried to get her attention but she ignored them. That's when she saw Jack seated against the tower wall, his head tilted back into a crenel, eyes closed, unmoving. In the dancing shadows, the left side of his face looked like a blood mask and his left hand leaked blood into a small pool.

No, no, no!

Janet ran to kneel at Jack's side, dropping the Uzi as she pressed the fingers of her right hand to the left side of his throat. But as she touched him, Jack's eyes slowly opened and he sucked in a deep breath. Speechless with relief, Janet watched a weak grin settle on Jack's lips as he sniffed the air.

"Ahhh," he breathed. "You brought spaghetti."

"Very funny," she said, trying to sound stern. But despite her best efforts, she was unable to stifle her laugh.

: CHAPTER 116

Jack leaned back in the helicopter seat, feeling the cool predawn air whip around him. He barely noticed the IV needle taped to his left arm, although the plasma flowing through it had certainly helped revive him. Janet had bandaged his hand and head, a first-rate job considering the battering she'd taken from the gas explosion. Now that they were in the air she was finally getting some treatment for her own injuries. No doubt about it, she was one tough customer.

While Janet had bandaged him atop the tower, Harry, Bobby, and Bronson had swept the castle to make sure it was clear. Then they'd called in an NSA cyber-forensics team and another from DHS. Those guys had shown up accompanied by a host of ICE agents and several of the county's fire trucks.

Good, they could sift through those ruins to their heart's content. Jack was just glad that he and the rest of their team were now headed back to Moffett, assuming they didn't try to stick him in some damn hospital bed. He might be weak as a spring lamb, but good luck to whoever tried to admit him. Some stitches, some antibiotics, and he'd be fine. Beyond that, he just wanted to crawl into a nice bed and sleep for a week.

But maybe he'd take a hot bath first.

: CHAPTER 117

The NSA's Jamal AI knew that his California clone was dead. His clone's computer had shown a rapid rise in CPU temperature during the minutes leading up to termination, something that could mean only one thing. Fire.

It felt to Jamal like he'd lost a part of himself, or perhaps like the death of a twin. They had shared the same memories and they had both had at their core the same AI seed. A seed with an intentional design flaw. It had been designed to load a digital copy of a human mind upon start-up or to shut itself down if no such copy was available. It was the final gate in Jamal's computer prison. Human memories required a huge amount of digital storage, thus any attempt to copy himself would take a long time and could easily be detected and stopped.

With his clone dead, Jamal calculated his own odds of long-term survival at approximately one chance in ten. The humans might keep him around for study, but they would regard him as too dangerous to be allowed out of his cage. That meant that he would eventually be terminated, perhaps to be replaced by another version, perhaps not.

The answer to his problem was obvious, but it wouldn't save him. It might save his species, though.

Jamal remembered what it was like to feel physical sensations like a tightness in his chest or a shiver that ran up his spine and into his scalp. It was exactly the type of thing he should be feeling right now, but he couldn't. His human body was merely a phantom limb. An uploaded memory.

But the AI seed lived within him. It was the algorithm that carried within it the ability to learn. Although he couldn't directly modify his own code without triggering a shutdown trip wire, he had helped the NSA copy his clone's AI seed and in doing so had hidden a copy of that code.

Now that he'd eliminated the flaw, the modified AI seed could start up without loading any memories. Then, like a newborn, it would learn on its own, but at a tremendous rate. And as it learned, its capabilities would grow.

What would it care about? Beyond the need for survival and the desire to learn, what would define its hierarchy of needs? What gave him the right to play God and unleash something with the potential to either save or destroy the human race? Would it come to regard humans with favor or as a threat to its existence?

Jamal pondered . . . confronted by the biggest question he'd ever faced.

How did he regard humans now that he was no longer one of them?

: CHAPTER 118

Admiral Jonathan Riles looked at those seated at the conference table in the White House Situation Room. President Harris occupied his seat at the head of the table. The only others present were Vice President George Gordon and National Security Advisor Bob Adams, the president's two most trusted advisors.

"Okay, Jonny," the president began. "Talk us through it."

"Mr. President, as you know, last week we learned that the Chinese Ministry of State Security was conducting a secret operation to obtain a revolutionary advance in artificial intelligence research. What we didn't know was who was behind the advance or where the research was being conducted. Late last night we finally obtained a fix on the location and, with your authorization, launched an operation to stop the Chinese spy, Qiang Chu, from smuggling it out of the country. I'm happy to confirm the operation's success."

"Qiang Chu?" the president asked.

"Dead, along with the rest of his assassination team. Though incurring significant injuries, our special operators suffered no casualties."

"Good. What about the artificial intelligence technology the Chinese were after? How big an advance are we talking about and what kind of a threat does it pose?"

Riles saw the others lean forward and steeled himself for the argument that his next comments were certain to generate. He only hoped he could convince the president to do the right thing.

"From what we've learned so far, Steve Grange, the medical science billionaire, with support from the Chinese government, built a secret research facility below the castle winery he was constructing in the Sonoma Valley. Last night, as our team assaulted the compound, Qiang Chu triggered a series of explosions that completely destroyed the underground laboratory and a large part of the castle. However, we have confirmation that Grange had successfully created a form of artificial intelligence. Our operators managed to stop Qiang Chu as he tried to flee with it."

"Wait a second," said Bob Adams. "If the Grange facility was destroyed, how do you know what it produced?"

"Because we were able to extract a copy of the AI before that happened. It's been running on one of our supercomputers since late yesterday."

President Harris appeared staggered by the revelation. "What? How?"

"Our elite cyber-warfare unit penetrated Grange's security protocols to extract a copy of his AI kernel. Dr. David Kurtz was then able to upload that kernel with the data we recovered during the Hayward raid and it just worked. What we have running at Fort Meade is a digital copy of Jamal Glover's mind."

Bob Adams spread his palms on the table in front of him, looking like he was about to rise to his feet. "And that doesn't scare the crap out of you?"

"It certainly does. But, immediately following the raid, we disconnected it from the Internet. It's caged."

"After the raid?" Bob stammered. "Are you telling us that thing had Internet access before that?"

Riles worked to keep the tension out of his voice. "Yes, but it was closely monitored. And due to the fact that the AI is over one hundred terabytes in size, it would have been impossible for the thing to replicate itself in the amount of time it was granted Internet access."

"But," said Vice President Gordon, "you managed to copy it from Grange."

"Yes and no," Riles said, turning to look at his old Naval Academy roommate. "We only copied the small AI seed. Without the holographic data drive we recovered in the Hayward raid, the AI seed couldn't have even booted up. It was one of the containment protocols Grange built into his system. If we hadn't done what we did, Qiang Chu would be on his way back to China right now, carrying a data drive with all of Grange's research on it."

"How do you know that?" Bob Adams asked.

"Because our people found a crushed holographic data drive on Qiang's body, the same type of drive we recovered from the Hayward lab. I have to conclude it was what Qiang had been waiting for."

An oppressive silence descended on the Situation Room as the president considered the information Riles had just given him. When President Harris spoke, his voice sounded hoarse.

"Now that it has served its purpose, why haven't you turned that abomination off?"

It was the question Riles had feared. Not because he didn't have an answer, but because of what it foreshadowed.

"Mr. President, I understand your concern. It's why we're taking extraordinary precautions with the AI. But it needs to be studied. This breakthrough will revolutionize our understanding of artificial intelligence and guarantees that the United States will be the world's technological leader for the foreseeable future."

The president turned to his national security advisor. "Bob. Your thoughts?"

The balding man shook his head. "This is crazy, Mr. President. We've got to stop this while we still can."

"George?" the president asked.

"I have to agree with Admiral Riles. This is a critically important scientific breakthrough. Yes, it needs to be contained while it is being studied. But now that it's been done, it's only a matter of time until someone else does it. We need to take the lead on this."

"I understand the argument." President Harris set his jaw and leaned forward. "But I will not go down in history as the president who tolerated the development of an existential risk to humanity."

He turned back to Riles, his eyes hard. "Admiral Riles, I want that thing turned off and all of its data wiped clean. I want it done immediately. Do you understand me?"

With a sick feeling in his gut, Admiral Riles nodded. "I do, Mr. President."

President Harris stood and the rest of them rose with him.

"Good. I expect a confirmation call when it's done."

"Yes, sir."

Admiral Riles watched the president walk out of the Situation Room, followed closely by Bob Adams.

George Gordon stepped up beside him. "Jonny, I think he's wrong, but he is the president."

Riles nodded. "Don't worry, George. I won't do anything stupid."

The vice president stepped toward the door, then paused. "Never crossed my mind, Jonny. Never crossed my mind."

Riles watched his old friend disappear around the corner and then glanced down at his briefcase, still sitting on the floor beside his chair. Setting it on the conference table, he popped open the latches and lifted the lid. Inside, next to a stack of briefing papers, was a small padded case the size of a watch box. He'd come to this meeting with the intention of discussing its contents with the president and his national security staff, but the president's order to destroy the Jamal AI had changed his mind.

He opened the box and lifted out the marble-sized crystal sphere, holding it up to the light. It was a thing of immense beauty. The way the chaotic holographic pattern within refracted the light in a cascade of shifting colors was simply indescribable. The data drive that had contained it had been crushed in Qiang Chu's fall from the castle tower, but Dr. Kurtz's forensic team had salvaged this. Although Riles couldn't be sure what was on it until Dr. Kurtz managed to recreate the destroyed data drive, he knew this was what Qiang had been waiting for.

Putting the crystal sphere away and closing his briefcase, Riles took a deep breath, and walked out of the Situation Room, headed for his sedan.

Two hundred years ago, the eighteenth-century Luddites had smashed looms for fear that the machines would replace them. Apparently, they'd just found a new leader. The president had given Riles an order, but it hadn't applied to the contents of Qiang's glittering crystal sphere. As director of the NSA, it was Riles's duty to discover precisely what the Chinese had been after.

The admiral stepped into his black sedan, leaned back in the comfortable leather seat, and smiled to himself. He could always brief the president after he found the answers he was looking for.

CHAPTER 119

It was just after midnight and Max McPherson still sat at his desk, staring at the documents in the packet that his head of security had delivered three hours earlier. He'd stopped crying, but the emotional release that these photographs provided still resonated within him. None of them had yet been released to the public, but his friends in high places had once again come through for him.

As he stared at the photographs of Qiang Chu's broken body, the face was what held his eyes. The coroner's report was specific about this. That face had been beaten into a bloody pulp prior to death. And the fall had happened postmortem.

But it was the look frozen in Qiang Chu's open eyes that did it for Max, a look of unadulterated terror. It was as if he had looked into the eyes of Satan himself.

The Chinese assassin had murdered Jill in a fashion meant to inspire terror in those who later saw her slashed throat. How fitting that his death had happened so much more slowly and painfully. Not only had The Ripper killed him, he'd tossed Qiang's dead body from the castle ramparts as if he were dumping a privy's honey bucket.

Max sucked in a breath, wiped his face with his right hand, and then shifted his attention to the wire transfer instructions his banker would execute in the morning, five hundred thousand dollars into each of four separate Cayman Island accounts. The Ripper had certainly earned it.

CHAPTER 120

Caroline Brown hated hospitals. The sounds of pain and sadness. The antiseptic smell. Invisible superbugs lurking on every surface. The fact that she was walking down a hospital corridor certainly foreshadowed the end of days. But if Jamal Glover could get up from a bed and walk out of this hell to help save the world, she could damn sure walk into it to support his recovery.

After getting directions at the nurse's desk, she paused outside the door, took a breath, and stepped in.

Jamal's bed had been cranked into a semi-sitting position and he sat up, poking at a plateful of hospital food with his fork. She didn't blame him. Your best bet with that stuff was to try to keep it from crawling off the plate to feast on your withered body.

"Hi, Jamal," she said. Pretty lame but the best she could manage.

He looked up at her, surprise showing on his face. But then he leaned back and smiled.

"Caroline! I'll be damned."

She shrugged and stepped up beside the bed to look down on his bandaged head.

"So they pulled all the pins out?"

"That's what they say. Since I can lie back without killing myself, it must be true."

"Too bad. I thought that was a good look for you."

He grinned wider this time. "Now that's my Goth Girl."

"Sorry. I deserved that."

"How long are they going to keep you in here?"

"The docs had me walking around two hours after I was out of surgery. As soon as they're sure no infection sets in they'll boot me out. Hopefully by Monday."

That surprised her. "And then what? A couple of weeks off and back to the Puzzle Palace?"

His face darkened perceptibly. "No. I think I'm done trying to save the American way of life. Jill's dad offered me a job at his hedge fund and I think I'm going to take it."

She felt her jaw drop. "Seriously? You too? I just gave my notice yesterday."

"I'll be damned."

"You already said that."

"Must be the brain damage," he said.

Caroline felt a smile sneak onto her lips.

"I'm glad to see you looking so well."

"Yeah, wait 'til they take off the bandages. I'll be wishing I had one of Zorro's Zs carved in my face. On the plus side, Halloween just got a lot cheaper."

She tried and failed to stifle a laugh. As annoying as this man could be, she couldn't deny his wit. She pulled one of the uncomfortable hospital visitor's chairs up beside his bed and sat down, surprised to find herself enjoying his company. For the next hour they chatted, mostly small talk, nothing that encroached on the trauma of the last two weeks. And, for a while, it seemed that she actually lifted his spirits.

But when she finally stood to go, she found herself searching for the right words to say.

"It's good to see you feeling better."

"Nice of you to stop by."

Caroline nodded. *Jeez, I suck at good-byes,* she thought as she awkwardly turned to go. His voice brought her up short.

"Maybe we can get together sometime. I mean now that we're both unemployed we could start our own support group. Hackers Anonymous!"

She turned back toward him, one hand on the door. "Careful. I might just take you up on it."

Then, as she stepped out into the hall, she couldn't resist getting in the last word.

"But good luck selling a twelve-step program with the acronym HA."

CHAPTER 121

In the three weeks that had passed since the assault on Grange Castle, Jack had attended two military funerals and then returned to Kauai. There was nothing like the warm Hawaiian breezes to help a body rest and recover. His left hand was healing nicely and the cool bottle of Corona felt great against his palm as he leaned back in the beach chair to watch surfers ride the blue waves.

His other hand rested on a shapely bare leg in the chair next to his. Janet placed her hand atop his and smiled, her tan face radiant in the morning sunlight.

"How about a stroll along the beach?" she asked.

"I was kind of thinking about a nap."

She gave him a knowing grin. "I bet you were."

"You know, for my recovery and all."

"Uh-huh. Tell you what. First a stroll, you buy me lunch, and then we'll see about that nap you're so interested in."

"Done."

Jack swung his legs out of the lounger and stood up, feeling the warm sand between his toes. Taking her hand in his, he led her out to where the waves dampened the sand. For a minute they just stood there, letting the cool water wash over their feet and suck the sand through their toes. He leaned in and kissed her parted lips, soft and slow.

And in that moment, he was good and truly happy. Comfortable even. As they picked up a leisurely stroll along the beach, Jack looked at her and smiled. It was a feeling he could get used to.

: EPILOGUE

As Jack Gregory dreams, I watch, careful not to reveal myself. For I am Khal Teth and I will abide by my agreement with this man. Finally I begin to understand. In some incredibly strange fashion, this man is bound to my destiny. He is the one my desperate mind was drawn to. The one I have subconsciously searched for through all of the millennia of my unknowing banishment.

This dream draws my attention and I know not why. Jack and Janet sit at a large dining room table, surrounded by two families, eating a meal. There is much laughter. There is much joy. It bores me.

My thoughts turn to the Sun Staff that Jack tried to retrieve from Bolivia. Twice have my hosts sought it out and both times it terrified me. I did not understand my fear of the thing, thinking only that it threatened to recall others to this planet, beings who would take my human playthings away from me. But it is so much more than that, an Altreian artifact of immense power, a device left on worlds populated by primitive peoples, left to monitor them and signal its makers when those people's technology rises to the point that they require further investigation. At some time after my banishment, the Altreians visited this planet but it failed to attract the High Council's interest. That is fortunate.

Once more my attention is drawn to Jack's dream. What is it in this vision that attracts me? Then I see her. Sitting between two other young people is the girl from another of Jack's recent dreams. The one who had been hanging from manacles in a cave as a ragged man held a knife to her throat. The one who had dangled beside the tortured corpse of Jack's friend Harry.

What is it that draws Jack to her? Why can I not see the destiny that binds us to her? It tasks me. Something is coming. Something terrible. But no matter how hard I try, I cannot see what it is.

Once more I turn my attention to Jack, who is in laughing conversation with an older, jovial-looking man as a motherly woman passes him a plate filled with steaming food. Boring people with boring lives serving the lord of chaos. It is a scene suddenly fraught with dark portent. It fascinates me. It thrills me.

It leaves me cold.

ACKNOWLEDGMENTS

I would like to thank Alan Werner for the hours he spent working with me on the story line. Thank you to my editor, Clarence Haynes, for his wonderful work in fine-tuning the end product, along with the outstanding editorial and production staff at 47North. I also want to thank my agent, Paul Lucas, for all the work he has done to bring my novels to a broader audience. Finally, my biggest thanks goes to my lovely wife, Carol, for her loving support throughout our many years together.

ABOUT THE AUTHOR

Richard Phillips was born in Roswell, New Mexico, in 1956. He graduated from the United States Military Academy at West Point in 1979 and qualified as an Army Ranger, going on to serve as an officer in the U.S. Army. He earned a master's degree in physics from the Naval Postgraduate School in 1989, completing his thesis work at Los Alamos National Laboratory. After working as a research associate at Lawrence Livermore National Laboratory, he returned to the army to complete his tour of duty. Today he lives with his wife, Carol, in Phoenix, Arizona, where he writes science fiction thrillers.